Dark Companion

Dark Companion

MARTA ACOSTA

TOR*
TEEN

A TOM DOHERTY
ASSOCIATES BOOK
NEW YORK

DARK COMPANION

Copyright © 2012 by Marta Acosta

Reader's Guide copyright © 2012 by Tor Books

Grateful acknowledgment is made to Paulette Jiles for the use of her poem "Paper Matches."

A Tor Teen Book
Published by Tom Doherty Associates, LLC
175 Fifth Avenue
New York, NY 10010

www.tor-forge.com

Tor® is a registered trademark of Tom Doherty Associates, LLC.

The Library of Congress has cataloged the hardcover edition as follows:

Acosta, Marta.
    Dark companion / Marta Acosta.—1st ed.
        p. cm.
    "A Tom Doherty Associates book."
    ISBN 978-0-7653-2964-6 (hardcover)
    ISBN 978-1-4299-8829-2 (e-book)
 1. Supernatural—Fiction. 2. Orphans—Fiction. 3. Boarding schools—Fiction.
 4. Schools—Fiction. I. Title.
    PZ7.A18656 Dar 2012
    [Fic]

                                                                  2012011656

ISBN 978-0-7653-2965-3 (trade paperback)

Tor books may be purchased for educational, business, or promotional use. For information on bulk purchases, please contact Macmillan Corporate and Premium Sales Department at 1-800-221-7945 extension 5442 or write specialmarkets@macmillan.com.

First Edition: July 2012
First Trade Paperback Edition: June 2013

Printed in the United States of America

0 9 8 7 6 5 4 3 2

With love to Sam Gough,
who is an exceptional girl

My aunts washed dishes while the uncles
squirted each other on the lawn with
garden hoses. Why are we in here,
I said, and they are out there.
That's the way it is,
said Aunt Hetty, the shriveled-up one.
I have the rages that small animals have,
being small, being animal.
Written on me was a message,
"At Your Service,"
like a book of paper matches.
One by one we were taken out
and struck.
We come bearing supper,
our heads on fire.

—Paulette Jiles, "Paper Matches" (1973)

Dark Companion

Prologue On the night that I die, a storm rages, and the thin glass of the cheap windows shudders as if beaten by fists, and the wind howls like someone calling *come away, come away.* I wrench open the back door and run outside.

The darkness is unfathomable and rain pounds down and I am small and terrified.

I slosh toward my secret place among three enormous trees at the far end of the yard. It is too dark to see, yet I know when I have reached the largest, and I creep around it, hiding behind the wide trunk.

An earsplitting blast throws me back against the third tree. I think it's lightning. A moment later, pain radiates from below my shoulder to every part of my body. My knees buckle with the agony. I know that if I fall to the ground, I will die.

I twist toward the tree and blood seeps from my shoulder to the trunk. Rain washes my blood down to the soil, the tree's roots. *Help me,* I think, *help me.*

As I begin to black out, I feel arms—no, not arms. I feel *something* take me and lift me high into the wet green branches.

Later, I hear sirens approaching and then voices amplified by bullhorns. The storm has passed and rain falls through the branches in a soft drizzle. I want to sleep.

"The girl, the neighbors said there's a kid here," someone says.

They call my name and I hear them rushing through the house and into the yard. "Jane! Jane!"

I don't answer because I am safe.

"Here," a man says. "A shoe."

They are close now and they move below me. A woman says, "On the tree. Blood. Oh, God, a lot of blood."

"Where does it lead?"

"Up. Is there something up there? Turn the light this way."

"Where?"

"In the tree! Way up there."

I nestle closer to the trunk, so they won't find me. I feel as if I'm drifting somewhere.

Then the pain in my body vanishes. I can't hear the noise or the voices any longer.

I open my eyes and I'm in a glorious shady wood. I inhale air that smells of green things—pine, cedar, newly cut grass, sage and mint, the aromatic anise scent of wild fennel. I want to stay here forever.

I see someone coming toward me. I know she's a woman by her gentle movements, but she's not human. Her dress falls down to the brown earth and tendrils of the hem burrow into the soil. I can feel her kindness as she begins leading me out of the lush world.

"I don't want to leave," I tell her.

"You've found the way here. You can find the way back whenever you need us," she tells me in a language that is like a breeze. "Breathe, Jane."

I gasp and open my eyes. Pain suffuses my body.

Then there is the pandemonium of an ambulance, blinding lights of an operating room, the metallic clicking of instruments, tubes attached to my body.

Then I'm in a pink room filled with machines and electronic noises. I can see a stenciled border of butterflies and hear the doctors talking.

"Poor little thing," says a woman in a hushed voice. "It would be best if she forgets what happened."

And so I did. As I sank into the sightless, soundless, motionless void of a drug-induced coma, I tugged away that memory as if I were tugging at a loose thread, little knowing that I was unraveling the entirety of my brief existence. Because who are we without our memories?

Chapter 1

When I was six, I was entered into the foster care system because there was no one to care for me.

I was small and plain without the puppyish cheerfulness that makes grown-ups love a child, so I was passed from one miserable foster home to the next. I scurried in the shadows, away from the predators in the violent neighborhoods where I lived. I existed without love, without safety, without hope.

One sweltering Saturday in August when I was sixteen, I said good-bye to my roommates at the group home where I had spent the last four years. I picked up a ratty vinyl sports bag that contained all my worldly possessions: thrift-shop clothes, two pairs of shoes, a paperback dictionary, my SAT workbooks, a worn leather-bound Bible that had belonged to Hosea, and a tin box of trinkets. I had my life savings, $7.48, in my pocket.

As I walked to the front door of the ramshackle house, Mrs. Prichard grabbed my arm, her maroon nails digging into me. Her spray-on orange tan scaled on her rough skin while her inner arm was as pasty as a reptile's belly. She wore a purple t-shirt and new jeans with rhinestones and embroidered flourishes.

"Jane Williams, aren't you gonna thank me for everything I done for you?" Her yellow frizz of hair bobbed each time she snaked her neck.

I jerked away from her grip. "Don't you *ever* touch me again." I kept my eyes on her dirty dishwater-brown ones. "You've never done anything for me that you didn't *have* to do so you could keep getting money from the state. You would have thrown me in the street the second I aged out."

She flushed under the fake tan, her cheeks turning copper red. "There was no use spoiling you when you're gonna wind up like the rest of these stupid girls, another baby-mama on the public dime, hooked on the pipe."

"I never asked you for a single thing except kindness, but that's not in you. You don't know me at all."

"Don't you put on airs with me! Your fancy book-learning and phony manners might fool others, but I know that you're still what you always were—low-class garbage from no-account people. The apple doesn't fall far from the tree."

My anger was cold and dense. I leaned so close to Mrs. Prichard's face that I could smell the stale coffee and strawberry gum on her breath. "And I know what *you* are. You're a heartless, soulless waste of human life. When I'm older, I'll make sure that your license is revoked. I hope you burn in hell after what you did to Hosea. *You're* the reason he died, and I will never forget that. I will see that you pay."

Mrs. Prichard's lower lip quivered and she stepped back. I felt a spark of something unfamiliar: it was power and it warmed me as I imagined a mother's caress might.

Outside, the sun blazed on the ugly street, revealing the paint peeling on houses, dried blood on the cracked sidewalk, and trash in the gutters. The hood was a volatile mix of the destitute, the dangerous, and the desperate. I knew that the men on the corner, who seemed so nonchalant, noticed me with my bag, because they noticed everything and everyone. I kept my head down as I neared them.

One of the other men said, "Squeak, squeak, squeak," and they all laughed, but there was nothing I could do about it.

I walked past the liquor store, the check-cashing shop, and houses with chain-link fencing and pit bulls that lunged and snarled. I made sure to keep close to the curb when I went by a crack house, and then I reached a lot with junked appliances.

A tall, skinny Goth girl, incongruous in her short purple tube-dress and platform flip-flops, smoked a cigarette and leaned against a busted washing machine. Her straight waist-length hair was dyed black with shocking pink streaks. She wore chalky makeup, but her shoulders and legs had colorful tattoos.

When she spotted me, she shouted, "Janey!" and dropped the cigarette.

"Hey, Wilde!" I put down my bag and, as we hugged, I felt the thinness of her body and smelled her sugar-sweet perfume. My hand on her bare shoulder blade touched the raised surface of one of the small round scars that marked her body.

We finally let each other go and smiled. The thick blue eyeliner around her gray eyes and her sharp cheekbones made her appear old. She said, "So you're finally making a prison break from Mrs. Bitchard's?"

I grinned. "Hosea *hated* when we called her that. Remember how he'd frown that way he did and say, 'She's trying as best she knows.'"

"He was always schoolin' us to act ladylike." Wilde deepened her voice and said, " 'Sis, you're too pretty to say such ugly words.' Heck, I *still* feel bad when I cuss."

"Me, too." We both were quiet for a moment. "The school's sending a car to get me."

"High styling!" Wilde had a wide-open smile with a small gap in her front teeth that made it special. "Well, good on you."

"I'm going to miss you, girlfriend." I wondered when she'd last slept or eaten a real meal. "How are you doing? How are you *really* doing?"

"Oh, you know. You know how you been riding me to get my GED?"

"Because you're as bright as a new penny."

"That's what Hosea used to say. Anyways, I'm gonna get my degree and go to beauty school."

"Seriously? You'd be an amazing haircutter. You're working those pink streaks."

She flipped back her hair. "I did it myself. They've got videos online about cutting and styling and the other girls let me practice on them."

"Wilde, maybe now's a good time to clean up . . . because when you apply for those beautician licenses, I think they drug test you."

Her eyes narrowed in warning. "Let it go, Jane. I *already* told you, I'll clean up when I clean up."

"Sure, I know you will," I said, because Wilde got defensive every time I brought up this subject. "Hey, I'll come back to visit when I can."

"You do what you have to do and get settled in, baby girl. I'm gonna be fine even *without* you checking on me twice a week, and don't deny it. My man, Junior, takes care of me."

I gritted my teeth so I wouldn't say what I thought about the midlevel thug.

When she gave me another hug, her hand snuck into my front pocket. "Some cash for your stash."

"Wilde, you don't have to . . ." I began, but she cut me off, saying, "Janey, you gave me running-away money when I needed it."

I gazed around at the dismal surroundings. "It wasn't enough to get you out of this place."

"Well, you were always more ambitious than me. I got away from Mrs. Bitchard and that's all that matters." She shrugged her narrow shoulders. *"Quid pro quo."*

Laughing, I said, "Where did you learn that?"

"My clientele. See, I can talk Latin, too."

A gray Volvo slowed on the street and the car's window

rolled down. The man inside leered at Wilde, who waved her hand at him and said to me, "Sorry, Mousie, I gotta get back to work. Now get outa here and show them rich girls that Hellsdale girls got brains, too!" Hellsdale was what we called our city, Helmsdale.

My friend sashayed to the car, swinging her hips widely as she called out, "Need some company, sugar?"

In another life, Wilde would have been a model instead of working the streets. I patted the bills she'd put in my pocket and walked slowly back toward Mrs. Prichard's foster home. A shiny black Lexus was parked in front of the house. The men on the corner stared at me as I hurried to it, and I knew that they had already called in the license plate to their informant at the police station.

A driver in a blue suit got out of the Lexus just as I reached the front of the house.

"Hi, I'm Jane Williams. Sorry I'm late."

"Good afternoon, Miss Williams. I'm Jimmy." He tipped his cap. "I'm a little early. Mrs. Radcliffe didn't want me to keep you waiting if there was any traffic. May I take your bag?"

As he was placing my ratty bag in the trunk, I saw that 2Slim, the local boss, had joined the corner crew and was now ambling toward me.

I told Jimmy, "I'll be a minute. Do you mind waiting in the car?"

"No problem." Jimmy glanced at 2Slim and got in the car.

I stood on the sidewalk and 2Slim seemed to take forever to walk to me. I admired the jaunty tip of his straw hat and the creamy suit that was loose enough to cover a shoulder holster. His skin was a rich caramel and his expression was friendly. "Hey there, Mousie. Going somewhere special?"

He'd never spoken to me before, and now I stood straight and spoke respectfully, because I wasn't out of here yet. "Hello, sir. I'm going to Birch Grove Academy on a scholarship. It's in Greenwood."

"Birch Grove." He hissed out a soft whistle through his even white teeth. "I heard of it. We had another Hellsdale girl go there before, a long time ago."

The school's headmistress hadn't mentioned anything about another girl from Helmsdale. My confusion must have showed, because 2Slim said, "Nasty little thing left and never looked back. I don't like people who forget where they from."

"No, sir, I won't forget."

"Rich folk. You know the difference between them and us?"

I thought, *Yes, education, money, manners, culture, decency,* and waited for him to speak.

"It's not only that they talk like they just sucked a lemon and dress uptight." He pointed to a street memorial of plastic flowers and posters for the victim of a recent drive-by. "The difference is that we honest about who we are, what we *do*. They hide the bodies and think they so clean and *nice*." His laugh had the staccato rhythm of automatic gunfire.

I smiled, because when 2Slim made a joke, it was best to smile.

He said, "I remember when you came here, all skittery and spitting mad, like you was rabid. Wasn't sure if you'd want to get in the game like your girl Wilde, but I didn't expect you to take the long view. You don't have it all figured out yet, Mousie, so take care you don't get your little neck snapped in a trap."

"Yes, sir."

He reached into his pocket and brought out a gold money clip holding a thick wad of bills. He counted out five twenties and held them toward me. "Here's some cheese for little Mousie. No one from *my* turf's gonna show up without a dime and shame Hellsdale. Can't do nothing about your clothes now, but at least you neat and decent."

I took the money, feeling the thick crispness of the paper. "Thank you, sir."

"You remember me. You ever make good, you remember me. You know my name."

"2Slim."

"Too light to fight and too slim to win," he said. "I was like you, Mousie, puny, so I had to use other resources." He tapped one finger to his temple three times. "But for reals, the name's Norton Barrows Blake. You remember that and I'm sure gonna remember you. Jane Williams, Little Mousie, the orphan girl with the spooky eyes."

"Thank you, Mr. Blake." I didn't want to be remembered as Little Mousie, the puny orphan girl who got shoved around and hassled. I wanted to be someone else.

2Slim stared at me curiously. "You never been like the others, you know. I could tell that from the start. Well, I got business to tend." Then he flicked his bony fingers toward the car. "Go on now."

2Slim stood there as I got in the front seat of the Lexus, and Jimmy, the driver, said politely, "You can sit in the back if you like, Miss. There are magazines and refreshments."

I *should* have known to sit in the back. "I get a little carsick. Is it okay for me to stay here?"

"Of course, Miss Williams." He moved to get out, but I closed the door before he could do it for me. He started the car, and I gazed out the window as we drove past a playground with broken swings and a toppled slide. We went by dirty walls and street signs all tagged with WTH, Welcome to Hell.

I'd heard that Eskimos have a hundred different words for snow; we should have had a hundred different words for filth because everything in Helmsdale was covered with grit and grime.

Jimmy said, "You can listen to the radio if you want, Miss."

"Thanks." I clicked it on to fill the uncomfortable silence. It was preset to a news station, and we listened to the entire broadcast twice as Jimmy steered along a series of freeways that led away from the group house, through the city, and beyond. I was conscious of my shabby clothes against the leather seat, but the fold of bills in my pocket reassured me.

Road construction slowed the trip, and three hours later we finally arrived in the town of Greenwood. It was set in a small valley below wooded hills draped with gauzy shawls of fog.

Jimmy turned on his headlights. "This place is in a fog belt. It's overcast all year-round."

I didn't answer because I was too busy staring at a tree-lined main street with a row of shops, each with gleaming windows and colorful flower boxes. Jimmy took an avenue up a hill where enormous older homes were set back behind hedges. The color green was everywhere: deep green trees, vivid green lawns, and lush green bushes. I suddenly felt queasy and closed my eyes, but I could still see green, green, green, and I clasped my hands together and squeezed my eyelids tight.

"Feeling carsick, Miss Williams?"

Jimmy's voice snapped me out of the weird feeling, and I blinked. "I'm fine."

"Here we are, Miss. Birch Grove Academy."

It was the first time, in a manner, that I had known space and air and freedom, all the music of summer and all the mystery of nature. And then there was consideration—and consideration was sweet. Oh, it was a trap—not designed, but deep—to my imagination, to my delicacy, perhaps to my vanity; to whatever, in me, was most excitable.

Henry James, *The Turn of the Screw* (1898)

Chapter 2   Jimmy turned right at a private drive marked by stone pillars and a lacy black ironwork archway in a leaf and branch design. A square brass plaque read BIRCH GROVE ACADEMY FOR GIRLS. The car's tires crunched on the gravel road as we passed a garden. It looked like a park for the wealthy, with endless emerald lawns, flowering borders, and a pond with a fountain.

As the car rounded a curve, I gasped as I glimpsed Birch Grove for the first time. Towering evergreens framed a magnificent dusky coral building that rose three stories against the leaden sky. The photos in the glossy brochure hadn't prepared me for how . . . how intimidating it was. I clenched my fists so tight my chewed-up nails dug into my palms.

Jimmy parked in front of the building, where wide white marble steps led to massive wood doors. I was so excited that I jumped out of the car before he even undid his seat belt. I walked to the steps, trying to take in all the details while Jimmy got my bag out of the trunk.

Above the ornate doors, a carved banner with BIRCH GROVE ACADEMY FOR GIRLS arched over a shield with a lantern, a fox, and branches. I read aloud the motto beneath the shield, *Ut incepit fidelis sic permanet,* and then translated the words in a whisper to myself. "As loyal as she began, so she remains."

I tore my gaze from the building and saw sprawling sports fields to the right and a more modern building set back on the left.

"There you go." Jimmy handed me my bag. "Mrs. Radcliffe said that she would meet you here. Would you like me to wait with you?"

"I'll be fine. Thank you, sir."

"Good luck, Miss Williams."

The car drove off and I stood there alone in the fog, feeling bewildered and incredulous. I patted my pocket, making sure the folded bills were still there. I wanted to take them out and count them, but someone called out, "Hello, Jane!"

I turned to see Mrs. Radcliffe, the headmistress, walking around the side of the building, carrying a basket filled with branches. Despite the weather, she wore a wide-brimmed straw hat with a white blouse, navy sweater, and navy slacks.

The first time we'd met, I'd been puzzled when I was called out of class and sent to my academic counselor's office. An unfamiliar tall, slim woman waited for me. She had smooth ivory skin, clear blue eyes, and sleek sienna-brown hair twisted back into a bun. She'd smiled graciously. "Hello, Jane. I'm Mrs. Radcliffe, the headmistress of the Birch Grove Academy for Girls. I'd like to talk to you about a scholarship."

It had seemed too good to be true, but here I was.

"Hello, Mrs. Radcliffe."

"Welcome to Birch Grove. Let me put these inside. Then I'll give you a tour of the school and show you the cottage."

I wanted to see the cottage where I'd be living right away, but I said, "That would be great," and we went up the steps to the building.

"How was your drive here?"

"Fine, ma'am. It's a long way."

"Yes, it is. I don't suppose you'll be able to visit your old friends often, but I know you'll make wonderful new friends here."

"I hope so." I slowed down my speech and movements so she wouldn't see my nervousness. I wished there were someone who could cue me in on how to act with rich people. "I heard that someone from Helmsdale came here once. Do you know who she was? Maybe I could say hello to her if she lives nearby."

"That's an excellent idea, Jane. I'll try to find out her name, but it may be a while. We lost records in a recent computer upgrade and some of our older information hasn't been digitized yet." She guided me down a hallway with shiny indigo-blue linoleum. Awards and trophies filled glass cases, and portraits of white-haired women hung on the walls. "Birch Grove girls become friends for life."

Mrs. Radcliffe opened a door that had ADMINISTRATION in old-fashioned gold letters on the glass inset. A counter separated the front reception area from desks and file cabinets. She directed me around the counter. "This is my office."

She opened a door to a room with antique furniture, Oriental rugs, lamps with amber shades, and gold-framed certificates. It could have been a room in one of the *Masterpiece Theatre* shows we had to watch in English class. Although everything seemed to be very old, there were no chips, cracks, or dirt.

"Excuse me while I put these in water." As Mrs. Radcliffe passed close to me, I recognized her fragrance from our earlier interviews. It was a pleasant smell, like a newly mown lawn. She went through a doorway, and I heard running water.

Rows of yearbooks stood on a nearby shelf, and one was open on a polished table. I flipped through it and saw photos of girls with funny old-fashioned names: Emily, Susana, Grace-Ann, Roselyn . . . I was about to check the date of the yearbook when Mrs. Radcliffe returned with the slender arching branches in a vase.

"There." She placed the vase on her desk.

The arrangement was unexpectedly pretty. "Those are so graceful."

"I think so, too. They're from the European White Birch tree. Our school's founder planted a grove of them here because they'd grown in his village in Romania. Now let me show you the school."

I walked beside her to the end of the hall. "I was quite pleased with your end-of-term grades, Jane, and with your excellent health exam. I hope you didn't mind the blood test."

"No, I'm not scared of needles, ma'am. Does everyone go through medical testing?"

"We keep health records for all our students, primarily to take precautions if someone has a condition. We want the best for our girls."

Mrs. Radcliffe showed me homerooms, the teachers' lounge, and the nurse's office, which had one wall covered with degrees and certificates. We doubled back to the middle of the building and she stopped at a series of tall carved doors. "Here's the auditorium, where we hold assemblies and student performances."

The auditorium at Helmsdale City Central had looked and stunk like a prison dining hall. This one had pale wood paneling on the lowest section and murals of white-barked trees that stretched all the way to the curved balcony. Midnight-blue velvet curtains on the stage matched the leather seating.

"The paneling here is birch, and when we meet here, it's as if we're gathering in our grove." Then the headmistress took me to see the classrooms, which had older-style oak desks and chalkboards, and the gym. I'd never seen anything like the locker room, which had individual shower cubicles and private dressing rooms.

Mrs. Radcliffe noticed my baffled expression. "Young ladies were quite modest in the days when this school was built, and we've been discussing a renovation since *I* was a student."

"It's like stepping back in time here, isn't it?"

"You might find us a little anachronistic, but we believe that quality is timeless."

We visited a small plain chapel with windows of yellow glass that let in golden light. "Services used to be held here when most of our faculty lived on campus. Although Birch Grove is not a religious school, we encourage spiritual development. Do you follow any faith, Jane?"

"No, but I once had a friend named Hosea and he was . . . well, someone described him as having *grace*. He would have liked the peacefulness of this chapel. He could have read his Bible without being disturbed."

"Hosea. Was he the boy who died of meningitis?"

"Yes, he was in my group home. How do you know that?"

"Your social worker told us that it was a difficult time for you."

Each foster kid was assigned a social worker, and I'd given permission for mine to talk to Mrs. Radcliffe. The same social worker had previously refused to take any more of my daily phone calls demanding that Mrs. Prichard be investigated for malicious negligence.

"Hosea sounds very special, Jane."

"He was amazing." I swallowed hard. When I next spoke, my voice was calm. "Your students probably don't die of infections."

Something—maybe disapproval—flickered in her eyes, and I knew I should have kept my mouth shut. Then she said, "Bacterial meningitis can progress so rapidly that nothing can be done to save a victim. We are grateful for our many privileges here, Jane, but no one escapes death."

Mrs. Radcliffe led me out of the main building to the more modern building, which held classrooms and art studios that were set up with long working tables and easels. After touring the building, we went outside and I took a deep breath. Even the air here was better—damp and fresh and clean.

"Let's go to your cottage. It used to be for the grounds-keeper." Mrs. Radcliffe took me on a path around the art building and toward the back of campus. I was so excited about living on my own that I didn't care if the cottage was a cardboard box with a sleeping bag.

"Here's the grove I told you about," the headmistress said, and I saw the birch trees for the first time.

The three-acre grove seemed as large as a forest to me, as it stretched up the hill and became lost in the mist. Ferns as tall as my shoulder lined a path and shrubs grew all around, making me feel enclosed by the greenery. The towering birches had ghostly white trunks with black markings, and their branches swayed gracefully and rustled in the mild breeze. The trees' outermost layer of bark, as delicate as parchment, peeled away from the trunks.

I shivered in the cool darkness.

"Jane, are you all right?" Mrs. Radcliffe's brows knit together.

"It's all so different than Helmsdale." I smiled. Adults liked it when you smiled.

As we walked along a shady path, Mrs. Radcliffe told me that registration would take place on Monday and classes would begin Tuesday, but I couldn't stop listening to the *shush, shush, shush* of the branches.

"My house is right up the hill there." Mrs. Radcliffe pointed to a trail that continued into the deep shadows of the grove. "Please come by if you need anything or want company. Here we are."

The little white house had a porch with two wooden chairs and a clay pot of purple and white pansies. Mrs. Radcliffe opened the door and I followed her inside to a living room with robin's egg blue walls and white trim.

"It's so pretty!"

A loveseat and chairs with floral cushions faced a fireplace and built-in bookcases. A wooden desk with a vase filled with pink daisies was placed by a window with a view of the grove. A small television was tucked into the corner of the room.

"We've tried to make it cozy. Here's the bedroom."

Through the doorway was a pale yellow room that was barely big enough to hold a full-size bed with a white head-board and a white dresser. Next to it was a blue-and-white-tiled bathroom with a deep white tub.

On the other side of the cottage was a tidy kitchen with a narrow stove, a refrigerator, a microwave, and a square table and two chairs.

Mrs. Radcliffe opened a cupboard. "You're stocked up with the basics. Cereal, milk, juice, eggs. Do you know how to cook, Jane?"

"I helped make meals at the group home."

"What do you think?" she asked. "Will it do?"

"It's perfect and wonderful. Thank you, ma'am."

"It's no more than you deserve, Jane." She placed her pale hand on my arm and gave a gentle squeeze. "Please come to dinner at my house tomorrow, six o'clock. Follow the path up the hill and you'll see it. Will you be all right by yourself tonight?"

I nodded. "Thank you."

"I thought you could use a few days to adjust and prepare before registration day. My home number is programmed in the phone and you're welcome to call for anything. I'm really happy you're here."

"Me, too."

When she left, the first thing I did was count the money in my pocket. Wilde had given me $70, and I hoped that Junior wouldn't miss it and punish her. I put the money back in my pocket and then went from room to room, astonished that this was mine.

I discovered lavender-scented sachets in the closet, brand-name shampoo and tampons in the bathroom, and cupboards filled with good food. The desk drawers were stocked with paper, notebooks, pencils, pens, and a calculator. A navy canvas book tote with the school emblem hung from the back of the desk chair.

There was a tiny room behind the kitchen with a stacked washer and dryer and a rack to dry small items.

I unpacked my clothes, which barely filled a dresser drawer, and placed Hosea's worn Bible on a bookshelf where I could see it and think of him. Even though there was no snooping housemother or klepto roomies here, I put my money in a manila envelope and slid it in the narrow space behind the washing machine. I covered the envelope with lint from the dryer; only someone with a hand as small as mine would be able to reach it.

The simple meal I ate—a grilled cheese sandwich, grapes, and chocolate chip cookies—seemed fantastic because *I* was the one who decided what and when to eat. I turned on the television and surfed the channels, watching junk celebrity shows that my classmates at Helmsdale City Central had talked about, but I'd never seen. I stayed up until two, when I couldn't keep my eyes open any longer.

After washing up, I slipped between the crisp sheets, moving my legs to feel the smoothness of the fabric. I pulled the comforter up to my chin, closed my eyes, and listened to the trees outside. The branches shifted and brushed against the roof as if they were whispering.

A weird sensation ran through me, and I remembered sleeping by a campfire long, long ago, but the memory was so faint that it felt as if it belonged to someone else.

A tree gave a loud creak that sounded exactly like a door opening, so I got up and crept to the living room. The front door was closed and locked. When I peered out the window, there was only darkness and the darkness seemed impenetrable. I checked the locks on all the windows and the doors. Then I went back to bed and covered my head with the comforter so I wouldn't hear the trees.

Before I drifted off to sleep, I thought of all that I had done to get here. Mindless with fury at Hosea's death, I'd started sitting in his seat in the cafeteria with the smart kids. They had ignored me at first, then jeered at me, trying to get me to leave, but I'd stayed there, seething, hating them and the world.

One day I'd heard someone say "full scholarship with living expenses." I'd looked at the kids at the table: they were from the same lousy neighborhood as I was. If they could escape Hellsdale by getting good grades, why couldn't I?

I'd started doing my homework and paying attention in class. It had been a struggle to grasp simple lessons and then harder ones. My school had kept me tracked with the bad students, though, and my guidance counselor had said, "Be realistic about your abilities." I'd sat in the hallway outside her office day after day until she transferred me into better classes.

I'd spent hours after school attending free tutoring sessions at the library. I'd studied videos so I could learn how to speak properly. When a teacher offered extra credit for more work, I'd done it. The hardest—the most humiliating— thing I'd learned was to say, "I don't get it. Will you explain it?" because I hated the smart-ass smirks from the other kids.

Mrs. Prichard hadn't believed I was at the library most nights. She'd follow me through the house, screeching that I was a slut, a drunk, a junkie, trash. I couldn't have dinner until I'd finished my chores and sometimes it was midnight before I finally microwaved leftovers. I'd eat in five minutes, wash up, fall into bed, and start the whole thing all over again when the alarm clock buzzed at six the next morning.

By the time I'd left Helmsdale City Central High, I'd transformed myself from an inarticulate loser foster kid to a college-track student who aced every test. I still sat in Hosea's old place in the cafeteria, but the others didn't ignore me anymore.

Now when people met me, they saw an unassuming, hardworking, well-spoken girl. But inside I was still shrieking with rage for everything that I'd had to do merely to have the crumbs that others carelessly dropped.

I'd pressed down my fury until it metamorphosed, as soft messy carbonate does, into a diamond so hard it can cut through steel and with such clarity that I could use it as a lens to see the world as it truly was, cruel and capricious.

It was rage that got me to Birch Grove Academy for Girls and out of Hellsdale. I nestled into my bed, knowing that rage would help me survive here, too.

The strange little figure there gazing at me, with a white face and arms specking the gloom, and glittering eyes of fear moving where all else was still, had the effect of a real spirit: I thought it like one of the tiny phantoms, half fairy, half imp, Bessie's evening stories represented as coming out of lone, ferny dells in moors, and appearing before the eyes of belated travellers.

Charlotte Brontë, *Jane Eyre* (1847)

Chapter 3

I'd never been allowed to sleep in before, so I lingered in bed thinking about what the week would bring. Tonight I was invited to dinner with Mrs. Radcliffe's family, but other than that, I was free until Monday, which seemed an eternity of time by myself. Something seemed off and, after a moment, I realized that it was the silence. I was used to slammed doors, rumbling buses, shouting, snarling pitties, police sirens, and Mrs. Prichard's and my roommates' furious arguments.

I didn't have to mop floors, do the laundry, or scour the bathroom. When I remembered that I had my very *own* bathroom, I got up.

At the group home, we were allowed five-minute showers every other day. The boys always cut ahead in line, leaving only tepid water and a spray too weak to wash the cheap shampoo out of my hair. Now I filled the bathtub with steaming water and eased in, savoring the almost painful heat. I soaked until my fingers and toes puckered and the water cooled.

I dried off with a thick, soft towel, and then examined myself in the steamy full-length mirror on the bathroom door. I could never keep myself from rubbing hard at the scar below my left shoulder, wishing I could rub it away. It was oval-shaped with a higher ridge running lengthwise, crossed horizontally with narrow pale marks caused by hasty stitching. I had had it as long as I could remember.

I touched the tattoo of the *H* below my left breast. Hosea would have been eighteen now. I remembered him sitting on his bunk bed and scrunching his face while puzzling over the Old Testament, eventually saying, "Why did Leviticus hate pigs so much? I love me some ribs."

"Who cares about Levit . . . whatever his name is? I never even ated ribs. Mrs. Bitchard wouldn't give me no money for the goddamn Fourth of July barbecue."

"Don't be disrespectful, Little Sis, and talk proper. Say 'Mrs. Prichard couldn't afford to give me money for the Fourth of July barbecue.'"

He'd taken my small hand in his big brown hand. "God gave us brains to think things out. I *want* to understand Leviticus, even though he thought hatin' God's creatures was part of believing. He was confused, I suppose, and maybe God wants us to figure out *why* he was confused. When we get outa here, I'm going to take you to eat ribs, so many that you fall asleep with your hands on your belly."

I smiled at one of my few happy memories.

He'd been sixteen then and looked grown-up to me. Now that I was sixteen, would anyone think that I looked grown-up? I doubted it.

My eyes were an unremarkable brown, as was my hair, which fell in waves down my back almost to my waist. My nose was a nose, and my cheeks were cheeks. I thought my best feature was probably my mouth, because my lips were full and my teeth were straight and white. My skin was an unenthusiastic tannish color.

I shoved my small breasts together, but the resulting cleavage looked like a luxury accessory on an economy car. I twisted around and checked out my butt. It wasn't completely flat, but it wasn't curvy, either. I was as I'd always been, plain Jane, the type people thought of as a sexless friend.

I dressed in clothes that Mrs. Prichard had gotten from the free box at the community center. My jeans were too big, so I folded up the legs and pulled my vinyl belt tight to keep the bottom from drooping. I put on a cotton-blend lime shirt that was only a little faded. As I ate a bowl of granola, I read the Birch Grove Academy Handbook. The schedule for classes was an elaborate grid of short and long blocks, and no two days of the week had classes in the same order. After I skimmed the handbook, I decided to explore the campus.

It was another overcast day. I walked cautiously on the path through the gloomy birch grove, and the silence and solitude made me uneasy. I kept twisting around, expecting that someone dangerous was hiding in the wavering shadows. I tried to memorize my way in case I got lost, but I couldn't distinguish one tree from another and the paths were lined with shrubs that obstructed my view. A sudden chittering made me freeze, but it was only a squirrel.

I went to the main drive and veered onto paths that wove through a rose garden and a terrace with a vine-covered trellis. A stone statue of a nymph stood in a fountain. I cut through a sports field and found myself out back by the birch grove.

In the center of the grove, I discovered a clearing that was about thirty feet in diameter. Two concentric tiers of white marble benches surrounded a flat empty space with the remnants of a fire in the center. I sat there listening to birds and watching squirrels scamper. A leaf wafted down in the breeze and brushed against my cheek. Then a memory, or rather an impression, flashed in my mind: of leaves, dampness, and joy. It was gone before I could register any details or identify the memory's origin.

I realized that I'd been absentmindedly rubbing a bump on the surface of the bench. It was a drop of wax, and other wax droplets marked the marble. Someone must have brought candles out here, maybe for a hook-up or nighttime barbecue.

The sky above cleared for a moment and sunlight flickered through the moving branches. I thought I saw something, *someone*, but it was only the shadows of the branches dancing in the breeze.

I stood and continued staring up, losing myself in the swaying branches that sounded *shush shush shush* like brushes against the sky. I walked slowly while gazing upward, almost hypnotized, when a loud crunching noise ripped me out of my daydream. I twirled around to see a bicycle hurtling straight at me.

"Look out!" the rider shouted as he swerved to avoid hitting me. His tires skidded on leaves and loose soil and slid sideways, and he went flying off the bike, tumbling into the underbrush.

I ran to him. "Are you all right?"

The rider was sprawled on the ground. He lifted his head and I saw a tangle of long dark curls and a scruff of beard. He wore khaki shorts and a gray t-shirt. A silver chain around his neck dipped beneath the collar of his shirt.

I studied him while he sat up. He glared at his bike and cursed it. His hair was the bittersweet chocolate shade between brown and black. He had strong features and thick straight eyebrows over wide green eyes with lush black eyelashes. His body was sturdy and muscled, from his broad shoulders to his sun-browned calves.

"You came out of nowhere," he said, grimacing as he stood. He was about a head taller than I was, more if I counted the wild curls, which had bits of twigs and leaves from his tumble. He leaned to one side, then swiped the dirt from the torn skin on his leg, exposing long, bloody scratches.

"Are you hurt? I can get help."

"First you try to kill me, now you offer help."

"You were the one going too fast!"

"Going too fast is the whole point. Get my bike for me."

I narrowed my eyes at the stranger. "You have a lot of attitude for someone who nearly ran me over."

He made a face and I couldn't tell if he was sneering at me or wincing in pain, but he finally said, "*Please* get my bike for me."

"Okay then."

As I picked up his mountain bike, he asked, "What the hell are you doing out here?"

"What business is it of yours?" I held on to the bike, ready to push it down the slope. "I live here. *You're* the one who doesn't belong at a girls' school."

"You're awfully touchy for someone who tried to kill me. Birch Grove is a day school and it's still on summer break."

"That shows how much you know. I moved into the cottage."

"So a pixie is living in the fairy-tale cottage." When he tossed back his head, his curls bounced and his laugh boomed in the quiet grove. "Okay, you live in the cottage, but that still doesn't explain why you're up this way. Where were you going?"

"You ax a lot of questions," I snapped, and flushed with embarrassment. "I meant, you *ask* a lot of questions. I was exploring the grounds and thinking of walking up to Mrs. Radcliffe's house. She's the headmistress."

"Have you met the Radcliffe family yet?"

"Why do you care?" I stared at him and he stared back. The contrast of his black lashes with his green eyes made them luminous. We stood motionless as the trees rustled and birds called out.

He broke first. "We're not going to get anywhere if you keep answering questions with questions."

"I don't want to get anywhere with you!" I blushed again because it came out wrong, and he grinned lopsidedly. "I mean, I don't have to answer any of your questions and I don't know why you're grilling me."

"I'm not grilling you. We're having a conversation. That's a friendly exchange of information, you know, saying things and asking and answering questions. 'How are you doing?' 'Fine, I was enjoying my afternoon walk in the woods. How are *you* doing?' Don't you have friendly conversations where you come from?"

I scowled, but he kept waiting for an answer, so finally I scoffed, "How are *you* doing?"

"Well, fine, thanks for asking, except that my knee's shattered."

"If your knee was shattered, you wouldn't be able to stand. Where *I* come from, people don't cry like big babies when they fall down."

"Your sympathy is overwhelming." He tried to swing his leg over the bike and had to grab on to a tree trunk to keep from falling over. "Maybe my kneecap isn't *technically* shattered, but I could use some help. Come here. Please."

I reluctantly went to his side. He smelled like pine and warm earth. When he leaned on my left shoulder, the heat from his hand went through the thin fabric of my shirt and my scar pulsed like a heartbeat to the pressure of his hand, something that had never happened before. Warmth bloomed through my body like sunshine.

"Later, pixie." He pushed off so that I had to take a step back to get my balance.

"Stop calling me that!" I yelled at his receding back. I peered down at the place he had put his hand and saw a smear of blood and dirt on my t-shirt. "Stupid jerk."

Instead of going to Mrs. Radcliffe's house, I went back to the cottage and took off my shirt to wash it before the stain set. I glanced in the mirror at my bare skin. His blood had soaked through the shirt to my scar; it was mottled rosy red and scarlet like an autumn leaf.

I scrubbed the blood and dirt off my shirt, but when I went to wash off my shoulder, it was clean and my scar was its normal pale color. The blood must have been a trick of the light, perhaps from the pink towels' reflection in the mirror. I changed into my nicest pants, maroon corduroys, a blue blouse, and fake leather sandals that were too big. I wished I had a necklace to wear, or makeup.

When I walked up the hill, I heard the individual notes of birdsong and noticed the serrated edges of the birch leaves. Colors seemed more intense and even the modulated shades of earth were remarkable. I felt as if the grime of my old life had been dulling all my senses and now my perceptions were heightened. I heard running water—from a creek or stream?—in the distance and felt the softness of a fern frond across my hand.

The Radcliffes' house was easy to find. The two-story building stood apart from its neighbors and was the same deep coral hue as the school with the same classic style. The main entry to the house was a turnoff from a street that ran above it at the top of the hill. Towering dark green pines surrounded it, and when I walked on their fallen needles, they released fragrant oils.

I wiped my sweaty palms on my cords before I rang the doorbell. I expected to see Mrs. Radcliffe, but the door was opened by a tall, lean young man so beautiful he took my breath away.

"You have a wonderfully beautiful face, Mr. Gray . . . And beauty is a form of genius—is higher, indeed, than genius, as it needs no explanation. It is of the great facts of the world, like sunlight, or spring-time, or the reflection in dark waters of that silver shell we call the moon. It cannot be questioned. It has its divine right of sovereignty. It makes princes of those who have it."

Oscar Wilde, *The Picture of Dorian Gray* (1890)

Chapter 4 He wore a teal polo shirt, and his eyes were the same blue as Mrs. Radcliffe's. His hair was thick and honey-gold. Although it was the end of summer, his skin was pale and creamy with a hint of pink on his cheeks. His features were fine and perfectly symmetrical in a way that struck me as elegant yet masculine.

He was like those boys who used to brush me aside as they walked down the halls at City Central because I didn't even register as being there. But I could tell that he was different from those boys just as the luster of real silk was different from the cheap sheen of my synthetic shirt.

He smiled broadly, showing dimples. "You must be Jane. I'm Lucian." He reached out and shook my small, sweaty hand with his firm, dry one, and I felt almost sick with tension.

"Hello, Lucian," I said, my voice cracking.

"Everyone calls me Lucky. Mom's all excited about having you here. Come on in."

He led me through the foyer, where a large vase of burgundy dahlias was set on a circular table, and then past a sumptuous ivory and slate-blue living room. Although the interior of the house was dim, I glimpsed polished wood furniture, luxurious fabrics, and framed paintings. Thick rugs muffled our footsteps.

"Mom thought you'd be more comfortable in the family room. That's where we usually hang." His voice was pleasant and clear.

I followed him to a broad room with windows facing Birch Grove Academy below. The furnishings were casual and modern, and the dining area opened to a large kitchen, where Mrs. Radcliffe stood over a six-burner stove, checking the contents of a pot. "Jane, good to see you. Lucian, offer Jane a drink."

"Water or soda?" he asked.

I didn't know if Lucky would judge me on my choice. "Anything is fine."

Lucky took a bottle out of the wide glass-fronted refrigerator. "Try this lemon soda. It's kind of tart. Makes your mouth go *smack*."

"Pour it into a glass for Jane, dear." Mrs. Radcliffe opened the oven and pulled out a tray of breadstick-type things.

Lucky tipped the soda into a glass, plunked in ice cubes, and chose a strawberry from a bowl on the counter and dropped it in. "There you go." He winked at me.

It was only a friendly wink, and a strawberry was only a piece of fruit. Most girls, pretty girls, were accustomed to attention. But I wasn't one of those girls, and I had no idea what to make of Lucky's gestures.

I couldn't even meet his eyes when I spoke. "Thank you."

"Lucian, please ask your brother to join us."

"I'll try to drag him out of his den." When Lucky looked directly at me, I felt my heart jump. "Jack's a caveman, completely unevolved."

"No name-calling," Mrs. Radcliffe said as her son sauntered off.

I sipped the soda. It was a little sour, yet tasty. "Do you have more children, ma'am?"

"Only Lucian and Jacob. Of course, I have all my Birch Grove girls, too." She put the breadstick things on a platter.

"Would you mind taking these cheese straws to the table, Jane?"

I was glad I'd put the platter down before Lucky came back with his brother. The bicyclist, still wearing his dirt-smeared shorts, limped in with a bandage on his leg and a smirk on his face.

"This is the bad little pixie who crashed my bike."

"Jacob!" Mrs. Radcliffe said. "That is no way to greet our guest."

"It's not my fault she knocked me over." He grabbed a handful of the cheese straws and popped one in his mouth. "Yow, hot!"

"I did *not* knock you over! You were riding recklessly."

"She defends herself like a lawyer!" Jacob said. "She'll probably want to sue me for libel with a talking frog as her witness and a troll king as the judge."

Lucky slugged his brother on the shoulder. "Don't let Jack bother you. He's an idiot."

"I believe I said no name-calling, Lucian, but, honestly, Jacob." Mrs. Radcliffe inspected her grimy son from head to foot and crossed her arms. "Not everyone is entertained by your teasing."

He ate another cheese straw. "These are great, Ma."

I tensed, waiting for her to yell at him, but she only brushed his curls off his face.

"Jane, this young man is Jacob, my oldest son. It's no secret that a headmistress's biggest challenge is her family. Jacob, say hello to Jane."

"Hello to Jane," he parroted. He yanked out the pockets of his shorts and held them sideways as he dipped his knees in a curtsy.

It was stupid, but I almost laughed anyway.

"Jane can materialize out of nowhere, Mom." Then he turned to me. "Also, I prefer Jack unless I am in trouble."

"You *are* in trouble, Jacob," Mrs. Radcliffe said.

He ignored her and kept talking to me. "Jake is when

I'm playing poker. Jackie is only for my grandmother, but you can call me that if you pinch my cheeks and palm me a twenty."

"Jacob, please stop being inane and go make yourself presentable," his mother said. "Jane, would you mind helping with the salad while Lucian sets the table?"

"Sure. What do you want me to do?"

The headmistress set me in front of a cutting board and I began slicing tomatoes and cucumbers.

I observed how Lucky placed the plates, cloth napkins, glasses, and silverware on the long rectangular table. I memorized the arrangement: two forks on the left and on the right were the knife, spoon, and napkin.

"What year are you?" Lucky asked.

"I'll be a junior."

"Me, too. What's your favorite subject?"

"It's a tie between math and science. They make the most sense."

"I hate science. I'm stupid that way."

Mrs. Radcliffe placed a basket of bread on the table. "You're not stupid. You simply don't apply yourself. In fact, I thought that Jane might like to tutor you in chemistry to earn some pocket money. Would you consider that, Jane?"

I waited to see how Lucky would squirm out of this situation, but he said, "That would be cool," as if it were the most normal thing in the world for some geeky poor kid to teach the headmistress's son.

"I could tutor," I said quickly. I was thinking, *money and Lucky,* instead of paying attention to what I was doing. The knife slipped and sliced into my finger. I cried out more in anger at my carelessness than pain, which registered a second later.

I was watching the blood ruining the food when suddenly Lucky was standing right beside me. His voice was hoarse and low when he said, "Let me see."

I held my hand toward him. He stood so close that I

smelled the same fresh, herbal scent that his mother wore. He seemed mesmerized at the blood dripping from my finger and his finely curved lips opened slightly. I felt the whisper of his exhalation on my cheek.

"Lucian!" Mrs. Radcliffe said sharply. "I'll take care of that." She put her hand on my wrist and inspected the wound. "It looks worse than it is. Let's rinse it off. Lucky, get a Band-Aid. Your brother has a box in his bathroom."

Lucky rushed away, and Mrs. Radcliffe turned on the faucet and washed the cut with soap. Her manicured fingernails with their clear polish made me embarrassed about my chewed-off nails and bitten cuticles.

"I'm really sorry, Mrs. Radcliffe. I should have been careful."

"No apology necessary, Jane." She didn't take her eyes from my hand. "Most accidents happen in the kitchen. I should have a first-aid kit here." She folded a paper towel and handed it to me. "Apply pressure."

I was pressing down on the cut with the towel when Lucky came back with a box of Band-Aids. Mrs. Radcliffe reached for the box, but Lucky held it away. "I can do it, Mom."

"It's nothing," I said. "I'll put it on."

"You're the patient." Lucky shook a Band-Aid out of the box. "Hold out your hand."

I put the blood-splotched paper towel on the counter and held out my hand. "It's only a small cut."

Lucky tore the waxy envelope from the Band-Aid and peeled off the slick white backing. He gazed at the cut again before carefully wrapping the bandage around my finger. His fingers were as pale as his mother's, and his nails were clean and squared off. Again, I felt his breath on my cheek. He made me so anxious that I could barely stand it, but then he stepped away. "There you go. You can thank Dr. Lucky."

"Thank you, Dr. Lucky."

Mrs. Radcliffe said, "Thank you, Lucian. However, you'll have to put a little more energy into your studies if you intend to earn a medical degree."

He shrugged and offered the plate of cheese straws to me. I took one and bit into it. It was warm and buttery. Lucky ate several, then held the plate toward me again. I accepted another and ducked my head, uneasy with his thoughtfulness.

Mrs. Radcliffe opened the oven and brought out a roast chicken with shiny, golden skin that made my mouth water. A whole chicken, not frozen wings in ten-pound bags with packets of hot sauce. "Lucky attends Evergreen Prep, the all-boys companion to Birch Grove."

"Jack graduated from public school last June." Lucky said *public school* the same way college-track kids at Helmsdale City Central said *youth correctional facility*. "Now he's slacking."

"You'll give Jane the wrong impression." Mrs. Radcliffe gave Lucky a stern look. "The local public school has an outstanding music program, and Jacob is a talented guitarist. He's taking off a year to focus on his music, perform with his band, and consider his options."

"Now my brother has options like sleeping in late or sleeping in *really* late."

"Jane, now you can see why I'm happy to work with my Birch Grove girls. I know you're especially interested in the sciences, but you test extremely well in the language arts. I'm sure you'll enjoy our wonderful literature courses."

"I don't really care for literature, ma'am. I prefer subjects that teach useful information."

"But literature has many lessons we can apply to our daily lives, Jane."

"Now you've got her started," Lucky said, and he was right. Mrs. Radcliffe talked for another ten minutes about the importance of fiction and poetry. I pretended to listen while I peeked at Lucky slouching against the counter, gazing out the window. His nose was long and straight and he had a small cleft in his chin.

When I carried my glass to the sink, I looked for the bloody paper towel so I could throw it away, but it was already gone.

Then Jack, wearing a cleaner version of his previous outfit, returned with a handsome older man by his side.

"Right on time for dinner, dear," Mrs. Radcliffe said to the older man. "Jane, this is my husband, Mr. Radcliffe. Tobias, this is my new student, Jane Williams."

"Pleased to meet you, Jane." Mr. Radcliffe flashed the briefest of smiles. His blond hair was threaded through with silver, and his eyes were the light blue of the early morning sky. He was almost as tall as Lucky, but thin, and there were dark circles under his eyes. On his wrist, a heavy steel watch slid loosely, as if it was intended for a bigger man.

The dinner was more lavish than Christmas dinner at the group home. We had roast chicken, crisp green salad, red cabbage slaw, buttery mashed potatoes, and warm crusty bread. It would have been perfect, except that when I cut into the chicken, blood seeped at the bone. I tried to eat around the raw part and then hid the barely eaten meat under lettuce leaves.

Mr. Radcliffe was pleasant but caught up in his own thoughts, often staring into the distance. Mrs. Radcliffe chatted with her sons and me about weather, the neighborhood, school. They said things like "Allison's sister is visiting from Duluth," things that weren't special in any way, except that there was no animosity or nastiness.

The oddest thing about the family was Jack, who looked so different from the others. He wasn't a caveman, but there was something a little wild and unpredictable about him.

When Lucky finished telling us about the new basketball coach at Evergreen, he turned to me. "Jane, what sports do you play?"

"Jane doesn't like to be *asked* a lot of questions," Jack said.

I wanted to stab him. "I don't do sports."

"We'll have to find one for you," Mrs. Radcliffe said. "We're happiest when we engage both our minds and our bodies in vigorous activity." She watched her husband as he refilled his glass to the brim with red wine. "Tobias, what do you think?"

His eyes skimmed over me. "I don't know. Golf?"

Lucky hooted. "The clubs are bigger than she is! I've still got my kiddie set, though."

"I'm not interested in golf."

"Get a bike," Jack said. "It's a sport and transportation and it doesn't spew toxic fumes. You can build your own. I'll show you."

"These hills are too steep for a beginner," Mrs. Radcliffe said. "Jane, you can talk to the sports clubs at registration on Wednesday and see what interests you. If you don't want to join a team now, you can do it later. We have something for every girl."

"Anyone can ride a bike," Jack said. "Even an elf." The corner of his mouth went up in amusement. "She can ramble through the grove, her natural habitat, and visit her animal subjects."

I fiddled with my knife in a way that only Jack noticed, but he just smirked more.

"Jacob, stop teasing," Mrs. Radcliffe said. "Jane, did you see much of our campus?"

"I walked all around the buildings and sports fields and I saw that clearing with the benches."

"Our amphitheater. The clubs use it for events, like the Drama League's annual sonnet recital. The faculty sometimes holds informal meetings there."

Then Mrs. Radcliffe served dessert—strawberry short-cake oozing with ruby-red juice and topped with whipped cream. At first I thought this must be a special meal for them, but they acted like it was no big deal, and that amazed me. I wanted to shovel down my shortcake before anyone snatched it away, and I wanted to nibble it in tiny bites so that it would last forever. The brothers wolfed down their desserts, but I matched my pace to Mrs. Radcliffe's.

"That was delicious, Mrs. Radcliffe. Thank you."

"You're welcome, Jane. I'm so glad to have you join our family."

Mr. Radcliffe finished eating the berries out of the dessert, leaving the rest. "Very nice meeting you, Jane. If you'll excuse me . . ." He ruffled Lucky's hair as he walked by him, but Jack ducked away from his hand with a laugh.

Mrs. Radcliffe said, "My husband likes to relax in his study in the evenings." She glanced out the window. It must have been sundown because the overcast sky was dark. "How the evening has passed!"

"I better get going." I watched how the boys set their napkins on the table and copied them. "Thank you again."

Jack stood when I did. "I'll walk you home, pixie."

Something about Jack set my nerves on alert. "Isn't your knee supposed to be shattered?"

"I'm recovered. It's a miracle!"

I peeked at Lucky, who was serving himself seconds of dessert. "It's a short walk. I'll be fine."

"Jacob, don't try to get out of cleaning up," his mother said. "Boys, clear the table. Jane, I'll see you out."

We went to the front door and she said, "It's best to stay on the path and go straight to your cottage. The wildlife here forages at dusk. There's nothing dangerous, though Jack has an unfortunate talent for surprising skunks. To-morrow I want to take you into town. We'll pick up a few things you need, and you can open a bank account and deposit your stipend."

The school gave me a stipend for living expenses. I couldn't believe I'd be getting an allowance and had a chance to earn more money. "Okay."

"Shall we meet in front of the school at ten?"

"Yes, ma'am."

"Good night, Jane. Sleep well."

I was glad to be alone so I could mull over the evening and play back memories of Lucky bandaging my finger. I wanted to memorize the way he'd smiled when I first saw him in the doorway and how he'd winked. I wanted to think of the way his lips had parted when he held my hand and his loose-limbed grace as he'd leaned against the counter. I cupped my hand over my cheek, wishing I could preserve the feel of his breath there.

Images of smirking Jack kept intruding on my reverie, though, and I unwillingly recalled the slyness on his face when he'd said "ask" and called me stupid names. I didn't want to think of grimy, grubby Jack, but of gorgeous, sweet Lucky.

I said his name softly to myself. "Lucky. Lucian Radcliffe." His name must come from the Latin *lucianus*, meaning light, and that's what he was, golden and bright.

I didn't care what Jack's name meant. Probably jackass. I ignored the memory of his gleaming eyes and the heat of his hand on my shoulder, and I focused on Lucky again.

Tutoring him meant that we would spend time alone together, and the idea of being near him again made me so excited that I was partway down the path before I realized how dark it was in the grove.

Shadows shifted with the movement of the branches in the wind and there were so many noises, so many creaks and swishes, that I got spooked and started running. My feet slid sideways in my too-big sandals, so I paused to pull them off and ran barefoot the rest of the way to the cottage.

Once inside, I shut the door quickly and locked it.

As the night got later, the wind increased and branches swept against the roof. When I finally fell asleep, I dreamed that the branches were stretching around to encircle my cottage. They were squeezing tighter and tighter, bringing the walls close in on me. I tried to get out, but the doors were jammed shut as the small house began cracking under the pressure.

I awoke gasping for air, and goose bumps covered my arms.

I was not frightened, for I was one of those happy children who are studiously kept in ignorance of ghost stories, of fairy tales, and of all such lore as makes us cover up our heads when the door creaks suddenly, or the flicker of an expiring candle makes the shadow of a bed-post dance upon the wall, nearer to our faces . . .

J. Sheridan Le Fanu, *Carmilla* (1872)

Chapter 5

The next morning, when I met Mrs. Radcliffe at the school's front steps, she was dressed in navy slacks and a long-sleeved white blouse. A white canvas hat shaded her face. "Good morning, Jane. Are you ready?"

Her car was an older model cream Mercedes with a Birch Grove Academy emblem in the rear window. I sank into the burgundy leather seat and Mrs. Radcliffe drove down the hill and told me about the town. I nodded and kept hoping that she'd say something about Lucky.

She pointed out the stop for the shuttle uphill, and we went to a tailoring shop, where a seamstress marked and pinned uniforms for alterations. My school wardrobe consisted of navy V-neck sweaters, a navy cardigan, navy slacks, navy-and-tan plaid skirts, and white cotton blouses. The jacket bore an embroidered Birch Grove crest on the pocket.

I felt sweaty and itchy by the time we went to the bank, where Mrs. Radcliffe opened an account for me and deposited my first stipend check. Fifteen minutes later, I was given a bankbook and checks. A debit card would be sent in the mail.

Our next stop was a shoe store, and I came out carrying a big bag with loafers, flats, tennis shoes, slippers, and flip-flops. I'd never expected shoes. I kept bending down to pry open the box lids so I could see them nestled in crisp white tissue.

We had lunch in an old-fashioned drugstore, sitting at a counter. Mrs. Radcliffe suggested a roast beef sandwich and raspberry lemonade. The meat was so rare that the juices soaked through the wheat bread, but I was hungry.

In the mirror over the counter, I watched three teenage girls come into the store, arm in arm, giggling. They stopped when they spotted Mrs. Radcliffe and exchanged whispers. They were pretty, with nice figures, shining, long hair, and smooth skin. Two wore shorts and tank tops, and the third wore a long gauzy white skirt, lilac blouse, and a straw hat.

The girls approached in that friendly yet wary way that you do with people you like who have authority over you. "Hello, Mrs. Radcliffe," they said in unison.

"Hello, girls. How has your summer been?"

Even though they tried to be subtle about checking me out, I was acutely conscious of my hand-me-down clothes and I resented the girls as they described their vacations in a jumble of words, tumbling over one another's sentences. One had been sailing, and one had traveled to Italy. The prettiest, the auburn-haired girl in the skirt, had spent the summer in Montreal with relatives. She was as pale as the headmistress, and I caught a whiff of the same herby scent. I glimpsed into the overhead mirror to make sure that I was keeping my expression friendly.

Mrs. Radcliffe said, "This is Jane Williams. She'll be joining us this term."

We exchanged hellos awkwardly and then Mrs. Radcliffe said, "I won't take up any more of your last precious minutes of freedom, girls. See you on Monday at registration." When the trio had drifted off to the cosmetics section, out of hearing, she told me, "I know transferring during your junior year isn't easy, but I think you're going to adjust smoothly, Jane. Now let's pick up a few basics."

She took me to a prissy women's clothing store, but I wasn't going to turn down free clothes. I let Mrs. Radcliffe pick out shirts and tops, a skirt, cargos, and jeans. She plucked simple but pretty underwear from racks. Then she called over a clerk, and soon I was in the dressing room holding my arms out while a salesgirl used a measuring tape to find my bra size. She had me try on a lace-trimmed bra that made me look like I had a shape.

Mrs. Radcliffe popped her head through the curtain and nodded to the salesgirl. "That's quite nice. We'll take three white, two beige, one pink, and one black." She waited until the salesgirl left the dressing room. "Jane, no more tattoos, please. They are unseemly and unhealthy. You can get a blood-borne infection, and we wouldn't want that."

"I was careful and I'm fine."

"Still, we don't want you catching anything. We want you as healthy as can be."

When she'd left the dressing room, I ran my finger across the tattoo and wondered what Hosea would think if he could see me at Birch Grove. He wouldn't be impressed by the money. He wanted me to be a kinder person, not a richer person.

Our last stop was Greenwood Grocery, where I stocked up on cheaper store brands of foods that would fill me up.

Mrs. Radcliffe went to the entrance while I waited at the register with my checkbook. When she turned to chat with a store manager, I scooped up a dozen candy bars and threw them in my basket.

The clerk was a cute Latina, about twenty and wearing a neon pink shirt under her Greenwood Grocery apron. "I got a sweet tooth, too. You're not from around here, are you?"

"I'm new. I'll be starting Birch Grove."

"Good on you. See you around."

❧ After saying good-bye to Mrs. Radcliffe, I walked along the path to my cottage, my bags of new clothes bouncing against my legs. The birch leaves fluttered in a faint breeze, revealing the pale green on the reverse side. Even in nature, there was one side that was shown to casual observers, and another side beneath.

Once inside, I put away my groceries before spreading out all my new clothes on the sofa and chairs. I arranged them in different combinations, figuring out the most useful. I put those away and placed the unnecessary items back in the shopping bags. I watched TV while I slowly ate a Snickers, savoring each tiny bite so it would last a long time.

I reviewed a chapter of my SAT vocabulary book and wrote out the words in sentences like "He has an avuncular mien" and "We were habituated to the pedagogue's acerbity." I read them aloud until the words rolled easily off my tongue and I'd memorized the definitions.

It felt like a long day, but when I checked the time, it was only six.

Wilde would be working, but I wanted to talk to her anyway, so I picked up the phone and dialed her number. I got a message that said, "This number is no longer in service," which wasn't unusual because she changed numbers whenever cops hassled her. I chewed at a ragged thumbnail as I worried about all the sketchy situations she put herself in.

I'd have to e-mail her and get her new number. The map in the student handbook didn't show a computer lab, and I couldn't recall any computers in the library.

The knock on my door startled me.

I went to the front window and peeked through the curtains. Scruffy Jack Radcliffe stood on the porch, holding a pizza box. His bike was propped against the banister.

When I opened the door, he said, "Hey, Jane, thought you might want some chow. I couldn't find any of your natural diet, shamrocks and moonbeams, so I brought pizza." He was wearing those old shorts and rusty scabs had formed on his most recent injury. His chest was rising and falling from exertion, but he seemed perfectly comfortable being grubby, sweaty, and uninvited.

Enticing aromas wafted from the box. "Your mother took me to the grocery store today. I have food."

He walked right by me into the cottage. "I know what my mom's groceries are like. Full of antioxidants, roughage, and upright moral character." He glanced around the living room and then went into the kitchen and put the box on the table. "Get plates for us, changeling." He pulled off his backpack, unzipped it, and took out two cans of root beer.

"You're making up that word." The smell of the food overcame my irritation, so I got plates and napkins.

"It's as real as you are. A changeling is a magical creature who has been raised as a human. But I'm guessing you're probably a halfling—half human and half magical creature. Which magical creature, I'm not sure. I'm guessing that you're a pixie, hopefully not one of the evil ones. Are you?"

"Am I what?"

"Are you half evil pixie?"

"If you want to say that I'm puny, *say it,* because I'm used to it. Pipsqueak, pocket pal, peewee, munchkin, midget, Mini Me. I've heard it all before."

"Pixies are also magical beings that are almost human size. Sometimes they're helpful to people, but sometimes they play tricks. Do you ever hear anyone knocking at your windows at night? Because they do that when they want to take you back to their world."

His resonant voice drew me in and I had an eerie sensation as I imagined small hands beating against a windowpane.

"Then you'd live with them and never get old. They like music and dancing and pretty ribbons." He paused to see my reaction, but I kept my face deadpan. "Nope, you don't strike me as a pretty-ribbons type, Halfling."

"If you keep calling me that, you might find out if I'm evil or not. You've spent too much time playing RPGs and reading Tolkien."

"Who doesn't enjoy a good sword battle?" When Jack

grinned, his whole face lit up and the corners of his eyes crinkled. "Yeah, I've read Tolkien, and my mother told us fairy tales every night. I'm an expert on magical creatures and I can recognize one when I see one."

"Does anyone think you're funny, Jack?" I twisted my mouth to keep from smiling.

"I do and that's enough, isn't it?" He flipped open the lid of the box. The pizza had slid to one side and much of the topping was stuck to the cardboard. He shrugged. "This is why people don't deliver pizzas by bike."

We sat down and Jack said, "Mom told me she dragged you clothes shopping. She loves shopping with girls. It kills her that she can't dress Lucky and me in matching sailor outfits with little white hats."

As we lifted out slices of the gooey mess, I asked, "What else does your mother like?"

"Besides her family? Her *girls*." He pitched his voice higher, mimicking her. "A Birch Grove girl is an exceptional girl."

He waited to see if I'd play along. I stared right back into his wide green eyes. They were the moss color of the school's pond, with bronzy flecks like sunlight glinting on the water.

"Well, Jane?"

I bit into my slice. I'd only ever had frozen microwaved pizza before, and this was completely different, so delicious that I couldn't believe they were both called by the same name. "The pizza makes your conversation almost tolerable."

"And by 'tolerable' you mean the most awesome conversating in the world. What are your favorite subjects?"

"Your brother *asked* me the same thing." I hoped he would say something about Lucky. "I like math and science."

"Why? Tell me in complete sentences, the way you'd answer in a college interview, although you do that anyway, don't you, at least when you talk to my mother?"

"You're *axing* a lot for a few pieces of pizza."

"Is that the way you really talk?"

"I talk the way I talk. I haven't had the advantages that spoiled rich kids have, and I taught myself proper English, so, yes, I talk different. Or different*ly,* if you're going to nitpick. Your mom is always formal, so that's how I am with her. With my pals, I'm more kicked back. Everyone is."

"I'm not."

"Well, good for you that you can talk foolishness about fairies and elves and fluffy bunnies and people put up with it because you're Jacob Radcliffe." Why did he make me react?

He considered for a moment. "I never thought of it that way. But I usually don't talk to people about fairies and elves and, what was the other thing?"

"Fluffy bunnies. You forgot the foolishness." I expected him to be annoyed, but he nodded amiably.

"Yeah, I knew there was more. I bet you're good at tests. Anyway, you set my mind thinking in a very foolish direction. But you haven't answered my question about math and science."

"I like science and math because they're always reasonable, logical, and fair. The rules apply no matter who you are, or who you know. They make sense."

"And people don't. We're irrational and unreliable."

"Some more than others. But the rules of science apply when we die. When our bodies decompose, it doesn't matter if we were rich, poor, smart, stupid, good-looking, or ugly . . . None of that matters, because our chemical components are all the same. In death, we're all equal."

There was a long silence and then he said, "I don't know when I've had a more cheerful dinner companion."

I shrugged. "You asked."

He was able to keep quiet for only a few minutes. "Tell me about yourself, Jane."

"I came from a group home and now I'm here."

"I already know that. Why were you in a group home?"

"What did your mother tell you?"

"You're kinda cagey, Jane. The only thing she told us was that you're here on scholarship and that Birch Grove helped get you out of foster care."

"I'd tried to get emancipated from the system before, but no one listened to me until Birch Grove's lawyer helped me file the papers," I said. "My mother died when I was six and I don't have any relatives, so I became a ward of the state. I got shuffled around until my last group home, where I lived for the last four years."

"Where's your father?"

"He bailed before I was born. I don't even know if Williams was his last name." I moved my leg, accidentally brushing Jack's under the table. I felt a jolt from the contact and thought of his muscled thighs and calves, the hair on the browned skin. A smile flickered on his lips, and I quickly tucked my legs under my chair. "As far as I'm concerned, he doesn't exist."

"You're all alone then."

"Save your pity for someone who wants it," I said sharply. "You probably don't know or give a damn, but lots of kids don't live with their birth parents. Kids get taken from crackheads and psychotics. Parents get locked up. They take off. They die."

"I know that, Jane." His somber tone gave me the strangest feeling that he actually did understand.

But I didn't want Jack's sympathy, so I changed the subject. "I'd like to get in touch with my friends, but I didn't see the computer lab on the school map."

"You mean my mom didn't tell you?" He tossed his head, sending his long curly hair swinging. "Birch Grove has a no-computer policy for schoolwork."

"No, it doesn't."

"Yes, it totally does. There's research that shows that writing out information by hand helps you process it. At least that's what my mom says, and she's usually right. Read your handbook, because I'm sure it's in there with the million other insane rules."

I wouldn't give him the satisfaction of thinking I couldn't handle the work, and I could find a place in town with Internet access. "Fine. I'll write out my work. Let them try to decipher it."

"Evergreen Prep is almost as bad. Now you know why I went to public school." He leaned back in his chair, stretched his arms out, and rolled his shoulders. "Do you like living by yourself here?"

"Who wouldn't?"

"You're very taciturn, Jane. Cagey and taciturn and unpredictably sparky and possibly evil pixieish."

I sighed. "Of course, it's great having my own place, but it's an adjustment. I'm used to more noise, city noise, cars and people. And at night, when the wind blows, the trees make sounds. I'll become habituated to it."

"*Habituated?* Really?" A smile played on his lips. "Well, look who's been studying for the SATs."

"Jacob, why should I want to talk to you when you throw things in my face and act all superior?"

He raised his hands in surrender. "Okay, okay, I'm sorry! I do think you're my equal—even before we've both decomposed into our chemical components—or I wouldn't have come here to talk to you."

"Why *did* you come here?"

"I thought you might want company, but it didn't occur to me that you might not want *my* company." After a minute, he said, "There are lots of folktales about birches. Do you know what they say about them? They say they lift their roots from the earth and walk at night."

I had that unidentifiable sensation again of almost remembering something. Then one corner of Jack's mouth lifted in amusement.

"Oooh, spooky, Jack. I'm so scared." *They're only trees,* I kept telling myself.

"No, I don't suppose it's easy to scare you." The last of the evening light coming through the kitchen window caught Jack's face as his expression grew more serious. "There's something in your eyes, Halfling, and I'm not teasing about this, but it's like you've seen things that we aren't meant to see."

"You're imagining that."

"Maybe I am, because I imagined that you appeared the other day on the path. It was clear and then I saw a shimmer and then you were standing right in my way."

"That's impossible. You were going too fast to see anything anyway. Isn't that why you keep getting sprayed by skunks?" I looked anxiously at the leftover slices in the pizza box. Some people threw good food away.

"Skunks don't make the air around them shimmer." Jack finished eating and stood up. "Keep the rest. Don't wander around the grove at night and make sure you lock the door when I leave."

"I thought this place was safe."

"It is, but sometimes people party in the amphitheater before the school year starts. Besides, it's easy to lose your way on the side paths and fall in a creek or a gully. See you around, Halfling."

I followed Jack to the front door and locked it. I looked out the window and saw him straddle his bike and take off into the dusky wood. He'd made the evening pass quickly. I thought of the feel of his leg against mine and the way his hand had warmed my shoulder when we'd first met. I thought of how his teasing made me let down my guard and say things I shouldn't say when I'd spent years training myself to control my behavior.

I'd have to be careful around Jacob Radcliffe.

Strange and various were her conjectures respecting the lights she had seen, and the accountable noises she had heard . . . she did not suffer her mind to dwell on the causes being supernatural, she conceived there must be some mystery which, on the following day, if her health permitted, she resolved, if possible, to explore.

Eliza Parsons, *The Castle of Wolfenbach* (1793)

Chapter 6

Mid-morning the next day, Friday, Mrs. Radcliffe stopped by to drop off my uniforms and a round box. "These are your school hats. Our founder's wife had the good sense to protect our girls from sun damage."

I imagined Mrs. Radcliffe trying to wrestle Jack into a sailor suit and hat, and I almost laughed. "Thank you, ma'am. For everything. Um, I know I should have asked before—but is there a computer around that I can use, not for schoolwork, but so I can contact my friends?"

"The Greenwood Library has public computers. Once you settle in, we can certainly evaluate getting a laptop for you, Jane. I know it seems like a hardship, but people did exist for millennia without electronic communication." She smiled, so I guessed this was her idea of a joke, and I returned her smile. "Well, I'll be off. See you Monday, Jane. Blazers and skirts are worn on registration day."

After I had lunch, I got the shopping bag with all the clothes I didn't need, walked down the hill into town, and located the library. I applied for a card and was issued one labeled *Birch Grove Academy*.

I got on a computer and logged into a private group shared by my Helmsdale City Central pals. I wasn't that close to them because Mrs. Prichard rarely allowed me to visit anyone, and I wondered if they'd miss me. I wanted to tell them about the incredible campus, gorgeous Lucky, my amazing cottage, and weird Jack, but I didn't want to sound boastful about Birch Grove when they were still stuck in Hellsdale. I sent them a general "thinking of you" update.

When I went to my e-mail, I was excited to see that Wilde had sent me a message. "I got a nu website, Mousie. Check it!" When I clicked on the link, an X-rated page blazed on the screen, and I immediately closed the browser. I opened up a new session and sent a reply: "You're hilarious. What's your phone number?"

I checked out a chemistry tutoring book and imagined sitting side by side with Lucky. I thought of how we'd lean together to read a lesson, and I wondered if he'd come to see me as someone special, not merely a mousy geek girl.

My next stop was the women's clothing shop. The clerk didn't want to give me a cash refund without a receipt, but then one of the other women recognized me. "I'm sure it's fine to give her cash back. Mrs. Radcliffe brought her in the other day. She's a new Birch Grove student."

I was so pleased with the money in my pocket that I didn't mind just missing the shuttle. I plopped onto the bench to wait for the next one, and I was thinking about Lucky when an older gray Nissan stopped in front of me.

"Hey! Hey!" It was the girl from the grocery store. She was leaning across the front seat so she could yell out the open passenger window. "Where ya headed?"

"Up to Birch Grove. I missed the shuttle."

"It'll be another hour 'cause it's still on the summer schedule. I'll give you a lift."

"Thanks." I got in the car, which had fuzzy pink seat covers. "I'm Jane."

"Hey, Jane. I'm Orneta, but you can call me Ornery, 'cause I'm kinda cranky." She told me she lived in Millerton, close to the local community college.

I asked, "Is there decent shopping there? Because everything is crazy expensive here."

"Yeah, but you have to get there by car because there's no bus lines. Greenwood people try to keep outsiders away. Where you from?"

"Helmsdale, and they don't like outsiders, either."

She let out a hoot. "I dated someone from there and he told me about *Hellsdale* City Central."

After she relayed a few stories, I admitted, "It's all true. At least it's safe here."

"*Too* safe. It's not natural. Everyone is always up in your business. I'm getting out as soon as I find another job."

"I'll take this over Hellsdale any day. It's so different, though. Like all the greenery and space here. I was jumping each time the wind blew."

"If it was just wind, heck, that's nothing. But the old buildings and the trees at Bitch Grave freak me out. People say the place is haunted."

"Bitch Grave, that's what it's called?" She nodded and I said, "Well, City Central was called Mandatory-Sentencing Prep. You can't take that stuff serious."

"Maybe, but there was that lady that killed herself last year."

"Who died?"

"A teacher or maybe a counselor? It didn't happen here though. Her car was by a cliff near the ocean, so maybe it doesn't count. Why are you up at the school so early?"

"I'm living there. They gave me a place to stay."

Orneta rolled to the main gate and squinted up at the ironwork of leaves and branches. "Is it okay to leave you here? Because this place gives me the creeps."

"Sure. Thanks for the lift." I followed her sightline, trying to see what she was seeing. Thick fog draped over the trees. "There's nothing scary."

Ornery pursed her lips and drummed black fingernails

on the steering wheel. "Not the same kind of scary as Hellsdale, but my feminine intuition says something's wrong."

"There's no such thing as feminine intuition."

"Knowing things isn't only in books. All I'm saying is, be careful."

"Hey, Hellsdale girls are *always* careful." I grinned to show her that we were cool.

Chapter 7   On Monday, I was so nervous that I couldn't eat breakfast. After years of wearing oversized hand-me-downs, my uniform felt uncomfortably snug. At 8:15, I walked along the drive to the school and watched a stream of expensive cars dropping off students dressed exactly like me, in blue blazers and skirts. By the time I got close to the main entrance, I could hear high-pitched voices.

A herd of girls moved through the main entrance of the school. I didn't see any extreme piercings, wild hairstyles, doorknocker earrings, or protruding bellies. The "discreet makeup" permitted in the handbook seemed to be mascara and lip gloss, although some girls wore more and some wore none at all. Most of the girls had their hair long and loose.

They struck me as exceptionally attractive, and I tried not to panic as I followed them into the building and to the gymnasium, which was set up for registration. I stood in line at the W-X-Y-Z table. When I got to the front, the woman at the table smiled. "You're Jane Williams, right? Good morning, Jane!"

"How did you know my name?"

"We study all the new girls' files and photos so we can make them feel welcome." The woman shuffled through a file box and pulled out a navy folder with the school crest on the cover and a sticker with my name. "Williams, Jane, no middle name. These are your classes and here's today's schedule and a map. After you sign up for your extracurriculars, you need to have your photo taken for your student ID. The Refreshment Break is in the cafeteria, and the headmistress will give her welcome speech in the auditorium."

"Thank you, ma'am."

"Certainly, dear. Next!"

I moved to a clear space by one wall and read the contents of the folder. My schedule listed Honors Chemistry, Trigonometry, Western Classical Literature, Latin IV, and Western Culture and Civilization. There was also something called Z Block that I could fill from a variety of courses. I decided to take Expository Writing as my elective so I could improve my essay writing. I wove through the crowd to the sign-up table. A poster board displayed the school newspaper, *The Birch Grove Weekly,* and cheesy photos of students busy in a classroom.

"Hello, Joan, right?" The teacher at the table was almost as small as me, dressed in navy slacks and a blue button-down shirt. She wore a daring slash of ruby-red lipstick and had a short, spiky haircut.

"Jane Williams, ma'am."

"Nice to meet you, Jane. I'm Ms. Chu, the journalism teacher. Are you interested in our newspaper?"

"I thought this was expository writing."

"Yes, that's what journalism is: expository writing." Ms. Chu handed me a pen and a clipboard with a sign-up sheet. "What are your career plans?"

"I'm thinking about going into forensic science." I tapped the pen against the clipboard.

"Really?" Ms. Chu brightened. "Which field of forensic science? Are you interested in being a medical examiner?"

"No, I would like to be a crime lab analyst. It would all

be lab work, but I'd have to write reports, too. I wanted a course that would help me write essays for college applications."

"Then you've *got* to take this, because journalism can help train you to write lab reports. You'll learn to be objective and accurate, and meet deadlines," she said. "It's exciting to put the paper to bed. That's what we call it when we meet our deadline and go to press."

Although I wasn't completely convinced, Ms. Chu seemed nice enough, and I signed the sheet and then had my photo taken for my school ID. I went to the restroom and washed my hands for too long, then smoothed down the unruly waves of my hair. When I could no longer avoid the inevitable, I headed to the refreshment break.

The cafeteria was a long, open, bright room. At one end was a lounge with rugs, potted plants, and sofas. Between old black-and-white photos of the school were student-made posters extolling excellence, honor, and duty. Tables with food and drinks were set along a wall. Girls mingled in groups and I felt their eyes on me as I got a plate of fruit salad and a glass of juice.

"Hi, Jane."

I turned to see the pretty auburn-haired girl I'd met in the drugstore. Her shining hair was in a sleek ponytail and she wore small gold earrings with pearls. Her hazel eyes were framed with long, thick lashes. She was several inches taller than me and slim, but with curves.

"Hello. We met in town, right?"

"Yes, I'm Hattie, Harriet Tyler." She smiled with even white teeth. "I'm a junior, too, and Mrs. Radcliffe asked me to show you around. Come meet my friends."

She wasn't the type of person who was usually friendly to me, so I was wary as I followed her to the lounge area, where older girls were hanging out. She introduced me to a dozen girls and we exchanged bland hellos.

A beautiful, plump girl named Mary Violet asked, "Are

you living in the groundskeeper's cottage?" Her hair was a cloud of silver-blond curls and she had a golden tan. She was wearing shiny pink lip gloss and thin gold chains around her neck and wrists. She leaned toward me eagerly.

"Yes, I moved in last week."

"It must be *fabulous* to live in your own place!" She raised her cornflower-blue eyes toward the ceiling. "If I lived alone, I would have many passionate affairs with debonair *men*!"

The other girls giggled, and someone said, "You'd have a short commute."

"Yes! I would rise from my silk sheets late after a night of untamed sexual coitus, bid my lover adieu—he would beg me to stay—and then I would dash breathlessly to class as the last bell rang. My hair would be romantically tousled." Mary Violet waved her arm, sloshing juice over the rim of her glass.

"You mean you'd be a disaster and wouldn't have the common courtesy to shower," said Constance, a thin girl with dark brown skin, braids, and huge glasses that magnified her almond-shaped eyes. She had introduced herself with a handshake, saying, "I'm Constance Applewhaite. Pleased to meet you." Her voice had an attractive lilt, and I wondered where she was from.

"Let me have my fantasy!" Mary Violet said. "Bebe got up only ten minutes before class. She was hardly ever a mess. Well, there was that time—"

The group became quiet, and Hattie said quickly, "We don't need to gossip."

Mary Violet pouted. "Why can't I mention Bebe? She's the one who dumped us after promising we'd go to the Ivies together and stay BFFs."

"MV, we don't want Jane to feel that she's a replacement." Hattie looked at me. "Bebe was here on full scholarship, too. She moved overseas at the end of last year."

"And she's never written to one of us, not even me!"

Mary Violet said. "That is utterly heartless. All our slumber parties and cram sessions meant nothing, nothing, nothing to her. She was all talk-to-you-*never*-biatch!"

"Stop being so self-centered, MV," Hattie said. "Bebe's too busy. Mrs. Radcliffe's heard from her twice this summer and she really does miss us."

"Huh!" Mary Violet twirled a silvery gold curl around her finger. "Where did her mysterious uncle come from anyway? I thought she didn't have any relatives."

Constance said, "*Everyone* has relatives, Mary Violet. We don't appear out of thin air. You might know that if you paid attention during biology."

This was enough to divert the girls onto Mary Violet's study habits.

Hattie remembered that I was there. "Jane, how's your class schedule?"

"It's okay, except that I was supposed to be in AP Chem, but it says Honors Chem on my schedule."

"It counts as the same as AP Chem, but Birch Grove doesn't offer courses that 'teach to the test,'" Hattie answered. "Honors Chem is more in-depth and ex—"

"Exceptional classes for exceptional girls!" the others said together, and cracked up.

Mary Violet told me, "The joke is that we pretend we don't believe it, but we totally believe it."

"Well, *you* are exceptional, MV," Constance said. "Exceptionally absurd."

"You're exceptionally no-fun," Mary Violet retorted, and stuck out her tongue.

I tried to step away as the girls teased one another, but Hattie kept me in the conversation by addressing comments to me. I was herded into her group as they left the cafeteria and went to the auditorium for the welcome speech.

"Juniors get balcony privileges," Hattie told me, and we went upstairs and into the first row of the balcony.

"You can see everything from up here." Mary Violet

peered over the railing. "I'm so glad I'm not a lowly under-classman. It's tragic we can't haze them and make them grovel like the miserable worms they are."

"Mary Violet Holiday, you're the most appalling girl I've ever known." Constance shook her head, which caused her glasses to slide down her elegant long nose. I could see she was trying not to laugh.

"Can't I ever say anything?" Mary Violet huffed. "What about freedom of speech?"

Hattie stared at her friend. "Mrs. Radcliffe always says, 'Freedom of speech does not excuse freedom *from* thought.'"

A bell chimed and Mrs. Radcliffe walked in front of the blue velvet curtains to the podium. "Good morning, ladies."

As one, the students answered, "Good morning, head-mistress."

"Let us rise for the Pledge of Allegiance."

After we recited the pledge, an elderly woman in a boxy blue suit came from the wings and stood center stage. She blew a little round whistle and then began leading the students in the school song about the birch trees that ended:

Let us bend in the storm, yet never break
Let us offer others more than we take
Let us live for the truth and act for the good
Hail, Birch Grove, hail!

Mrs. Radcliffe returned to the podium. "Students, I am honored to be the headmistress of this exceptional school and all of you exceptional girls. I know you have come back to Birch Grove refreshed and ready to meet the challenges of this year. It will be intellectually stimulating and often emotionally demanding. The faculty, counselors, and I always have our doors open to you."

She talked for several minutes about campus news and then said, "I am so happy to have you all back for the new academic year. I hope you will arrive every day eager to become the very best you can be."

She waited for several seconds and a feeling of anticipation grew in the room. Then she began speaking in a quiet voice that grew stronger with each phrase: "Because I *believe* in your intelligence, talent, and goodness. I *believe* you are exceptional. I *believe* in you. I hope that you will learn to trust in *yourselves*. Trust in *goodness*. Trust in *Birch Grove*."

She nodded and there was a moment of silence. Then the students began clapping and I was clapping, too, and when they stood and clapped louder, I clapped harder, too.

When we were dismissed, the atmosphere seemed energized as students streamed out of the building.

"She's inspiring," I said to Hattie.

"I know. She always makes me feel as if I can do anything."

"She has that je ne sais quoi." Mary Violet tugged my sleeve. "That's French for 'I'm totally clueless.' French is the language of *amore,* and *amore* is Italian for love. What language are you taking?"

"Latin IV. It helps with scientific terms."

"Do you want to be a doctor?" Hattie asked.

"I'm interested in forensic science."

"Since all Romance languages come from Latin, it must be *terribly* romantic," Mary Violet said. "I can come to you when I need details for my mysteries. Maybe I'll write one about a Latin scholar who exhumes mummies and solves ancient murders."

Constance said, "Mary Violet claims she's going to be a novelist."

"Why do you find that so difficult to believe?" Mary Violet demanded.

"Because you are the sissiest female in existence and I can't see how you plan to write gory scary stories."

"That's why it's called *creative* writing, because you make it all up. Let's do lunch."

They began walking toward the parking lot and I turned to go back to my cottage. Hattie came back and hooked her arm through mine. "You have to come with us. Our treat, as a welcome to Birch Grove."

Hattie stood in the shadow of a tree, so I couldn't read her expression. "It's okay, Hattie. You don't need to babysit me."

"It's not babysitting. It's . . ." She shrugged. "It's hard changing schools and figuring things out. I'd want someone to give me the dish."

"Okay." But I thought that she was being overly friendly.

As I walked with them to Hattie's gleaming red BMW, a stunning tall girl with long, wavy tawny hair crossed the parking lot in front of us. She saw our group and sneered. "Hi, sad little juniors."

"Hi, Catalina," Hattie's group responded.

The girl's amber eyes settled on me. Her full lips curved downward sullenly. "You're new. Who are you?"

"I'm Jane Williams. I transferred in," I said with a sharp edge in my voice. I almost preferred her direct hostility to the other girls' unnatural friendliness.

"She's living in the groundskeeper's cottage," Mary Violet said.

Catalina frowned. "What happened to Mrs. Radcliffe's charity project?"

"If you mean Bebe, she went to Europe." Hattie opened the car door. "See you later, Cat."

"TTF Never." The tall girl walked off with a swing of her hips.

Mary Violet said, "I call shotgun."

We got in the car, and I asked, "Who was that?"

Hattie started the engine while Mary Violet fiddled with the music. "I'm feeling Pink today," she said, and "Trouble" began playing. "That was Catalina Sachs-Montes, the Argentine princess. Not that she's really a princess. She just acts like one. She speaks five languages, including Russian, so she thinks she's special."

"I speak four languages," Constance said.

"Five is the tipping point," Mary Violet answered. "Cat's little sister, Adriana, is starting this year. She's much nicer. She had class after me at Miss Harlot's School of Croquet."

"Mary Violet means Miss Charlotte's School of Ballet," Constance said. "That's where we met when I was six and moved to Greenwood from Barbados. All the other girls wore leotards, but MV was a roly-poly thing flouncing in a pink tutu."

"I was as graceful as a swan and I had a fabulous sense of style even then." Mary Violet adjusted the rearview mirror so she could see me.

"Why are we always talking about you, Mary Violet?" Hattie moved the mirror back as she maneuvered around students to the street. "Jane, Catalina's a senior and she's very . . . very Catalina. Don't let her get to you."

Mary Violet twisted to face me. "She's one of those foreigners who thinks Americans are gauche, which is French for oh-my-gawd-how-tacky. Unlike Constance, who thinks Americans are frivolous."

"Not all Americans, only you," Constance said.

I automatically scoped for cops as Hattie drove us off campus, but no one else seemed concerned. "I thought you had to be eighteen to drive other teens."

"Oh, no one pays attention to that here," Hattie said. "It's fine as long as you live in Greenwood."

Mary Violet said, "My grandparents let my mother drive when she was fourteen. She was an excellent driver and hardly ever got in accidents. She did run over a possum once and we can make her cry about it if we pour her a second tipple of Dubonnet and ask her about its darling furry paws and adorable whiskered snout."

I tried to remember *dubonnay* and *tipple* so I could find out what they meant later.

"You don't," Constance said.

"We absolutely do! My father is the worst. He always

talks about the heartbroken possum husband searching for his dead possum wife. Sometimes I recite my poem 'Requiem for a Marsupial.'"

Mary Violet switched off the music, and then threw out her arms as far as she could in the confines of the car.

"Oh, once you gamboled happily in a wood
Living, loving, gathering food . . ."

Constance said, "*Food* doesn't rhyme with *wood*," but we were all laughing, and Mary Violet continued:

"You cross the road exploring afar,
When you are crushed by a speeding car!
Alas, poor possum, you draw a last breath,
A Birch Grove girl has crushed you to death!"

She bowed her head.

"Brilliant as always, MV," Hattie said. "Jane, as long as you're wearing your uniform or you let people know that you go to Birch Grove, they're okay. If bigger problems come up, Mrs. Radcliffe can take care of them. It's easiest for everyone that way."

Hattie parked in front of a small café called the Tea Stop, but the girls called it the Free Pop and explained that Birch Grove students always got a free soda with meals.

When I opened one of the laminated menus, Hattie said, "They don't actually serve anything that's on the menu. You have to order from the chalkboard. Our favorite is crab sandwiches on toasted white bread and Caesar salad."

"I always get the cup of soup," Mary Violet said. "Salad gets stuck in your teeth."

Constance said, "Soup gets dropped on your boobs."

"At least I *have* boobs," Mary Violet snipped back.

"Or you are a giant one."

I hoped they'd just let me listen to their conversation,

but Mary Violet asked, "Jane, where is your family? Do they mind you living away from them?"

People usually dropped the subject after I gave them a few basic facts. "My mother died and I have no idea who my father is or where he is."

Mary Violet's eyes went wide. "How tragic! You could hire a detective to find him. Think of how excited he'd be to find out that you're attending a top school. You're the crème de la crème. That's French for 'all that and a bag of chips.'"

"I think if he cared, he would have stuck around," I said uneasily.

Hattie said, "Jane is doing okay on her own and we'll be her family. She won't be able to get rid of us!"

I stared at Hattie in disbelief. "Hattie, you know, I'd be more comfortable if you were straight up with me. I'm not interested in being a charity project."

"I *told* you that inviting Jane to lunch was overkill," Mary Violet said to the others before turning to me. "Mrs. Radcliffe asked us to include you in things so you won't hate Birch Grove. I want her to give me a letter of recommendation for college. She only gives out a few each year so we're being completely extorted to be your new bestest friends. I only hope Mrs. Radcliffe doesn't ask me to murder someone for her, although I'm sure I'd commit the perfect crime."

"Mary Violet!" Hattie gave the girl a hard look.

"Wasn't that you five minutes ago yodeling about living for the truth?" Mary Violet answered obstinately. "Jane, another thing is that we're so tragically bored with one another that we're thrilled to meet anyone from the outside world. Greenwood is like one of those luxury prisons, where inmates can decorate their rooms and play tennis, but only get day passes."

"I wish Mrs. Radcliffe hadn't done that, because I'm fine on my own and besides, I'm not that exciting."

Constance said, "I'm not doing it for the letter of recommendation."

"Well, Constance, you're friendly to *everyone*," Mary Violet said critically. "You're such a friendship slut and I find that deeply disturbing. Jane, I hope you aren't as wildly promiscuous with your friendship."

"No one's ever accused me of that," I said, which made her giggle.

Hattie shook her head. "I'm not doing it for the letter, either—"

"Because you already know you're getting one, headmistress's pet," Mary Violet cut in. "You always do everything Mrs. Radcliffe wants."

"Excuse me, but *you* were ready to plot the perfect murder for a letter of recommendation!" Hattie said. "So, Jane, we're happy to show you around and if we all get along, fine. If not, that's okay, too, and we'll act friendly in front of Mrs. Radcliffe so she lets it go. Deal?"

I shrugged. "Sure."

"Good. Have you met Mrs. Radcliffe's family yet?"

"I had dinner at their house. They were really nice."

"Especially one of them." Mary Violet pinched Hattie's arm. "Your loverrrrr!"

Hattie looked away. "It's not that serious."

My heart dropped, but I kept my expression even. "Lucky seems like a cool guy."

"Not Lucky," Hattie answered. "His brother, Jack."

"Jack? Really? He doesn't seem . . ." I paused awkwardly.

"He's really smart and talented," Hattie said. "And mature."

"Why do you think he didn't go off to college?" Mary Violet asked. "He's psychotically in lust with Hattie. There's something terribly intriguing about him, as if he has a dark and depraved secret."

Constance sighed. "Mary Violet, if we cut open your

skull, I have a feeling all we'd find would be hair products and chick flicks."

"And silk lingerie and chocolate truffles!" Mary Violet said.

Constance asked me, "What do you think about our no-tech rules?"

"I think that because older people grew up without all the technology, they're incapable of multitasking and refuse to believe that we can."

"If you say that to Mrs. Radcliffe, she'll show you a dozen studies that say that technology is destroying our cognitive and analytical skills. We always agree with her and do whatever we want anyway." Constance shuffled through her tote and lifted out a silvery blue phone. "Let's all sync up. What's your number, Jane?"

"I only have the phone in the cottage."

"Oh, we've already got that," Mary Violet said. "It's Bebe's old number. She didn't have a real phone until last spring. We have to sit through an assembly once a year about how it's more important to live life than text it, blah, blah, blah, because Mrs. Radcliffe is so viciously anti-TSGs."

"Do you mean STDs?" I asked.

"TSGs are trendy status gadgets," Hattie said. "TSAs are trendy status accessories. Mrs. Radcliffe dislikes obvious logos and labels."

"I adore labels, because they tell you whether something is good or not." Mary Violet applied lip gloss using the napkin dispenser as a mirror. "What I want is a TSB."

Constance and Hattie seemed puzzled for a few seconds and then said together, "Trendy status boyfriend?"

"Yes! I'm drawing up a list of candidates and starting with A for Ashton and working my way to Z for Zach."

Hattie said, "I'd love to hear them, but I've got to get home."

When I glanced at the teakettle-shaped clock on the wall, I was surprised to see that two hours had passed.

Hattie drove us back to the Birch Grove parking lot, and the girls shouted good-byes. As I walked back to the cottage, I brooded about how these privileged kids expected and received special treatment with the same blasé attitude that City Central kids expected and got violence and grief.

"I will be as good a friend as such a mite of a thing can be to such a noble creature as you. And be a friend to me, please; I don't understand myself: and I want a friend who can understand me, very much indeed."

Charles Dickens, *The Mystery of Edwin Drood* (1870)

Chapter 8 The next morning, I joined the other students filling up the hallways and located my locker, which was on a top row because I was an upperclassman. I twirled the combination, opened the metal locker, put my books inside, and headed to the day's first period, which was homeroom. I was glad to see Hattie already at a desk. She waved me over and I sat beside her.

A short man with thinning brown hair and glasses stood at the oak desk at the front of the room shuffling through papers. On the blackboard, he'd written "Mr. Albert Mason." He wore a navy blue jacket, a white shirt, a navy-and-maroon-striped tie, and gray trousers. He was thin all over except for a small round belly. His nose was like a deflated balloon drooping on a string, his cheeks were hollow, and his ears protruded, yet there was something very likable about his intelligent expression.

When the bell rang at 8:30, he said, "Good morning, students. I'm Mr. Mason, your homeroom teacher." He had a pleasant smile, but I could tell that it was like mine, something he was wearing to please others. "Let's go around and make sure we're all here." He read a roster aloud, and when he came to "Jane Williams," I raised my hand and said, "Here."

"Welcome to Birch Grove, Jane, and I'm happy to have you in Honors Chemistry."

As he finished the roll call and went through announcements, I gazed out the window at the greenery beyond. None of this felt real. I'd known that there was a world outside Helmsdale, but my conception of that world had been flat, like the image on a television. I felt as though I had stepped through the screen into another dimension, and I was astonished that everything had depth and detail. I noticed the grain of the wood desks, the scent of floor wax, and the burnished brass doorknobs.

As we left homeroom, Hattie asked, "What do you have next?"

"Western Classical Literature."

"Me, too. I wonder what else we have together." We compared schedules and saw that we were also in the same history course. "I love studying the past," she said. " 'Whereof what's past is prologue.' "

"Is that a quote from something?"

"It's Shakespeare. It means that what's happened in the past determines what will happen in the future. That's why history is so important."

"But whoever wins battles gets to write history, so history is the winner's version."

"You're terribly cynical, Jane."

"I'm realistic. The only lesson in history is that it's better to be stronger and more vicious."

"Like I said, you're cynical. I kind of agree, but I still think it's important to study history."

I followed Hattie to the classroom and we sat at desks in the front row. When the teacher, Mrs. Baybee, handed out the syllabus, it was even worse than I had thought: Homer, Virgil, and Sophocles, readings from the Bible, Chaucer, Milton, and Shakespeare. Mrs. Baybee spoke in a mind-numbing drone, and I jotted down notes that were totally incomprehensible to me.

How could I possibly keep up with girls who'd been to excellent schools all their lives? I dreaded going to my next class, Honors Chem on the third floor.

Mary Violet was sitting at one of the tall black lab tables, sighing and staring out the window to trees beyond.

I sat at her table. "You didn't tell me you were in Honors Chem."

She smiled cheerfully. "Yes, I'm a Chem Ho, too. My parents are totally draconian and make me take all this math and science because they've got some delusion that I should be a surgeon, but I don't want to deal with the insides of bodies, ew. I wish I had nothing but English and history classes."

"I've got the opposite problem. I just had Western Classical Lit with Mrs. Baybee." Usually I hid my inadequacies, but Mary Violet was looking at me with such friendliness that I said, "I couldn't make any sense of what she was talking about, even if I cared about the subject, which I don't at all."

"I would be mortified if you were a cultural barbarian, Jane. That's exactly what my mother tells my father when he complains about the symphony, though she doesn't call him Jane. Mrs. Ooh-baby-Baybee is notorious for being boring. Her voice always makes me think of a mosquito buzzing somewhere in the room. Allow me to demonstrate." Mary Violet made a buzzing sound.

"That's *exactly* what she sounds like. I thought it was just me."

"Oh, no, she's always voted Teacher Most Likely to Inspire Mass Catatonia in our secret annual poll. Of course, I'm the one who invented the category. I keep hoping we'll get a Teacher Most Likely to Spontaneously Combust. Why don't you transfer to something more interesting?"

"I could do that?" Of course I could do that—and it's what I would have done immediately at City Central. "What else is there?"

"I'm in Civility and Propriety of the Victorian Woman because I want to write fat, juicy historicals with lots of mayhem and I need to learn all about hysteria and corsets. But that's at the end of the day and you'd have to shuffle your whole schedule. Constance is in Night Terrors and that's the same block as Western Classical Lit."

"What's Night Terrors about?"

"It's totally fabu. Fabulous to the nth degree," Mary Violet said. "See, I also *parlez* geek! I'm multilingual, which sounds so *dirty*, don't you think? Night Terrors is the only class Mrs. Radcliffe teaches. I'm taking it next semester."

Mr. Mason came into the room, hung up his blazer, and put on a white lab coat as the bell rang.

I felt more confident now that I had a heavy chem book in front of me and sat in a room with shelves of specimens in display jars and racks of test tubes. An old cloth banner of the periodic table was stretched on a standing wooden frame.

When Hosea had taken chemistry, he asked me to quiz him on the table of elements and I'd somehow memorized it along with him. He'd counted out the groups on his fingers, saying, "Alkali metals, alkaline earth metals, lanthanides, actinides, transition metals, poor metals, metalloids, nonmetals, halogens—"

I'd cut Hosea off and put down the book. "This is *so* fu— I mean, soooo dang boooring."

He'd laid his big hand on my head, and I'd leaned toward him, like a dog enjoying a petting. "Little Sis, these are all the things that make the universe, and that's a beautiful and amazing thing."

"I don't get it." I'd pointed at the Bible on the wooden crate he used for a bedside table. "How can you believe the world was made in seven days *and* believe that dinosaurs lived hundreds of millions of years ago? Pick one or the other."

His deep chuckle had rumbled through the room. "You

been paying more attention than you let on, Little Sis. God created everything, including this universe and its scientific rules. Why can't both religion *and* science be true?"

"It can't be both because they, uh . . ." I'd struggled to remember the term I'd heard him say once. "They're mutually exclusive."

Hosea ruffled my hair. "You got a fine mind in that little head of yours. Pity if you didn't use it. Promise me you'll try."

I hadn't tried, though, not until after Hosea had died.

Mr. Mason began talking about our curriculum and I opened a wire-bound notebook. I'd already drawn a vertical line through each page. On the left side, I scribbled notes. Later, when I reviewed my notes, I would add details on the right side of the page.

Despite Mary Violet's complaints about chemistry, she was writing diligently with a fountain pen that had purple ink. Her script was old-fashioned with big loops and swirls. While Mr. Mason was handing out the week's assignments, she drew a small flower on the page border.

"It's a violet," she whispered to me. "My trademark."

I didn't know why I liked Mary Violet so much, and I couldn't help returning her bright smiles. I liked her pink and golden plump cherub prettiness and the way she blurted out anything that came to mind.

Class seemed to go by quickly. Mr. Mason spoke clearly and paused for questions, which he answered easily. As we were leaving, he stopped me. "May I have a word, Jane?"

"Yes, Mr. Mason?" I moved to the side of his desk.

"We go at a brisk pace in this class, and I want you to know that I'm here to help if you find yourself getting swamped."

"Thanks. I can keep up in Chem, but I'd like to transfer out of Western Classical Lit."

"Is there a problem with it?"

"I can't really connect to the subject. Mary Violet Holiday suggested Mrs. Radcliffe's nightmare course."

"Night Terrors. I'm surprised the headmistress didn't sign you up for that. It's an excellent course. I'll talk to the registrar at my break, and you can stop in at her office after school today to get your revised schedule."

"I really appreciate it. Thank you, sir."

Mary Violet was waiting in the hall for me. "Mr. Mason's so valiant and tragic. What did he want?"

"He was checking on me. He's going to talk to the registrar so I can transfer to Night Terrors."

I wanted to ask her why she thought Mr. Mason was tragic, but she said, "You were staring at the periodic table. Which element are you?"

"You're perplexing me. Do I have to pick one?"

"Perplex is a good word. You can have any element but potassium. That's mine."

"I thought you might pick something, um, noble like neon instead of a humble poor metal."

"Oh, so you think I'm gaseous! Really JW, you wound me deeply." She bumped my hip. "I'm potassium because when it comes into contact with water or air, it instantly combusts—kaboom!—into violet flames. *Violet.* You should have figured that out. Knowledge is power."

"Or I could have guessed because metals are sonorous and I bet you make a ringing sound when you're smacked hard."

"Don't you dare, Jane Williams! Do you have lunch now? Let's go to the café-teria."

As we walked down the stairs together, Mary Violet told me that they usually went off campus for lunch. "We go to the Free Pop or get something from the deli in the market. Everything else in town is too slooow and takes too long. On days with long blocks, we're stuck here."

"Why aren't there any fast-food places around? At my old school we had them right on campus."

"The Birch Grove Alumnae Club makes the mayor's life

a living hell any time there's a rumor that a fast-food place might move in."

We went into the cafeteria and I smelled the wonderful aromas of Italian food and something baking, like cookies. "I'd rather use my lunch pass anyway. What's good?"

"The salad stuff is always fresh, and the pasta's good. Everything's homemade and organic since the alumnae are terrified that we'll have mutant babies if we eat anything with pesticides."

"You sound like you'd *like* a mutant baby," I said as we served ourselves mixed lettuces that I didn't recognize.

"I'd prefer an alien baby with soft fur, like a kitten, but violet, of course." Her big blue eyes opened wide. "Quick! Tell me what you're thinking."

"In Helmsdale, they would say, *You hella crazy, bitch!*" Which made her burst into giggles.

"See, that's why I adore new students. Hattie would never say that or threaten to smack me. Constance always *says* she'll hit me, but she hasn't done it since we were seven and I stole her black Barbie to add to my collection. What color are you, by the way?"

"I'm a tannish or brownish, I guess."

"I would call you a café au lait shade. If anyone asks what color I am, you can say that I have a peaches and cream complexion—doesn't that sound yummy? But what *are* you?"

"Mixed up, like someone poured all the leftovers from soda bottles into a glass. My mother was part Mexican, and everyone thinks I'm whatever they are."

"It's called 'projection' in psychology. Why did your mother name you Jane?"

"I have no idea. Why are you named Mary Violet?"

"It was a grand-aunt's name and you have to pay tribute or else you're cut out of the will. When she died, all I got was her collection of Tom Jones memorabilia. She used to go to Las Vegas and throw her underwear at singers, but we only learned that after she passed away, which is tragic because I have *so* many questions."

"I noticed that about you."

"I'm intrigued by mystery and you're *so* mysterious, Jane! You could be anything—even part Laplander."

"That's everyone's first guess," I said, which sent Mary Violet giggling.

We split up at the hot entrées counter. I got something called pasta primavera, warm bread, and an apricot bar. I looked around for a place to sit, and Mary Violet came back and jabbed me with an elbow. "Come *on*, slowpoke." She headed to a table near the lounge area. "This is reserved for juniors, although a few underclassmen might be allowed if we decide they're worthy. Naturally, I was invited to sit here last year because I'm so fabulous."

Hattie had a later lunch period, but Constance was already there. I sat at the end of the table, kept quiet, and observed the clusters of students. I'd been to enough schools to know that they all had the same cliques. Birch Grove was different, though, because geekishness was a common denominator, and no one seemed embarrassed by it.

I must have looked puzzled at some of their slang, because Constance explained, "Everything here has a nickname. The main building, Birch Grove Hall, is B-Gro, and the other building, Founder's Arts Building, is Flounder."

The other students told me that the nickname for the gymnasium was the Gin Nauseum, and the Founders Memorial sports fields were called Fo-Mem or Foaming at the Mouth.

Mary Violet said, "Do you have a nickname, Jane?"

"No, I'm just Jane." Plain Jane.

"We'll have to get to know you better and we'll give you one. My grandfather was Horrible Holiday because he was a terror of the football field."

Constance asked to look at my schedule and said to Mary Violet, "Jane's got Ms. McSqueak for Trig!"

"Oh, you'll love her," Mary Violet said. "Especially when she says 'hypotenuse.' You have to count how many times she says it before Thanksgiving break and then guesstimate the total number over the semester."

"We have a pool and it only costs a dollar to enter," Constance said. "Whoever's assigned the front right desk has to keep track, and then there's a prize to whoever guesses the closest."

Mary Violet said, "My mother won when she had Ms. McSqueak. She guessed one hundred and sixty-seven and she was right. We're all so proud of her."

I discovered what they meant when I went to Trigonometry. My teacher, Ms. McPeak, was a tiny ancient woman who gesticulated wildly and was covered with chalk dust. Her reedy voice broke upward on the last syllable of each word, especially hypotenuse. I counted four times and wrote it on the corner of my notebook cover.

Then I had history, which was mind-numbing, but at least the tests didn't ask for personal interpretation. When the bell rang at the end of the day, I went to the registrar's office and waited behind other girls trying to fix their schedules. When it was my turn, I asked to change classes.

"Hmm," the registrar said. "Mr. Mason talked to me about that. Students reserve their spot in that seminar one or two years ahead of time."

"But I just transferred in, ma'am. If there's a space . . ."

"I can put you on the list for next year."

I was trying to judge what tactic would work with her, whether I should get whiny, friendly, or demanding, when a voice behind me asked, "Jane, how was your day?"

I turned to see Mrs. Radcliffe. "Hello, ma'am. It was good, thank you."

"Can I help you with anything?"

The registrar said fussily, "Miss Williams wanted to transfer into your class, and I explained that it was full and requires a reservation."

"You're quite right, but I think we can make an exception for Jane. Would you please handle the paperwork, Mrs. Dodson? Thank you so much."

"Of course, Headmistress."

As the registrar printed out a new schedule for me, Mrs. Radcliffe said, "Jane, I'll have Lucian call you soon to arrange his tutoring sessions."

"Okay." I was amazed that she had both the desire and ability to help me—and I was excited at the thought of spending time alone with Lucky.

My homework kept me busy all evening. I spread all my books and papers on the floor and worked there. When night fell, I went outside and gazed up toward the Radcliffes' house, thinking that I might be able to see their lights through the grove. The black splotches on the white-barked trees looked like pale, amorphous faces. The more I stared at them, the more they seemed to be gazing back at me.

I focused on the trunk of one tree and, when the clouds overhead moved, the shifting shadows seemed to reveal the face and body of an ethereally lovely woman. Her dress was made of the paper-thin bark and her eyes were as black and shining as anthracite. The scar on my shoulder suddenly burned as hot as fire.

The branches thrashed in a gust, altering the pattern of moonlight on the bark. In that moment, I thought I saw the woman smile at me.

I spun around and raced into the cottage.

I slammed the door shut and locked it quickly. My heart pounded and I was trembling because, because . . .

Because I thought I recognized her.

I slid to the floor and clutched my left shoulder hard, pressing against the pain, and it faded away. When I stopped shaking, I stood and opened the door. All I saw were trees.

Whilst he was petting the horses and trying to quiet them, dark clouds drifted rapidly across the sky. The sunshine passed away, and a breath of cold wind seemed to drift over us. It was only a breath, however, and more of a warning than a fact, for the sun came out brightly again.

Bram Stoker, "Dracula's Guest" (1914)

Chapter 9 I thought my morning would be manageable because I had Latin, but when I walked into the classroom Catalina was there arranging her books on a desk. Her luxurious amber hair hung in curls down her back and gold earrings gleamed on her earlobes.

"Please sit at your assigned seat." The teacher, Ms. Ingerson, was looking right at me. She was a sturdy woman with cropped hair the color of a dead lawn and brownish yellow eyes behind gold-rimmed glasses.

To my dismay, I spotted *Jane Williams* on a piece of paper atop the desk beside Catalina's. The stunning girl raised her eyebrows in disdain, and I rolled my eyes at her in response.

The moment the bell sounded, Ms. Ingerson began class. *"Salvete, discipulae. Latine colloquamur."* Hello, students. Let's speak in Latin. She put us through a series of rapid drills. I could barely follow what she was saying, and I kept flipping through my dictionary, trying to translate. When the bell rang an hour later, I felt as if my brain had run a marathon.

Catalina gathered her things and stood gracefully, watching me as I scribbled down what I could recall of our homework assignment. She waited until I shut my notebook and then said, "Maybe this isn't the right place for you."

"Thanks for your condescension. Guess what? I don't care." I shoved my books in my tote and stood.

"You *should* listen to someone who knows something." She tossed her head dismissively. "So the headmistress has enrolled a new scholarship student, another poor little homeless thing." Her accent was barely discernable, only evident in the full rounded vowels. "Harriet Tyler has adopted you, no?"

"No one's 'adopted' me. I can take care of myself."

"Hattie was friendly to the other scholarship girl, too. Another *pobrecita* like you."

If Wilde were here, she would shriek "Get the bitch!" and jump Catalina, hauling out hanks of her hair. I spent a moment enjoying that fantasy before saying, "The world has as many poor girls as it does nasty snobs."

"The world may be full of poor girls, but not Birch Grove Academy. One poor girl vanishes, and another quickly replaces her. But why?"

"The scholarship was available."

"Then why not a freshman, instead of someone who will always be behind? As for snobs, your so-called friends are among the worst at the school."

"I don't need your concern." I resisted the urge to swing my tote at her head, and I walked away.

❧ When Constance invited me to go off campus, I told her I was going to eat in the cafeteria. She said, "Next time then. How was Latin?"

"It would have been better without Catalina. She told me I shouldn't be here."

Constance grinned. "Welcome to the club. Being insulted by Catalina is a rite of passage here. She called me Rotten Applewhaite for weeks. Once she told Mary Violet that if she didn't stop sitting at the upperclassman table she would slap her like a maid who steals jewelry. Of course, Catalina said it in French because she thinks MV actually speaks French."

"I thought she did, too."

"No, she takes German, but she thinks French is more glamorous. MV made me translate and I told her Catalina thought she had the most beautiful hair at Birch Grove."

"At least Catalina didn't jab me with a pin while her friends made a video."

"Did that happen at your old school?"

"Frequently. I think it was offered for five units as a performing art."

❧ My last class of the day was Expository Writing. The classroom was in the Founder's Arts Building, aka Flounder. I got lost in the hallways before finding the classroom in the basement, so I was five minutes late. The first thing I noticed was a row of computers on tables against the wall. Wooden file cabinets lined another wall.

Ms. Chu reviewed editing symbols and the newspaper production schedule. "The file cabinets are our archives and they have every article *Birch Grove Weekly* has ever published. Always make a hard copy, no excuses, because we lose records whenever the technology changes. Your assignments will not be accepted as complete until they are filed in the archives."

Ms. Chu talked about the five *w*'s of reporting: who, what, where, when, and why. "Our first issue comes out in two weeks and your five-hundred-word story is due Wednesday. I want succinct prose. Quote at least two sources, and if *any* of your facts are incorrect, you *will* fail the assignment. I don't have to tell you to proofread now, do I?"

When a student asked about the computers, Ms. Chu said, "You'll get access to the *Weekly* account, and your use is restricted to submitting articles and formatting the paper."

I stayed after class to ask her about a topic for the first assignment. She suggested a feature on the lacrosse team, and when I frowned, she said, "Or write a piece about the

Birch Grove Foundation, which administers our scholarships. Twenty percent of the student body receives some form of financial aid. A student started a feature on it last year, but she got the flu and never finished it. You can ask Mr. Shaunessy in the administrative offices about the foundation."

❧ I forgot the frustrations of my day when I unlocked the door to my cottage and heard the phone ringing. I ran inside and grabbed it up. "Hello!"

"Hey, Jane? It's Lucky."

My throat constricted. "Oh, hi, Lucky!"

"How's it going?" His voice was lighter than Jack's and didn't have that annoying, sardonic edge. "School okay?"

"It's good. I'm taking Night Terrors with your mom."

"Everyone loves that class. Okay, you know that tutoring thing? Chemistry? My parents say I should start it right away and not fall behind. I can come over there on Saturday around noon if that's okay."

"That would be great." I spoke too fast in my eagerness. "I mean, I'm available then."

"Okay, see you then."

"See you."

I hung up and thought, *Lucky and me and money for tutoring.* I closed my eyes so I could imagine his face, his long body, the wink he'd given me, the smell of him, the feel of his breath against my cheek. I knew absolutely and without any doubt that girls like me never got guys like Lucky, but that night in my own bed, I imagined him and what it might feel like to kiss him and to have his hands exploring my lonely, unloved body.

As the evening comes on, an incomprehensible feeling of disquietude seizes me, just as if night concealed some terrible menace toward me. I dine quickly, and then try to read, but I do not understand the words, and can scarcely distinguish the letters. Then I walk up and down my drawing-room, oppressed by a feeling of confused and irresistible fear . . .

Guy de Maupassant, "The Horla" (1887)

Chapter 10 The next day, Constance and I had Mrs. Radcliffe's Night Terrors. The headmistress stood in front of us holding a thick book with a maroon leather cover. "Let's begin with a poem written in 1748 by Heinrich August Ossenfelder. It's called 'Der Vampire.'"

She waited until the room was completely silent and then she recited the poem:

"And as softly thou art sleeping
To thee shall I come creeping
And thy life's blood drain away.
And so shalt thou be trembling
For thus shall I be kissing
And death's threshold thou' it be crossing
With fear, in my cold arms.
And last shall I thee question
Compared to such instruction
What are a mother's charms?"

She opened her hands, letting go of the book, and it hit the floor with a loud slap. Many of the girls jumped in their seats and several laughed nervously. Mrs. Radcliffe smiled. She said, "Does everything that goes bump in the night have a nasty bite?" We laughed more comfortably.

"Why does every society, every culture have stories about monsters, such as those that drink blood?" she asked. "The universality of these tales says something about our own humanity, but what? Are we afraid of what is outside lurking in the night, or do we dread the darkness of our own souls?"

We went through the poem line by line, and I discovered it was about a man threatening to give a vampire's kiss to a pure maiden. Mrs. Radcliffe caught my eye and I thought, *No, please don't call on me,* but she did. "Jane, what are your thoughts?"

"Well, he's like, um . . . He's like a pimp. He seduces the innocent girl and she thinks he loves her, but he's only using her. He's taunting her even at the end about her powerlessness to resist him and about everything she's lost . . . a mother's love."

"That's a good analogy, Jane, but could the author have used the supernatural to represent a more real fear? What could blood symbolize?"

I brooded on the poem through the discussion that followed. When someone mentioned menstrual blood, I expected giggling, but the students were serious as they made associations between fertility and blood, fear of death, and the penetration of a bite and coitus. They even used that word, coitus, and the only other time I'd heard another girl use it was Mary Violet, when we'd met.

"Thus life, death, blood, sex, power, innocence, and corruption all come together in these two brief stanzas," said Mrs. Radcliffe. "Please read Johann Ludwig Tieck's 'Wake Not the Dead' for our next class."

The bell sounded and we began leaving the classroom. Mrs. Radcliffe stopped me as I passed her desk. "I'm glad you participated, Jane. Did you enjoy the class?"

"It's definitely more interesting than Western Classical Lit." I paused. "The poem's disturbing."

"It is, isn't it, even after more than two centuries. I've

always been fascinated by our perception of those things outside the norm."

"Jack told me you read fairy tales to them at night."

"Lucian wasn't interested, but Jacob always loved hearing folktales from the Old World about goblins, elves, will-o'-the-wisps, magical kingdoms . . . Some kids have an imaginary best friend, but my son had a whole grove of make-believe creatures. He was less interested when I discussed fairy stories as a reaction to the Industrial Revolution." Mrs. Radcliffe handed me a few pages. "Here's the syllabus, and you can pick up your books for this course in the administrative offices."

"Thanks, Mrs. Radcliffe." As I took the pages from her pale hand, I thought of the line "in my cold arms" and I also thought of Lucky's warm hands as he bandaged my cut.

After class, I went to the admin offices, got my books, and visited Mr. Shaunessy to interview him about the scholarship fund. The older bald man rattled boring facts and statistics before walking me to the door. "A pity that Bebe isn't here for your story. She was on full scholarship, like you, but abandoned the school for a European jaunt with some unreliable relative." He sniffed.

I wanted to slap him, but I kept my voice calm. "Every foster kid I've ever known would give up anything, *everything*, to be with their family. I know I would."

"Birch Grove *is* family." He shut the door before I could respond.

I stormed into the hallway, where Mary Violet was using her reflection in the glass of a framed portrait to fluff up her silver-gold curls. "Why are you vexed? That's what my mother always says. She says, 'Why is my family determined to vex me?'" Mary Violet accompanied this statement by placing the back of her hand on her forehead, and I laughed.

"I'm vexed because I've had to deal with vexatious people. Mary Violet, do you know that Catalina had the nerve to say that my 'new friends' were snobs?"

"Oh, it's absolutely true. If someone doesn't think I'm fabulous, I'll have nothing to do with her. Catalina's not all bad, though. She thinks my hair is splendid. Why were you talking to Mr. Shaunessy?"

"I interviewed him for my story on the student aid program."

"He's a darling. My mother loooves him. She has him for tea, and they moan about how no one cares about culture anymore and Art with a capital *A*, and then she gives him massive checks."

"Your mom donates money to the school?"

"Oodles. As fast as Daddy makes it, she gives it away."

"Do you think I could talk to her for my assignment?"

"Sure. You can come to my house if you promise not to scream when you see my mother's paintings. They're *scandalous*!"

Mary Violet lived nearby and we walked to her house on narrow streets that didn't have sidewalks. Often a car would slow down and the driver would call out a hello to her or a kid on a bike would wave and shout to her.

"It's an itsy-bitsy little town," Mary Violet said. "We know all the tedious details about everyone else. That's why I was ecstatic that you came to Birch Grove. Of course, it would have been *more* fun if you were secretly a super-dreamy guy dressed in girls' clothes and hiding out from the Mafia."

"Sorry to disappoint you."

"Oh, I'm already over it. Not every transfer student can be a super-dreamy guy on the run from the mob." She sighed. "There isn't any interesting new talent in Greenwood."

"Talent?"

"You know, guys. You go to preschool and primary school with these boys and you can't even think of them *that* way. It's like incest without the thrilling wrongness. It's boring wrongness. Brongness."

"I used to feel that way about the boys in our group home. The fastest way to get over a crush is to share a bathroom with a guy. It's way too much information."

"Was it a horrible orphanage? Did you eat moldy gruel?"

"We ate stuff that came in giant cans from the dented warehouse store and could be microwaved. It was a group home, not an orphanage." I told her a little about the ramshackle house and the rules.

"That sounds hideous! I could never ever get up at six every day. I'm sure it's child abuse. How did you get to be so smart?"

"I had a friend who liked science and told me I should use my brain, so I started sitting at the nerd table in the cafeteria. They decided to use me as the subject in an experiment to see if anyone could be smart. That's why I freaked out when we had to read *Flowers for Algernon* last year. I was paranoid that I might revert back to the feral kid I was."

"That book is freaky anyway. I swear, the people who pick assigned reading must be high. *The Stranger*, ugh. How were you feral?"

I shrugged and my book bag slid from my shoulder. I pushed the strap back up while I thought of my answer. "I didn't know how to communicate so all I did was cuss."

"You?" Her blue eyes widened. "I don't believe it."

"It's true. If you removed the obscenities from my vocabulary, the only things left would be *you, can,* and *go*. I didn't have the words to express myself so all I felt was an inchoate anger. Now I know when I'm aggravated, frustrated, anxious, exasperated, exhausted, fretful, infuriated . . ."

"*Inchoate* is an excellent word, but those are all negative feelings. What about when you're hilarity-ated?"

"Do you make up words all the time?"

"Yes, because William Shakespeare made up words and he wrote poems, too, just like me. I believe I'm his spiritual heir."

"I don't think he wrote any poems about roadkill." I

watched a woman walking with a toddler across the road. "I got vexed when I talked to Mr. Shaunessy because he didn't understand why a foster kid would do *anything* to be with family. I'd be happy to have even one relative."

"Are you talking about Bebe leaving school? It is a little odd, but she had her own agenda. She's the reason we have to be super careful about texting, because she was caught sexting."

"Everyone who has a phone sexts." I wondered what Lucky sexted.

"Not me, because I believe women must have mystique to be truly alluring." When I stopped laughing, she said, "Bebe must have been sexting with someone from the *outside* because there was a humongous brouhaha that wouldn't have happened with a Greenwood boy. I think it was someone older, because she was always going on about *mature* men."

"If Bebe ran off with an old guy it would explain why she hasn't contacted you."

"You have a very naughty mind! We thought of that, but Bebe loved it here. We thought she was great, too."

"I'm the replacement."

"Don't be like that. I like you *more* because you have a fabulous sense of humor and, besides, Bebe always seemed like she was only half listening to me while she was secretly plotting world domination."

One thing caught my attention. "You think I have a sense of humor? Really?"

"Mais certainment!" Mary Violet opened a gate in a hedge. "That's French for 'true dat.' Home sweet home."

The house was painted taupe and the paned windows had snowy-white trim. Ivy grew up to the second-floor balconies, and a brick path curved through a lush lawn to the red front door.

"It's wonderful," I said.

"It is, isn't it? But wait until you see my mother's Exposition of Vulgarity. She doesn't call it that, though, so just tell her how lovely everything is."

Mary Violet walked to the side of the house. "My mom says children shouldn't use the front entrance because we are too messy, even though I've explained to her that I am an elegant young lady now." She opened a door and we walked onto a back porch. MV dropped her bag and book satchel on the floor beside a coatrack. Through the doorway ahead, I glimpsed stainless steel, pale stone countertops, and a huge butcher block island.

"I'm home, Teresa!"

A short, stocky woman came to the kitchen doorway. She wore high-waisted mom jeans and a pink sweatshirt. She scanned the floor. "Hang up your bag, baby." She spoke with a Spanish accent.

"Yes, boss." Mary Violet sighed loudly and went back to pick up her things. "Teresa, this is Jane. Jane's new at school."

" 'ello, Yane."

"Hello, *señora*," I said as I followed Mary Violet. My mother had cleaned houses and now the image of yellow rubber gloves and a bucket of soapy water came and went as quickly as a billboard sighted out of a moving bus.

"Teresa thinks she is the boss of me," Mary Violet said.

The woman made a face and then tapped her own cheek. *"Besito."*

Mary Violet gave her a hug and kissed her cheek. "Who's home?"

"Your mama is in her studio and Bobby is upstairs. The Baby is at practice."

Had my mother been close to another family? I wondered, and felt an ache inside.

Mary Violet said to Teresa, "Okay. We're going up to my room for a while."

On the other side of the kitchen was a narrow staircase and we went to the second floor. "Teresa's from El Salvador. Her kids are still there because she wants them to be with their family."

I was sure the reasons were far more complicated.

Mary Violet led me down a hallway decorated with photos. "Behold, the family gallery. Thank God, my mom hasn't put her paintings here. *Yet*. We live in terror that she will."

A thick rug in shades of blue and butter-yellow cushioned our steps. We walked by a bedroom with an open door and my friend called out, "Hey, Bobby," and then said to me, "That's my little brother, and he's a pestilence upon this earth. My sister, Agnes, aka the Baby, is okay. She's always off doing one of her sports things."

We went past a wide staircase with polished wood bannisters, and I glimpsed a luxurious living room below. "Is Agnes at Birch Grove?"

"She'll be coming next year. She's in eighth grade now at Town School, which is where we all go before the boys and girls are separated because our parents believe raging hormones turn us into crazed sex fiends."

At the end of the hall was her room, all done in pink and white with gilt-trimmed mirrors. Makeup and accessories completely covered the top of a dresser, and clothes spilled out of a closet.

"Are *all* these clothes yours?"

"They pile up somehow. I think they have coitus while I'm asleep and replicate."

"Why do the girls here say 'coitus' all the time?"

"Because you can tell someone to coitus off and you won't get detention. Besides, everyone uses the F word now, so it's not special anymore. I'm *fanatical* about special words." She kicked clothes into the closet. "My mother says that one day I'll be buried under an avalanche of clothes and no one will ever find my body." She forced shut the double closet doors with a small grunt.

"MV, I heard that one of the teachers here committed suicide. Who was it?"

She leaned against the doors. "Mr. Mason's wife. That's why he's such a disaster. Mrs. Radcliffe was devastated, too, since her family, the Belvederes, sponsored Mrs. Mason to Rich Loathe. She was like an aunt to Jack and Lucky."

"I thought the school was nicknamed Bitch Grave."

"Yes, but *polite* haters call it Rich Loathe, even though it's a crummy rhyme."

I noticed a slim lavender laptop set on a mirrored antique vanity table. "I can't believe we can't use computers at school. Would you mind if I checked in with some friends?"

"Go ahead, but don't download anything because my parents spy on all our online stuff since the PTA had a consultant come in last year to warn them about the dangers of the Internets."

"There are ways to bypass monitoring, but it's harder when you're all on a private ISP. It's the same thing with phones. Dealers use burners, you know, those prepaid phones they can toss away." I tried to sign into my e-mail, but I got a message saying *ID Closed.* "Oh, coitus. City Central must have cancelled my student account."

"Don't you have another e-mail account?"

"Yes, but I had phone numbers and addresses on this one. I guess this is why Ms. Chu makes us print out hard copies. I'll have to get the information again somehow because I want to buy a phone." I closed the laptop.

"Well, when you get one, don't tell Mrs. Radcliffe because of her issues," Mary Violet said. "Come on and I'll introduce you to my mom. Try not to stare."

"I don't stare."

"Uhm, maybe not stare, but you have a uniquely piercing look as though you've got a caustic and contemptuous interior monologue going. Quick, tell me what you're thinking!"

"I'm thinking that you should come with footnotes so I can understand what you're saying." I followed her out of the room and down the main staircase. "Also, you let your imagination run amok."

"I adore that word, *amok*. What's the fun of having an imagination if you don't let it run amok?"

"I think reality is difficult enough to deal with."

"Jane, it will be my life's mission to funnify you."

"Now I'm the one living in terror."

As we went through the luxurious living room, I glanced up at an enormous painting in beiges and pinks above the white stone fireplace. After several seconds, I registered that the painting was of a nude woman in way too much detail.

Mary Violet gave a small shriek. "You *are* staring! The art studio is horrifyingly gynecological, and my mother uses explicit anatomical terms like they're perfectly normal, so whatever you do, *don't* ask her about her *Art*."

We went down a hall to a sunroom and I felt the marvelous heat of the room seeping into me. All around us were easels with paintings similar to the one in the living room. I was so embarrassed that I didn't know where to look.

"Hello, honey." A woman came from behind an easel. She was wearing paint-smudged denim overalls and her curly auburn hair was cut close to her head, making her appear young and boyish. She looked at me and said, "Hello. I'm Mrs. Holiday."

"Hi, Mommy. This is Jane Williams. Remember I told you she transferred in? She wants to interview you for a story she's writing for the *Weekly* about the scholarship program."

"Nice to meet you, Jane. I'm happy to talk to you about the school fund. Come sit with me. Mary Violet, would you get us some tea, please?"

"Everyone thinks she's the boss of me," MV grumbled cheerfully as she left us.

I wove through a maze of paintings to join Mrs. Holiday at a yellow wicker patio set. This close, I could see the small wrinkles radiating from the outer corners of her gray eyes, like she'd smiled a lot. "What would you like to know, Jane?"

I took a notebook and pen from my school tote. "Why is it important for you to donate money for scholarships?"

She said the things I expected and then sighed. "Between us, no matter how much I give, I'll never be in the inner circle since I'm only a second-generation Birch Grove girl. Hyacinth Radcliffe and her family go all the way back to the founding of the school."

"Does it really make a difference? It's only a high school."

"Oh, it's much more than that. Our lives in Greenwood revolve around it in one way or another. Sometimes I feel, I don't know, *left* out. Maybe I make these donations for approval and acceptance."

"But you also paint these, uhm . . . you express yourself in these paintings and they're very individual."

Mrs. Holiday patted my hand. "Jane, I appreciate what you're not saying as much as what you are saying. Yes, there is a dissonance in my individualism and my desire for acceptance. I still don't know all the reasons I do the things I do."

"Why is it important to know why we do things so long as we do the right things? The result is the same."

"Alexander Pope wrote that the proper study of mankind is man. In my case, it's woman. If we don't scrutinize our own psyches, how can we expect to truly comprehend others? The internal and the external are all of a piece."

"I'm interested in what people do, not why they do it."

"Why do you do what you do, Jane? You must be exceptional to have been invited to Birch Grove."

"I'm not. I'm ordinary, but I'm diligent because I want to succeed and have a secure career and a home."

"That's a practical approach to life. But where's the joy in practicality?"

I hesitated. "There's not much joy in living without security, Mrs. Holiday."

She put her fingers together like a teepee, the apex touching her lips. After a few seconds, she said, "I didn't mean to romanticize poverty, Jane, but I believe that joy is essential to a worthwhile existence. Finding joy is a survival skill."

I thought of how Wilde's lively personality got her through dark days. "Mary Violet has a plan to funnify me."

Mrs. Holiday laughed. "Come, let me show you my Art while we wait for our tea." She tried to explain her paintings to me and talked about the "ripeness and fecundity of the female body."

I nodded my head like I was listening, but I was focused on a painting that was set on the floor, leaning against other canvases. It had vivid splashes of grassy green, yellow-green, and streaks of sooty black and ivory. "What's that?"

"Ah, my Lady of the Wood series." Mrs. Holiday wrested out the painting and the canvases behind it to show several variations of the theme. "These paintings are based on the mythology and folk stories about birches. Birches grow all over the world, and they're one of the first trees to leaf out in spring, so they symbolize rebirth to many cultures. They also represent a connection with the world of the dead."

"So they're ghost stories?"

"Oh, no! The Lady of the Wood is a good spirit who inhabits the trees. She helps those in need."

"The bark makes them look like they have faces. Especially at night."

"That's why I love the grove. I never feel alone there. It's as if the Lady of the Wood is with me. I know it's only my fantasy."

A chill ran down my spine as I thought of the way I'd imagined a woman smiling at me. "I've had strange moments in the grove when I could swear I see something . . . but it's only the shadows."

Mrs. Holiday scratched at a splotch of paint on her overalls. "You may have learned in Biology that the human eye actually sees the world upside down, but our brains reverse images so they make sense to us. I sometimes wonder what *else* our brain tricks us into seeing differently."

"I don't understand."

"Maybe our brain only lets us see what we are *prepared* to see." She smiled. "Well, it's one of my theories."

Mary Violet came in with a tray of tea things and almond cookies and set it on the wicker table. After serving us, she asked innocently, "Did you enjoy my mother's paintings?"

"They're very interesting." I kicked her foot under the table.

"Jane liked my Lady of the Wood series."

Mary Violet stood, knocking against the table and making the teacups rattle on the saucers. She threw out her arms dramatically and recited:

"So was I once myself a swinger of birches.
And so I dream of going back to be.
It's when I'm weary of considerations,
And life is too much like a pathless wood
Where your face burns and tickles with the cobwebs
Broken across it, and one eye is weeping
From a twig's having lashed across it open.
I'd like to get away from earth awhile
And then come back to it and begin over."

The poem sent an eerie yet hopeful sensation through me, and we were all silent for a moment. Then Mary Violet sat, bumping the table again. "That's from Robert Frost's 'Birches.' I did a term paper last year on poems dedicated to the birch and I *should* have gotten an A-plus, but I got a B. It was a dreadful travesty of justice."

"Your teacher told you not to use purple ink," Mrs. Holiday said. "I'm sure your prose was purple, too."

"It was violet, not purple, and that is my trademark."

Her mother rolled her eyes exactly the way Mary Violet did.

We talked about our classes and teachers, and when Mrs. Holiday got up to switch on the lights I noticed how late it was and said good-bye. Mrs. Holiday asked, "Would you like a ride?"

"It's only a few blocks. I'll walk."

"Try to celebrate the trees, Jane."

I nodded even though I had no idea what she was talking about.

Mary Violet went outside with me. "My mother's an intellectual so we don't expect her to act like a normal person."

"Like you're a judge of what's normal. She's wonderful. See you tomorrow."

"Au revoir."

I'd walked a little ways when Mary Violet came skipping after me. "Jane, I'm really glad Mrs. Radcliffe extorted us to hang out with you."

"Me, too." I felt oddly shy. "Au revoir."

The streetlights came on while I was walking back to campus. The neighborhood was quiet except for occasional noises—the slamming of a car door, the *swish-swish* of automatic sprinklers. Ahead, the school was a dark mass looming against the sky. The lights at the school's entrance cast ominous shadows of the stone angels.

As I approached the main building, I looked up and saw a man's silhouette in the window of a third-floor classroom. Mr. Mason was working late, and I felt a twinge of empathy for him in his solitude and his heartache.

The breeze grew stronger, as it had every evening, and now the night was no longer silent but filled with the sounds of the trees—rustling and sighing, stirring and creaking, so *alive*. Mrs. Holiday had told me to celebrate the trees, so

I stood and listened until I understood why some people talked about how they loved the roar of the ocean.

Then my skin goose bumped all over because the noises began to take on the rhythms of a language. I raced frantically to my cottage. My hand was shaking as I fitted my key in the lock. As I stepped inside, I fumbled for the light switch. Light filled the room, diminishing the shadows to nothing more than the absence of light.

My creepy feeling intensified as I read the assignment for Mrs. Radcliffe's class, "Wake Not the Dead." Although I had to refer to the footnotes constantly, I soon became so engrossed that I hurried through the paragraphs.

A powerful lord is passionately in love with his beautiful bride, who dies young. He marries a kind woman and they have children, yet he remains obsessed with his dead bride. He forces a wizard to bring her back to him even though the wizard warns, "Wake not the dead."

The bride returns from the grave and the lord is enchanted by her, but death and destruction soon come to his castle. She kills his children, his wife, his servants, and the villagers. He discovers much too late that she's a bloodthirsty vampire.

A loud *creeeeak* made me jump. It was only a tree. I needed to hear another voice, a *human* voice, so I called Mary Violet.

Her sister, Agnes, answered her phone and told me MV was taking a bubble bath. "Do you want me to give her a message?"

"Yes, tell her that imagination is highly overrated."

Agnes snickered. "Now she'll try to drown herself, but she'll keep popping up like an inflatable raft."

I put the phone down, reassured that I could contact people in an emergency. My night was restless, and I put my pillow over my head so I would not hear the wind and the trees.

In the morning, I walked out my front door into the misty morning. The heavy pot of flowers on the porch had been knocked over and broken. Dirt spilled out and the pansies were trampled.

After my lonely life I dare say I should have loved any one who really needed me, and from the first moment that I read the appeal in Mrs. Vanderbridge's face I felt that I was willing to work my fingers to the bone for her. Nothing that she asked of me was too much when she asked it in that voice, with that look.

Ellen Glasgow, *The Past* (1920)

Chapter 11   No one was here now, but someone *had* been here last night while I slept. My heart raced and then I calmed myself enough to think. Catalina was nasty, but straight up about it, not sneaky. Jack had come by before and parked his bike against the porch railing. Could he have visited again and knocked over the flowerpot by accident?

I searched the ground for clues, but the dry soil was hard and didn't show anything but old bike treads. I continued to examine the ground as I walked to the amphitheater. I came across empty vodka minis, a candle stub, a flattened cigarette box, and a rusty razor blade. So people visited the grove and maybe someone got curious about the cottage.

I considered the possibilities and the probabilities. Someone could have been walking by and decided to see if the cottage was empty, as it had been before. Someone might have been spying on me. Someone might have dropped by to visit me. The potted plant could have been knocked over intentionally or accidentally, or maybe one of the animals that lived here broke it somehow.

I thought of the impossibilities and improbabilities. Jack would say that elves had broken it when they came to take me back to the wood.

I wasn't going to give in to my imagination. I'd find out more before I made any conclusions. I arrived at Latin class before Catalina. She came in with waves to her friends. Her amber eyes skimmed indifferently over me, like I was a piece of furniture. I spent the rest of the day trying to discern any laughing or stares directed my way. I was tense when someone touched the back of my arm in the cafeteria. I jerked away and saw Constance behind me.

"Wake not the dead!" she whispered in a spooky voice. "What a sick story."

Hattie and Mary Violet joined us. "We've decided to have a sleepover at your cottage tomorrow night," Hattie said. "If that's okay with you."

I wanted company. "That would be great."

Mary Violet said, "I can arch your eyebrows and trim your hair."

Constance waved her hands, palms outward and fingers splayed. "Under *no* circumstances should you let MV near you with scissors. I made that mistake once and my mother cried when I came home."

"You looked like a Parisian model with your hair so short," Mary Violet said.

"I did not. I had to get an emergency weave because my ears stick out like handles on a jug." Constance raised her braids to show us.

"Embrace your flaws. I would if I had any," Mary Violet said.

"Right, Miss Thing." Constance pinched her friend's plump pink cheek.

Hattie offered to bring spaghetti, Constance would bring Caesar salad and garlic bread, Mary Violet would bake brownies, and I would get the drinks.

Hattie gave me a ride to Greenwood Grocery after school. Under the fluorescent lights, her pale skin had the slight blueish tinge of nonfat milk. This was my first time having my friends over, so I chose two six-packs of the Italian lemon soda that Lucky had given me even though it cost twice as much as the store brand of soda.

"We all like that," Hattie said. "Mrs. Radcliffe always has it at her house."

"That's where I had it." I tried to sound casual. "Lucky's coming over tomorrow at noon for chemistry tutoring."

"Really?" She tilted her head.

"Yes, and it's cool because I can add it to my résumé and earn money, too. I was thinking of making lunch."

"I'm sure Mrs. Radcliffe doesn't expect you to teach *and* feed him."

"Maybe not, but it will be lunchtime. What do you think I should make?"

"Lucky likes roast beef sandwiches, extra rare. Mrs. Radcliffe says good beef shouldn't be overcooked."

Hattie walked to the store entrance to make a phone call while I went to pay. I spotted Orneta at the far register. I steered my cart there, and she said, "Hey, Jane from Hellsdale, how's it going?"

"Hi, Ornery. It's a major transition."

"No kidding." She picked up the package of beef and pointed to the price label. When I leaned in to see what she was trying to show me, she whispered, "They been watching you here." Her eyes went toward the corner of the store and I saw a convex mirror there, reflecting the store aisles.

"I didn't boost anything!" I whispered back.

She glanced back. "Maybe cuz you're from outside." In a louder voice, she said, "Yes, that's a dollar sign, not a five! Sorry, miss."

A man in a store smock with "Manager" on a lapel pin came up. "Is there anything I can help you with, Orneta?"

She smiled at him. "No, sir, my contacts blurred up for a second, but I'm fine now."

When I went to Hattie, she asked, "Who was that?"

"Her name's Orneta. I met her when I came here with Mrs. Radcliffe."

"The checkers at the store are always nice."

On the ride back to campus, Hattie talked about her

favorite places in town and again mentioned how nice the locals were.

"Hattie, everyone does seem really friendly, but do they really like outsiders?"

"No one likes, you know, a bad element. Why?"

"Just curious. See you tomorrow."

By the time I got inside my place and unpacked my groceries, blood from the roast beef had soaked through the white butcher paper package. I placed the meat in a plastic bag and put it in the fridge. I went to the porch and cleaned up the mess from the broken flowerpot.

Then I vacuumed, dusted, scrubbed out the bathroom, and emptied the trash. I gathered branches, twigs, and fern and did my best to arrange them in a vase. When evening came, I closed the curtains so that no one could spy on me from outside. I dragged and pushed the small sofa so that it blocked the front door. After checking all the locks, I flicked off the lights in the living room and left on a bedroom lamp and the porch light.

Now no one outside could see me in the dark living room, but I would see anyone prowling close to the porch. I gathered the comforter and pillow from the bed and set myself on the sofa to sleep.

❧ As soon as I awoke, I thought, *Lucky's coming!* I checked outside, but everything was the way I'd left it. I shoved the sofa back into place, and my thoughts bounced from Lucky to the slumber party as I showered and dressed in new jeans, a clean white t-shirt, and my new black tennis shoes. I wore my hair loose and parted on the side, like Hattie. It didn't fall smoothly like Hattie's, but it shone more than it had when I lived at the group home because now I had time to wash out the shampoo and use conditioner. I let it dry without messing with it so the waves were even and almost pretty.

I made two roast beef sandwiches, sliced them diagonally, and placed them on plates with potato chips. I set the table with glasses and napkins. I checked the time. It was only ten A.M.

I drafted my article on the financial aid program, but I couldn't stop watching the minutes ticking slowly by, which was so pitiful because it was only a tutoring session. I tried to recall every detail about Lucky, from the way he lounged against the counter, to his wink, and the concentration on his face as he bandaged my finger.

Then noon came. I paced up and down the small living room, biting my ragged nails, and ten minutes later there was a knock at the door. I counted *one hundred, two hundred, three hundred* before opening it.

Lucky stood there in a snug long-sleeved Evergreen Prep t-shirt holding a chem book and a paper bag. "Hey, Jane." His smile was so bright that I thought it would illuminate all my defects: the uneven surfaces, blemishes, and dullness of my insignificant person.

"Hi, Lucky."

"Bet you hate spending Saturday teaching a knucklehead."

"Of course not. I'm happy to help." The words sounded stiff and boring to my ears, like a customer service rep's response.

"Yeah, right. You don't have to be polite about it, because I'd hate having to tutor a dunce." He held out the paper bag. "My mom sent cookies because she thinks we're ten years old."

When Lucky Radcliffe walked into my cottage, it seemed smaller. While he wandered around, I surreptitiously stared at him. He looked like he'd just gotten up; he had stubble on his jaw, his clothes were rumpled, and his gold and honey hair was tousled.

"You moved things around."

I imagined that long body stretched out on a bed, and I

nervously bent down to arrange the paper and pencils I'd put on the coffee table. "You were here before? When Bebe was here?"

"Yeah, and when it was empty, too. I helped fix it up. I painted the bedroom." He walked to the fireplace and touched the mantel. "Mom wanted it to be like new for you."

He didn't say anything else, and I realized that I was standing there stupidly when I was supposed to be in charge of our session. "I made sandwiches. We can eat and study."

"I ate cookies on the way here. I'm thirsty, though."

I nodded, hiding my disappointment, and went to the kitchen. I put the sandwiches in the fridge and returned to the living room with two cans of soda. Then it seemed too late to go back and pour the drinks into glasses, the way he was used to at home.

We sat on the sofa and I opened his textbook. "Okay, we'll go over the basics, so I can figure out where you're at."

"My head hurts already." He reached for the bag of cookies. "Oatmeal with dried cranberries. Even Mom's desserts are good for you." He handed it to me and took one for himself.

"I thought you weren't hungry," I said, annoyed.

"There's always room for a cookie." He winked at me, and I forgave him.

I flipped open his textbook to the first chapter. "Did you bring your calculator?"

"I guess I should have, huh?"

"It's okay. You can use mine."

As we leaned over the coffee table to read the book, our shoulders occasionally touched. Although I was painfully sensitive to each contact, I tried to act casual.

"Jane, Jane, how can you like this stuff? My mind goes into overload." He leaned back and threw his arm over the back of the sofa, brushing my shoulders.

My heart beat faster. "You're doing fine. You get it. You

should spend some time reviewing exponential numbers and memorizing chemical symbols."

"No wonder my mom likes you, because you're all business. How's school going? Who are you hanging out with?"

"Your mother sort of set it up for Hattie Tyler to introduce me to her friends, Mary Violet Holiday and Constance Applewhaite."

"That's what I mean about treating us like we're ten. Do you like them?"

"Actually, I do, but I would have been okay meeting people on my own. They're coming for a sleepover tonight."

"Sounds like fun. Should I crash?"

I turned my eyes down to the textbook as I felt the heat rise in my face.

"Relax. If Mary Violet's coming, it's going to be too girly for me. Girly movies and girly gossip. Don't tell them how stupid I am about chem."

"I would never say that!"

"I was joking, Jane. You can say whatever you want. They're cool girls, especially Hattie. She goes out with Jack."

"She told me. I was a little . . . surprised."

"Because he's so grungy and she's a goddess? Yeah, but Hattie doesn't care that he's a slacker. She thinks he's artistic."

"Being artistic is nice, I guess, but I'm more interested in real things."

"You haven't seen Jack play yet. He's like a grimy, hairy Pied Piper, only instead of rats, he attracts girls. Hey, I'm taking up all your time." He picked up his textbook and stood. "How about next Sunday around four thirty? Mom says you should come to the house and stay for dinner."

I nodded and walked him to the door. "We can go over any assignments you have then."

"I hate chem, but I'm okay in biology." Lucky suddenly grasped my hand. Turning it over, he ran his finger on the inside of my wrist, tracing the blue veins. My wrist was so narrow in his large hand, and I felt vulnerable and nervous.

"Jane, did you know that the human body contains about five liters of blood?" His voice was quiet and intense. "It travels twelve thousand miles through your circulatory system every day." His finger pressed on my wrist. "I can feel your pulse. It's strong. The blood inside is warm, Jane, full of oxygen, minerals, and protein."

I gazed into his eyes, able to see each eyelash and the gradations of silver and blue.

He wasn't smiling anymore. His lips were parted and his expression was deadly serious and I thought he might lean over and . . . Then he dropped my wrist. "See you next week."

Lucky walked out the door and sauntered off along the path.

My knees were weak from my desire for him. I went over and over what Lucian Radcliffe had said and done, but I couldn't make any sense of it.

I came to an open spot of ground in which stood a little cottage, so built that the stems of four great trees formed its corners, while their branches met and intertwined over its roof, heaping a great cloud of leaves over it, up towards the heavens. I wondered at finding a human dwelling in this neighborhood; and yet it did not look altogether human . . .

George MacDonald, *Phantastes:*
A Faerie Romance for Men and Women (1858)

Chapter 12 Hattie and Constance arrived in the early evening, and Mary Violet showed up ten minutes later, saying, "*Bonne soirée, belles dames.* That's French for 'What's up, my bitches.'" She threw a sleeping bag on the sofa and set a platter of brownies on the coffee table. "This cottage is like something in a fairy tale."

Constance said, "I'm sure you'd be happier if it was made out of gingerbread and candy."

"True, but getting boiled alive isn't my idea of fun. Honestly, the old fairy tales are as bad as reading *The Stranger.*"

"Were halflings awful?" I asked MV.

"No, they were usually delightful. I meant gruesome old folktales, like the ones that inspired the Grimm brothers."

"Don't ask how MV knows these things," Constance said. "She never remembers my birthday."

"Yes, I do. It's in one of those *M* months, March or May. Maybe Mebruary or Maugust." Mary Violet smirked. "Someday I'm going to write stories with terrifying monsters and werewolves."

"I thought you were writing mysteries and historicals," Hattie said. "Besides, no one needs to hear scary stories about make-believe monsters."

Mary Violet scrunched up her face as she thought for a

moment. "I think we do because fear makes us feel alive. Besides, the supernatural is really about the id."

"I don't know what the id is, but *id* guess it's something ridiculous," Constance said.

"*Id* is not." Mary Violet tugged one of Constance's braids. "The id is your unconscious desires and fears. It's your instinct for pleasure and survival. That's what my mother says and she did her minor in psych."

Constance said, "That sounds like something Mrs. Radcliffe would lecture about in Night Terrors. I think there must have been some huge psych fad when they were at university."

"They probably had study sessions to analyze Madonna songs and danced like this." Mary Violet began hopping around and swinging her arms up.

"And once again, MV's dragged us completely off topic," Hattie said. "I bet you love living here, Jane."

"Totally, even though Jack Radcliffe tried to scare me about the trees walking at night. Please."

"That's his twisted sense of humor," Mary Violet said as she continued hopping and swinging her arms. "It's not as refined as mine."

"Yes, I could tell that he's a . . ." I paused to think of the right term. "He's a major excrement-disturber."

After dinner and after I'd let Mary Violet trim an inch off my hair (which became three inches because she kept trying to make it even), she said, "Mr. Mason seems so lonely since his wife died. Jane, when did your mother die and how long did it take you to recover?"

"She died when I was six and I had an accident then. The doctors put me in a coma while I healed, and when I woke up, I didn't remember anything—not the accident, not my mother, not my life before. The official name is retrograde amnesia, and because my brain went without oxygen for a long time, those memories are gone forever."

There was a long and awkward silence, and my friends

switched the conversation to the guys at Evergreen and how they'd changed during the summer.

"None of them is much improved," Mary Violet said. "Jane, tell us about your boyfriends in the hood. Was it like those movies with the smart girl and the dangerous boy, hopefully with a big dance-off?"

"Not hardly. I'm always in the friend zone because I look like a little kid."

"You mean you have had no carnal knowledge at all?"

"Mary Violet!" Hattie said. "Let a person have some privacy."

"Just because you won't talk about your lover doesn't mean Jane doesn't want to talk about her experiences." Mary Violet pouted. "I confided in you how Teagan Bartholomew stuck his tongue down my throat and then dropped trou with no warning whatsoever. After my mother's paintings, I'd assumed everyone had a hoo-ha and I was so shocked that I screamed. I thought he had a disfiguring tumorous growth. True story!"

"You're totally making that up," Constance said, and Hattie spit out her soda, and we were all howling.

"I've been deeply traumatized ever since," Mary Violet continued. "I'll probably die a virgin."

Hattie's phone trilled and she answered it with a terse "Hello." Then she said, "How did you know I'd be here?" She went out to the porch to talk, closing the door behind her.

Constance said, "MV, *you're* the one with the crazy dentist theory."

I tried to puzzle this out. "Okay, I give up. What do crazy dentists have to do with anything?"

"I'm so glad you asked!" Mary Violet brushed brownie crumbs off her shirt. "Your wisdom teeth get removed only once in your lifetime. Some people have them taken out too early because they want to get it over with, but the surgery's more complicated if your teeth are impacted. And some people go to any old dentist as if it doesn't matter, but a bad dentist can make it a horrible, *horrible* experience."

"Okay, I get that," I said, "but you can't compare the sex with dental surgery, because dental surgery is always going to be scary and painful, but—"

MV shook her head, tossing her curls. "My point is about the *memory* of a unique and significant incident. You can't control each individual factor, but you can wait for the right time and choose the right dentist, because you'll live with that memory for the rest of your life. That's my dentist theory and it's not crazy."

I searched her earnest face before telling Constance, "I hate to say this, but she's making sense."

Constance sighed. "Sometimes she does. That's the danger of hanging out with her."

We crashed about two A.M. Mary Violet slept on the sofa, and Constance had gone to the bedroom to escape her friend's snoring. I awoke under my comforter on the floor. Hattie's sleeping bag was empty.

I checked around, but she was gone, so I put on shoes and a sweatshirt, got my flashlight, and walked outside. "Hattie, Hattie," I called in a whisper. I began walking along the trail toward the Radcliffes' house. "Hattie!"

"Over here!" Hattie's voice came from the direction of the amphitheater.

The blackness wasn't as dense in the clearing. A full moon was barely visible through the clouds. Hattie sat on a bench, cloaked in a blanket. She was as still and pale as a statue. The lace hem of her long white cotton nightgown skimmed her bare, narrow feet.

She saw me and smiled. "What are you doing out here?"

"I was wondering where you were." I sat beside her, the cold stone bench chilling me through my thin cotton pants.

"I woke up and felt like taking a walk. Isn't this place magical? In the moonlight it's like a black-and-white photograph."

"How did you find your way here?"

"I know the grove and, besides, I have great night vision."

We sat quietly, listening to the whispering of the trees and feeling the damp air on our skin. Then Hattie said, "I know things are different for you here, Jane. Whenever you want, you can talk to me." The moonlight caught the shine of her eyes as she turned toward me. "I'm good at keeping secrets."

"It's been so long since I've had someone I could really talk to that I forget what it's like for most people." Peaceful moments always reminded me of Hosea. "I had a friend, Hosea, at the group home and I could tell him anything. He was a few years older than me, and he was brilliant in a way that went beyond book smarts. His girlfriends never understood why he always let me tag along, but I loved being with him."

"Did he get adopted?"

"No, he got bacterial meningitis and died. One day he had a fever and stayed in bed. By the time I got home from school, he was burning up." My heart ached as I thought of seeing Hosea being wheeled on a gurney though double doors at the ER. "He died that night."

"I'm sorry."

I nodded, not trusting myself to speak for a few minutes. "He was the best person I ever knew."

"When you were changing clothes, I saw that tattoo with an *H*."

"One of my housemates did it for me. Her name's Wilde. Well, her real name is Tiffany and she hates that. She read some graffiti in a bathroom that said 'More is not enough. Oscar Wilde' and that's how she lives."

"How did she do the tattoo?"

"With ink from a ballpoint pen and a needle."

"That sounds painful."

"Sometimes you suffer for the things that are important to you." We were speaking very softly. I listened for other sounds, but heard only the wind in the trees. "Who comes to this place? Because someone broke the flowerpot on my porch while I was asleep the night before last."

Hattie's brow furrowed. "Sometimes locals come here, but no one should have been on your porch. Did you tell Mrs. Radcliffe? She'd really want to know."

"Maybe it was the wind, or an animal. Please don't say anything to her."

"I think you should tell her, but it's your call." Hattie watched the play of shadows from the birch branches. "How did your tutoring lesson with Lucky go?"

"Good. He doesn't seem to care about chem, but he solves the problems easily."

"Lucky pretends to be incompetent and other people fall over themselves to do things for him because he's so gorgeous," she said bitterly.

"Hattie, good-looking people always get special treatment. So do rich people and people with connections. *Everyone* at Birch Grove gets special treatment."

"We must all seem completely self-centered to you."

"You seem . . . incredibly lucky. I think it's hard not to believe you deserve the best things in life when you're told you're extraordinary all the time. People say that anyone can make it, but rare exceptions don't make it true."

"But you made it, Jane."

"I've made it this far. But I can name dozens of kids at Helmsdale City Central who are amazing students and they're trying to succeed without, well, everything. Saying that anyone can make it is an excuse for ignoring all those who need a little help."

"I've thought about that. Bebe sometimes told me about what she went through. She'd laugh like it was nothing, but I could tell it still hurt. I think that people like me, people with advantages, should do something to make the world better."

"The problem is finding a way to actually make a difference when there are so many obstacles in the way. I haven't figured out how I can help yet, but I want to make a difference."

In a lighter voice, Hattie said, "I hope Lucky will find friends who'll bring out the best in him, instead of feeding his egomania. He's got a good heart and he's smart . . . But why are we talking about Lucky anyway? I'd rather talk about Jack. He looks out for me and he can make me chill out when I get riled."

"What sets you off?"

"The usual stuff. Being treated like my opinions don't matter. Being treated like I'm just a girl. *Just a girl.* Whenever people say that, it makes me want to punch them. What makes you angry, Jane?"

"Pretty much everything," I said casually, as if it weren't true. "Life isn't fair, so you have to play the best game you can with the cards you're dealt." The wind gusted and I crossed my arms over myself.

"You're cold." She took off the blanket and placed it over my shoulders. "Let's go back."

I used the flashlight, but Hattie walked as surely as a cat on the path. The hem of her white nightgown drifted behind her in the breeze.

I rearranged the blanket over me. "Anyone seeing us would think we're ghosts."

"You aren't superstitious, are you?"

"No, there's a rational explanation for everything."

"I stood here, and saw before me the unutterable, the unthinkable gulf that yawns profound between two worlds, the world of matter and the world of spirit; I saw the great empty deep stretch dim before me, and in that instant a bridge of light leapt from the earth to the unknown shore, and the abyss was spanned."

Arthur Machen, *The Great God Pan* (1890)

Chapter 13   I became accustomed to my new school and my new home. Sometimes I glimpsed the beam of a flashlight in the grove at night, or heard faint voices carried by the wind, but I no longer pushed my sofa against the door at night. Catalina ignored me in Latin class, and I stopped paying any attention to her, too. My most difficult class was Mrs. Radcliffe's seminar. I struggled with my essay on "Wake Not the Dead." The day after I handed it in, Mrs. Radcliffe stopped me as I was leaving class.

"Jane, I read your paper last night." She came from behind her desk and smoothed her skirt. "It was quite businesslike. I'd hoped for a more personal analysis."

"I thought the assignment was about story comprehension," I said, hiding my irritation.

"Comprehending literature requires more than grasping the plot. Fiction offers insights to the human condition. Don't tell me what happened in the story, but how you *feel* about what happened and the characters." She handed me my ungraded paper. "I know you can do better, and I'd like you to try again."

That night, I started the essay three times, getting more aggravated with each effort. Why should I be graded on my *feelings* for an assignment? Finally, in my clumsy cursive hand, I scrawled, " 'Wake Not the Dead' is not a story about love. It is about one man's thoughtless and cruel self-ishness. He believes his position and wealth entitle him to do whatever he desires, irregardless of the consequences for everyone else." I read the paragraph over and changed "irregardless" to "regardless." The rest of the essay came rushing out as I thought about love and desire, and the way I wanted Lucian Radcliffe and the things that I would be willing to do if I thought that I could have him.

❧ Mary Violet invited me to stay over on Friday night, and we set up cots on a second-floor balcony. I stared up into the sky, the stars hidden by a layer of clouds.

"JW, I'm jealous you get to tutor Lucky. I've got dibs on marrying him, though."

"He might want to marry someone he hasn't even met yet."

"He doesn't have much choice. Radcliffe men only marry Birch Grove girls, and Radcliffe girls only marry Evergreen boys. At some point, the inbreeding is going to show up in rare blood disorders or prehensile toes. Maybe even a tail."

"Why are you obsessed with genetic mutations?"

She pointed upward. "I always wonder what's out there and what's *here* on Earth that we don't know about. I saw a documentary with a scientist explaining the theory of mul-tiverses. He said that an infinite number of universes can exist, and that they can each have their own rules of physics. Maybe in one universe, E *doesn't* equal MC squared, and maybe in one there's magic, and maybe in one, time moves backwards or in circles."

"So that realities that seem mutually exclusive could co-exist?"

"Yes." She sighed contentedly. "Maybe there are alien girls talking right now about the possibility that girls as fabulous as us exist somewhere."

I thought about how Hosea would have loved that theory. "Jane?"

"Yes, Mary Violet?"

"Do you mind sleeping outside? When you lived in the hood did you ever go camping?"

I vaguely remembered nights sleeping outside and the scent of fires. "Sort of, but it wasn't anything fancy."

"Camping isn't supposed to be fancy. Whenever we go camping, the days last forever, but summer vacation seems really short. Someone should do a study on the theory of relativity and holidays." She was quiet for so long that I thought she'd gone to sleep. "We always go to my parents' alumni camps and see the same people every year. Did you camp at a state park?"

"It was a long time ago," I said. "There's another thing. When I had my accident, I didn't just lose my memory. I might have had brain damage. I had to go through testing. The doctors said I'm fine, but sometimes I wonder."

"Maybe you *are* fine." I heard MV's long exhalation of breath. "It's probably easier to remember things when parents remind you about them, always saying 'remember when you did this' and 'remember when you did that.' You're such an enigma."

A mockingbird sang somewhere in the distance, and I wondered why the species evolved to mimic other birds' songs. "MV, you asked me if I had a nickname and I said no. But back home they called me Mousie or Mousie Girl, because I'm mousy and plain."

"But you're not plain! You have lovely colors, like an old sepia photo, and mice are so petite and exquisite, like you."

"MV, I may be brain damaged, but sometimes I worry that you're clinically insane. Don't tell anyone about the accident or my nickname, okay?"

She sighed again. "Okay."

❧ At breakfast with Mary Violet's family, the kids fought over the last pieces of bacon while Mr. Holiday tried to devise a plan to share equally based on prior consumption.

Mary Violet leaned over to me. "He's *such* an alpha nerd. We love that about him."

He was so different—smart, involved, and reasonable—from the other fathers I'd known that I was studying him like he was an exotic animal.

Mrs. Holiday asked me to come into her studio. She handed me a large package covered in brown paper. "It's one of my Lady of the Wood paintings, Jane."

I was speechless for a moment. "You're really giving this to me?"

"Art isn't alive unless it's seen and loved." She ruffled her short locks. "I hope it will bring some joy to you, Jane. Make sure to take the time to explore your inner self and learn who you are."

She looked at me with her smoky gray eyes and I thought that perhaps she did know things I couldn't yet understand. "I'll try. Thank you for the painting."

As I was leaving, Mary Violet shoved a glossy black bag into my tote. "I get all these gifts-with-purchase when I buy makeup and perfume. I put things in there for your coloring. What are you doing tonight?"

"Thanks, MV! I'm not doing anything except studying."

"I have to go to my grandmother's for a family birthday. Grand-mère calls me Marie-Violette and she's always asking me about my beaux, which is French for players with trust funds."

"Have fun. I'll see you Monday." Although the painting was big, it was light, and I carried it back to my cottage and propped it on the mantel. Mary Violet's gift bag contained samples of makeup, lotions, and hair and bath products. I was so thrilled by them that I lined them up on the bath-room vanity so I could play with them later.

Then I walked down the hill to Greenwood Grocery.

The manager was near the front door and he watched me as I came in. "Good afternoon, miss."

"Hi," I said, but not in a friendly way. I scanned the

registers, but didn't see Ornery. As I went to get milk, cereal, and fruit, I peeked to the mirrors mounted on the market's ceilings. Each time, I was able to see the manager. Which meant that he was standing so that he was always able to see me.

I went to a register, chose a handful of candy bars, and paid. The manager had once again moved to the doors at the store's entrance. I went up to him, set down my grocery bag, and opened up my tote. "Go ahead and search it."

"I'm sorry, I don't get your meaning."

"You've been surveilling me the whole time. I *didn't* steal anything from your store. I don't need to steal. I have money to pay for things now."

He waved his hand palm outward toward my tote. "Oh, good heavens, no, I didn't think you were taking anything, miss! I recognized you as the new Birch Grove girl. You're a friend of Orneta's, aren't you?"

"We've met," I said, suspicious of his interest. "I didn't see her here today."

His lips moved up and down, from a smile to a frown to a smile again. "She quit rather abruptly a few days ago. She didn't happen to tell you anything about why she was leaving, or any problems she had with the store? She seemed very happy here."

I shook my head. "We weren't that close." Ornery must have been thrilled to get away from this creep.

"Well, I hope you won't stop shopping with us! Enjoy your afternoon."

I was thinking about my conversation with Ornery when I went to the library and did a search for any Birch Grove suicides. There was one newspaper story dated last March.

Claire Dana Mason, 43, of Greenwood, Calif., was presumed dead when her car was abandoned on the highway shoulder at Devil's Slide. After drivers reported the vehicle as a road hazard, CHP officers found a note addressed to Mrs. Mason's husband, Albert Mason. The contents of the note have not been disclosed. An acquaintance believed that Mrs. Mason had been depressed after a miscarriage.

The Coast Guard is conducting searches on nearby beaches, but an unnamed officer stated that a fall from the Devil's Slide promontory "has a zero percent chance of survival."

Mrs. Mason was a nurse at the exclusive Birch Grove Academy for Girls in Greenwood. She was also an alumna of the school. Birch Grove Academy's representative said, "Our prayers and thoughts are with Mr. Mason at this difficult time." Mrs. Mason had no other living relatives or children.

I wanted to find out more, but an older woman was impatiently waiting for the computer, so I picked up my groceries and took the shuttle back to Birch Grove. As I walked by the main building, I stopped to consider what would happen if someone jumped from the building. A fall from the third floor or the roof would certainly be fatal.

I knew nothing about Claire Mason except that she was a nurse, married to a science teacher. In other words, she was practical. Would a practical person take a long and treacherous drive to throw herself off Devil's Slide when she could have jumped off the building here or overdosed on meds from the nurse's office? The official story was possible, but seemed improbable.

I didn't know why or how, but I had a sudden gut feeling that Claire Mason had run away from Birch Grove.

Why did they bring me here to make me
Not quite bad and not quite good,
Why, unless They're wicked, do They want, in spite, to
    take me
Back to Their wet, wild wood?

Charlotte Mew, "The Changeling" (1916)

Chapter 14 By late afternoon, the cottage was gloomy and I felt cramped. I turned on a few lamps and went outside to stretch. Then I heard someone calling my name.

"Jane! You home?" Lucky was coming down the path.

"Hi!" My heart leaped, and I pulled the rubber band from my hair and shook it out. "Did you want to change our lesson? Or cancel? You could have called." Anxiety ran through me.

Lucky stepped onto the porch and his height made me feel much smaller. "I was just coming by to say hi, but if I'm bothering you . . ."

"No, I thought . . ."

"I had to get out of the house." He pushed back his thick honey-colored hair.

"Come on in."

We went inside and Lucky sat on the sofa and patted the space beside him. I sat close, but not too close to him, noticing the way he spread his legs, in the way boys do, taking up space. Then he pivoted toward me. "Do you want to know something about me, Jane? I don't have any friends."

At first, I thought he was joking, but his expression was serious. "Lucky, you talked about all the friends you supposedly don't have when I went to your house for dinner."

"Okay, I have lots of casual friends, but not anyone close to me, someone I can really talk to."

"You have your brother."

"Brothers don't count. They have to talk to you."

"Are you seriously trying to get *me* to feel sorry for *you*?"

"No, but . . ." He rubbed the stubble on his cheek and I couldn't help staring at his long, strong fingers. "What I mean is, I'd like to talk to someone who likes me for me, not because I'm a Radcliffe or because my mother's the headmistress. Money doesn't solve loneliness, Jane. It makes it harder for me to figure out who my real friends are. People here assume they know exactly who I am, already. I want a friend who doesn't come with any ideas of how I'm supposed to act, or be."

So he had come here wanting to talk to Jane, the friend. I sighed. "I like you for you, Lucky."

"Maybe once you really know me, you won't like me. Would you like me no matter what?"

In the soft light of the lamps, I could see the angles of his perfect face. I imagined what it would be like to slip my hands under his shirt and feel the skin and muscles beneath. "I wouldn't like you if you were stupid or mean, and I know you aren't stupid, and you've been nice to me."

He edged closer to me until our knees touched and I felt that slight contact run all the way up my leg and thigh. "Jack says I'm selfish. Yeah, maybe he's right. Maybe I do use people sometimes. Maybe they're okay with that. Would you mind?"

Pretty girls got used for sex and rich girls got used for money, and I was neither pretty nor rich. "You're not using me, Lucky. I'm getting paid a lot to tutor you."

"What I mean is—" he began, and then we both heard the sounds outside of skidding and metal clanging against wood.

I'd left the front door open and now Jack strolled in,

wearing his ragged shorts and an old t-shirt. "Hi, Jane. Lucky, I was looking all over for you."

"Well, here I am." Lucky moved away from me on the sofa.

"So I can see. You've gotta go. Dad wants to talk to you."

"He'll see me later."

"He said *now*."

When Lucky stood and walked to the door, I followed him. He scowled back at Jack. "Aren't you coming?"

"Dad wants you, not me."

"Whatever, jackass." Lucky's face flushed with anger. "See you tomorrow, Jane."

"Okay, bye."

Jack's bike was propped haphazardly against the porch steps and Lucky kicked it as he went by. I watched him until the trees hid him from view. When I turned back to the living room, Jack was sitting in the armchair with his feet on the coffee table.

"Get your damn feet off the furniture."

"Ooh, snappish." He swung his legs down.

"I didn't ask you to stay."

"Do you have other plans?"

"I might go out with Mary Violet."

"That'll be news to her. Hattie told me that MV's stuck with her crazy *grand-mére* all night. How've you been?"

I sat on the sofa. "If you thought Lucky might be here, you could have called."

"This is more neighborly," Jack said, and I noticed the warm timbre under the teasing of his voice. "You didn't answer my question."

"All you ever have is questions. I've been fine."

He tipped his chin toward the mantel. "Is that one of Mrs. Holiday's paintings?"

"She gave it to me. It's the birches."

"She must have a high opinion of you. Mrs. Holiday's

kind of famous and that's probably valuable, so take care of it."

"I'll take care of it because it's wonderful."

"That's an even better reason. I think so, too, but I love the birches." He picked up my Latin book from the coffee table and flipped it open. *"Nihil boni mihi hic inveniri potest,"* he read slowly. "How was that?"

"Terrible. You're supposed to pronounce the *v*'s like *w*'s."

"Vhy?"

"Because that's how it is."

"Vhat does it mean?" He repeated the sentence.

I translated the words in my head. "Nothing good can be found here in my opinion."

He gave a hoot. "That sounds about right. That should be the Birch Grove motto." He repeated the sentence as if memorizing it. He slapped the book down on the table. "Why Latin instead of a modern language?"

"It will help with my science studies. I like it because it's specific—the declensions break things down into gender, number, tense, and mood. English is too ambiguous and you're always guessing what people actually mean."

"Do you think everyone should say exactly what they mean?"

I glared at him. "I wish *you* would. You'd probably benefit from taking up Latin."

"Maybe I vill. Everyone at school treating you all right?"

"Yes."

"Because these schools can be a bit, you know, elitist and controlling. That's why I decided to go somewhere else."

"Yes, you already told me you didn't like the rules, but your mother told me you went to public school for the music program."

"And for the friendly girls, of course."

As he sat there, I studied him and his out-of-control curls. His eyes were light and clear against the dark lashes and his strong nose was balanced by his broad forehead, wide cheek-bones, and square chin.

"So, Jane, do you approve of what you see?"

"Your hair is a mess and you've got bike grease on your leg."

He raised one thick eyebrow. "That's another reason I couldn't go to Evergreen Prep—my hair is too messy. Do you think I'm better-looking than my brother?"

"No one thinks you're better-looking than Lucky."

"You could at least pretend. You could have said that I was good-looking in my own unique way, like a snow-flake."

"You're not a snowflake, and it's obvious that Lucky is really good-looking."

"Yeah, that's what the mirror tells me, too. The girl I'm crazy for tells me that. Appearances are so important. And Lucky's nicer than me, right, Halfling?"

"He has better manners. He doesn't call me ridiculous names." When Jack talked to me, I felt wide-awake because I had to be completely alert to follow the twists in his con-versation. "But you did bring the pizza that time."

"It was the neighborly thing to do, like this. A visit to chat. You should chat more."

"I believe that we're allotted a limited quota of words in our lifetime and you're using all of mine up."

"I'm borrowing them since you've got so many getting dusty in the attic." He lifted his hand and wiggled it, say-ing, "I like your hair that way, like ripples in a stream. You're as small and elusive as a fairy creature, yet you're as silent and mysterious as a sphinx. Mary Violet would call that a sphinxling. Tell me something in your native wood-land language. Or, since ve're switching *v*'s and *w*'s, *vood-land*."

"My native language would get me detention."

His pond-green eyes sparkled with humor. "Jane, one day I'll discover the magic words to win your trust. They may even be in Latin, although I think your tongue pre-dates human history." Then he stood up. "Guess I'll go and get ready for my date. I'm taking Hattie out tonight. She's gorgeous, don't you think? She's as gorgeous as Lucky is handsome."

"What's important to me is that she's friendly and not stuck-up."

"Not many girls are gorgeous and smart and talented, and her family has truckloads of money. Have you heard her play the piano? Like an angel, and she speaks French like Marcel Marceau. She draws extremely well."

"You better not be late then." I stood and walked him to the door. "Jack, did you break my flowerpot with your bike?"

"I don't think so, but go ahead and blame me anyway. Aren't you going to give me a hug good-bye?"

Jack stood waiting, holding his arms out, and I suddenly knew why Hattie would think he was sexy, with his eyes sparkling with mischief and wide, sensual mouth that was always curling up in amusement, his strong shoulders, his muscled legs, and his scent of fresh green things and earth.

"Jane, a hug is the *neighborly* thing to do."

I thought of what it would be like to be pressed up against his body. "I come from a different neighborhood." I swung the door shut before he could answer.

Then I wondered what had just happened. Why did everything the Radcliffe brothers said seem to have an alternative meaning?

I sat at the wooden desk and took out a new composition book. I drew a line vertically down the page. On one side, I wrote down everything I'd remembered Lucky telling me. On the other side, I wrote possible interpretations. Why had Lucky asked if I would mind if he used me? People who used people didn't ask permission.

I didn't have enough information, so I added all the bewildering things Jack had said, too. While I was doing this, all sorts of other questions came to me . . . including all the peculiarities around Bebe leaving the school and Claire Mason's disappearance. I'd never even met them, but when they were mentioned, I got an uneasy sensation, like walking into a cobweb and feeling the invisible sticky threads catching at me.

There might be reasonable explanations for everything, but the more I thought about the unanswered questions, the stranger they seemed. I hid the notebook in the laundry room with my stash.

A nameless spell seemed to attach him to her; even the shudder which he felt in her presence, and which would not permit him to touch her, was not unmixed with pleasure, like that thrilling awful emotion felt when strains of sacred music float under the vault of some temple; he rather sought, therefore, than avoided this feeling.

Johann Ludwig Tieck, "Wake Not the Dead" (1800)

Chapter 15 On Sunday afternoon, I filed my short nails until the edges were even. I carefully stroked on the clear pink nail polish that was in the bag that MV had given me. Some smeared on my cuticles, and I had to start over again. When the nail polish dried, I got dressed in my best jeans and a black t-shirt under a purple sweater. I used some of the hair care samples and my hair waved glossily down my back.

I patted concealer on a red spot on my chin that had erupted overnight. I stroked on mascara, rubbed on a little blush, and slicked on lip gloss. I smelled the perfume samples and dabbed on the flowery one I liked best.

I left the porch light on and locked the front door as I left. The days had quickly become shorter and cooler. As I walked up the path toward the house on the hill, I passed the amphitheater. A faint ray of sunlight flashed off something on the ground among fallen leaves.

At first I thought it might be a bottle cap. With the edge of my shoe, I pushed aside the dry leaves and saw a silver penknife. As I leaned over to pick it up, I noticed two brownish maroon spots on the marble bench. On impulse, I licked the tip of my finger and dragged it across one of the spots. My finger came away rusty red. It was blood.

I examined the area nearby, but there were no signs of

serious injury, like a trail of spots or splatters or a damp splotch.

The knife, less than four inches long, had the soft glow of old silver and a delicate floral etching. I thought of Hattie sitting here at night. The cutters I'd known had been like cracked glass, able to shatter at any moment, but Hattie was sure of herself. I put the knife in my pocket and walked up the hill to the headmistress's house.

Mrs. Radcliffe answered my knock. "Hello, Jane. Don't you look nice today!"

"Hello, Mrs. Radcliffe." Once again, I was struck by how dim the interior of the house was.

"Lucky is in the boys' study. Go upstairs, turn right, and it's the second door."

As I walked upstairs, the penknife in my pocket hit my thigh. My footsteps were muffled by a woven rug in shades of deep reds and browns, the color of dried blood and dead leaves. The door was open, and I walked into a comfortable room with windows facing the pines that crowded the house. There were desks against the walls and built-in bookcases. The back of a long blue sofa faced me. Opposite the sofa were a navy blue leather chair and an ottoman.

"Lucky?"

His blond head popped up from behind the sofa's back. "Hey, Jane. Come on in." His head dropped back out of sight.

I went around the sofa, where Lucky was lying on his back, tossing a baseball from hand to hand. I admired the tendons on his arms for a moment before saying, "You have your own study?"

"I'd rather have a home theater. My mom thinks the bigger the screen, the smaller the brain." He swung his legs down and sat up. "I guess we better get to chem."

I followed him to a desk and struggled to keep down my emotions as we spent an hour reviewing metric units of mass and volume. I helped him prep for his next chapter on the physical properties of matter. He kept up easily with the problems.

"You don't need my help," I blurted.

"I do need you, Jane." He put down his pencil and faced me.

"I mean, you don't need me to explain. You can do all this on your own."

His blue eyes held mine for nerve-racking seconds. "You smell nice."

I blushed and I kept my eyes on his.

Then he reached for my hand and held it, and a shiver went through me. "I can do the chemistry on my own, but I'll do better if you keep me on track. I need someone beside me for support, someone I can confide in who won't judge me. Don't you want to be that person?"

We both jumped at the sound of someone in the hall. I leaned away from Lucky as Mrs. Radcliffe came in.

"Hope I'm not interrupting. Lucky, would you please unload my car now? I've got files in there that I've got to review," she said. "Jane, dinner will be ready in about ten minutes." Lucky tossed a glance at me as he and his mother left the room.

I stared at the chem book but could only think of Lucky's hand on mine and the frustrating obscurity of his comments. I was so tense that I needed to move and decided to walk down the hall and see what was up here.

There was a small blue-and-white guest bath, linen closets, and then a spacious and neat black-and-white bedroom with sleek modern furniture. Dozens of sports trophies filled glass cases, and an entertainment center had game systems and a flatscreen. One wall was covered with baseball and ski team photos and photos of Lucky and his friends at parties. I tried to imagine myself in a picture here, but couldn't.

I left the room and wandered to the end of the hall. A door was ajar, so I pushed it open to see a cluttered, sun-filled room as big as my cottage. Black, gray, and khaki clothes were strewn across the floor, and bicycles hung from hooks on the ceiling. Music equipment and guitars were everywhere, and club flyers covered giant bulletin boards.

Albums were sorted on shelves with handwritten labels: WINTER, SANDSTORM, MELANCHOLY, WILD ANIMAL JAMBOREE, TANTALIZE ME, RUMINATE ON THIS, and more. I tilted my head sideways and ran my fingers over the spines to read all the unfamiliar titles. A bookshelf was crammed from top to bottom with sci-fi and fantasy books and books about music.

On one side of the room, French windows opened onto a wide balcony. I wandered over to see the view but froze when I spotted Jack sitting on an old wooden chair there. He faced out toward the trees while he plucked a guitar. Beside him was a table with a notebook and a pencil. He'd play a few seconds and then write in the notebook.

A soft breeze blew back his bittersweet chocolate hair and when he dropped his head to write, I saw his profile. His lips twitched upward before he replayed an altered version of the tune.

I was unaware of how much I'd edged forward until he stopped playing and turned toward me. I felt like I'd been caught spying as I stood at the open doors and the breeze cooled my skin. We stared at each other too long and then Jack smiled slowly.

"So you came to see me, Halfling. I've been hoping you would."

His expression was so earnest that he almost fooled me, almost made me believe that he'd been waiting for me. "Very funny, Jack. Why would I come to see you? I'm here for Lucky." I saw the disappointment in his face—I guess since I hadn't fallen for his teasing.

He played a few notes that gave me a strange sensation, like fingertips softly brushing the back of my neck. "I know that, that you're here for Lucky."

"I was, uhm, just seeing what's on this floor," I stammered. "Why do you organize your music like that, instead of alphabetically or chronologically?"

"Because that's what music is to me, an emotional story." He began playing a slow, intricate song that made me feel melancholy.

"What kind of music is that anyway?"

"Classical modern. The notes would be crisper if I took care of my hands, but people keep crashing me into bushes."

"Like I said, very funny. Is that song for your band?"

"No, my band's mostly rock. The song can be for you if you like. It can be 'Into the Wild with My Brown-Eyed Nymph.'"

Did he mean Hattie in the woods at night? Had he been the one who called her at the slumber party? Had she met him out there? "Hattie has brown eyes."

"Hazel, actually. Yours are brown as chocolate. Or coffee, a medium but sparky blend."

He was so weird. "An 'emotional' system sounds like a 'random' system. I don't see how you find anything that way."

"Sometimes I don't, but that's what makes things interesting. I find music I forgot I had and hear new things in old songs. The way you experience a song changes with your own experiences. It changes with your moods."

"It sounds like a way to waste time."

"It's not the destination; it's the journey, Halfling. How would you organize emotions?"

"Well, I'd assign each elemental emotion a code, like the periodic table, arranged by weight, property, and charge. Compound emotions, like sibling rivalry, for example, could be easily broken down into base elements, including competitiveness and envy, and I'd factor in family dynamics."

Jack sighed loudly and twanged his guitar. "Why do you need to break everything down into boring components? I mean, you could take something amazing like . . ."

"Pizza."

"Yes, pizza." The right corner of Jack's mouth lifted. "It's tomato sauce, and the crust has flour in it, and then there are the toppings. None of those ingredients is especially interesting on its own, but together they're awesome. The whole is greater than the sum of its parts."

"You must have been terrible in math."

"Maybe you could tutor me."

"I think you're beyond help."

"I'm incorrigible?"

The word startled me. "Why did you use that word?"

He shrugged. "Isn't it right? You're the vocabulary genius, not me."

"It's fine. Dinner's ready."

The peculiar conversation with Jack somehow helped me get my act together enough to sit through dinner, and I had to stop myself from staring at Lucky. I stalled leaving by helping wash the dishes and then Lucky came to my side. "Jane, I'll walk you home."

We were silent until we walked into the darkness of the grove. Like Hattie, he had no problem finding his way, but my steps slowed because I didn't want to stumble. To my amazement, Lucky swung an arm over my shoulders and helped me on the path.

My breathing quickened. "Lucky, what did you mean about using me?"

"I want you to be there for me. To be my friend and my . . . and more. I want you to be loyal to me and to stay with me through anything."

"Do you mean as a friend?"

"More."

My heart raced. "A girlfriend?" I desperately hoped that he wouldn't sneer.

"Girlfriends are temporary." His arm over my shoulder tightened. "Will you be loyal to me, Jane?"

I wanted to please him, to make him like me. "I'll be loyal to you so long as you are deserving of loyalty."

Lucky's voice was husky as he said, "I knew I could count on you." We were at the amphitheater and he paused. "I like this place. Sometimes I come here at night to chill."

"Lucky, you said girlfriends are temporary, and I was wondering . . . Are you seeing anyone?"

"Are you asking for yourself or did Mary Violet tell you to snoop? I'd never hook up with such an attention whore."

I drew away from Lucky so quickly that his arm fell from my shoulder. "That's really harsh and unjustified. She's . . . she's *fabulous.*"

"I didn't mean it in a bad way. I meant, like, she's an extrovert and I like girls who are quieter, you know, quiet like you." There was enough light for me to make out his smile. I wanted to believe he'd merely been careless with his words. Then he put his arm over my shoulders again, and we started walking.

At the cottage porch, Lucky faced me and I couldn't breathe anymore. He pushed my hair back behind my shoulder, and his mouth went to the side of my throat, and my knees went weak with astonishment. He wrapped an arm around my waist, drawing me close.

I arched my neck back, astounded by his mouth on my skin, thrilled by the feel of his tall body against mine, and I closed my eyes.

When he nipped my throat sharply with his teeth, my first reflex was to jump away.

"Did I hurt you?" he asked anxiously.

"You surprised me." And made me nervous and excited and confused and unsure.

He put his arms around me so that my body was tight against his. "Jane, don't tell anyone what I said to you before, about us."

"Lucky, I don't go telling everyone my business."

"No, I know you don't. But everyone gossips here. Some of the girls would be jealous because they've been after me and they'd get nasty and go mean-girl on you.

Once people get to know you, we can be more open about our . . ."

"Our what?"

"About *us*. I'll see you soon, Jane."

So there was an *us*.

I replayed his words, the press of his body, the kiss—and the nip—obsessively in my head. I wrote down everything that had happened in my composition book. All through the night, I imagined things I could have said, things Lucky could have said, the ways we could have touched each other.

My biggest question was *Why me?* Why had Lucian Radcliffe chosen Jane Williams, Mousie Girl, as a special friend? And what exactly did he expect?

On Monday, I asked Hattie if we could talk for a minute. We stepped into an empty hall, near the chapel. I pulled the silver penknife from my blazer pocket. "Hattie, I found this at the amphitheater."

She took it from me. "Thanks! I must have dropped it when I was out there. It was my great-grandmother's."

"There were spots of blood on the bench. If something's bothering you . . . if there's anything I can do to help, just ask."

"I'm not a cutter." She rolled up her sleeves, revealing flawless skin so pale that the blue veins showed clearly. "See." Then she hiked up her skirt, so I could see her slim, perfect legs. "I carried the knife out for protection, which was silly since this is the safest place in the world. I was playing with it and I nicked my finger." She held up her forefinger. "All better now."

"Sorry. I had to ask, in case."

"It's okay. I'm glad you cared enough to say something." She smiled. "Hey, I wanted to tell you, there's a party on Friday at the country club. Jack's band is playing. Do you want to come?"

"Sure."

"Great. Constance and MV are coming." We began to walk back to the main hallway and she added casually, "Lucky will be there, too."

And those five words made my heart stop. I stole a peek at Hattie, but to her it was merely a comment. Lucky said we had to wait to let others know about *us,* but maybe he'd change his mind at the party. Maybe he'd put his arm over my shoulders as he introduced me to his friends. Maybe he'd hold me close for a slow jam. I thought of how I'd look up into his perfect face. I imagined Lucky's golden hair falling over his forehead and his blue eyes meeting mine as he leaned down to kiss me.

I went through the next days trying to act normal, but Lucky was always on my mind, like a favorite song that you play over and over in your head. I had the delirious feeling that the party would be a changing point in my life—and that the headmistress's son would declare his feelings for me in front of everyone.

By one of those caprices of the mind, which we are perhaps most subject to in early youth, I at once gave up my former occupations . . . In this mood of mind I betook myself to the mathematics, and the branches of study appertaining to that science, as being built upon secure foundations, and so worthy of my consideration.

Mary Shelley, *Frankenstein* (1818)

Chapter 16 As I was leaving homeroom on Thursday, Mr. Mason called me over. "Jane, would you come see me after school today? We should touch base to see how things are going." He removed his glasses, huffed on the lenses, and polished them with a handkerchief.

Every time I saw him, I thought of MV's description: tragic and valiant. "We have to put the *Weekly* to bed this afternoon. Ms. Chu said we'd be busy until after five."

"Come as late as you like. I have papers to grade and I'll be in the lab."

When I went to the chem lab a little after six P.M., Mr. Mason was standing at the window staring out to the lush trees beyond. He startled at the sound of my footsteps and then smiled.

On the surface, he seemed fine. A closer inspection showed that his shirt was badly ironed and his graying hair had grown shaggy. His white lab jacket was missing a button. There were bags under his eyes and his complexion was dull.

Mr. Mason set a batch of papers on the ledge under the window. "Will you have an article in this issue of the newspaper?"

"I wrote a piece on the scholarship program."

"A *piece*, hmm? You're already speaking the jargon," he

said warmly. "My wife was an orphan who won Birch Grove's Belvedere Scholarship, which paid for her tuition and housing. You probably heard that she passed away last year."

I thought he actually believed that story. "Yes, I'm very sorry, Mr. Mason."

"Like you, she had an aptitude for science, although her specialty was biology. She decided to return here as a nurse and we met my first year teaching. That's the wonder of Birch Grove. We all become part of one another's lives. But I really wanted to know how you're doing. How do you like Night Terrors?"

"Thanks for helping me transfer in. It's much better than the other course."

"But?"

"But I still don't see the purpose of studying superstitious fiction when we have so many really interesting scientific mysteries that need to be solved."

"I feel the same way. Let's not tell anyone though, because people always think something's wrong with you when you'd rather conduct an experiment than read a novel."

I grinned. "Deal."

"If you'd like any assistance, I could set up sessions with tutors or counselors."

"It's hard, but I'm keeping up."

"Terrific. You're my top student in Honors Chemistry, you know, and that's quite remarkable for someone who hasn't had the advantages of good schools."

"I work hard." I felt shy about his compliment but really happy, too.

He took a red pencil from his pocket. "I suppose we both better get to our homework. I've got to finish grading and then set up for tomorrow's Frosh Chem."

"Can I help, sir?"

He smiled gratefully. "If you have time. It's an easy experiment on chemical changes." He gave me a printout of the experiment, and I set up each station with test tubes, beakers, reagents like sodium bicarbonate and aluminum chloride, and solutions. I marked off each item after I placed it on the lab tables, and then I checked again.

"All done!" I said.

Mr. Mason, who had been glancing at me from time to time as he graded papers, came to inspect my work. "Very good, Jane! Thank you for your help."

"Well, if you're not part of the solution, you're part of the precipitate."

It was a corny old joke, but he chuckled. "Nerd alert!"

"Nerds unite! If you ever need help, I can come by."

"I'll hold you to that, Jane. You better go along now and get to your homework."

I was still savoring Mr. Mason's praise as I went down the stairwell. The building seemed so different when it was vacant. A few low-wattage bulbs provided dim circles of light, and each footstep echoed in the empty hall. I began walking softly in the creepy gloom.

As I turned toward the lockers, I saw someone down the hall, a darker shape against the shadows, and the little hairs on the back of my neck went up. She wore jeans and a black sweatshirt with the hood up over her head and she was fiddling with a locker. I stepped forward and realized that she was by *my* locker.

"Hey!" I shouted.

She ducked her head so I couldn't see her face and dashed off in the other direction. My foster-kid attitude kicked in and I sprinted after her. She turned down the hall with the music practice rooms.

The slick soles of my shoes slowed me down, and when I rounded the corner, the shadowy hallway was empty.

The hall dead-ended at an emergency exit door with a glowing red light still active. My heart pounded and every nerve was alert as I went up and down the hall, searching each practice room. They were empty.

She *couldn't* have disappeared, so I checked the rooms again. She must have gone out the emergency exit. Which means that she knew the access code for the exit. I rushed back to the other hallway. My locker was closed and locked. I opened it—everything looked the same.

Was I letting paranoia affect my reasoning? The light here was so faint that she could have been at someone else's locker or even at her own locker. She might have been freaked out when I surprised her and yelled.

But if she was trying to get in my locker to snoop or steal something of mine, then she might have been snooping around my cottage and broken (on purpose or by accident) the flowerpot.

But this wasn't Hellsdale. After all, a store manager might watch you without thinking that you were a shoplifter.

I left the building and glanced back. The only lighted room was the chemistry lab. Mr. Mason was still silhouetted against the front window.

❧ I was eating my dinner of scrambled eggs when Mary Violet called. "What are you wearing tomorrow for the soiree? Don't answer that because I already inspected your closet and you don't have any dresses."

"I don't know. I guess I'll wear my cargos and a tee."

"No, *all* the girls wear dresses. Did you know that my mother has a room like a museum where she keeps all our evening and special occasion wear? We should have a directory like in department stores, you know, Women's Intimates, Third Floor."

"Your clothes wouldn't fit me, MV."

"State the obvious, please! You're about the same size as Agnes and she's got dozens of dresses that she won't wear."

"Really?"

"*Really.* My *grand-mère* and all the aunties keep buying

them hoping she'll be more feminine, which is like, ugh, why do they need *her* to be feminine when they've got me?"

"Good point."

"Come over tomorrow after school. We can get ready for the party together and then you can stay overnight. My parents don't care what time we get home so long as no possums are killed between here and the country club. Constance is coming, but Hattie's going out to dinner with Jack first. He'll probably take her to that depressing old-people restaurant in town."

"Are you sure? You keep giving me things, MV."

"I know—isn't it fabulous? Aren't *I* fabulous? The answer is yes! Until tomorrow, darling!"

🌸 I awoke early and gathered all the things I needed for tonight. I didn't have any heels, so I put the black flats and the ratty plastic sandals in a bag with my overnight things. Classes seemed interminable, and I bolted from my desk the moment the bell rang and hurried to meet Mary Violet and Constance by the front entrance.

MV skipped over to me. "JW, you will *not* believe the ensembles I've put together for you to try on. I will transform you into a mini-diva."

"MV, repeat after me: *Jane is not a Barbie doll.* I'm not even a Bratz."

"Jane is not blah, blah, blah. My mother told me I can't dress like a courtesan. Courtesan is French for high-society ho. They could discuss politics and art and also knew techniques to make men insane with desire and lust." Mary Violet widened her big blue eyes and puffed out her pink cheeks. "Can you imagine! Maybe I can discover their secrets."

Constance moved a garment bag to her other hand. "MV, you should restrict your fantasies to entries in your Hello Kitty diary."

"You are so unambitious. If you had been in charge of the space program, we never would have put a man on the sun."

"We haven't . . ." Constance began, and then smiled.

We rounded the drive and my friends waved and called out to all the other girls going home. It wasn't until we were on the Holidays' street that Mary Violet said, "Constance thinks that Lucky won't ever fall dementedly in love with me. She thinks I'm too ugly and stupid."

"I did *not* say that!" Constance narrowed her almond eyes. "I said you're too girly-sissy."

"That's the same thing."

"It is not," Constance answered. "Jane, tell her it's not the same thing."

"It's not the same thing." I kept my tone nonchalant. "It's okay that you're a sissy. You're really good at it. Exceptional even."

Constance said, "Even if Lucky finally notices that you're . . ."

"Fabulous and fascinating and sexy." Mary Violet fluffed her hair.

"Sure, why not? Why would you even want to date the headmistress's son? It would totally complicate everything at school for you."

"Hattie dates the headmistress's son, and you don't give her grief."

"That's different. Hattie's a Tyler. They've been here as long as the Radcliffes and the Belvederes. Mrs. Radcliffe couldn't object even if she didn't like Hattie." Constance frowned. "Why do you care about Lucian Radcliffe anyway? He's kind of . . ."

"He's spectacular!" Mary Violet cried. "Jane, tell Constance he's spectacular."

"Lucky's spectacular," I said as if I didn't care, but my heart was pounding. "Constance, he's kind of what?"

"A little *too* perfect. He's all polished surface, like a mirror reflecting what you want to see, and I seriously doubt if there's anything below the bright shiny."

"Con, you're crazy!" Mary Violet said. "His manners

are divine. Don't you remember in sixth grade when the boys came to Miss Harlot's School of Croquet? Jack put on his blazer backwards because he thought it was funny—"

"It *was* hilarious," Constance said. "You laughed so hard you peed your tutu."

Mary Violet's cheeks turned bright pink. "We do not need to bring that up *ever* again. Lucky was the only one who bowed after a waltz. He was the best at the two-step."

This was finally my chance to ask questions. "Has Lucky ever gone out with anyone at Birch Grove?"

"Frosh year he was a total womanizer," Constance said.

"A cougarizer," Mary Violet said. "He was going through all the juniors. Mrs. Radcliffe heard about it, though, and Lucky got sneakier about whatever he does. I always thought he'd date Hattie."

Constance waved her narrow fingers like she was shooing away a fly. "MV, I don't know why you find it impossible to believe that Hattie would choose an interesting personality over a pretty face, although I think Jack's way hotter than Lucky."

"It's just that I've never sensed a real spark with Hattie and Jack. Where's the chemistry?"

"Not everyone wants to have dramatic fireworks," Constance said. "Jane, you must think we're pitiful. We have so few guys here that we get worked up over the headmistress's sons."

We arrived at the Holidays' house and went through the back entrance. Mrs. Holiday was in the kitchen swirling chocolate frosting on cupcakes. We all said hello and MV stuck her finger in the bowl of frosting to swipe a taste before saying, "Mother, dearest, we'll be in the Wardrobe Museum."

Mrs. Holiday gave her daughter a stern look. "You are not allowed to borrow any of my gowns. Nothing with a low neckline."

"I know, I know, no displays of my décolletage." MV winked at me. "That's French for bodacious tatas."

As soon as we were away from the kitchen, Constance said, "Mary Violet is still in trouble for wearing a halter dress to the Spring Frolic that was too scanty."

"It was only a little side-boobage. Meanwhile, my mother does scandalous things like making pink cupcakes with Hershey's strawberry kisses in the center of each one."

"They tasted good," Constance said.

"I had to close my eyes to eat them. We had an intervention and begged her never to make cupcakes that resemble her paintings."

"No, you didn't!"

"We did, and I recited my poem 'Ode to an Artistic Mother.'" Mary Violet dropped her bag, and threw out her arms.

"Your cupcakes are tender and taste quite delightful
But please don't decorate in ways most unsightful.
You zealously guard us from X-rated crudeness
Extend this policy to baked dessert lewdness
We celebrate all your creative expressions
But lady-parts cupcakes will cause insurrection."

Constance and I doubled over with laughter, and Mary Violet huffed. "And she has the nerve to tell me not to dress skanky."

"Please don't ever change, MV," I said.

"Only my clothes." She opened a door to a room that was so astonishing that I stopped and stared. Clothes, shoes, and accessories filled shelves, racks, and stands like a boutique. There were full-length mirrors, and chairs and benches with pale blue velvet cushions. MV waved to a rolling rack with several dresses. "*Voilà!* That's French for *Ta-da!* Agnes won't wear these even though I tried to convince her that jocks glam up occasionally."

"MV, this is amazing!"

"I know, although my mom locks away her couture in her bedroom." Mary Violet fluffed the skirt of a sleeveless sky-blue dress. "What about this one?"

Constance liked a scoop neck with a peach-and-white geometric pattern. "This is cute. Try it on."

When I stripped down, I made sure to let my hair fall over my shoulder and the scar, and I was self-conscious of my friends looking at my body.

Mary Violet said, "What an interesting tattoo! What's the *H* for?"

"A friend of mine named Hosea, who got sick and died."

"I'm sorry, Jane. Did you do the tattoo yourself?"

"MV, how could she do it herself on that place? She's not a contortionist."

"My friend Wilde did it for me. I lay down on the bed and she drew it in first and then used a homemade tat kit."

Mary Violet made me describe the process. "How very crafty! Maybe we should all make a pact and—"

"No way, MV," Constance said. "I will not ever get a tattoo of your face for any reason."

I tried on a dozen dresses, wondering which one Lucky would like best. There was a blue print that was the same color as his eyes, and a dress that matched the teal shirt he'd been wearing when we met. Maybe he liked really sexy girls, and I pulled out a slinky black spaghetti-strap mini.

Mary Violet said, "An aunt gave that to Agnes for her last birthday. I thought my mother would have a heart attack, but it would be hot on you."

"It's not quite my style." I eventually decided on a sleeveless emerald-green dress with a narrow cut and empire waist that made me appear taller.

My friends approved and Mary Violet said, "You can totally work the Audrey Hepburn–elfin-waif thing."

"I never know what you're talking about, MV." I gazed

at the shelves of beautiful shoes, all too big for me, and I was about to put on my flats when Constance said, "Wait!" She went to her garment bag and brought out a lumpy cloth sack tied at the top with a big red ribbon. "This is from us to you."

I untied the ribbon to find a pair of sleek black open-toe heels. "How did you . . ." I began, touching the smooth leather. "They're my size."

"Well, duh," Mary Violet said. "I told you I inspected your closet. We all pitched in."

"Thank you." My eyes welled up.

My friends put their arms around me and said, "Group hug!"

They helped me pick out a copper velvet evening bag and a copper cashmere shawl that was so soft I couldn't stop stroking it.

Mary Violet's younger sister, Agnes, poked her head in the wardrobe museum. She nodded at me. "That fits you just right. Keep it. I hate dresses."

In a few minutes, I'd put on my makeup and fixed my hair. When I stepped into the high heels, I was suddenly four inches taller. Jack wouldn't be able to call me any stupid pee-wee names tonight and I hoped Hattie would keep him from interfering with me and Lucky.

I practiced walking in the heels while Constance got ready in a turquoise-and-white-print dress and clipped up her braids with silver combs that matched her dangling silver earrings.

Mary Violet changed into a dozen pink dresses that all blurred into sameness after a while. Constance used her phone to snap pics of Mary Violet's outfits and send them to Hattie. She was texting and grinning. "Hattie says you look like a Teletubby cousin, Pookie Pinkie."

Mary Violet said, "That's so hilarious, *not*! I look *fabulous*."

Constance set down her phone and told me, "We can take pics at the party, but nothing incriminating or all of our TSGs will get taken away."

"It's draconian the way Birch Grove treats us." MV twirled around. "How's this?"

I squinted at the pink dress. "MV, isn't that the *first* thing you tried on?"

"Maybe." MV spent ages messing with her blond curls before letting her hair down as it had been when we left campus. When she was finished, she inspected me and snapped her fingers. "Jewelry."

She wanted me to wear big hoop earrings. "Even Constance is wearing earrings and a bracelet and she's practically a Puritan."

"Jane, tell her I'm not a Puritan."

"Constance isn't a Puritan, and I can't wear the hoop earrings because I don't have pierced ears, and don't offer to pierce them with a needle and a potato."

"You can pierce ears with a potato? *Interesting*." Mary Violet fastened gold bracelets on my wrists. "Okay, baby steps. Are we ready?"

We leaned our heads together so Constance could take a picture. I could ask for a copy of it later and keep it as a memento of a night that I would remember forever.

I looked, and had an acute pleasure in looking—a precious yet poignant pleasure; pure gold, with a steely point of agony: a pleasure like what the thirst-perishing man might feel who knows the well to which he has crept is poisoned, yet stoops and drinks divine draughts nevertheless.

Charlotte Brontë, *Jane Eyre* (1847)

Chapter 17 As Mary Violet drove us to the country club in her Saab, she blasted a silly musical song where someone trilled, "I feel pretty, oh, so pretty!" I kept touching the silky material of my dress and the soft shawl as MV navigated winding, unlit roads into the hills. She stopped at a gate with an elderly guard at the booth. A narrow sign read GREEN-WOOD COUNTRY CLUB in small white letters.

Mary Violet rolled down her window. "Hi, Mr. Haggerty."

"Hi, sunshine." He pressed a button so that the big gate swung open. "Have a good time."

"Thanks! See you later." Once through the gate, we drove along the golf course. "Mr. Haggerty has been here since the dawn of man," Mary Violet said. "He once caught my mother and her friends skinny-dipping, and she still gets as red as a tomato when she sees him. That's why you should never ever skinny-dip near where you live."

"I think I lose brain cells whenever I spend time with you, MV," Constance said.

"Someday you'll appreciate my important life lessons." MV parked in a lot by a low building near swimming pools that glowed aqua in the night. Another older and more impressive building was set farther back.

Constance said, "This depressing warehouse is the Teen Center."

"They keep us away from the civilized people," Mary Violet added.

Kids were getting out of cars and going into the building. The guys wore suits, most of them with loosened ties and tennis shoes, and the girls darted to greet one another, as vivid as butterflies in their party dresses.

I asked, "Where's the security? I mean, besides Mr. Haggerty, to handle people who crash?"

"No one crashes," Constance said. "The police watch any car that comes into town."

"And I'd thought this place was so different from the hood."

We walked inside to a cavernous hall. A DJ, stationed on a platform in the corner, was spinning an indie tune that sounded familiar. Strings of lights radiated out from central points on the ceiling, like starbursts. Chairs, sofas, and trees in large pots created nooks around the periphery of the room. Tables with refreshments were set up at one end of the hall. At the other was a stage with band equipment.

Most people clustered in small groups, and there were so many tall guys here that I couldn't see over the crowd as I searched for Lucky.

Constance led the way, speaking loudly so we could hear her. "What were the parties like at your old school, Jane?"

"A lot like prison riots. I'd get away before anything serious went down." When I was thirteen, I'd whined until Hosea agreed to sneak me out of the house for a back-to-school dance. We'd walked by the police cars parked at the entrance, been patted down by security, and passed through metal detectors into City Central's packed gymnasium. Excitement and danger had electrified the atmosphere. We hadn't been there half an hour before a shouting match started. I'd wanted to see what was happening, but Hosea had put his arm around me, protecting me with his big body, and calmly maneuvered me through the mob, saying, "'Scuse me, bro," and "Pardon, sister." The guards had been barreling inside, but Hosea shielded me, saying, "Just leaving, thank you, sir."

We'd gotten halfway down the block when we heard the sharp crack of gunfire. Hosea had kept his arm around me. "Listen up, Jane. In an emergency, this is what you do. Try to stay calm. Figure out where the danger is. Don't show fear and talk respectful. Get away as soon as possible. You listening, Sis?"

I'd nodded and he'd made me repeat his instructions all the way home.

Mary Violet, Constance, and I claimed a spot near the DJ's stand and put our sweaters and shawls on the chairs. Mary Violet and Constance left their clutches, but I kept hold of my small bag.

We went to the refreshment table, where people were ladling red punch from big silver bowls to glasses. "It's the famous Greenwood Country Club punch," Mary Violet said. "In the old days, someone always had the decency to put rum in it. Now the club's so strict that we have to drink outside like animals."

Constance said, "You can't drink anyway. You're the designated driver."

"They let you drink in the open?"

"Only if everyone pretends it isn't happening," Constance said. "It's part of Greenwood's see-no-evil, hear-no-evil moral code."

"Hey, guys!"

We saw Hattie coming toward us, holding hands with Jack. Hattie's tousled dark hair hung down her back and she wore a strapless scarlet dress that exposed her pale and perfect skin. Glittering gold earrings with red gems dangled almost to her shoulders.

I felt a complicated pang of admiration for my friend and self-pity because I would never be beautiful.

Standing beside Hattie, Jack seemed less ramshackle and

more arty and rakish. He wore a battered old tuxedo jacket over a black t-shirt, ancient jeans, and black boots. He hadn't shaved and his curly hair looked like he'd been cycling in a hurricane.

I hung back as MV squeezed Jack's arm. "Oooh, muscles! I can't believe your mother let you go out like this."

"I'm a grown-ass man." He gave MV a loud smacking kiss on her cheek. "You're very *blond* tonight, Mary Violet."

"I hear that sarcasm in your voice, Jacob Radcliffe, and I'll have you know that Albert Einstein was very blond as a child."

"Is that true?" he asked suspiciously, and MV turned her head and winked at Constance and me.

"Speaking of spectacular blondes," she said, "is your brother here yet?"

"Not that I've seen. Don't look so disappointed. He always shows up eventually." Jack was facing MV, but I thought his comment was directed at me. "Jane, did you come to hear Dog Waffle?"

"Dog *what*? You never make any sense."

"Dog Waffle. It's my band. I guess the answer is no. Doesn't Hattie look amazing?"

"Yes," I said, but I was thinking, *jackass*, because he always needed to remind me that I didn't look amazing. "Very."

Hattie touched my hand. "You're so pretty in that dress. I love that color."

"I thought red was your favorite," Jack said. "Valentines, roses, strawberries, blood—"

Hattie interrupted him. "Red lipstick, rubies, beets."

"No one likes beets," Mary Violet said.

"MV, you always make these grand pronouncements," Constance said. "With you it's always *everybody* or *nobody*. You have a binary approach to life."

"That's because my mind is like a super computer," MV said. "Let's do a lap of the room. Hattie, are you coming or will you be acting all groupie with the band members?"

Hattie said, "Thanks for reminding me, MV. I better get started on that."

Jack waggled his eyebrows. "How do I get in on the groupie action?"

Hattie slapped his arm and said to us, "I'll catch up with you."

I followed Mary Violet and Constance as they began making their way around the room, which had quickly become packed with mostly upperclassmen and lots of college-age people. My friends were so busy that it was easy for me to edge away, keeping to the comfort of the periphery, where I could observe things and hear bits of conversation.

The music stopped, the stage lights came on, and the other lights dropped further. Jack and three other guys hopped onstage. One guy went to the drum set, another carried a bass, a guy with bleached white-blond hair and a guitar went to the center mic, and Jack picked up a guitar from a stand.

The DJ announced, "Greenwood's own . . . Dog Waffle."

The crowd clapped and hooted as the singer at the center thrummed his guitar and shouted, "*Uno, dos,* three, four . . ."

I moved back around to where my friends had left their things. I stood half hidden by one of the potted trees and watched the band as best I could between the people standing.

At City Central, most everyone listened to hip-hop, much of it performed by students who used their closets as recording booths and sold their CDs out of their backpacks. I didn't know much about rock, and the acoustics of the room were so bad that I had to listen hard to make out the lyrics. It was a song about deceit. The more I listened, the more I liked the band.

Even I could tell that Jack on lead guitar was the best musician. He played with his head down, his curls tumbling over his face, but then he'd lift his head, and the light would catch the gleam of his eyes. Even when the songs rocked hard and fast, each note he played was clear and distinct.

The singer was good, and everyone else seemed to like all his posing and preening. But I could tell the lyrics were Jack's because they sounded exactly like him, with lots of wordplay. For the last song of the set, the bass player picked up a stand-up instrument and another guy came onstage with a cello. The singer stepped up to the mic and said, "Jack and I are gonna switch it up for this one, even though I'm a better singer."

Jack gave the singer that one-sided grin as he went to the center mic. "You mean you're a better screamer." He waited until the singer had moved into place before saying, "This is something I just wrote for someone special." Everyone looked at Hattie, who looked shy and happy as she stood near the stage. "It's called 'My Titania' and it's for the most extraordinary girl I've ever met."

The crowd grew quiet as the cellist sounded out the first deep melancholy notes of the song and Jack began singing in a resonant, gravelly voice.

Tangled in the darkest woods, the paths twisting,
All direction lost,
I try to follow my Titania,
As she slips from reach and grasp
Like a dream that wants to be forgotten
Like a ghost condemned to wandering
I turn my head and she is gone.

The song sent a shiver through me and Jack's eyes searched the crowd and seemed to meet mine and I felt as if he were singing right to me.

Titania, stop for me, Titania, stay for me.
Let me take your cloak of pain
Let me hear your laugh again

Titania, stop for me, Titania, wait for me
She bewitches and bewilders me,
Hesitates, then flees from me,
Titania, stop for me, stay for me
Titania, I can't bear you away from me.

I thought, *It's about Hattie sitting in the amphitheater like a ghost,* as the crowd clapped and stomped until the floor and walls reverberated.

Jack and the singer traded places again, and the singer said, "Okay, one more before our break." The music cranked up with a harder, faster edge. Someone shouted out to Jack and he laughed, and I got a completely different sense of who he was.

I caught sight of Lucky's golden head near the front of the stage and I hurried through the crowd, excited to see him. And that's when I saw a tall, amber-haired person beside him: Catalina. Lucky was leaning close to talk to her. His hand went up to stroke her hair. She was smiling at him, her hand on his shoulder.

I stood transfixed by the sight of them flirting and felt as if someone were squeezing my throat.

How completely *stupid* was I to believe Lucky's "girl-friends are temporary" speech? How *stupid* was I to think that I might have meant something to him when he was only playing me . . . because he wanted adoration from the pathetic, lonely, desperate foster kid.

I tried to find the anger that would overcome the pain, but all I could feel was the agony of rejection because I knew the truth: that no boy would ever choose me when he could have Catalina. I needed to get out of here fast.

"Jane! There you are. What's the matter?" Hattie caught my arm as I reached the door.

"Nothing! I have to go. I'm . . . I don't feel well." I despised myself for letting my crush on Lucky make me so vulnerable.

Hattie hooked her arm in mine and headed to the exit. "There's no air in here. I'll go with you."

Outside, I gulped down the cold air. Across the lot, the swimming pools glowed pure and bright, the blue of Lucky's eyes. Voices floated from behind a tall hedge. Glass crashed and shattered somewhere, and drunken laughter followed.

"Jane, what's up?"

"Nothing. I'm fine."

"I can tell you're *not* fine." Her expression was too earnest and she wavered slightly. She'd been drinking.

"I'm not really good at social things, Hattie. I'd rather be home."

"If you stay at home, you'll never learn to deal with social things. People here are okay, but you have to put some effort into getting to know them."

I nodded even though I didn't want to *ever* get to know them. Finally, I admitted, "I saw Lucky in there. With Catalina. She'll probably talk smack about me to Lucky just when we're starting to be friends."

"Is that all? Hey, Lucky knows that she talks smack about everyone. She even told him that he was 'too provincial' for her to ever date." Hattie laughed. "I don't think he'd ever been so insulted. She did it in front of everyone and MV told Lucky that provincial was French for ignorant hick."

"Then why is he all over her?"

"Lucky gets a kick by making other girls jealous, because it keeps all the attention on him." She twisted her lips to show her disgust. "As if I give one damn about who Lucian Radcliffe hits on."

I wanted to believe her. "He said the girls here are all jealous."

"Let's go back in. Unless you want to get your drink on first. Some of my friends set up a bar behind the pool house."

"No, thanks."

"Don't you ever get loose, Jane?"

"It's not fun for me, because . . . thinking clearly is all I have." I tried to explain. "If you're small and live in a sketchy place, you've got to keep your wits about you all the time."

"You might not think so, but I have to stay cautious, too, Jane." She was so serious that I assumed it was the vodka talking, and I followed her inside.

The band had ended their set, and Jack jumped off the stage, high-fiving friends as he made his way to Lucky. Hattie hauled me by the hand as she went to meet the Radcliffe brothers.

Lucky was in a slate-gray shirt, a gray blazer, and black jeans. He and Catalina were insanely glamorous together. She was now leaning against the stage. Her lustrous caramel satin halter dress flaunted her golden skin, the curves of her breasts, and her long legs. In heels, she was six feet tall.

"Hi, Catalina, Lucian," Hattie said breezily as she dropped my arm and leaned against Jack.

"Hello, Harriet." Catalina rolled her *r*'s in a way that seemed sarcastic. Then she noticed me. "Oh, who let the little mouse sneak into the party?"

For one awful second, I thought that Catalina had discovered the nickname I hated. My paranoia threw me off my game. I lamely snarked, "It's always so *nice* to see you, Catalina."

Lucky acknowledged Hattie and me with an apathetic "Hey."

Hattie frowned at Lucky and said to me, "Isn't Dog Waffle great?"

Jack pushed a curl off his sweaty forehead. "Hattie, it's no use pressuring Jane to compliment me. I've tried and all she does is hurt my feelings. She hates me."

"I don't compliment unless I mean it. You're really good."

Jack raised an eyebrow. "Good like pizza?"

"Pizza's great, not good, so there's a qualitative difference."

Jack clutched his heart dramatically. "See what I mean?"

I smiled, but I was acutely aware of Lucky nearby. He was

already talking to some other guy who'd come up. Then more kids joined us and somehow I was standing in the center of people talking over my head.

One guy mentioned the midterm break and another said that they should go on a group vacation. Lucky wanted to visit Portland because he'd never been there, and Catalina said she would be visiting relatives in Barcelona. Hattie voted for the trip to Portland.

No one invited me to come along, and I was moving away when a long-faced college student named Sage stared at me. "Who are *you*?"

"I'm Jane. I transferred in to Birch Grove."

Catalina sneered, "She's the new Bebe because Bebe left."

"She probably flunked out." Sage grimaced in disgust. "Or maybe she got knocked up by one of her thug boyfriends and sent back to the ghetto." She dipped her head and peered up at Lucky. "Lucky, I'd think your mom would get tired of rescuing these sad orphans."

I held my breath, thinking that this was Lucky's opportunity to stand up for me and to show everyone that we had a connection—but he slapped his brother on the shoulder. "This one's all yours, bro," he said, and walked away.

I stared at Lucky's back incredulously and Jack suddenly said, "I'm a sad orphan, too, Sage."

He stepped forward and stared down at Sage. "Yeah, I'm adopted. Do you feel sorry for me? Can I cry on your shoulder? My nose gets snotty when I cry, but snottiness turns you on, doesn't it? Makes you feel so very *special*, am I right?"

"I, uhm, I didn't mean . . ." Sage said nervously while the others watched her distress as avidly as a pack of stray dogs eyes an injured member. "I didn't know, uhm . . ."

"It's not your fault. Only our close friends knew. Like Jane." Jack put his arm over my shoulders, drawing me toward him, and when he touched me, I got that jolt that made me tingle all over. I felt the heat from his body and smelled his intriguing scent, like the morning dew evaporating in the grove.

"I'm sorry, I, uh . . . didn't mean . . ." Sage stepped away from the group.

"Don't ask to cry on my shoulder, Jacob," Catalina said. "Hattie is already so jealous of me."

"It's because you're so hot for me. Say the word, Cat, and I'll rock your world," Jack said in a sexy growl, and she burst into laughter.

I was on the edge of tears, and kids were still looking at me. I wanted to run away, but Jack kept his arm firmly around me. I could feel the pressure of each individual finger on my shoulder.

He smiled at me and said, "Shorty, I know you were forced to listen to my band, but if you've had enough, I can give you a lift home."

He was giving me a cover so I could leave. "Don't you have to play again?"

"Not for another hour."

Even though I didn't want to go with him, I didn't want to be here, either. "I was going to spend the night at Mary Violet's."

"She'll stay here until three. Our music gets worse by the hour," Jack said. "Your choice."

"Let me tell her I'm going to my place." After a brief search, I ran into Constance by the refreshment table. "I'm burned out and Jack's giving me a lift home. I can pick up my things at MV's tomorrow."

"You sure?"

"Sure. See you in the morning." As I went back to Jack, I searched the room for Lucky's golden head above the crowd. He and Hattie were talking by the steps leading onto the stage. At least he wasn't with Catalina.

He had large, wild, gazelle-like eyes: his hair, like mine, was in a perpetual tangle—that point he had in common with me, and indeed, as I afterwards heard, our mother having been of gipsy race, it will account for much of the innate wildness there was in our natures. How shall I describe the grace of that lovely mouth, shaped verily "en arc d'amour."

Count Eric Stanislaus,
"The Sad Story of a Vampire" (1894)

Chapter 18

Jack and I went outside to the parking lot, and he pointed to an old green Vanagan. "Ain't she a swell ride?"

"I thought you were against cars."

"I can't even deliver a pizza on a bike, how am I going to handle amps? It's our drummer's van."

He opened the passenger door for me. I tried to step up and sit without my dress hiking up, and I had to pull at the hem, which caught on the ripped seat cover. The van smelled like stale potato chips and motor oil and weed. There were curtains in a daisy print on the side windows. A plastic Batman with a missing arm dangled from the rearview mirror.

Jack got in and after a couple of wheezing cranks, the engine rolled over. He struggled with the stick shift and said, "I'm driving, so it's your job to make small talk."

"Oh."

"Not that small." He waved at the security guard as we left the club. "Make medium talk."

"I didn't know you were adopted."

"It's not a big secret, but it's not the first thing I tell people. Most people take one look at my family and say, so who's the Jewish kid?"

"I guess I'm used to mixed-up families. What happened to your parents?"

"The short story is that my birth mom was the book-keeper for Birch Grove. She died of an aneurysm when I was born, and my father gave me up to the Radcliffes because he couldn't stand the sight of me and knew they hadn't been able to have kids. A few years later, Lucky came as a lucky surprise."

"That's why you asked me about my family and my father."

"I was wondering if you'd ever met him. I got in touch with my birth dad when I was fifteen. He's in Vermont, remarried, no kids."

"How'd that go?"

"He told me that whenever he saw me, all he could think was that I'd killed my mother."

"That's awful!"

"Yeah, actually it was awful. I raged out for a while," Jack said matter-of-factly. "But I love my family, my *real* family." He drove along the winding road with an occasional grinding of gears as he shifted. "You may not think I'm a prize, but the Radcliffes always act like they've won the lottery with me."

"I'm glad for you, Jack."

"So am I. All families have problems, though, Halfling." He glanced over at me. "My mother works really hard trying to keep everything in order. My father gets stressed and down. Lucky has his own major issues. He's not just some smiling, Abercrombie-looking dude, so don't expect him to act like a hero."

"Jack, if there's something you want to tell me, tell me. Don't speak in elliptical terms."

"Elliptical." He gave a short, sharp bark of laughter. "That's odd coming from you with all your mysteries, Halfling."

"All I have is a lousy childhood. That's no mystery, and if I don't talk about it, it's because I don't want to live in the past." We drove through the main entrance of Birch Grove Academy, and I tried to think of a safe subject. "You described the rest of your family, but what about you?"

"I'm the one who tells them that it's not all about success and image."

"In other words, you're the slacker."

"Or the king's fool."

"What does that mean?"

"Read your Shakespeare."

"Why don't you tell me straight out?"

"No cheating on the test. Eyes on your own paper, Jane Williams." He parked on the drive. "I'll walk you to your cottage."

He stretched across me to open the glove compartment. As he took out a flashlight, his arm grazed mine, sending that reaction through me, so potent that it threw me back into a cool, shady place that I could *almost* remember like one might remember the coolness of a drink of water, but not be able to recall the taste. I froze and thought, *What was that?*

"Don't panic," he said. "Being a jackass isn't contagious." He hopped out of the van, and went around and opened the door for me. He took my hand to help me down. As soon as I was standing, I pulled away from him.

He angled the beam of the flashlight on the uneven soil of the path. I stepped carefully in my high heels. The thick fog swirled around us. The wind grabbed at the ends of my cashmere shawl and the branches of the birches thrashed. Other than the porch light, the cottage was dark.

Jack walked with me to the steps of the porch. "Don't you ever get scared out here by yourself?"

"You asked me that before."

"I asked you if you got lonely, not scared. Different question." He clicked off the flashlight and put it in his jacket pocket.

"There are worse things than being alone. There are real dangers and I'd rather be aware of them than oblivious, even when they frighten me." We stood still, facing each other, and his face grew serious.

"You are a strange and remarkable little creature, aren't you, Jane?" The wind whipped my hair across my face and Jack reached over to me and brushed my hair back. Then he held his warm palms against my cheeks. "You're very fierce and very beautiful and very brave."

My skin tingled all over, from the heat of the party and his hands now and the cold wind, causing such turbulent emotions and sensations that I trembled. The world beyond seemed to drop away: Jack and I were alone in this wood and I imagined it stretching on endlessly. There was only us, the rush of the wind in the swaying trees, and this black night.

For a brief moment, I imagined that if I took Jack's hand in mine, we *really* would be in a place where the trees lifted their roots and danced in the night, a place where I really was fierce and beautiful and brave. The illusion was so overwhelming that long seconds passed before I could form a sentence. "Do you talk to Hattie this way?"

"No, only you, Halfing. You make me say foolish things. You make me think impossible things."

"That's why I never believe a word you say."

Jack sighed and dropped his hands to his sides. "Here is a word you can believe. I found it for you, a word that's like music. Susurration."

"Susurration." The word tasted like wind in my mouth.

"Aren't you going to *ax* me what it means?"

I was so relieved he was openly teasing again that I played along. "What *do* it mean?"

"A whispering sound. Listen."

We were silent, but the grove was not. The leaves rustled and sighed and branches crashed and creaked. Jack's long curly hair flew in the hissing breeze and he looked half-wild, like he belonged here in the woods, and I thought of his song, of him running through the forest after his elusive

Titania. I thought of him as Pan, the Greek god of music and love and the woods.

I became lost again, staring in his green eyes and listening to the wind swirling and eddying around us.

My thoughts and feelings were so unlike me that I wondered if the punch had been spiked. I stepped back. "Susurration. Thank you for the word and the ride. Good night, Jack."

He gazed at me in such an odd way, as if he were seeing someone other than the Jane Williams that everyone else saw. "Good night, Halfling."

I unlocked and opened the front door, and I flicked on the light before I stepped into the living room. I shut and locked the door, making sure I was safe from . . . I didn't know. I peeked out through the front curtains. Jack stood at the edge of the path. He must have seen me, because he waved before walking away.

He looked so alone that I wanted to call him back. But his solitude was temporary and soon he'd be surrounded by all his friends at the party.

I was the one who was alone.

I unzipped the dress and hung it in the closet, and then placed my new heels neatly beside my other shoes. I put on a cotton tank and pajama pants. The mirror showed me a plain girl with smeared mascara.

When I went into the medicine cabinet to get facial cleanser, I saw the sunscreen there. I unscrewed the cap. It smelled like Lucky so I rubbed some on my skin.

I curled up on the sofa with a comforter because my thoughts were spinning in circles. I had a hundred questions, most of them beginning with *why?* Why, why, why, why. I don't know when I fell asleep, but a banging on the door shocked me awake.

"Jane, let me in! It's me, Lucky! Jane!"

I ran to the door and opened it. Lucky fell into my arms, drunk and laughing.

He felt her sharp kisses upon his white throat, and he knew that her lips were red. So the wild dream sped on through twilight and darkness and moonrise, and all the glory of the summer's night. But in the chilly dawn he lay as one half dead upon the mound down there, recalling and not recalling, drained of his blood, yet strangely longing to give those red lips more.

F. Marion Crawford,
"For the Blood Is the Life" (1911)

Chapter 19

"Jane, you're awake!"

"I am now," I said as I helped Lucky inside and he collapsed onto the sofa.

He smelled of beer and cigarettes. He slurred when he said, "Why'd you leave?"

I sat on the chair facing him and crossed my arms over my breasts. "You should know—you were there. Or you were until you walked away."

"That's because Jack could handle it. Stupid Sage, what a wannabe." He made a scoffing sound and began coughing.

I went to the kitchen, filled a glass with tap water, and carried it to him. He swallowed several gulps. He tried to set down the glass on the coffee table, but missed. Before it hit the floor, before it even sloshed over, he caught it. He put it down more carefully. "Jane, come over here."

I sat on the far side of the sofa. His hair was tousled and the different shades of gold, honey, and amber caught in the soft lamplight. His cheeks were flushed and his lovely lips were slightly open. Even drunk, Lucky was dazzling.

"Janey, are you mad at me?" When he took my hand, I jerked away even though all I wanted was his touch.

"You completely ignored me."

"I said hi. You saw how they can be."

"Yes, but I don't care what they think!"

"I do, and I'm protecting you." He leaned toward me. "I'm protecting us."

"There is no us. I don't even know what you want from me."

"I'll show you what I want." He fumbled with his jacket and brought out a gold penknife, similar to Hattie's.

I jumped off the sofa and skipped back, out of his range. "What the hell do you think you're doing?"

"Don't be scared, Janey. I only want to have a blood oath with you. It'll only be a drop or two."

"Why?"

"To seal *us*, Lucky and Jane. You can even do it yourself, if it makes you feel safer. Come here, baby."

I wanted there to be an us.

"Don't you trust me, Jane?" He held out the knife and said, "Here, take it."

I wanted to trust him just as I had wanted to believe that there was nothing between him and Catalina. I sat beside him and accepted the penknife. "What do you want me to do?"

"Prick your finger. That's all." He held my forefinger steady.

I counted silently to three and jabbed the point of the knife into my fingertip.

He squeezed the flesh until a bead of shiny crimson blood welled up.

Lucky raised my finger up and into his mouth, biting down on the nick and pressing his tongue against it. I dropped the knife on the coffee table as he sucked. I gasped and his arm went around my waist and jerked me hard to him. My body thrummed with desire, and a moan came from low in Lucky's throat.

After minutes, he let my finger slide out of his hot, slick mouth. "Jane, you're delicious." His eyes shone with excitement.

He picked up the knife again and then pulled me so easily that I nearly flew off the sofa. "Come on." He led me to the bedroom, turned on the lamp by the bed, and dropped the knife on the bedside table. He yanked off his jacket and dropped it on the floor.

He caught my hand as he fell back on the bed, seeming huge in the small room, and he drew me down on the mattress. When he rolled on top of me, I savored the crushing weight of him, the solidity of his body. I thought that now he might kiss me, but his mouth never went to mine.

His face tucked in toward my neck. His warm lips were on my throat, at first nipping gently, in a way that made me crazy with desire for more. I wanted his hands to caress me, to taste his tongue in my mouth. I wanted him to hold my face in his hands and to gaze into my eyes like . . . like . . .

And then Lucky bit harder.

I shoved his chest. "No, that hurts!"

"Sorry," he mumbled. He propped himself up on one elbow and placed his broad, sweaty hand palm down above my breasts. I waited for his fingers to move under my clothes, but he only said, "You're as small as a bird. I can feel your heart pounding."

He stroked the inside of my arm, making my whole body quiver. "Close your eyes," he whispered.

"No."

"It'll nick for only a second, a small cut. I *need* you so much, Jane. Can't you tell how I need you?" His lips went to my inner arm and his nips were gentle but urgent. My skin flushed and my breathing quickened. "Won't you let me have a few drops?"

"Why? Tell me why?"

"I like the taste. I *need* the taste. It's my strangeness and I can't share with anyone but you. It's what we have. It's our secret, Jane."

He seemed so vulnerable and his desire was overwhelming. It surrounded me like fog so impenetrable that I couldn't see anything but the desire. "Please, Jane, *please.*"

"Okay," I said, and closed my eyes.

I flinched as the knife pierced the tender skin on the inside of my elbow. Lucky latched his mouth over the cut.

Outside the wind grew loud, howling through the trees, and branches lashed against the cottage as Lucky sucked at the wound, opening the cut more with his perfect white teeth, his persistent tongue pushing into me.

I wove my fingers into his thick golden hair and when he shoved his body against me, I could feel his excitement, but Lucky's lust was for my blood. I tried to take pleasure from the strength of his body, from the fact that he was here now with me, Jane Williams, instead of any other girl. But the sharpness of his teeth made me squirm, and the trees beat so violently against the windows that I thought the glass would shatter.

I wanted to block out everything outside this room and this moment. I pressed my face against his shoulder. I tried to touch inside his shirt, but he shoved my hand away and sucked harder at the cut.

Then Lucky groaned and shuddered. When he raised his head from my arm, blood was smeared on his lips. He licked at them with his red-streaked tongue. Then he laughed wildly. "That was incredible!" His eyes were half-shut, like a cat dozing off. He rolled onto his back, crowding me against the edge of the bed, and passed out.

I eased off his shoes and his belt and covered him with a blanket. I thought I'd never seen anyone so perfect. I stroked his hair and traced my fingers along his cheek. The wind had died down and the trees made a sad, low *shush-shush-shush.*

A buzzing woke me about four A.M. I found Lucky's phone in his jacket pocket and Jack's picture was on the screen. He was probably wondering where his brother was, and I didn't click on the video because I didn't want him to see me like this. "Hi, Jack. It's Jane."

"He's with you? Let me talk to him," Jack said sharply.

"He showed up and he's sleeping now."

"I can't believe you let him in. I thought you were smarter than that."

"He's my friend."

"What kind of a friend? The kind who blows you off in public and then shows up for a . . . *whatever*. Why are you letting him use you, Jane?"

"It's none of your damn business, Jack, how I choose my friends and what I do with them." I felt myself flush with anger and something that felt like shame.

Jack was silent for a moment. "Let him sleep it off and I'll cover with my parents." He hung up without saying good-bye.

I thought of snooping through the phone, but Lucky had said he needed someone to trust. As I stretched to place the phone on the bed table, I saw the ugly red-purple wound on my arm. It was mostly bruising, but there was the bright red ragged edge of the cut. I went to the bathroom, washed the cut, and dressed it with a Band-Aid.

I returned to the bedroom and slipped under the blanket beside Lucky. I was too shy to put my arm around him, so I let my leg lie against his. Then I clicked off the light and listened to his steady breathing.

❧ I woke to see Lucky sitting on the bed beside me. My blanket had fallen down to my waist.

"Morning, Jane." He was fresh and bright-eyed even though he'd had only a few hours' sleep.

"Morning."

He pushed the strap of my tank off my shoulder. "What's this?" He touched my scar and I jerked away.

"I had an accident when I was little." I pulled the blanket up to my neck.

"It's not that bad. You should see my friend Brad's leg. Crashed into a rock snowboarding and needed forty stitches. Now that's something." Lucky put on his jacket and shoved his phone in the pocket.

"Jack called while you were sleeping. He said he'd cover to your parents."

"Thanks. But don't answer it again. *I'll* handle my calls."

I shrugged. "Whatever. Jack doesn't like our . . . our friendship. He knows about your secret, doesn't he?"

Lucky took my hand and stretched out my arm, looking at the bandage. "Hope I wasn't too rough. I got carried away."

"Have you done that with anyone else? Anyone here?"

"No, but I've thought a lot about it. Maybe I mentioned something to Jack about wanting to do it." He put down my arm reluctantly. "I gotta go. I can't wait until the next time."

"Lucky." I paused and then said carefully, "Do you think you're a vampire?"

"A vampire? The undead kind that sleeps in coffins and is hundreds of years old?" His laugh seemed forced. "No, I *don't* think I'm a vampire. Do *you* think I'm a vampire?"

"Of course not, but I thought you might believe it. You always wear sunscreen and . . ."

"Multispectrum sunblock, not sunscreen. I sunburn worse than an albino."

"Did you get the idea from the stories your mother teaches?"

"Jane, it's a total turnoff when you bring up my mother. This is between us. I thought you liked it, too."

"I like being with you, not the hurting part."

"We'll figure out a way so it doesn't hurt, so you can enjoy it, our secret." He walked out of the room.

I followed him to the living room. I wanted him to kiss me good-bye at least, but he patted my head. "Later," he said, and left.

I went back to bed and raised the comforter over my head because I wanted to think over every second of my night with Lucky, from the moment he'd stumbled into the cottage to the way he'd told me he needed me, to the heat of his mouth on my arm.

One thing I'd learned going from all my foster homes: everyone had secrets that they hid. Some were dangerous, while others were silly. Lucky hadn't hurt me, not really. He hadn't done anything without my permission.

He'd heard vampire stories all his life and he'd wanted to experience the power and sensuality of taking another's blood.

And, of all the girls at Birch Grove, Lucian Radcliffe had chosen me. He'd trusted me alone to understand his strangeness. I wouldn't betray him.

"Arrayed in humble weeds she offered herself as a domestic to the consort of her beloved, and was accepted. She was now continually in his presence: She strove to ingratiate herself into his favour: She succeeded. Her attentions attracted Julian's notice; the virtuous are ever grateful, and he distinguished Matilda above the rest of her companions . . . yet she wished not for Julian's person, she ambitioned but a share of his heart."

Matthew Gregory Lewis, *The Monk* (1796)

Chapter 20 Mary Violet called and invited me for a "post-soiree shenanigans review" with Hattie and Constance. I dressed in my cargos and a long-sleeved shirt that covered the Band-Aid on my inner elbow. I put my library books and borrowed clothes in a tote, and walked through the cool morning mist thinking about Lucky.

I daydreamed while Mary Violet gave a detailed recitation of clothes, hookups, and mishaps, and Constance and Hattie sent texts and pictures to their friends.

"Here's a nice pic of Lucky." Constance handed around her phone to show us. I wanted to ask her for a copy of it. "You left too soon, JW. Even though everyone's saying that Sage was her usual odious self."

Hattie said, "I can't believe I wasn't there when Jack shamed her."

"Jane, you should have yanked her hair out," Mary Violet said. "The boys are crazy for catfights."

The image of Jack standing up to Sage intruded on my thoughts of Lucky. "Yeah, Jack was kinda cool stepping up like that."

"He's such a *beast* when he's playing," Mary Violet said. "Not glamorous like Lucky, but he's totally the business. That song he wrote for Hattie was sooo romantic!"

As the others gossiped, I rubbed my thumb across the inside of my elbow, feeling the bandage under the fabric and the ache of the wound. After breakfast, Mary Violet walked me to the front door. "You should stay and do your work here. I'll tell you more about last night."

"There is something I want to know. Well, two things. Did you tell Catalina my nickname?"

She blanched and said, "No, never! I promised you and I keep my promises."

"I'm sorry, but . . . she called me a little mouse."

Mary Violet's pale eyebrows knit together. "Maybe she was referring to the story of the city mouse and the country mouse since you're new here. What's your other question?"

"What did the king's fool do in Shakespeare?"

"The fool is the only one who's allowed to tell the king the truth about things, but he has to do it in a joking way. He's protected by the king unless he goes too far and then he's exiled to some godforsaken place. Why?"

"I heard someone say it and wondered."

"I'm glad you're finally getting interested in literature. We should totally take Shakespeare's Critical Works together next year and for our performances, I'll be a comic heroine and you'll be a girl masquerading as a boy."

"You make education terrifying, MV. See you Monday."

"Au revoir, JW."

I walked to the Greenwood Library, dropped my books in the return bin, and went to a computer stall. But when I tried to log in, *Invalid User* flashed on the screen. I tried another computer and had the same problem.

A man at the information desk came over. "May I help you?"

"Would you? I'm trying to get into my library account and the system won't let me log in. I double-checked the log-in and the password." I handed him my library card.

He scrutinized it and said, "So you're at Birch Grove. It will be a few minutes."

"Okay. I'll look around."

While he was tapping away at his computer, I went to the psychology section of the nonfiction stacks. I was scanning the index of a book about fetishes and perversions when the librarian suddenly appeared at the end of the aisle.

"Excuse me!" he said in a loud whisper. "These books are for eighteen and over."

"I'm an emancipated minor."

"Be that as it may, you are *not* over eighteen." He snatched the book from my hand and snapped it shut.

"Libraries are supposed to *promote* freedom of knowledge, not censor it."

"It's not censorship. It's an age-appropriate restriction. Your library privileges have been revoked because you have been accessing pornographic Web sites."

"I haven't been . . ." I began, and then I remembered Wilde's Web page. "That was accidental. I closed it immediately."

"I think you better leave now, Miss Williams, or I'll have to call Mrs. Radcliffe and tell her about your disruptive behavior and your misuse of library property."

I glared at him and said, "This town is *too* nice," and stormed out.

❧ I stayed inside the cottage the rest of Saturday, working on my assignments and hoping that Lucky would call or come by. At midnight, I gave up and went to bed. I dreamed of the birch trees walking toward me, marvelously graceful for their enormous size.

Mrs. Radcliffe was sitting high in their branches, as if she were riding them. "All my Birch Grove girls are exceptional. Jane, you're the *most* special of all because you're already dead!"

"I'm not dead! I'm alive," I shouted. "I'm alive! I want to live!"

I awoke then to a dark room. I thought I heard voices in

the distance, and then the sound vanished beneath the howl of the wind.

❧ On Sunday, I tried to be patient, but I couldn't wait to see Lucky again, so I went early for my tutoring session.

Mrs. Radcliffe answered the door. "Come on in, Jane. Lucky's not back from the movies yet. He went to a matinee with his friends."

"Oh," I said, thinking, *The friends he says he doesn't have.* "I can come back later."

"Please stay. Would you like to wait in the family room?"

I followed Mrs. Radcliffe and she gave me a glass of juice and asked, "Did you enjoy the party?"

I couldn't tell from her tone what she'd heard about it. "It was nice. I've never been to a country club before."

"It's the center of a lot of our social activities. Jack's bored with it, but he can't play at most clubs—or venues, as he calls them—until he's twenty-one."

"I liked his band. What does the name mean?"

"Whenever I made waffles, the neighbor's old dog would come begging for his waffle. Jacob says it's also a play upon *dogging,* following faithfully, and *waffle,* to go back and forth between things. He may be joking."

"I can't tell when he's kidding and when he's serious."

"His humor and his seriousness are intertwined. He loves to laugh, but often when he's joking, he's trying to make a more serious point."

"Like the king's fool?"

She seemed a little surprised by the comment. "My Jacob is nobody's fool, not even a king's."

When I heard the front door open, my heart leaped.

Lucky came into the family room. He was wearing a narrow-brimmed hat, aviator sunglasses, a long-sleeved navy t-shirt, and jeans. I pressed at the bandage under my sleeve so I could feel the tenderness.

"Hi, Mom. Hey, Jane."

"Jane's been waiting for you, Lucian."

"I'm on time." His expression was so bored that I had to set my teeth to keep from cussing at him.

"Dinner will be in an hour and a half," his mother said. "No hats in the house, young man."

Lucky plucked off his hat, twirled it around on his fingers. "Come on, Jane." I followed him upstairs and into the study. He dropped onto the sofa with his long legs sprawled out. His eyes were hidden behind the sunglasses. "Could you be any *more* obvious?"

"I haven't said anything!" What had happened to the sweet woozy boy who'd slept beside me?

"You don't need to say anything. Anyone can read it on your face."

He sat there judging me, and I said coldly, "Be specific: you mean your *mother* could read it on my face. You want me when it's convenient for you, but you're embarrassed to be seen with me."

My tone got his attention. He slipped off the shades and sat up. "You're right. But you have no idea how upset she'd be if she found out that I was . . . that *we* had this special relationship. She'd be disappointed in you, too, Jane. She wouldn't let us see each other anymore."

"You should be getting treatment for it, this blood-drinking disorder."

"Is that what you really think, Jane?" He slumped once again. "My bad. I thought you of all people knew what it means to be different. That you don't have to play by the rules all the time. I thought you actually cared for me."

He looked up at me with a forlorn expression and my heart ached for him. I sat next to him and put my hand on his leg. "I *do* care for you, Lucky, that's why I think you should get professional help."

Lucky reached for my hand and lifted it to his mouth, dragging his lower lip across the inside of my wrist. "I know all the psychological terms for what I did, and there's a difference between a preference and mental illness. Lots of gourmet restaurants serve raw meat and some people eat blood sausages. How is that any different from my craving?" His voice dropped lower. "I like *your* blood, Jane."

I considered his point. Logically, blood was blood.

Lucky pulled me onto his lap. "I don't want to lose what we have, okay?"

I smelled his herby sunscreen and put my hand on his firm chest. "Okay, but you have to be nicer to me, Lucky."

He smiled, happy again. "How's your arm? Let me see." I pushed my sleeve up above my elbow. He slowly peeled off the bandage. The area was purple and yellow around the red-brown scab. He bent his head to lick the cut, making me quiver with anticipation, and I pressed against him.

Then he lifted me off himself as easily as lifting a pillow and set me beside him. He fell back against the sofa, breathing heavily. "Not here. Someone could come in." He stared out the window for a minute before saying, "You are so good to me, Jane, and I'm such a tool."

"Are you putting yourself down to make me feel sorry for you?"

"No, I'm putting myself down because I know I should be a better person."

"Then *try* to be a better person," I said. "Lucky, why does Hattie have a knife like yours?"

"Lots of people have them. Didn't your friends have knives?" He took the penknife out of his pocket and ran the blunt edge of it over the rough surface of my new scab.

"Yes, but for protection, not to play with."

"Maybe it's a Greenwood thing. I can get one for you. Do you like silver or gold?"

"I don't need one."

He grazed the blade of the knife ever so lightly down the inside of my arm to my wrist and my breathing came fast and shallow. "The blood is such a rush. It's better than a drug because it makes me healthier and stronger."

"That's your delusion, Lucky. The amount you take is insignificant in terms of protein and nutrients. What if I had an infection?"

"You don't have an infection."

"I don't know why I'm agreeing to do this." I stood and crossed the room.

"It's an act of kindness. You trust me because you know I need you as much as . . . It's not one-sided. I'll take care of you, too, Janey. I promise."

We heard footsteps coming down the hall. Lucky folded the knife and put it back in his pocket. His father walked by without even glancing in, and I said, "Your parents are paying me by the hour. Did you get back any of your assignments?" Lucky showed me his work and I tried to focus on the numbers and symbols.

Dinner was quiet because Jack wasn't around. We had homemade lasagna with thick tomato sauce. I looked at Lucky just as his tongue tipped out to lick a spot of sauce, and I thought of what he'd done to me. I *had* liked some of it. I'd liked his body's weight against my body. I'd liked the feel of his lips and his hands. I liked knowing that I had the stunning boy that all the other girls wanted.

I liked that we shared a secret, something special.

I looked at the scrumptious plates of food on the dinner table, Lucky's elegant parents, and their wonderful home. I liked all these things, too.

❧ Lucky walked me home after dinner. He talked about his school and his classmates. I tried to remember the names of his friends. Most of them had been at the country club: tall, loud guys with longish hair and lots of attitude.

"So like Julian, he borrowed his dad's new Beamer and when he came out of this club, it's gone, stolen. Hilarious." Lucky laughed loudly. "So I do him a bro-*favor* and drive him home. He sneaks into the house and goes to bed. When the car is missing the next day, his old man thinks someone stole it from the garage, and Julian acts all shocked."

"He sounds like an ass."

"Oh, like you've never done anything wrong, Jane." Lucky's sneer made him instantly seem bigger and dangerous. "Whoever stole the Beamer is the thief, not Julian, and besides, the insurance will pay. No need for the J-man to get hassled." Once we got to my door, he said, "Maybe I'll come by sometime this week. See you."

As easily as that, Lucky Radcliffe taught me that he'd punish me if I criticized him or his friends. I could imagine it now, how our relationship was like an equation. On one side was the sum of his astonishing beauty, wonderful family, and social status. On the other side was my desire. The only way to balance the equation was to offer my total compliance.

He wanted me for my blood and loyalty, but everyone had blood and most girls would want to be loyal to Lucky. I was replaceable, *for now*. My fury flared as I thought of how people always underestimated my tenacity. I'd prove them all wrong. And I would prove to Lucky that I was irreplaceable.

🍀 On Monday, I raced home from class so I would be there if Lucky called or came by. I finished the rest of my homework before I read my Night Terrors assignment, a story called "The Vampyre" by John William Polidori.

I pored over the pages, searching for clues about Lucky's behavior.

The story was about a young man named Aubrey, his best friend, mysterious Lord Ruthven, and a lovely young woman. Aubrey goes into a dangerous forest even though it was "the resort of the vampyres in their nocturnal orgies."

When vampires kill the lovely girl, Aubrey becomes sick from grief, and Lord Ruthven cares for him. Lord Ruthven dies and comes back to life, causing Aubrey to go insane because he's promised never to tell. Then Aubrey's sister is slaughtered: "Aubrey's sister had glutted the thirst of a VAMPYRE!" The end.

I hated the story and thought that it was typical that spoiled people, like the story's author, had nothing better to do than imagine stupid scary fantasies. I was angry that I had to waste my time looking up the words I didn't understand, reading the story again, and composing a 350-word synopsis. But learning all this junk was part of succeeding, so I powered through and did the work as meticulously as I could.

Lucky didn't call that night, and I fell asleep thinking, *Tomorrow he'll come, tomorrow he'll call, tomorrow he'll hold me, tomorrow he'll tell me how much he needs me . . .*

"What ails my love? the moon shines bright:
Bravely the dead men ride through the night.
Is my love afraid of the quiet dead?"
"Ah! no—let them sleep in their dusty bed!"

Gottfried August Bürger, "Lenore" (1790),
translated by Dante Gabriel Rossetti

Chapter 21

"Jane? Jane?" Mrs. Radcliffe was at the front of the classroom waiting for a response. Her navy suit had white piping along the edges. She always dressed so stylishly.

"I'm sorry, ma'am, could you repeat that?"

"I asked what you thought of Aubrey and his predicament with Lord Ruthven."

"The story makes no sense. Why does Aubrey keep a promise to Lord Ruthven when he believes Ruthven's a vampire? Ruthven is a caricature of a monster with no motivation besides sadism."

Mrs. Radcliffe tilted her head. "What other motivations could he have had?"

"I don't know. Maybe he needs to drink blood to survive. Maybe he has no soul. Maybe he wants revenge for an ancient wrong."

"Do you think Aubrey should have broken the promise?"

"Absolutely, especially since his secrecy endangers others and he gets absolutely nothing from the relationship." I paused to reflect on the characters' dynamic. "If Lord Ruthven *needed* Aubrey in some way, if there was reciprocation and affection, it would be different. But there's no unique bond between them, so why is Aubrey so delicate that he goes crazy?"

"It's a metaphor," a senior said.

"A metaphor represents something, and I don't think this does," I answered. "The author believes Aubrey's stupid, too, because he describes him as trusting poetry over reality."

Constance raised her hand. "I agree with Jane. I don't think the author put a lot of thought into the story. The structure was clumsy, the writing awkward, and the characters were cliché. The young girl is described as . . ." Constance skimmed her notes and read, "having an 'almost fairy form,' and being so innocent that she is 'unconscious of his love.' How could she be so oblivious of Aubrey's passion for her? Is she a complete idiot?"

Mrs. Radcliffe said, "She's young and naïve. There are always things that we don't recognize due to inexperience, as well as those things which we consciously or unconsciously choose not to see because they don't fit our expectations and desires."

Her comment echoed what Mrs. Holiday had mentioned about vision and perception.

The other students began speaking up about "The Vampyre." "The vampire is only used as a mechanism. The author could have used a werewolf, or a ghost, or any Big Bad. It doesn't matter, because he has no larger meaning to the story."

Mrs. Radcliffe looked at all the raised hands. "Do you see any similar themes running through these works?"

We all began discussing how the main characters' pursuit of pleasure caused them to dismiss forewarnings of danger. Mrs. Radcliffe steered the discussion to the symbols for life and death. She was tying together themes and I remembered Jack saying that the whole was greater than the sum of its parts.

I was thinking of this, feeling that I only had a few pieces of a large puzzle and wondering how they fit together as I walked to Latin class and bumped right into Catalina in the doorway.

"Sorry." I stepped back to let her go through first.

She pursed her full lips. "Clumsy girl!"

"I *said* I was sorry." I followed her into the room and we both sat at our desks.

"You require too much attention for such a tiny thing." She arranged her books and took out her silver pen. "Sage is envious of anyone close to the Radcliffes and she's always trying to climb the social ladder. You, at least, have no pretensions. I can't believe all this pettiness over Lucian, who's so handsome, but this is such a small town. *Mundus vult decipi, ergo decipiatu.*"

I had studied the quote before: The world wants to be deceived, so let it be deceived. "What do you mean by that?"

She tossed her hair back. "I'm bored with you now."

Mundus vult decipi, ergo decipiatu. It seemed to fit into the Night Terrors discussion, and I could use the quote in my essay on "The Vampyre."

🌿 The days that followed were agonizing. I kept my arms covered during school and tried to pay attention to my lessons, but all I could think about was Lucky. I thought about the shades of honey-gold in his hair, his voice, the stretch of his long body, and the way he moved.

I wanted to hear him tell me that what we had was special . . . that *I* was special and not merely some mousy girl. If only I could be patient, then he would let people know that Lucky Radcliffe and Jane Williams had a *thing*. I wasn't quite sure yet what that thing was.

When Mr. Mason asked me to help set up another lab on acids and bases, I was glad because it prevented me from obsessing . . . at least for a few hours while I set out the glass beakers, color pH charts, and protection goggles.

Mr. Mason checked on a completed station. "Nice work, Jane. I appreciate your help."

"It's calming thinking about how acids and bases neutralize each other." I aligned a box of borax with a bottle of alcohol. "When you know the rules, you can predict what will happen."

"Usually, not always."

"But when we can't predict, it's our own lack of knowledge—it's not as though things behave . . ." I paused to think of the right word. "Quixotically."

"You have an excellent vocabulary for someone who says she dislikes the language arts."

"I try to find words that are precise because language is so ambiguous. Why can't all words be qualitative and quantitative?"

"So that we could calibrate communication precisely?" Now he chuckled. He removed his white lab coat and hung it on a knob by the door. "I have to run off some copies of tomorrow's worksheet. If you finish before I come back, please lock the door on your way out. Thank you, Jane."

"Good night, sir."

When I completed setting up the experiment and went to get my book bag, I noticed a folded sheet of paper on the blue linoleum near Mr. Mason's lab coat. The edges were worn as if it had been handled a lot. I opened it to see a photocopy of a handwritten page. The heading read "Dearest Albert" and knew I should stop reading. But I didn't.

Dearest Albert,

By the time you read this, you will know what I have done. I did not want you or anyone else at Birch Grove to find me so I will leave it to the ocean to wash away what remains of the body that I offered as a map of my love.

You believe that my grief is the result of a chemical imbalance which requires medical and psychiatric treatment, a fresh start somewhere new. But my grief is real. I loved this last baby with every atom of my being, and I believed that my love could make him healthy and whole. He was the incarnation of my passion, everything I have hoped for since I first came to Birch Grove.

Love is a poisonous drug, Albert. The first drops were so intoxicating that I felt I could possess the world. But as time passed, I wasn't satisfied with those meager drops. It wasn't enough, not nearly enough. Even now that I have drunk the cup of poison, I still crave more.

You are a good and kind man and you deserved better. I now set you free to find another who will value your worth and give you a family. I ask for no one's forgiveness, but I hope that someday you will understand why I had no choice. My traitorous body has become a map of pain and I am trapped and lost within it. There is no escape. My heart and soul will always be at Birch Grove.

Ut incepit fidelis sic permanent.

Claire

By the time I read the signature, the page shook in my unsteady hand. I folded it quickly and put it in the pocket of Mr. Mason's lab coat. I hurried out of the room and was down the hall before I remembered to go back and lock the door. Then I ran down the steps, across campus to my cottage.

All week, Claire Mason's words repeated in my mind. I noticed that Mr. Mason patted his pocket the same way that I always did when I had money. How could this letter reassure him? I thought about Claire Mason and poisonous love after school, when I changed into jeans and a short-sleeved t-shirt, because I knew the mark on my arm excited Lucky, and I became more desperate with each day that went by. I didn't bother cooking dinner and subsisted on candy bars, which I could eat quickly and then be available. I turned down an invitation to go to dinner with MV and

Constance. Several times, I checked the phone to make sure it was working.

I couldn't focus on my schoolwork, so it took twice as long. Anger had motivated me in the past, but now I dreaded that if I didn't do well, I'd be sent away from Birch Grove and never see Lucky again, so I second-guessed everything I did. I regretted calling his friend an ass, scolding Lucky to be nicer, and revealing my emotions.

I'd go outside in the gloaming and stare up the hill at the Radcliffe house and think, *Please, please, please,* as if my desire and need could be transmitted if I only concentrated hard enough.

I was watching the sky grow darker when I heard the familiar sound of a bike's wheels crunching on leaves. A second later Jack came on his bike from the direction of the drive.

He skidded to a stop and hopped off his bike, propping it against the porch banister.

"Hey, Halfling, what are you doing outside in the cold?" He was breathing hard and his gray t-shirt clung damply to his wide chest.

"Are you going to tell me I shouldn't stand outside because you *always* know what other people should and shouldn't do?"

"Stand wherever you want, and, yes, I know what you *shouldn't* do, if it's letting a drunk jerk into your place in the middle of the night. Especially when the guy's mother could expel you."

"Why would she expel me when he was the one—"

"Moral turpitude. *Turpitude.* It's in the handbook. Your headmistress disapproves of impropriety and she also disapproves of the appearance of impropriety."

"You keep telling me how important appearances are, yet you don't care how you look or what you say."

"Irritating, isn't it?" He wiped his brow with the hem of

his t-shirt, showing a glimpse of his firm tanned stomach and abs.

I looked away before he caught me staring. "Yes, it's irritating."

He let the shirt drop back into place and sighed. "When I saw you standing here, so motionless, I was afraid an evil witch had transformed you to stone. What would bring a pixie back to life? A jar of angel's tears? Or maybe I'd have to answer three trick questions."

"I'm sure you could answer any trick question. You like playing with people."

"Not me. I don't play with people."

"You play with language, which is the same thing."

"No, it's not, but you know that," he said. "At night, I look down the hill and think of you here surrounded by the trees."

A frisson ran through me at the thought that Jack might have been staring down the hill at the same time that I was staring up toward his house.

"I think, *Has my halfling become habituated to the sounds? Should I visit her?* But I get the feeling that you don't enjoy our conversations and you don't like my friendly neighborhood visits."

"Why should I? One minute you're nice to me, and the next you're lecturing me. *You're* the one who asks trick questions, and talking to you is an exercise in futility."

His eyes darkened and his smile was as chilly as the breeze. "Hattie doesn't think so. I understand her and she understands me. Isn't that what love is, knowing another person so perfectly well that there are no surprises?"

"You always bring up Hattie as if you're complimenting her, when you're really just putting me down, Jack. I know Hattie's beautiful, talented, and sophisticated." I felt myself losing control even though I knew that's exactly what Jack wanted. "And I know that I'm small, plain, and no-class.

I *accept* those facts. I *accept* that no one will ever fall in love with me because I'm pretty and fun, but I hope that maybe someday someone will get to know me, and he'll find out that I have a heart and a mind just as good as any pretty girl's."

"And you would love him no matter what he looked like?"

"If he *needed* me, yes! I would be loyal to him and I would never give up trying to make him happy." I tried to blink back my tears.

"That's not love, Jane, that's letting yourself be used."

I felt as panicked as a bird caught in a room, battering against a closed window. "If you want to know what love is, ask someone who's been loved, ask Hattie, because I *don't* know what it means!"

Jack watched me somberly and then his green eyes moved down and he saw the yellow and violet bruising around the scab on my arm. Stepping to me, he gently put his calloused hands on my wrists and heat from him went through my body.

I tasted the salt of my tears as they slid down my face. I wanted to wipe them away, but Jack still held my wrists.

"Oh, Halfling, what have you done?" he murmured. "What have you let him do to you?"

Anguish rose up in me and I couldn't bear it anymore. Jack's head dropped so that his chin rested lightly on my head, and I had an inexplicable urge to lean into him, to have him hold me, to breathe in his scent of leaves and earth and sun, to weep until nothing was left inside of me but a void free from pain and aching need and loneliness.

Why did I feel this way? Why did he make me feel?

Then my phone rang, and I wrenched my wrists away from Jack's hands and ran inside, slamming the door behind me.

I got to the phone on the second ring, thinking *Lucky's calling,* and choked out "Hello?"

"Hi, Jane, this is Penelope from Latin. Do you want to join our study group?"

The phone call was brief, and when I peeked outside, Jack had left, and the last of the dim light was gone, leaving only night and the trees and my confusion and misery.

When I found that I was a prisoner a sort of wild feeling
came over me. I rushed up and down the stairs, trying every door and peering out of every window I could find;
but after a little the conviction of my helplessness over-
powered all other feelings. When I look back after a few
hours I think I must have been mad for the time, for I
behaved much as a rat does in a trap.

Bram Stoker, *Dracula* (1897)

Chapter 22 On Friday, I watched Hattie, wondering if Jack had told her anything
about Lucky and me, but she was the
same as always when we went to the Free Pop for lunch.
The café was crowded with girls excited about a six-day
break, because the teachers had trainings on Monday through
Thursday.

"They bring us back on Friday simply to torture us,"
Mary Violet grumbled. "If we had the whole week off *and*
two weekends, we could go somewhere fabulous."

Constance got off her phone. "Okay, it's on. Movies at
Spencer's tonight and we're all invited. You, too, Jane."

Mary Violet said, "His home theater's got the most gar-
gantuan sofa you've ever seen. It's orgy size. Twenty people
can fit on it. He's got one of those old-fashioned popcorn
machines. We have sexy nonversations and I've been saving
up devastating double entendres. That's French for 'Oh,
no, she didn't!'"

"Do I know any of the guys who'll be there?"

Constance named several guys, but didn't mention Lucky.
"You met most of them at the club. This is the last break
before the semester gets really hardcore."

Hattie said, "I'm not going because I want to ace Music
Theory and History so I have to listen to scratchy record-
ings and write essays through the break."

I was thankful that Hattie gave me an excuse to stay at my cottage waiting for Lucky. "I'm going to grind down and study, too. I have some catching up to do."

"You're both really disappointing Mary Violet," Constance said, and MV sighed dramatically and slumped her shoulders.

At home, I changed into my good jeans and a tank top even though my bruise had almost faded away. I brushed my hair into a high ponytail so that my neck was exposed, and I put on mascara and shadow. I dabbed perfume behind my ears and imagined Lucky nuzzling me there. It had been a whole week. He *must* miss me by now, or at least miss what we shared.

I ate cereal for dinner and watched television. The hours came and went. When I heard a rummaging sound outside, after eleven, I peeked through my curtains, thinking that he'd come.

A doe stood near my porch, nibbling on a shrub. I'd never seen a live deer before and I had no idea they were so lovely, with velvety fur and liquid black eyes. I got the flashlight and tiptoed back to the living room to watch her. Another deer grazed at the lower branches of a birch.

They moved off into the grove. I stepped out of my cottage, clicked on the flashlight, and followed them, staying as far behind as I could without losing sight of them. Suddenly the deer stood motionless. Their ears pivoted forward and with a flip of their tails, they bolted off. After a moment, I heard what had startled them: voices rising and falling. In the distance, people were singing.

Keeping the flashlight to the ground, I walked toward the sounds. Soon I spotted yellowish light flickering through the white tree trunks. Someone was having a party. I clicked off my flashlight and stepped slowly and carefully toward the voices, dreading that I would discover Lucky with another girl there.

What I found was worse.

Two dozen people wearing scarlet hooded robes stood in a circle and chanted in a strange language. The words were harsh, full of sharp consonants. The hoods hid their faces in gloom, and each held a lighted torch, the flames slanting in the breeze.

A man in a black robe with gold embroidery stood in the center of the circle beside a rough wooden table that was set with a glass decanter filled with purple-red liquid and platters of purple grapes, pomegranates, and red apples. The man next to him bowed and I made out a vaguely familiar profile under the hood.

When I inched forward, I saw that they'd made a fire pit with rocks. The chanting halted, and the man in the black robe spoke, then touched his torch to the wood in the pit. Yellow and orange flames licked upward.

He picked up something from the mounds of fruits. It caught the light and glittered. It was a gold knife with a long, narrow blade. He seized a pomegranate and cut into it. Rich crimson juices ran over his hands. He spoke again and tossed the pomegranate into the fire.

The other man presented his palm and Black Robe slashed it quickly with the gold knife. Blood dripped and sizzled in the flames.

I was too shocked to do anything but stare in horror as Black Robe picked up the decanter and poured the viscous purple-red liquid into a goblet, and the other man let his blood drip into it.

And then I heard a low sob nearby. The wind gusted, and the trees made so much noise that I risked turning toward the sound. I caught the glint of glasses and the silhouette of a long, droopy nose. It was Mr. Mason spying on the robed people. His hand covered his mouth and his shoulders dipped and rose with his sobs.

I edged over to him and put my forefinger over my lips. "Quiet!" I whispered, and put my hand on his elbow. I drew him away from the awful scene and when we were around a bend in the path, I clicked on my flashlight and grabbed his hand. "Run!"

He resisted at first, but I didn't let go. I hauled him behind me and didn't stop running until we were on the porch of my cottage. I opened the door, yanked my teacher inside, and slammed and locked the door.

Mr. Mason dropped onto the sofa as I walked back and forth, checking the locks and saying, "What was that! What was that!" I thought of the knife and the blood and Lucky's knife and my blood. Had Lucky been among the people in the circle? It was impossible to know since their faces were hidden, but I thought I would have recognized his build.

Mr. Mason took a handkerchief from his pocket and swiped his eyes before blowing his nose. "You scared me to death. I didn't see you there at all."

"Mr. Mason, tell me what that was!" Fright pitched my voice high and loud. "Because right now I'm thinking *vampire cult.*"

"Calm down, Jane. There's a rational explanation, and I'll tell you as much as I can." He smiled nervously, and I sat down in the armchair because my knees were weak.

Then Hosea's instructions came to me as clearly as if he were talking to me: try to stay calm, assess the danger, don't show fear, talk respectfully, get away as soon as possible.

I put my hands between my knees to stop them from shaking, and Mr. Mason said, "The founders of Greenwood, including those who founded the school, emigrated from Eastern Europe, where they had been persecuted because they practiced pre-Christian folk traditions. They remained secretive to protect themselves, but they continue to celebrate the ancient farming cycles. It's their cultural heritage, the same way we use pagan symbols like trees to celebrate Christmas and bunnies to celebrate Easter."

My nerves jangled loud warnings, but I tried to keep my

voice even. "That man cut the other one and dripped his blood in the fire."

"It's a surface cut, less than you'd get scraping your knee," he said, and I was aware of his eyes on my arm.

I pressed my elbow close to my side to hide the mark Lucky had made. "Do they kill people?"

"Good grief, no! The sort of violence you've seen in Helmsdale would horrify these people. Tonight is the autumnal equinox. The ceremony was in honor of the autumn harvest. My wife, Claire, was their friend. She used to participate and I went to watch because . . . to remember her, and how beautiful and solemn she was by the light of the fire." His voice caught and his eyes watered behind his glasses. "It made her feel like she finally belonged somewhere."

I wanted to tell him that I knew about her misery, but I couldn't without admitting that I'd read the letter. "I didn't recognize the language."

"Claire told me it's probably a dialect of Dacian, an ancient Slavic language. Like the Latin you study, it's long dead."

Assess the danger. "The founders moved here because it was foggy and they're sensitive to sunlight. That decanter was filled with blood."

Mr. Mason pulled off his glasses and massaged the bridge of his nose. "Yes, animal blood, probably lamb. They have an enzyme deficiency due to an autosomal recessive genetic disorder. UVA from direct sunlight fragments their DNA. A biological desire to replace the damaged DNA makes them crave blood. They can trick the craving with red foods and drinks, but only blood satisfies it."

His tone was so matter-of-fact, as if this were an ordinary genetic disorder like color blindness, that he took the edge off my first horrified reaction. But I had to ask the question, even though I knew the answer. "Including human blood?"

"Animal on a regular basis, but also human with consensual partners. Some drink daily and some abstain entirely. They aren't what the superstitions say. They're good people. They take care of their friends and we take care of them." He raised a shaky hand to his forehead. "Outsiders never see this. I shouldn't be telling you this, but . . ."

"But I was brought here to supply blood, like a farm animal to genetic mutants."

"That's really judgmental for someone with a scientific mind, Jane." For a moment, he looked at me as if I'd handed in a substandard assignment. "Claire was from Helmsdale, too. The Family selected you to honor her memory, to give you the opportunities she had."

Talk respectfully. I stood up and paced. "Mr. Mason, I like you, I really do. But what kind of opportunity is this? I came here for an education, and now you're telling me I'm only livestock, only one of the herd to be served up at mealtime."

"It's not like that and you wouldn't be passed around. You would have a special relationship with one person. I can't say any more now!"

"Whatever 'special' relationship these pseudo-vampires offer, it didn't make your wife happy."

My teacher twisted his handkerchief. "She *was* happy here until . . . her breakdown. I was the one who thought it might be good to take time off and travel for a year. That's why she killed herself . . . because she didn't want to leave. It's all my fault."

His eyes teared up again. "Oh, Claire, my wonderful Claire!" I got a box of tissues and handed it to him and we sat without speaking. Eventually, his sobs subsided.

What I'd thought was my secret with Lucky wasn't a secret at all—except to me. I felt sick with humiliation thinking about how others must have looked at me, knowing my personal stuff . . . that I was only at Birch Grove to provide these people with my blood. "Mr. Mason, does *everyone* here know? Does the Holiday family know?"

"No, not your friends the Holidays or the Applewhaites."

I felt both relief and a hysterical urge to laugh when I thought of how ecstatic MV would be that these freaks existed. "The people in town—they're part of it, too, right?"

"Only those most trusted and a handful of us at the school. A few students have the condition. It can only be passed on genetically. Their blood can be deadly to us normals in blood-to-blood contamination so they live extremely careful lives."

The isolated puzzle pieces began coming together: the drops of blood on the marble bench, the penknives, the hats and sunscreen, the meals dripping in blood. "The Radcliffes and Harriet Tyler have the condition, don't they?" When he nodded, I asked, "What do you call them?"

"Family."

Family. The word held immense power to someone who'd never had one.

"Jane, it's your life and your decision. They chose you because of your exceptional potential. They'll send you to graduate school and pay for everything so that you can pursue a scientific career. It will be a lifelong commitment, but you'll always be provided with a nice place to live, expense money, business connections, and friendship. You'll be part of the Family."

I panicked thinking about some creepy old guy cutting me and putting his mouth on my body. "You said I'd have a 'special' relationship. With whom?"

"I'm not supposed to be telling you any of this, Jane."

"Mr. Mason, I thought that you and I both valued facts, truth."

He closed his eyes for a few seconds. "You're right. Mr. and Mrs. Radcliffe are very impressed because you've excelled against all odds." He met my gaze. "Jane, you were chosen for Lucian Radcliffe."

I took in a sharp breath. Mrs. Radcliffe had planned

for me to be with Lucky. Why then had he wanted to hide our friendship from her? "Does *he* know I've been chosen for him?"

"Maybe, but I'm not sure. I've been preoccupied with . . . other things. Claire used to keep up on all the news and tell me. Trust me that nothing will be done without your consent, Jane. Your headmistress would be the one to invite you."

"I need to think about this for a few days, at least until the break is over. Promise me you won't tell Mr. and Mrs. Radcliffe that I know."

"I promise, Jane. But I *will* have to tell them soon. I owe them that."

"Give me a few days."

He nodded. "I know when you weigh all the facts, you'll realize how incredible this opportunity is. Jane Williams, Ph.D.—that sounds right, doesn't it?"

Then he stood and left.

It was as if these people . . . no, it was as if Mrs. Radcliffe had walked into my dreams and seen exactly what I wanted: money, a home, a Ph.D., a family, and especially to be with Lucky for ever and ever. I could let them take care of everything for me.

Then I caught myself. When had I become a person who was willing to accept such dark insanity just to be near someone else, even someone as gorgeous as Lucky? When had I become a girl who let adults determine and control her life?

I felt as if I didn't know myself anymore and that scared me more than the strange blood ritual . . . because I'd *already* lost myself once.

I packed essential clothes and got my stash and my composition book from my hiding place. I split up the cash and hid it in the bottoms of my shoes, in my bra, in my pockets. I messed up the bed and set a cereal bowl and a cup in the sink to make it look like I'd just had breakfast. I upended a drawer with all my candy bars into the glossy shopping bag that MV had given me.

I touched the frame of Mrs. Holiday's *Lady of the Wood* painting and wished I could take it. Then I locked the door and hurried off campus and down the hill, hiding in the shadows whenever a car came near.

I walked by the bank because I wanted to clear out my account, but I spotted the security camera over the ATM. I knew Mrs. Radcliffe monitored my account and if I withdrew money this late at night, she'd know I'd gone.

I saw a truck lumbering toward Greenwood Grocery. I crept toward the loading dock of the store and watched a trucker deliver milk and dairy stuff. I waited outside the entrance to the parking lot. When the truck was leaving the lot, I waved to the driver and went to his window.

"Hi, sir, may I have a lift?" I smiled politely.

He had a crew cut and a handlebar mustache. "You running away from home, girlie?"

"I'm an emancipated minor and I'm legally free to travel where I want. I need to get to a train station or a bus depot."

"Waall," he drawled, "I guess I know the lure of the open road, but don't get any ideas that I'm gonna take you across a state line, jailbait. Come on." He opened the passenger door and I had to climb up to the high seat, dragging my sports bag. "Buckle up. I'm heading south."

"So am I."

"Name's Biscuit."

"I'm Mousie."

"Biscuit and Mousie." He chuckled. "We sound like a corny morning drive-time duo."

I was glad that Biscuit didn't say much, because thoughts swirled in my mind like a tornado. With every mile that passed, I felt safer. I stayed in the truck while Biscuit made deliveries and then he drove me to a transit station. "Well,

Mousie, here you go. You can catch a train or bus here. What was so bad about Greenwood?"

"I didn't belong there."

"Me neither. You take care of yourself now."

I had to wait almost an hour for a train. When a cop walked into the terminal, I knew he'd wonder what I was doing there this late, so I hid in the ladies' room until my commuter train was about to board. I hurried onto a dull metal car and ran up the stairs to the upper level. Along the journey, I stared out the window at the desolate industrial landscapes of abandoned factories and junkyards. I'd been on the right side of the tracks and I was going back to the wrong side, where I belonged.

I transferred to a bus and then another bus before arriving at my destination. I was walking in the dingy ombre light that preceded dawn when I saw the first WTH tag—*Welcome to Hell*—spray-painted in yellow on a cinderblock wall.

Hellsdale's ugliness was out in the open and the people here were straight up about their motivations: survival, power, money, sex, and family. They'd kill for family and they'd die for family. They'd kill for a lot less, too, but I knew the rules here.

The Radcliffes played an entirely different game.

I'd never possessed anything that anyone wanted before—not beauty, or money, or power—so I wasn't used to being played. I'd never expected that someday someone would want my blood. As furious as I was at the headmistress of Birch Grove, I still felt a deep ache of longing for the gorgeous boy who'd told me he needed me. Now I understood why.

Chapter 23 Nothing had changed except my perception. I noticed each piece of trash, smear of filth, and grease stain. I noticed the stink of diesel exhaust and sewage. I saw a homeless guy in a sleeping bag in front of the plasma donation building, where he could sell his blood for enough money to get the next meal and the next fix.

I walked by the liquor store and one of the men out front said, "Squeak, squeak, Mousie. Whatchu doing back?"

"Morning, sir. Just wanted to see my girl Wilde."

"She's moved into another place. Hold up, peanut."

I put down my bag and waited while he strolled off and made a phone call. He came back and told me the address, adding, "She just clocked off. Don't cause any problems, you hear?"

"No, sir. Thank you, sir." I nodded and lifted up my sports bag. It got heavier with each step to a grimy six-plex. I walked up the exterior stairs to the second floor. Her apartment was at the back, farthest from the street. Before I raised my hand to ring the buzzer, the door flew open and Wilde stood there, taller and skinnier than ever in booty shorts, a halter midi, and platform boots. Her hair was now indigo blue with extensions that went to her narrow hips.

"Mousie Girl! Holy crap!" She threw her arms around

me and I smelled her sweet perfume and felt the skeletal thinness of her body.

"Girlfriend, I missed you."

"Me, too. Get your ass in here."

Inside the small apartment, the TV flickered soundlessly and candles burned into pools of wax. Oversized red velour furniture filled up the space and a glass and brass coffee table was cluttered with overflowing ashtrays, bottles, and drug paraphernalia. Wilde picked up a half-empty liter of vodka and swung it. "We should celebrate."

"I'm cool, but here's something for you." I handed her the glossy bag.

She looked inside the bag. "Candy! You remembered."

"Of course! It was the last time I ever shoplifted. Hosea was so mad . . . no, he was so *disappointed* in us when he caught us. I couldn't believe he'd gone to the store and paid for our haul."

"That's when you were still a little shady. I'd rather have a beating than see that look on his face." Wilde put the bag on the table and unscrewed the bottle, then swigged the vodka. "Seems like a long time ago that a candy bar was so important that we'd whisper in our beds about our favorites and dream of being rich enough to eat chocolate all day long."

We both sat on the stained sofa. "Wilde, can I hang here for a couple of days?"

"For sure, but I'll still have my appointments. Junior's strict about business." She dug through an ashtray and picked out a half-smoked butt. She lit up and sucked in the smoke, her cheeks concaving like a skull's. "You gonna tell me what's going on? Don't say it was the schoolwork, because you're as sharp as a razor."

"I liked the school, but they're sick, twisted. You've got no idea."

Wilde laughed until she coughed. "Oh, honey, I know *all* about kinks. You get paid more with the specialties. What's their thing?"

"They're sort of like a cult, I guess, but they make it sound all refined and cultured and they drink blood."

"I prefer foot fetishists because they buy me shoes, but I've heard of blood play."

"Well, this is a little different than role-playing. These people share a genetic anomaly. You know how blue eyes get passed down with genes?" I thought of Lucky's clear eyes gazing into mine. "But this makes them want to drink blood. They wanted to drink *my* blood."

"Anything else?"

"No, just a taste of blood occasionally."

"Seems like they're paying you better than the plasma center." She shrugged. "The one thing I've learned is that everyone's kink is different. Heck, every *body* is different. One of my regulars has a sort of tail, for real, and one has webbed toes."

"I have a friend who'd love that."

"I'll tell you the details later. I gotta crash and you look all wore out, too, Mousie."

When Wilde brought me a stained and pilled nylon comforter and a flat pillow, I saw that she had added more tattoos on her arms, elaborate roses and vines. "I like your new ink. You can't even see the scars."

She stretched her arms. "Now when I look at my arms, I see the flowers." Wilde's face went solemn. "You talk about freaks, what's more unnatural than a mom burning her kid?"

"She shouldn't have done that, Wilde Thang. Your body is your own and you should decide what you do with it."

"Damn right. I'll do what I want to do with my own body, whether it's tats, or piercings, or renting it."

I thought about that as I covered myself with the comforter, how the rich owned so many things, but the poor's only valuable possession was our own bodies, and then exhaustion overtook me.

. . .

❧ I awoke early afternoon, confused about where I was. Then all the memories came flooding back—the weird ritual in the grove, Mr. Mason's explanation, and my flight from Birch Grove.

I peeked into the bedroom. My friend snored unevenly with the empty vodka bottle beside her and the radio playing low. I closed her door and went back to the main room. Greenwood had spoiled me, and I hated myself for being bothered by the dinginess and the stale smoke and booze stink of the apartment. Wilde was doing the best she could.

I opened the drapes and the aluminum windows to air out the place, folded my comforter, dumped out ashtrays, and collected bottles and cans.

I opened up the laptop and Wilde's home page flashed on-screen, her Web site for "escort" services.

I searched for articles related to what I'd seen at the amphitheater and what Mr. Mason had told me. One of the first results listed was the kink that Wilde had mentioned. People who participated in blood play called themselves sanguinarians. The submissives were called blood donors.

I read about genetic anomalies, including some that caused sun sensitivity and biological photophobia, a painful reaction to sunlight. I learned about bizarre dietary cravings and deadly recessive genetic disorders that were carried by people who originated from specific regions, like Tay-Sachs disease.

I read boring essays about pre-Christian folk celebrations and learned that Dacian was a language of a farming region in what became Romania, which fit in with popular vampire mythology. The information about Dacian crop-based ceremonies—set in circular areas marked by stones and boulders like the amphitheater—was consistent with what Mr. Mason had told me.

Birch trees were used in Dacian ceremonies, as well as folk ceremonies throughout the world. As Mrs. Holiday had told me, they were a symbol of hope, renewal, fertility, purity, strength . . . I thought of the grove and my comfy little cottage. I remembered how happy I'd been when Lucky walked me home that night and asked me if I would be loyal to him, when he'd talked about "us."

I'd thought he had chosen me over everyone else in Greenwood because he knew he could trust me.

I couldn't find anything about this specific "Family," but there had been murderous anti-vampire hysterias well into the 1800s that would have forced the Family to go into hiding. All the information led me to believe that Mr. Mason had been telling me the truth about these people—and that meant that the Radcliffes' secrecy was necessary for their survival. I could understand the survival instinct.

I was drinking a soda, eating potato chips, and watching cartoons when Wilde stumbled into the room in a wifebeater and a thong. I hadn't noticed all the bruises and scabs on her legs last night.

She gaped in surprise. "Mousie! I forgot you were here. My head's gonna explode." She went to the fridge and drank a bottle of peach iced tea. She got a box of cigarettes out of a drawer and lit one before saying, "Sorry you got stuck sitting around."

"It's okay. I used your laptop to do some research."

"Research! Most people look for porn. Did you see my site?"

"Yes, it's a good start. I could help you with layout and design so it's more polished."

"It's *supposed* to be half-assed, so clients think I'm a nice girl who's experimenting. But you could organize it better and put in a contact form." She went to the coffee table and set two white pills on a mirror. After crushing and chopping them, she used a straw to snort a line. "Want some?"

I wondered what it would be like to numb out all the painful feelings. I shook my head. "I'm still a nerd."

"That's good, Mousie. I'm gonna get clean soon, when

I'm not feeling so run-down. But the only thing that stops me from feeling that way is using."

"What about beauty school? I bet you'd get energized working in a cool salon, making money styling 'dos, and being glamorous. Or, like a friend always says, 'fabulous.'"

"Fabulous. I'd like to be *fabulous*. In fact, next week I'm going to clean up," she said. "So, Mousie, you got any plans?"

"I was thinking of trying to get back to City Central and finding a place to live."

"How are you going to pay rent?"

"I can get jobs tutoring."

She lit another cigarette and puffed for a few minutes. "I can give you clients, the easy ones who don't ask for much, and you can set the rules and only do what you want. If you dress real young, you can make good money from the pervs. I'll show you the ropes."

She smiled innocently, and my heart broke. She was like someone lost on the highway who keeps taking the wrong turns and getting farther and farther away from her destination. I remembered Claire Mason's phrase, a map of pain, and I thought that's what Wilde's life had been. "Thanks, Wilde, but I want to be legit and finish school."

"Yeah, I know how you are. I was just throwing that out there." She paused before saying, "If it was up to me, you could stay here as long as you like, but my man won't have that. You have to be in the life, or . . ." She pressed her lips together. "Junior will *want* you in the life."

My blood chilled because she was warning me that if I stayed too long, I wouldn't have a choice. "I could use a few days to find a room share and some kind of job."

"No problem. You're a minor, so you can go on welfare and go back to school."

"I'd rather work." I made some quick calculations in my head about how far my stash would carry me. I couldn't withdraw money now, or Mrs. Radcliffe would know my location—and I wasn't ready for that until I got settled. "I can scrimp and have enough to cover me for a month rent-ing at the by-the-week motel. I can tutor, or work in a bookstore or a restaurant."

Wilde let out a long *sssss.* "Jobs are tight all over, Mou-sie. But you'll figure it out. Tell me about this rich-bitch school of yours."

So I described Greenwood, Birch Grove, the hills, and the fog. "It's like in those movies where trees grow over wide streets and blond kids ride bicycles. They all live in these mansions with their families and they all go to the country club for parties. The cops don't ever hassle anyone."

"It sounds unreal."

"It *is* unreal. It's antiseptic and protected. If they could build a moat around their town and pretend the rest of the world doesn't exist, they would." I thought about Mrs. Radcliffe's serene smile as she welcomed me to Birch Grove. "They're so polite that you can't tell which ones are being phony."

"What about the guy?" she asked. "Because I know there's a guy involved somehow."

As much as I tried, I couldn't see Lucky as twisted and deceitful. He'd *told* me that I might not like him when I really knew him. He had been as honest with me as he could be. I thought about the intensity in his blue eyes as he asked for my loyalty. "He's not interested in me that way."

"*All* guys are interested in *all* girls that way. Anyways, Mousie, you always act like you ain't hot."

"I'm not. I'm puny, and I don't have any bounce, and I'm plain."

"You're plain stupid about some things, that's for sure. You skipped out on all that because they're a little freaky?"

"They want me to be a part of that life, and . . ." I had to think about why I'd really been frightened. "It's like they're controlling me and I'm just going along with it. That's not me."

"Well, you always liked running your own schemes, Janey."

"Yes, my sinister studying-hard-to-get-ahead scheme. I plan to reap in a fortune any decade now."

Mary Violet would have giggled and told me that she was going to write a book about an evil mastermind, but Wilde smiled blankly and took another drink.

❧ I spent the next few hours on Wilde's laptop. First, I searched for a room I could afford. Most of the shared situations required a big deposit. I e-mailed a few people, but the only person who responded immediately sounded *too* excited by the fact that I was in high school and wanted me to send a photo.

I had time to apply for a few entry-level jobs, filling out extensive applications that kept bumping me out of the system when I left blank spaces. But I had no experience, no degrees, no references.

I left before Wilde's first client arrived and had dinner at a fast-food place. The gray hamburger meat tasted flat and salty, and the soda was syrupy sweet. It didn't make my lips go "smack."

I went to the movies and sneaked from screening room to screening room until the last show was over, but when I returned to Wilde's, she was still busy. I sat outside on the steps, remembering the last time I'd been out this late, with Hattie in the birch grove.

Saturday night in the city was so bright and noisy. I heard the diesel engines of buses roaring, cars and horns, music thump-thumping, sirens, laughter, and fighting. I counted out six rapid shots of a semiautomatic and the response of ten shots. When footsteps vibrated on the cement stairs, I'd draw my hoodie over my head and scoot to one side so the men could pass by.

Suddenly I began laughing as I realized that I was actually *worse* off than I had been at Mrs. Prichard's. My laughter turned to tears and I felt utterly hopeless and lost.

I had worked so hard, so *incredibly* hard to improve my life . . . and that's when I angrily swiped my tears away. I could figure this out. I *would* figure this out.

❧ Sunday was more of the same: going online to apply for jobs and look for a rental. Now I had to wait for responses, so I visited Cecile, a friend from City Central who lived nearby in a dilapidated Victorian house.

Cecile unlocked the iron gate at her front door and grinned. She was a tall girl with a watchful expression who hacked her hair short and wore a frayed flannel and torn-up jeans. "Hey, Jane! What are you doing here?"

"Hey, Cecile. I've got a few days off so I wanted to see how things are."

She gave me the sort of hug guys give, with one arm around my shoulders and another patting my back.

"Come on in."

We passed through the cluttered living room, stepping over kids' toys, and we went to her tiny bedroom. Books were piled on the ratty olive green rug, and the walls were covered with posters of Marie Curie, Sally Ride, Toni Morrison, and Susan Sontag. We sat cross-legged on the bed and I looked for changes since I'd last visited. A dozen snow globes were arranged atop her dresser.

"Where'd you get those cool snow globes?"

"Someone threw them out. My mom's got me Dumpster diving with her, mostly for food, but we check bins when people move. You can't believe the great stuff people toss."

"I used to find things in the trash, too." I was sure that Greenwood people threw out valuable things.

"You know, we were betting on whether you'd ever come back to visit or not."

"Well, here I am. I would have been in touch more, but I don't have a phone or computer access."

"You wrote about that and we didn't believe it, but we

saw it on Birch Grove's Web site." She eyed me top to bottom. "Nice clothes and sweet kicks."

I glanced down at my new jeans and tennis shoes, remembering my shopping trip with Mrs. Radcliffe. "The school bought them for me. So what's going on at Hellsdale?"

"You want a list of the dramas over babies' mamas, or what's happening in class? It's always the same crap—someone trashed the chem lab two weeks ago." Cecile's features tightened into anger. "Can't we have one damn thing that's decent? Is that too much to ask? They moved the class to a trailer, but we can't do our labs because of fire codes, and we're all behind. And AP classes got slashed with the last budget. All the languages got hit and European History, too."

"What about Latin?"

"Totally decimated. Is Birch Grove everything they say?"

"And more." I chewed at a hangnail. "But the people there have no idea of what the real world is like. They're smart, but not street smart because they don't have to be." I looked at one of the snow globes on Cecile's dresser. I reached across for it and shook it so the white flakes fell on a small cottage surrounded by trees. "They're like this, living in a bubble, and they never have to see anything outside the bubble. Violence, poverty, pain are abstract concepts to them."

"A microcosm. Isn't that the same way here? Most of the kids at school think the world ends at the bus terminal. It's like those ancient maps where unknown territory was marked *There be dragons!*"

"You're right." I shook the globe again, watching snow fall on the miniature cottage. "Some of the people there are really nice anyway, smart and even funny."

"You never liked funny much, Jane."

"I didn't, did I? Maybe I had too much to worry about."

"You look sorta worried now."

I hesitated before saying, "I'm thinking about transferring back to City Central."

Cecile's mouth dropped open and she stared at me. "You are out of your mind . . . unless the work's too hard. Is that it? Don't beat yourself up if you gave it your best shot."

"It's not that. It's that I didn't fit in there."

"It's a universal truth that geeks are always misfits, Jane." Cecile patted my knee. "Look, we're meeting up tonight. The crew will be glad to see you. Do you still have a curfew like in the old days?"

"No, I'm free to do whatever. I can fall off the face of the earth into there-be-dragons land for all anyone cares."

We went to a hookah bar in the mall that let in underage kids. My friends smoked shisha and asked about Birch Grove, like kids wanting to hear a bedtime story. Terrance, a good-looking senior I'd lusted after for years, said, "I told them you'd be back. Here, you're a wizard, but there, what are you? Nothing."

"I'm *not* nothing!" I glowered at him. "I kicked ass. I was the *top* Chem student. I was acing Trig and Latin."

"Yeah, that's why you're back," he scoffed.

"I have my reasons and I don't need to share them with you."

Cecile changed the subject to a pirate radio show she was hosting, and I sat back in the shadows, seething. I'd told the truth. I *was* as smart as anyone at Birch Grove. I'd earned my place there.

❧ On Monday morning, I took the bus to Helmsdale City Central to see about transferring back in. I made my way through the wild crowd milling at the chain-link fence around the school. Yellow police tape cordoned off a parking space that had rusty-brown splatters of dried blood.

Students jostled and cussed each other out as they lined up to enter the building. They placed their backpacks on a table to be searched and walked through metal detectors. I didn't have a City Central ID, so a security manager had to be called to let me pass through.

I waited in the admissions office to ask about a transfer and got bumped to an enrollment counselor who said she needed to check my records, left the room, and never returned. I did the whole thing over again with another counselor.

She gave me a folder with an application and district residency requirements. "The first-tier classes you want are filled, so you'd have to choose other courses and start another language since Latin is gone. Next!"

Back at Wilde's place, I searched online for other public high schools in the district, but they were already closed to transfers for the academic year. I tried to cyber-stalk my Birch Grove friends and Lucky, but Mrs. Radcliffe had done an amazing job of keeping them off the radar. I redid Wilde's Web site and compiled information about beauty schools and GED programs until she got up in the late afternoon.

Wilde seemed happy with the changes to her Web site and then asked me all about Greenwood and Birch Grove. She seemed so curious that I talked more than usual.

"I still don't get it, Mousie. You rave about the school and you're crushing on that hot dude, Jack."

"Not Jack, his brother, Lucky."

She twisted her lips and shut one eye. "Which one is the musician?"

"Jack."

"Yeah, the sexy one."

I knew that Wilde was too high to think straight. "He's in love with my friend Hattie, who is perfect."

"No one's perfect." Wilde went to her refrigerator and pulled a bottle of vodka from the freezer.

"I bought some juice today. Wouldn't you rather have that?"

Wilde very deliberately unscrewed the bottle and gulped the booze. She swiped her mouth with the back of her hand. "How's that room hunt going?"

"I'm still looking. I can be out today, though."

Her face clouded. "No, no rush. But don't judge, Jane."

"I'm not judging, but . . . I want to help you get clean. You've got so much potential and it kills me to see you living like this, dealing with sus people. I want you to have a better life."

"Maybe this is where we're supposed to be, Mousie. Maybe we should make the best of it and not expect too much and get disappointed."

"I don't give up."

"Then I must be hallucinating that you're back here in Hellsdale, back to your same old running ways."

That was as far as our talk went before Wilde started getting calls for evening appointments.

I fumed a little because I was sensitive about some things, too. Leaving Birch Grove because they were trying to convert me into their weird society was *not* the same thing as giving up.

Chapter 24 It was long after midnight, and I was
drowsing off on the concrete steps,
waiting for Wilde's last client to leave,
when I heard her scream.

I jumped up and raced into her apartment. Techno pulsed
behind the closed bedroom door where an angry man
shouted, "Filthy dirty whore!" and Wilde cried, "Please
don't hurt me!"

We are so sensitive to some sounds that we can perceive
them through all the random noise of life—music pounding
on a stereo, bickering nearby, TVs blaring, traffic on the
street. When I heard the distinctive sound of an open hand
striking flesh, something in me clicked, like a key turning
in a rusty lock, opening a door to a secret room.

And in that room, I saw my mother.

She was crying and cowering beside the refrigerator and
a bear of a man—my stepfather—was shouting and moving
toward her with his hand raised.

The memory stunned me, but that numbness lasted only
a moment. Then came grief so intense that I would have collapsed there on the floor and curled into a fetal position, but
another scream snapped me back to the present.

In Hellsdale, no one ever answered cries for help. I ran
to the window, shoved it open so hard that it jumped off its
cheap aluminum track, and screamed, "Fire! Fire! Fire!"

I grabbed a tall brass candlestick and rushed to Wilde's bedroom. The door flew open and Wilde bashed into me as she entered the room, clasping a shiny red kimono closed over her body.

"Where! What's happening?" she said as she looked around frantically.

Through the doorway, I saw a man yanking on his pants and picking up a shirt. I looked back to Wilde, who had a red welt across her cheek.

She stared at the candlestick in my hand. "What the hell are you doing, Mousie?"

"Are you all right, Wilde?" I moved to her side, still gripping the candlestick and keeping my eyes on the man. My childhood memory felt as real to me as this scene and my heart beat fast—because I had the insane idea that my mother was in Wilde's bedroom.

That she would step forward and say . . . what would she say to me?

But it was Wilde who stepped in front of me, glowering. "Is that what this is? You *shoulda* knocked and asked. Actually, you shoulda just kept out of my business!"

The man jammed his feet in his shoes and walked through the living room. He sneered at Wilde. "You're not getting paid, bitch."

Footsteps pounded in the stairs and Wilde's pimp, Junior, blocked the doorway. He looked from the man to Wilde and me and back to the man again. "What's going on?"

"The deal was special treatment and then this . . . this stupid kid screams fire," the man said as he squeezed by Junior.

"Hey, you gotta pay first!" Junior followed him down the stairs and their voices got louder and angrier.

Wilde grabbed a pack of cigarettes and lit up. "You've caused me a whole lot of mess."

I set down the candlestick. "I thought he was hurting you. He *was* hurting you. You shouldn't let him do that."

"I get paid for it, and now I won't get paid!" Wilde paced around me, jabbing the air with her cigarette. "You always think you know everything, don't you? You always think you're so damn smart."

"I'm not. I just try really—"

"Don't give me *that* line. You talk about people being fake, but *you're* a phony. You fake that you don't think you're smarter than everyone in Hellsdale, and I bet you fake with all those rich bitches, acting like you don't think you're better than them, when you do because you did it on your own."

I wanted to slap her and I wanted to cry. My voice shook when I said, "I'll talk to you when you're not wasted."

She laughed an ugly laugh. "Oh, yeah, Miss Holier-than-thou, that's another thing I'm *sick* of. Not partying and not putting out doesn't mean you're any better than me—it means you're *boring*. You're just jealous that I have a boyfriend and get lots of action, and no one wants a *boring* priss like you."

I stepped forward and stared disdainfully at her. "Because you're *so* interesting when you're passed out on the sofa, or rambling about what you're going to do *someday*, how you're going to get straight *someday*. You're *so* interesting when you're talking about your boyfriend when he's nothing but a cheap, nasty pimp who sells your body and keeps you hooked."

Her expression softened and her lower lip quivered the way it used to when her father didn't show up on his visiting days. The welt on her face was darkening into a bruise.

I looked around at the depressing apartment with its flimsy pay-by-the-month furniture and stained shag carpeting. I saw the cigarette burns on the tables, the faded silk flower arrangements, and a goldfish bowl half-full of murky water.

"You're better than this, Wilde. You can have a better life." I went to get ice from the freezer, but the plastic trays were empty. I took a can of frozen juice and handed it to her. "For your cheek."

She opened her hand, letting the can roll off her fingers and drop to the floor. "I *like* my life. Not all of us want to be Hosea. There was only one of him and you're not it, so get out!" Wilde pushed me toward the door. "Get the hell outa here!"

I almost tripped on the steps as I heard the door slam shut behind me. I stumbled into the night, looking for a place to hide.

I ducked into the carport, finding the deepest shadows behind a minivan on blocks, and pressed back against the rough wall. I slid down the wall and wrapped my arms around my knees. The misery was all too much to bear.

I could still hear the slap, as brief and forbidding as a thunderclap.

I turned my face to my hunched-up shoulder, and Wilde's injured face suddenly became my mother's face.

My mother had been so much smaller than my hulking step-father. She'd held her arms over her head to block his fists. There was blood on his hands, her face, and he was raging at her.

Blood splattered onto the yellow floor that she kept bright and shiny.

I crouched under the kitchen table, terrified and whimpering. I smelled whiskey and sweat and burned food.

Scenes of my early years in foster care rushed at me: a filthy house with rats that scurried out at night, a man who said to call him "uncle" and tickled too much, a woman who locked me in my room while her boyfriends visited.

I gasped, stunned that I'd finally *remembered* a few things. Could I have even more memories hiding within me? Could I remember who I'd once been?

I thought of what Wilde had called me, fake, and how I'd come back here to be my real self. Well, this was my real self—frightened and confused and lashing out at my oldest friend.

Suddenly I wanted to be in the grove and hear the wind and the trees whispering *shush, shush, shush*. I wanted the green to wash away the pain. I wanted to be with Lucky, who'd made all my senses come alive.

And I realized that my real self was someone who'd rejected the violence, cruelty, and ignorance of Hellsdale. My real self was also someone who sat in chem lab, happy with a big book, formulas on chalkboards, and knowledge of how the world worked. And my real self was someone who didn't give up even when she had to say, "I don't understand. Can you explain it to me?" and hear others laughing at her.

❧ I awoke at dawn when a car door slammed and someone drove out of the carport. I was stiff and shivering, smelling of exhaust fumes. I went upstairs to Wilde's to get my things.

She was sitting on the sofa and surfing through channels on the TV. Her dilated pupils showed only a narrow rim of gray iris, and a bruise marked her pale face. "Hey, Mousie! Whoa, you really freaked out. I should have warned you that I had a hitter coming." She jittered a leg and cut out a line of white powder.

"I'll just get my stuff and then I'll be out of here." My bag was in the corner. I folded up a t-shirt and put it inside, aware that Wilde was watching me.

"You were going to throw down for me, weren't you?" she said seriously. "You're a good friend, Mousie. I'm sorry for all that drama. I didn't mean those things."

"I'm sorry, too, Wilde Thang. I try not to judge, but I worry about you." I wished the apologies would make everything okay between us, but I knew things were more complicated than that. "You're right. I am fake. I act nice to adults to get what I want."

"That's not fake. That's part of your school business." Wilde wiped her nostrils. "Just like for my business, I act like whatever fantasy the client wants. It doesn't mean I'm fake."

I dropped on the sofa beside her. "Wilde, you know what you said about me doing a runner and coming here?"

She had to think awhile. "Oh, that. Yeah, you were a runner before I met you. What did the Baby Snatchers call you?" The Baby Snatchers was our nickname for Child Protective Services because they swooped in to take babies from dangerous situations.

"They used to call me incorrigible. It was stamped right on my file. Well, I guess now I'm *corrigible*. I'm not going to run from things anymore. I'm not going to bail on an opportunity like Birch Grove even if the people there are a little twisted. I'll figure out the rules of their game, I'll play to win, and I won't give up who I am."

"Now that's the Mousie Girl I know! What did you say their kink was?"

Mr. Mason had said that the Family needed secrecy. "Nothing. They're normal." I reached out and put my hand on Wilde's knobby knee. "I don't want to leave you like this."

Her gray eyes wandered before focusing on mine. "It's not like you can take me with you, is it? Be real—we never wanted the same things. I know what you think about Junior, but we've got something and he takes care of me."

"If he cared for you, he wouldn't pimp you out and keep you using. Pain isn't love." Even as I spoke the words, I thought of Lucky cutting me . . . but he always asked permission and he had a biological need. "Maybe Junior calls it love, but that kind of love can get you killed."

"I know what I'm doing." Wilde's hand was shaky as she opened a bottle on the table and finished the last two inches of alcohol.

"Thanks for letting me stay, Wilde. If there's anything I can do . . . when you decide to leave this—and I *know* you will—I'll do whatever you need to get out."

"Hey, I'm good. We can catch up later . . . when I'm

straight and you're settled. I'll cut your hair for free." Wilde smiled her gap-toothed smile, and in the next moment her dark eyelids closed and she slumped back against the sofa.

I got her into bed and kissed the cheek that wasn't bruised. She was snoring and her breathing was even. On her night table, I left a thank-you note with my address and phone number, the $70 she'd given me, and the folder with information about getting a GED and beauty school. I took a final look at my broken friend and walked out of her apartment.

I was waiting at the bus stop with my sports bag when a silver Navigator slowed down. I stepped back, hoping there wouldn't be trouble. The car parked a few yards up in front of a hydrant, and 2Slim stepped out. He wore a gray pin-striped suit with a pale lilac shirt and a dove-gray tie. "I thought that was you, Mousie Girl. Junior told me there was a commotion at your girl's place last night."

I nodded. "Yes, sir. I mistook the situation. I didn't mean to cause any problems. I apologize."

"Apology accepted. I'll square things with Junior," he said. "Where you going?"

"Back to Birch Grove Academy. My break is over."

"No driver this time?"

"No, sir."

"Why don't you call someone for a ride?"

"I don't have a phone."

"I got someone headed north can give you a ride most of the way."

"I'd appreciate that, sir."

"Ain't no thing, Mousie." He raised his hand to signal to one of the men up on the corner. "But it's for the best you don't interfere with my affairs, because I can't let that pass again, you get me?"

My stomach constricted in fear. "Yes, sir."

"I used to see you with that boy—what was his name?—Rev, walking to school."

"Hosea was his given name. They called him Rev for Reverend."

"That's the one. Me and my baby sister, Evie, used to walk to school like that, steering clear of any mess." He stared off, but I could tell that he was using his peripheral vision to keep tabs on the street. "Baby girl got in the way of a drive-by when she was only ten." Now he turned to me.

"I'm sorry, sir."

"I made a decision then and I got no regrets, but I'm mindful that things could have gone different." He flipped his key chain in his hand. "No one here heard a squeak from you, Mousie, until that boy got sick. Then one night you started screaming bloody murder at that Prichard woman. I was standing across the way when the ambulance came and you climbed right in with Rev. They peeled you off and you threw yourself back in."

I'd gripped Hosea's hand, burning with fever, as they put him on a gurney. Hosea had opened his eyes one last time and found me in the chaos. He'd said, "Don't be afraid, Little Sis. I believe. You got to *believe*." Those were the last words he ever spoke.

I told 2Slim, "Mrs. Prichard said it was the flu and she wouldn't get him to the ER. I had to grab the phone from her and call myself."

"Same as yesterday. Here you are a scary-eyed little mouse, but you step up when your friends need you. That's loyalty. If you'da been a boy, I would have recruited you then and there."

A blue Acura rolled to the curb and 2Slim told the driver, "Take her near Greenwood and give her a burner."

"Thank you, Mr. Blake."

"Only use the phone in an emergency, Mousie. I didn't keep your scrawny ass from being kicked every day at school so's you can start trouble for me now."

I'd thought I escaped beatings because no one noticed

me, but the moment 2Slim said he'd protected me I knew it was true.

His genial expression vanished for a moment. "They say I'm sentimental. That just means if you even *think* to cross me, I'll leave flowers on your grave."

"You're doing all this because I remind you of your sister?"

He laughed his gunfire laugh. "Hell, Mousie, you remind me of *me*."

I was still staring, amazed, at 2Slim as I got in the car. He shut the door, and the guy at the wheel hit the gas.

The driver chewed gum as he sped on the freeways north. He dropped me off at the edge of town.

"Thanks for the ride."

"No problem." He pulled a cheap phone from his jacket pocket and handed it to me. The driver gunned the engine and was off the second I closed the car door.

My heart was full when I saw the lush green hills draped in fog. I caught the shuttle uphill and gazed out the window at the trees, the lawns, the greenness of the town.

When I opened the door to the cottage, the red light of the answering machine was blinking. I dropped my sports bag and then punched the play button.

Mary Violet had left gossip about the movie night, and girls from my Latin study group wanted to review chapters. Then there was a dead air sound that telemarketers leave when they get a machine. I was about to hit delete when I heard "Oh, hey, Jane, it's Lucky. I wanted to know if we could do tutoring Thursday. Say five. See you."

I didn't care that Lucky had "a strangeness." He was glorious and golden and he needed me.

Ludovico went on to describe the great advantage which would accrue to the farmer and his family if the baron's proposal were accepted. Not only, he said, would Teresa be a lady of the highest rank, and in possession of enormous wealth both in gold and jewels, but that the other members of her family would also be ennobled . . .

William Gilbert, *The Last Lords of Gardonal* **(1867)**

Chapter 25   On Wednesday, I stayed in bed until past noon and then took a long hot shower, happy to have my own bathroom again. As I finished dressing, there was a knock at the door.

When I opened it, Mrs. Radcliffe was standing there, neatly dressed in navy slacks and a pale blue shirt. Her eyes were shaded by a broad-brimmed linen hat, but I saw tension in her mouth. "Good afternoon, Jane. May I come in?"

"Yes, of course." I guessed what was coming but hadn't expected it so soon.

We both sat on the sofa, angled toward each other. "Mr. Mason told you what I saw."

"I hoped that we would have time to introduce you more gradually to our world." She smoothed her pale hands over her slacks. "You were not chosen at random, Jane. You have great abilities, and you've proved yourself hardworking and honest. I wanted to bring another girl here from Helmsdale because Claire was quite dear to me and my family."

"Mr. Mason told me that."

"We failed her, Jane, but not for want of trying. She was suffering a type of post-partum depression and we were making efforts to get her into a recovery center. We have some excellent facilities both here and abroad." Mrs. Radcliffe smiled sadly. "We're all trying to cope, though poor Albert has had it the worst."

I became impatient. "But you're here to talk about me, not Mrs. Mason. I'd like to know what *exactly* you expect of me along with . . . with my blood and loyalty."

"You put it so bluntly!" she said. "I'll try to put our offer in context. In the past, our people were murdered by the superstitious and by those using that ignorance in order to steal our lands and property. We developed a system to help us survive and even thrive. We have friends, associates like those you saw at the ceremony, who protect our interests. We take care of them as well.

"At a higher level are the Companions. Each Companion has a lifelong bond with an individual Family member."

She had been glancing away occasionally as she spoke, but now she clasped my hands and looked right into my face. "Jane, we are asking that you be Lucian's Companion. If you say yes, we'll take care of you for the rest of your life. You and my son would go to college together and graduate school. We would provide you with comfortable housing and a generous allowance."

Hearing it from her made it real and momentous. I drew in a breath. "Is that a . . . a proposal?"

"No, our genetic anomaly makes traditional marriage with a Normal almost impossible. If our blood contaminates your blood, you could die. It's one reason we are so cautious in our dealings with Normals. Companions usually marry another Normal and most have families who enjoy the benefits of the relationship."

I felt uncomfortable, but she seemed so absorbed that I couldn't tug away.

"Jane, you'll have to make compromises, of course, but in exchange, we'll offer you all of our resources to ensure that your life is as enriching and fulfilling as possible. In fact, we hope that you will want to work at one of our medical research facilities. You'd never have to worry about buying a house, or paying tuition, or medical bills."

I slowly removed my hands from hers and tried to sound calm when I felt anything but calm. There was still the chance that Lucky had only wanted to taste my blood but didn't know what his parents had planned for us. "Does Lucky know you've chosen me?"

"He's very happy that you were chosen . . . although he certainly wasn't supposed to take any action until you agreed to join the Family."

Family. I'd wanted a family so badly. "And what would my responsibilities be?"

"Lucky will want to taste your blood now and then. Only a few milliliters at each feeding, which won't endanger your health at all. You are not expected to do his chores or his schoolwork. If anyone gets suspicious, or if you feel that he needs our help, you'll act to protect him and be a liaison to the Family."

"No one believes in supernatural monsters, or would hold a genetic anomaly against you," I said.

"Superstition is based on emotion, not fact, and even intelligent people are eager to destroy anything different. People fear the unknown."

"Is Jack . . . ?"

"Jacob's normal. Well, he's *a* Normal." Her expression became softer and warmer. "We have a very low birthrate and I'd lost all hope of having children when he came into our lives. I am so grateful that he did and I love him as much as a mother can love a child."

"Claire Mason wanted a child."

"I should have told you that Claire was from Helmsdale, but her loss is still upsetting. She was my husband's Companion and like an aunt to my boys. Poor Claire." Mrs. Radcliffe sighed. "We have things in common, Jane. We're careful, smart, decent."

"I would feel more comfortable about this if you'd told

it all to me from the start." I wanted to tilt the power of the negotiation to me. "What if my answer is no?"

"No one's ever declined the offer." Mrs. Radcliffe stood. "However, in that case, we would certainly honor our agreement to provide you with a Birch Grove education, and we would seek another qualified candidate who is interested in my son's well-being."

"The way I was asked here to take Bebe's place."

"Bebe didn't refuse the role, Jane. She left before we made the offer, although I believe she suspected that we were going to give her an exceptional opportunity. You can give me your answer tomorrow."

❧ I barely slept that night, and I was already dressed and staring out the front window at daybreak, when everything was sparkling with dew and birds flitted among the branches, singing out.

I loved this place, but I had an odd feeling that I was missing *something,* like taking a test and skipping a critical step.

So I did what I knew best: I organized information, trying to find any reason why I *shouldn't* accept the Radcliffes' offer. In a clean new notebook, I wrote down everything that had happened, everything I'd been told. I drew a chart of relationships and tried to construct a timeline of events.

The missing factor was how Lucky felt about me.

I knew how I felt about him. I wanted him. It was that simple: I wanted Lucian Radcliffe and my desire for him was so powerful that all the unknowns seemed insignificant by comparison.

To my Birch Grove friends, he was merely a pretty boy, the headmistress's son. They didn't see anything more because they didn't need anything else that Lucky offered. My friends took a family, home, comfort, and safety for granted. They took beauty and pleasure for granted.

But I knew that these things were precious. Lucky offered something else, too. He was someone I thought I could love. And I would do everything I could to make sure he fell in love with me, too.

I hid the notebook in the laundry room and went back to the living room window.

Lucky was coming down the curving path, light and shadow flickering over his face. My heart jumped because he was even more stunning now that I knew his secrets. *Our* secrets.

I opened the door and waited on the porch. When he saw me, a blush came to his pale cheeks.

"Hi, Jane. Come for a walk with me." He started up the path toward his house and then veered right to a narrow trail that had been hidden by thick shrubs. Leaves crunched under our feet and birds chirped in the trees.

I studied Lucky as he walked ahead of me. His shoulders were wide in a thin charcoal cotton sweater and his legs seemed longer in black jeans. Occasionally a ray of sunshine pierced the clouds and branches and brightened his gold-honey-amber hair.

Soon we arrived at a small creek that wound around a boulder. Lucky boosted me effortlessly atop the boulder, and then he sat beside me.

"Jack and I used to play here. We built dams and had sword fights. He was Sir Jacob, Defender of the Grove, and I was Prince Lucian, Heir to the Throne. He'd still be happy playing here, but I grew out of that a long time ago."

The water in the creek pooled down below, the same color as Jack's eyes, and the smell here was like Jack, vivid and green.

"My mom's really mad at me because I didn't wait until you were formally asked. That's the reason I was staying away. Because I wasn't supposed to . . . you know. Although, it's not my fault that you saw the celebration."

So *that* was the reason he'd kept away. "Your mother

was calm yesterday. She told me about all of you like it was completely normal."

"We're human beings with a genetic anomaly, not monsters."

"I don't think you're a monster, Lucky." I watched a water skeeter glide on the water, and I thought about surfaces and tension. "So Bebe was supposed to be here with you?"

"Yeah, I spent two years getting to know her, and then one day she took off with this uncle who shows up out of the blue." He sounded hurt and angry. "I didn't even get a good-bye."

"Were you in love with her?"

"Bebe? No way. But I could talk to her and she was cool. We were buds." Lucky hesitated. "My folks were waiting to ask her about being a Companion, but I'd told her already. She was psyched, but I guess she got a better offer from this *uncle*. Hell, maybe she really did have an uncle."

"You were upset?"

He nodded. "Hattie said I should get used to girls blowing me off, unless I straighten out my act. She knew I'd told Bebe. Jack, too."

"It's a little weird, knowing that Hattie was probably reporting on me to your mom."

"If you told Hattie anything in private, she'd keep it secret because . . . you can always count on Hattie. She probably told my mom just enough to keep her off your back. It's all tradition with my folks. They keep expecting villagers to storm Birch Grove carrying torches and wooden stakes."

Our laughter eased my tension. My leg was alongside Lucky's. His arm was beside mine.

"I like you, Jane. You're smart and levelheaded. You listen and consider stuff. You didn't completely flip out about the geezers' ceremony or with me that night." His gaze drifted down to my breasts, then my neck and my arms.

"Lucky, what you said about girlfriends being temporary . . ."

"A Companion is a lot more important than a girlfriend. A Companion is a bond for life. I know you want something different, but that's because you're used to a certain idea of a relationship." He paused before saying, "This isn't sex for me, but the feeling I get when I taste blood is amazing. That's the only explanation I can give."

He shifted his weight to one hip and then reached into his pocket for the penknife. He opened it with one hand. He moved his fingertips along my cheek, making me dizzy with desire. "But I'll try to make it good for you, too. I want you to like it." When his hand dropped, his fingers skimmed the tip of my breast and my pulse raced.

"I like being with you, Lucky."

"Stay then. Two more years and we'll get out of this stupid town and go to college somewhere cool. We'll travel the world and have adventures. We'll find someplace great to live and be successes. My family will pay for everything."

"That's a lot of money. I can get scholarships."

"They've *got* a lot of money. You won't have to worry about anything except being there for me, Jane."

He rubbed my earlobe between his thumb and forefinger. He put his lips near my ear so that I could feel the soft exhalations as he spoke. "Will you stay with me, Jane?"

And his words echoed Jack's song, *Titania, stay with me, stay for me,* and I remembered the heat of Jack's hands on my face, but I shoved away those confusing feelings because I wanted Lucky to keep touching me. I wanted one bright and beautiful thing in the misery and ugliness that had been my life. I was used to *wanting*, I could exist with *wanting*.

But Lucky's wanting *me* gave me a sense of power that was intoxicating. And so I said, "Yes."

"Thank you, thank you, thank you, Jane, my very own Companion," he murmured into my ear. "The lobe doesn't have many nerves, but it has so many capillaries." He bent my lobe to expose the back. Then he raised his knife and I felt the pain, like burning, as he cut me, and I cried out.

A burst of wind sent branches rustling and creaking as my blood flowed, sticky and warm and iron-scented.

Lucky watched with exhilaration as the thick blood trickled down my jaw and then along my throat. He pushed me back against the hard, cold rock and began licking my skin, his tongue rough and smooth at the same time.

The branches above us swayed as the wind grew stronger, and Lucky's tongue rasped upward all along my neck. Then he nipped my earlobe and tugged, worrying at the cut and making it bleed more.

I closed my eyes and I wrapped my arms around Lucky. I would pay attention only to this moment, and this beautiful boy's body against mine. I could feel the muscles moving in his back. His hand slipped under my shirt, and his fingers clasped my waist. I clutched his shoulders when he bit hard.

Then I opened my eyes and saw a blurry, transparent shape above in the white branches and fluttering leaves. I blinked and watched in wonder as the shape grew denser and dark. It didn't move even though the branches thrashed, raining narrow leaves down on us.

"Lucky . . ." I said, but he kept sucking at my earlobe and then he grunted and shuddered.

As he lay atop me, breathing heavily, the shadow dissolved into mist, into nothingness. It was nothing.

Lucky pushed my hair back and started dreamily licking the traces of blood on my neck and behind my ear. I longed for more from him, and pressed my body against his, but he only gave a groan and nestled his face against the side of my head.

I stayed still even though a bump on the boulder jabbed my shoulder blade. I lay there uncomfortably, conscious of slick sweat on my skin where his hand still gripped my waist. I wondered if I should feel happier because I'd given him what he wanted. After a few minutes, he sighed and flipped onto his back. He licked a smudge of blood off his lips and murmured *mmmm*.

I stared up at the branches, which had stopped rustling as the breeze died down.

"Goddamn noisy trees." Lucky swatted leaves off his shoulders with the same annoyance that people swat at mosquitoes.

"I thought I saw something up there. A shadow in the branches."

He glowered at the leafy canopy. "The trees are nothing but shade and mess. I'd like to take a chain saw to all of them."

"You wouldn't!"

"No, I wouldn't. My parents might get over it, but Jack would kill me."

"The trees are so graceful and now I love the sound— it's like they're whispering and singing." *Susurration*, I thought, but I didn't want to share that word with Lucky.

"I wish they'd shut the hell up. Let's go back and I'll take care of your ear." He lifted me down from the boulder easily.

"You're really strong."

"You're small." He put his arm around me. "We do have more muscle mass and faster reflexes, which gives me an advantage in sports. Not that I could ever be in competitive swimming because I can't take the chance that my sunblock will wash off. For every advantage, there's a disadvantage, but I'd rather be what I am anyway."

We went to the cottage and he got a tube of antibiotic ointment from the bathroom. He smeared the ointment on the back of my stinging lobe and massaged it into the cut, as cheerful as when we'd first met. "I really liked that, Jane, but it's between us until you officially agree."

"We could have waited."

"I couldn't. I waited for two years for Bebe." Lucky put his hand on my chin and tilted it up so that I was looking right at him. "That's why you always need to remember that you're *my* Companion."

"I'll remember, but you've got to remember that this is a reciprocal relationship. You're tied to me, too, Lucky."

His brows went up, startled, and then his smile returned. "I'll remember, Jane, and I'll take care of you as faithfully as my father cared for Aunt Claire."

It was when I was about sixteen that a certain dream first came to me, and this is how it befell. It opened with my being set down at the door of a big red-brick house, where, I understood, I was going to stay. The servant who opened the door told me that tea was being served in the garden, and led me through a low dark-panelled hall, with a large open fireplace, on to a cheerful green lawn set round with flower beds.

E. F. Benson, "The Room in the Tower" (1912)

Chapter 26

Mr. and Mrs. Radcliffe scheduled Thursday for me, starting with breakfast at their house. Lucky opened the front door and asked me to wait in the living room. I pulled my hair forward to cover my ear and went to the display of the family photos.

Lucky had been a striking child with silver-blond hair. Jack was a smaller version of himself, a sturdy kid with a mischievous expression and a mop of curls. Mrs. Radcliffe looked the same, displaying her familiar serene expression throughout the years. The only one who had changed noticeably was Tobias Radcliffe. He'd been robust and quite handsome, with a confident stance.

"Jane, come on." Lucky was standing in the doorway, dazzling me all over again.

We went into the family room, where his parents were drinking coffee. Mr. Radcliffe said, "Lucky told us the good news, Jane. Welcome to the family."

Or maybe he said *the Family,* but the term thrilled me—this gracious, attractive, and sophisticated family thrilled me. "Thank you, sir."

"My own Companion, Claire Mason, was a very important part of my life. We met when she was only fourteen." In that moment, he seemed years younger and handsome. "She was so bright and so eager to be my Companion."

Mrs. Radcliffe flashed a sharp look at her husband. "We *all* loved Claire. Jane, come have breakfast."

I sat at the table, which had a basket of pastries, a bowl of fruit salad with raspberries and blackberries, and a glass pitcher of red liquid.

Lucky picked up the pitcher and poured a glass for me. "It's orange juice from blood oranges. Different color, same taste."

Jack came in as we began to eat. He grabbed a cranberry muffin and said hi to no one in particular.

"Jacob, Jane has accepted our offer. Isn't that wonderful?" Mrs. Radcliffe smiled, but there was an edge of steel in her voice.

Jack's keen eyes caught mine for only a moment, making me feel . . . something like guilt, but I had done nothing wrong. "Jane, if that's what you want, congratulations. I've got practice." Then he left without another word.

"Jacob's not a morning person." Mrs. Radcliffe began talking about the improvements at the country club, a surreal twist to the morning. I tried not to stare at Lucky and kept touching my hair to make sure it covered my ear.

"We need to get a membership for you to the club, Jane," Mr. Radcliffe said. "You can't join on your own until you're twenty-five, so we'll sponsor you and cover the fees."

"Thanks, but I'm not really interested in joining."

"The club is part of Lucky's life, of life here in Greenwood, so it will be part of yours, too," Mrs. Radcliffe said. "Joining the right clubs and organizations is always a good idea. Knowing the right people can make your life much easier."

"I'd rather be judged by what I do, not who I know."

"Why not make things easier when you can?" Lucky said.

"In an ideal world, one is judged by one's accomplishments," Mrs. Radcliffe said. "And in an ideal world, friends help friends."

The doorbell rang and Mrs. Radcliffe said, "That must be Hattie."

Lucky jumped up. "I'll let her in."

His mother said, "Jane, I hope you don't mind that we shared our good news with Hattie. She can answer many of your questions, but you can't tell anyone else about us ever. Our lives depend upon confidentiality."

Mr. Radcliffe folded his newspaper and set it aside. "Eventually you'll be able to spot a Family member at a glance. We have friends among the long-established townspeople, too."

"Like the librarian and the grocery store manager," I guessed.

Mrs. Radcliffe said, "We had to be careful until we were sure of you."

A few minutes later, Hattie came in by herself. "Welcome to the Family, Jane!"

"Thanks!"

"I'm so glad I have another girl my age to talk to about this stuff. Where's Jack?"

"He went to practice," Mrs. Radcliffe said.

"He doesn't have . . ." she began, confused. "Oh, that's right. I forgot that he'd told me they were starting early."

Lucky didn't come back to the family room and no one asked where he'd gone. Mrs. Radcliffe refilled my juice glass. "Jane, we do have an initiation ceremony to formalize your relationship with the Family. It was scheduled for Lucian's Companion some time ago, and it's coming up in a few weeks. I know it's soon, but Hattie will coach you about your part. I hope you'll enjoy our traditions, although my sons think they're . . ."

"Hokey," Mr. Radcliffe said. "Lucky thinks they're hokey and boring, and Jack thinks they're hilarious, which is why he is excused from participating."

Mrs. Radcliffe sighed. "I told you a headmistress's own children were her greatest challenge. Jane, you'll need more clothes now that you'll be accompanying Lucian to functions and gatherings. Hattie's going to take you shopping and help you pick out the right things."

"I'll transfer over enough to your bank account right now, Jane, to cover your expenses." Mr. Radcliffe tucked his newspaper under his arm and left the room.

Hattie popped a berry in her mouth. "Jane, do you mind going now? I've got a ton of work."

"That's fine. Thank you, Mrs. Radcliffe."

"Be sure to be back by three, because you and Lucky have a meeting with a Companion counselor."

As Hattie and I walked outside to her car, she shoved on a canvas hat and put on sunglasses. "There's a mall near Millerton. I thought we could go there."

"Good, because the stores in Greenwood are too expensive."

Hattie leaned against the car. "Jane, we are a big extended family, but this is also a business relationship. Lucky is going to be asking a lot from you, so be sure to get what you need from us. Is he already taking your blood?"

I didn't answer and Hattie frowned. "I thought so."

She drove to the most luxurious mall I'd ever seen. Water splashed in big fountains and a jazz pianist played in a courtyard. We went into department stores I'd only heard about. She ignored price tags while she picked out clothes. "Most of these pants and skirts are too long, but we can have them altered in town. You'll need a few LBDs."

"What?"

"LBD is Little Blue Dress, the Birch Grove equivalent of the Little Black Dress. Blue is seen as more appropriate for young women and the Family likes us to dress for the events, which are things like birthdays and graduations, recitals and the holiday parties."

"What about the ceremonies?"

"They're optional and we have traditional robes for those."

As we left one store, Hattie said, "Oh, I think I left my sunglasses in the dressing room. I'll be back in a minute."

While I waited, I wandered away to look in the window of a bakery and then noticed someone inside waving at me. I went in and saw Orneta behind the counter. "Hey, Or-nery! I wondered where you went."

"Hey, Jane! Well, you know I wanted out of that place, and this job came up. It doesn't pay as good, but it's closer to home and a lot less creepy. How's everything?"

"Good. The school is amazing."

She gave me a free cookie and then some customers came in so we waved good-bye. I felt better now that I knew nothing bad had happened to her.

I ate my cookie and people-watched until Hattie came rushing up to meet me. She was holding a shopping bag and said, "Sorry! I made an impulse purchase while I was there. Let's eat."

Hattie and I had lunch at a chic little restaurant with white tablecloths and waiters dressed in white shirts and black slacks. After we ordered, Hattie said, "I'm surprised you didn't run away when you learned about us."

"Actually I did, but being away made me realize how much I missed Birch Grove and my friends here." I paused. "Besides, I want to help Lucky."

"Lucky is gorgeous, rich, and has everything he wants, Jane. Why would he *need* your help?" She spoke quickly and caught herself. "What I mean is, do this for yourself, Jane, not for someone else."

"But I *want* to help him, Hattie. Let's face it, everyone sells themselves somehow, and I'm getting something in exchange for what I'll give Lucky. I've never had a family before and . . ." I paused. "Is it only the men who have Companions?"

"Only the men. Girls have to control themselves and act like ladies, even when we want to rip someone's throat out and drain their bodies." She saw my expression and added,

"Kidding! Supposedly, the guys can be dangerous because they're impulsive and strong."

"Why do you say 'supposedly'?"

"Well, they are strong, but individuals within the Family have different characteristics. Some are more tolerant of the sun and a few abstain from human blood. So when the guys in our branch say they need a secure source of the fresh stuff, we women have to take their word for it. But maybe the men only say that they need Companions, when they really *want* them."

"Hattie, what's tasting blood feel like to you?"

She hesitated. "Animal blood is really pleasurable, like good wine, I guess. But human blood is more like the best drug in the world, and it can be, uhm, arousing with the right person."

"So it's not sexual?"

She shrugged. "It makes my body feel so good all over that I don't even have the words to describe what it's like." She looked away, and I wondered if she was thinking of drinking Jack's blood. The image of them together upset me, but I didn't know why. What Jack did with his Titania wasn't my business.

By the time we finished shopping, I had several new tops, pants, skirts, dresses, and shoes, from flats to heels to graceful sandals. Hattie steered me to the accessories section of a store. "Mrs. Radcliffe disapproves of showy Trendy Status Accessories, but you should have a few nice things."

"Won't people wonder why a scholarship girl has a TSA?" I asked. "Not to mention the new clothes."

"We'll say a donor gifted the clothes to you. The trick is to find TSAs that don't have obvious labels all over them." Together we picked out a tote, handbags, and evening bags that didn't have noticeable logos. The shocking totals gave me my first real concept of how my life would be different from now on.

On the way back, Hattie stopped in Greenwood and parked in front of a jeweler's. "I need to get something fixed."

While she showed the jeweler the broken clasp on a necklace, I looked at a display of men's watches, wishing I could afford to give Lucky something.

"Jane, come try these on," Hattie said as the jeweler brought out a blue velvet tray with rows of sparkling rings. Hattie pointed to an emerald ring. "This is your color."

I tried it on and it rolled sideways. "It's too big."

"You have delicate hands. This might fit better." The jeweler slid a sapphire and diamond ring onto my finger. "How does that feel?"

I held up my hand and admired the way the gems refracted the light. "Perfect. Thank you." I handed it back to him.

Hattie was playing with an ornate topaz and diamond bracelet. "This is the sort of big, shiny thing Mary Violet would adore." She waved her hands and mimicked Mary Violet's dramatic voice. "So tragic that the rest of the world isn't as glamorous as *moi*!" Hattie moved along the counter to a display of penknives. "Maybe Lucky will get you one. Wouldn't you like one?"

I checked to make sure we were out of the jeweler's range of hearing. "He offered, but then I'd be like all the Hellsdale girls who constantly threaten to 'cut a bitch.'"

"Oh, we say that, too, but we mean cut them off socially."

When we got back to campus, Hattie helped carry my shopping bags to the cottage. "You seem very okay about all this, Jane. I'd be tripping if someone told me there were werewolves and they'd chosen me to be a werewolf's BFF and feed him dog chow during the full moon."

"There *aren't* werewolves, are there?"

"I heard a story once, but it was completely ridiculous. It sounded exactly like something Mary Violet would write."

"She's obsessed with alternative realities, you know. She'd love to find out about the Family."

"Oh, she'd think we aren't glamorous enough because we don't wear capes and shapeshift into bats and say 'I vant to suck your blood.' "

My mouth twitched up as I remembered Jack's pronunciation of Latin. "Can I ask you something, Hattie?"

"Sure."

"What's Jack's problem about me and Lucky? It's my body and my life, and I can do what I want." I didn't want to tell her about my encounters with Jack and the crazy things he said to me, or the bewildering feelings he stirred within me. "One minute he's nice to me and the next minute, he's hypercritical. I don't think he likes me."

She unpacked clothes from a shopping bag and put them on a chair before speaking. "Jack likes you. He thinks you were brought here too soon after Bebe left, but Lucky insisted on having a Companion now. Jack and I both think Lucky needs more self-discipline and maturity before he makes that kind of commitment."

"The way that Jack has self-discipline?" I raised my eyebrows.

"Okay, you've got a point, but Jack's different. He's artistic and he is disciplined about his music. The important thing is that Lucky likes you." She checked her watch. "I've got to hit the books and you've got to meet with the counselor."

"Thanks, Hattie, for everything. For being so nice from the start."

"I know what it's like being different, Jane. Besides, as a Companion, you'll get all the Family as friends for life, and that includes me, too."

Maybe it was because of the way that Wilde and I had parted, but I put out my hand. "Friends for life, promise?"

Hattie hugged me. "Friends for life, promise."

I felt so happy that I'd never lose her, and when we stepped apart I said, "And I guess I get Jack for life, too." I rolled my eyes and laughed, although I was wondering how I would feel seeing Jack through the years at parties, birthdays . . . at his wedding.

And there she lulled me asleep,
And there I dream'd—Ah! woe betide!
The latest dream I ever dream'd
On the cold hill's side.

I saw pale kings, and princes too,
Pale warriors, death pale were they all;
They cried—"*La belle dame sans merci*
Hath thee in thrall!"

John Keats, "La Belle Dame sans Merci" (1820)

Chapter 27 I spent too long trying on my new clothes, wanting to dress right for my meeting with the Companion counselor. I decided on a plain navy skirt and a white blouse. When I arrived at the house, Mrs. Radcliffe said, "You're quite the young lady now! The counselor is in my husband's study."

She guided me to a wood-paneled room with a big dark desk and floor-to-ceiling bookshelves on three walls. Lucky was slouched in an armchair, his legs sprawled out, and an older woman sat at the desk.

She had a chic, short haircut and a small, angular face. Rimless glasses were propped on her button nose. She wore a soft yellow sweater, a floral print skirt, and a dramatic necklace of turquoise and amber stones.

"Nina, this is Jane Williams. Jane, this is Nina York," Mrs. Radcliffe said. "I'll be in the family room if you need me for anything." She left, closing the door behind her.

"Good morning, Jane! Please have a seat." Ms. York held her hand toward the sofa and I sat next to Lucky.

"Hey, Jane." He had an annoyed and wary look, like he'd just been handed a pop quiz.

"Hello, ma'am," I said to the counselor. "Hi, Lucky."

"Congratulations, Jane!" Ms. York said. "I know how exciting this is for you. My parents died when I was young, they were addicts, and I was on the streets before the Family rescued me." She didn't say that she had *worked* the streets, but that was the implication.

I peeked at Lucky, thinking about how I'd pleased him. "I'm glad they rescued me, too."

"Excellent! Now let's go over safety precautions. I cannot stress enough the importance of being careful in your interactions. Jane, never let a cut or open wound make contact with Lucian's blood. It's natural for Normals to want to try blood tasting in our special relationships." She saw my surprised expression. "Believe me, it's common. Simple ingestion will have no ill effects. However, if you have a cut in your mouth, the blood play can have . . . dire results. It's best never to take that chance."

"What happens if Lucky's hurt, or in an accident? Shouldn't I help him?"

"Lucian, would you mind showing Jane?"

"Sure." Lucky pulled out his penknife and, before I could stop him, he scored the back of his hand with the blade. The cut filled with blood and then, as we watched, the wound began to close up as the skin slowly mended itself. Lucky licked off the blood to reveal unmarked skin.

"Thank you, Lucian," Ms. York said. "Jane, members of the Family heal easily from minor injuries, so that's not a concern. If Lucian's badly injured, you must contact us immediately so one of our medical teams can get to him before anyone else. Never, *ever* rely on any outside medical assistance. It endangers both the Family and the unaware medics."

"Let's move on." She reached for a maroon leather satchel and placed it on the desk. She unpacked surgical gloves, antiseptic spray, rubbing alcohol, bandages, a scalpel, a hypodermic needle, disinfectant wipes, a length of rubber tubing, and small glass cylinders. "Here are some popular tools for safe and healthy bloodletting. Come take a look."

Lucky quickly went to the desk, a blush of excitement on his cheeks.

I went to the desk and picked up a cylinder with a needle at one end.

Ms. York said, "That's a venipuncture vacuum system, a highly efficient way of taking a sample. Of course, most partners prefer a more intimate transfer, which is acceptable since the condition isn't contagious through saliva."

"I like it warm and fresh," Lucky said.

"Then you need to come to an agreement about scarring. Some partners relish seeing evidence of their relationship, and others want to minimize scarring. Have you talked about it?"

When I said "I don't want scars," Lucky's eyes narrowed in irritation.

Ms. York noticed his reaction. "That's a wise decision. Over the course of many years, scar tissue builds up, Lucky, and will obstruct blood draws. I'm sure you don't want that."

She demonstrated the different ways to take blood. "Jane, while we don't condone underage alcohol consumption, we make an exception for use as pain management during more *intimate* withdrawals. A glass of wine or a cocktail can help you relax and, well, enjoy the submissive experience. There are also topical anesthetics. Obviously, they reduce your partner's pleasure."

"It hasn't been bad, Ms. York."

Lucky frowned worriedly. "I don't want it to hurt Jane." At that moment I thought he was the most wonderful boy in the world.

"That's very thoughtful, Lucky, and Jane may come to relish the intensity of a withdrawal without any dulling substances. It is how one chooses to interpret the sensations," she said suggestively. "We can discuss that another time."

After quizzing us on what we had learned, she smiled at Lucky, who was rolling a hypodermic in his long fingers.

"Now I've got a brand-new instructional video to illustrate recommended bloodletting techniques!"

I felt queasy watching the couple on-screen siphon red-purple blood with a needle and use a scalpel to cut skin. Lucky had a glazed look that I recognized. He could barely pay attention to the rest of the session, which dealt with the initiation ceremony.

"How nice that Harriet Tyler will help you with the ceremony, Jane! She's one of our shining lights." Then Ms. York gave each of us a bag with bloodletting supplies. "This is your starter kit. Once you get an idea of your needs and preferences, I'll set up regular deliveries."

"Great, thanks!" Lucky said. "Can I keep the video, too?"

"Of course. You may want to review the techniques together. Will your partnership—or does it already—include sexual activity? I can advise you about special precautions."

"No, that's not necessary," Lucky said quickly.

"In the old days, you know, it was a customary part of the relationship, and it's still not uncommon. I don't mean to shock you, Jane, but your relationship with Lucky will be closer and more permanent than that with any lover. You may come to see that offering him sex when he feeds adds a thrilling dimension in your experiences."

My face was hot with embarrassment, and Ms. York patted my hand. "All of our discussions and dealings are completely confidential, dear. Lucian's parents will not be told, whatever your decision."

Lucky stood and asked, "When can we start, Ms. York?"

"The Council's given their approval. You can start now, although your parents hope that you'll wait until after the initiation."

"What council?" I asked.

"The Council acts as our governmental body, since the Family can't go to the standard authorities for many matters," Ms. York said. "Let me put these things away and we can talk more at dinner."

"Thanks for the info." Lucky took my hand. "Come on, Jane."

I thought he was going to lead me to the family room, but he tugged me toward the front door, his large hand enveloping my small one. Jack, wearing clean jeans and a striped button-down shirt, was walking into the hall from upstairs.

"Jack, tell Mom we can't make dinner."

"Tell her yourself," Jack said.

"I have *Family* things to do."

"What? You're going to suck the elfkin dry of her vital fluids? Big man."

"Shut up, jackass. You don't know anything about my needs! You're not one of us!"

"What? Not a useless douche?" Jack flipped his brother off, and then he glared at me. "So you're going to drink the Kool-Aid, Jane? Why am I even asking?"

"You have no right to tell me what to do," I said, but something inside me felt . . . awful, like I'd done something terrible and stupid. Why did Jack always make me *feel* so much?

"Why do you give a damn what she does?" Lucky shoved his brother's chest.

Jack raised a fist, ready to swing, when Mr. Radcliffe came to the hallway. "Jacob!"

Lucky grinned at his father. "Hi, Dad. Jane and I are having dinner at her place. See you later."

I went with Lucky as far as the foyer before twisting my hand out of his and stopping. "No."

"No what?"

"No, you can't drag me around like a dog on a leash. I already said I'd be at dinner and I want to talk to Ms. York. When I say I'll do something, I do it."

"Are you lecturing me?"

"I'm stating facts."

For a moment, I thought he was angry. Then he nodded and his golden locks fell into his face. "Okay, you're right. That was totally rude. Jane, keep me grounded, okay? Tell me when I'm a jerk."

I felt huge relief. "Okay. You're being a jerk."

"I'm sorry. *Now* can we go and play with our new toys?"

"It's not playing and they're not toys. I do it because you need it and we can wait till later."

"Okay, we'll do it later. I'm going to talk to my dad." Lucky headed toward the study, where his father and Ms. York were meeting.

I went to the family room and saw Mrs. Radcliffe tossing a salad and Jack getting plates from the cupboard. "May I help with anything?"

She gave me a warm smile that made me grateful that this incredible woman would be in my life forever. "Why don't you help Jack set the table?"

He ignored me as I copied his placement of forks, knives, and glasses. But then, as we passed by each other, he leaned so close that his curls brushed my face as he whispered, "The Halfling rebels against her master."

I stomped on his foot. "Oh, sorry."

The others joined us, and Lucky was as friendly to his brother as if nothing had happened. *Is this what family is?* I wondered.

When Ms. York came into the room, she beamed at Jack. "Jacob Radcliffe, how wonderful to see you again!"

"Hi, Nina! So tell me, are you at all interested in a younger man?" He raised one eyebrow rakishly.

"Keep dreaming," she said, laughing girlishly and reminding me of Wilde.

If Ms. York had been able to make a good life for herself after being out on the streets, then so could Wilde. When I had a minute alone with the counselor, I said, "I'd really like to talk more about the Family and what's expected of me."

She placed her hand on mine and squeezed, and I noticed that she wore a gold ring with a red gem on her right hand. "I'll be coming for your initiation and staying a few days. I'll set aside a few hours exclusively for you. How about then?"

"That would be great."

Lucky waited through the long meal before asking, "Jane, may I walk you home?"

"I'd like that."

He tried to keep a relaxed pace, but halfway down the trail he said, "Come on," and began jogging. I stumbled in the darkness, and he dashed back and swung me up in his arms.

In a sudden panic, I shoved at Lucky's chest and he let me down, saying, "What?"

There was something about being outside in the darkness and being grabbed up. My heart raced, but it was only Lucky and only the grove. "I don't like it when you pick me up without asking! I don't like the way you drag me around like a possession, not a person."

"Chill, Jane. I was just trying to help," he said, irritated. "Okay, I'm sorry." He took out his phone and used it to light the way for me.

We got inside the cottage, and he waited while I turned on the lights and closed the curtains. "Jane, will you please let me have a taste?"

"All right."

"Do you want to try the topical anesthetic?"

"No, I don't need it, but try to be careful."

He opened my bag of supplies and selected the lancet. It was a scalpel with a two-sided blade. He disinfected it with the same anticipation I'd seen in the faces of addicts setting up their works. "Lie facedown on the bed."

I pulled off my flats and did as he asked.

He sat beside me and began to stroke my back under my blouse, and my anxiety and longing became almost unbearable. Lucky hitched up my blouse and unhooked my bra. He began rubbing my skin, all the way from my shoulders to my waist. His fingers kneaded the tense places. "Your skin is so smooth, Jane, so soft."

I closed my eyes and gave in to the petting and stroking, making those small animal sounds of pleasure as he caressed my legs, massaging them from my feet upward. His fingers moved in circles at the backs of my knees, then pressed the skin to make my veins appear.

His hands moved upward to examine the insides of my thighs, pushing up my skirt, and I held my breath wondering what he'd do next—and wondering what I wanted him to do.

"There are good arteries here, rich with your blood, Jane."

But his hands moved to my back again. He explored a spot under my shoulder blade and gently rubbed until I relaxed with a sigh. That's when I felt the knife slice into my skin.

I bit the pillow to keep from crying.

When Lucky groaned I knew he was watching the blood rise in the cut and then he put his mouth to it and began feeding from me. He fell to the bed beside me and gripped my shoulders as he alternately sucked the wound and probed it with his tongue.

He became more aggressive and his teeth nipped at the edges of the cut, sending darts of pain through me, but the pillow muffled the whimpers that escaped me.

When Lucky finally became aware of my discomfort, he began stroking my back again, soothing me while still latched on the wound.

I have Lucky, I have him, I thought, but I kept recalling the lust on his face when he'd seen the video.

Lucky's hand stopped massaging and he bit down hard, bringing tears to my eyes. And when he moaned, I felt the reverberations from his chest against me more than heard the sound. He took his mouth from my flesh, and his breathing was ragged.

Then he bent over me again and gently licked the cut

and the area around it. He smoothed a hand over my hair. He did this for long exquisite minutes until the pain was forgotten and all I felt was happiness at being the center of his attention.

Lucky sighed deeply and then he rolled to my side and dozed off.

I watched the rise and fall of his chest and the tiny movements of his eyelids. I admired the thickness of his pale lashes and the perfect arch of his eyebrows and the straight line of his nose. I put my hand on his arm and saw the contrast of my skin against his.

I got up and went to the bathroom. I struggled to put ointment and a bandage on my back before changing into a t-shirt and pajama pants. When I returned to the bedroom, Lucky was sprawled asleep on the bed.

An hour later, I shook him. "Lucky, we *still* have to go over your chemistry and I have work to do for class tomorrow."

"Hmm? Oh, we don't need the tutoring anymore. That was only so you'd get to know me."

"Oh."

"Well, okay, my folks *did* hope you'd push me to do better, but it's not like I'm going to major in the sciences. Do you want me to take care of your cut?"

"I already did that."

"Okay. I gotta get going. See you."

"When?"

"I'll want a taste again in a few days. We can try something new with our toys. I mean, medical equipment."

I stood on the porch as he walked up the path and out of sight.

I had a place to live, clothes, cash, a position, and security for life. I had a permanent relationship with a stunning boy. I'd dreamed about having all these things, but I'd never expected to get them so soon and so completely.

Why, then, did I feel so desolate?

In a moment she thought she heard the step of some person. Her blood curdled; she concluded it was Manfred. Every suggestion that horror could inspire rushed into her mind. She condemned her rash flight, which had thus exposed her to his rage in a place where her cries were not likely to draw anybody to her assistance.

Horace Walpole, *The Castle of Otranto* **(1765)**

Chapter 28   I had two weeks until the initiation and I became more anxious with each passing day as I tried to make sense of my place within the Family. In Chem class, whenever I noticed Mr. Mason patting his pocket absentmindedly, I thought of Claire Mason at my age, eager to become a Companion.

I carefully tracked the times Mrs. McSqueak said *hypotenuse* in Trig. I lost myself in the beauty of the equations and came to love the unit circle, the circle with a radius of one. I began to see how angles and circles on infinite planes could describe everything. Even Lucky's face, his voice, and his lanky stroll could be expressed by trigonometry.

Mary Violet caught me daydreaming once and whispered, "Quick, tell me what you're thinking!"

"I was thinking that I wish our personal identities could be expressed as a formula so that we could prove or disprove equality in relationships."

She put the back of her hand against her forehead. "You're making me nervous, Jane."

"I know—it's tragic."

Lucky stopped by on Thursday, just after I'd gotten home from class. He was wearing a forest-green Evergreen hoodie with a white polo and navy cords.

"Hi, Lucky! Come on in!" I could hear the frantic need in my voice.

He dropped his messenger bag on the sofa and sat down. "Glad you're home. I keep telling my mom she needs to get you a phone but she's holding off until after the initiation. You should ask her for a laptop, too. She won't give you a car until you're a senior though."

I didn't mention the burner I had hidden behind the washing machine. "I have the landline. You could call here."

"But what if you weren't here?"

"You could leave a message."

"*I* don't leave messages unless my mother is standing over my shoulder making me. You need to get a phone, so I can text."

He seemed to be in a mood, but I was still happy to see him. "Why don't you stay so we can study together and make dinner?"

"I'm going for burgers with Seasick tonight."

"What?"

"My friend, Christopher Sycamore. C. Syc. I *told* you about him. We're on a paintball team. I was passing by and wanted to say I'll come by tomorrow for a taste to hold me through the weekend."

"Tomorrow is Latin Skit Night and I don't know what time I'll be back."

"Latin is stupid. You should study a real language, maybe Japanese. I plan to go to Japan and if you knew the language, you could be my translator."

"Latin will be useful for my science career."

"Whatever." His bored expression quickly changed. "Hey, we've got the venipuncture kit. We can use it now and I won't have to stop by tomorrow."

I tensed. "I don't know. It just seems really clinical."

"Jane, it'll free up your time for studying because you

know you need good grades or my mom's not going to let me see you so often." His smile lured me in. "Okay?"

I nodded. "Okay."

He had me sit in the armchair. His pupils dilated as he wound the rubber hose around my arm and thumped at my vein as it grew full. He was transfixed as he filled the tube with deep red blood.

He drew out the needle and capped the vial. Blood beaded on the puncture wound and he licked it until it stopped bleeding. With his forefinger, he circled the wound. "That's going to bruise some. You'll have to show me later. You can clean up yourself, right?"

I nodded. "No problem."

He lifted the vial of blood close to his face and his lips parted. Then he put it in the pocket of his hoodie. "See you."

I washed and sterilized the venipuncture equipment and felt the throbbing of my arm.

After my dinner of a peanut butter and jam sandwich and fruit, I rehearsed my part for Skit Night. My study group was performing two scenes from Roman plays by Terence. Although I'd read the English translation, I got lost with the complicated plots of trickery and manipulation. Everything lately made me think of my situation with the Family, including one of my lines: *"Homo sum, humani nil a me alienum puto,"* or "I am a man, I consider nothing that is human alien to me." But the Family was both human *and* alien.

❧ Lucky was right, and I did have a plum-purple bruise on my inner elbow the next day. I had to wear a long-sleeved t-shirt under my toga, which Mary Violet had helped me fashion from an old sheet. The event was at Catalina's house. The girls from my study group picked me up and we drove to an imposing stone mansion. The interior was starkly modern with abstract sculptures on bare stone floors and huge paintings on vast walls.

Catalina's younger sister escorted us downstairs to the ballroom. I didn't even know that private houses could have ballrooms. A maid served elaborate nonalcoholic cocktails garnished with fruit kabobs and edible flowers. Catalina's salmon-pink toga draped so gracefully that it must have been made for her. Her smooth tan arms were bare and she wore heavy gold earrings and a gold collar necklace.

My teacher, Ms. Ingerson, in a saffron-yellow toga, was happier than I'd ever seen her. She got on the small stage and welcomed us in Latin. The seniors did their skits, with the girls wildly exaggerating their parts as both male and female characters. Then it was time for my group to perform our scenes.

After the skits and dinner, Catalina came to me. "I thought you might humiliate yourself. However, you performed competently although dully."

"I'm not stupid, Catalina."

"No, but still naïve, I think, and odd. A frog out of water."

"You mean a fish out of water."

"No, a frog, because a frog is so common, yet it has the peculiar ability to breathe in and out of water," she said with a spark of humor in her amber eyes.

It almost seemed like a compliment. When Ms. Ingerson had left and we were all saying good night at the front door, I heard a familiar voice. Lucky was coming into the house with several of his tall, loud friends. They were shouting, "Toga, toga, toga!" and were dressed in sheets. One hefted a mini-keg on his shoulder and others carried bottles.

Had he come because he knew I'd be here?

But Lucky and his friends went right to Catalina. They fell to their knees and bowed with their arms forward, saying, "Oh, goddess, we are not worthy! We are not worthy!"

She struck a pose, tossing back her long, tawny hair and

pointing at them. "Crawl before me, you miserable mortals!" Several of the senior girls giggled and danced around the guys, play-kicking them and then leaping away.

My heart was in my throat when I saw Lucky stand, pick up Catalina, and carry her back toward the ballroom while she laughed.

I dashed away from the doorway and out into the night, so my classmates wouldn't see my face. I pressed my thumb to the bruise on the inside of my elbow until the pain spread along my arm.

My classmates began talking excitedly and finally the word went around that juniors could stay. A girl in my study group saw me waiting by the car. "Jane, aren't you going to come back? God, did you see Lucky Radcliffe carrying Cat? He's so hot. I would do him in a heartbeat."

"Thanks, but I think I'm going to walk. See you Monday."

"Are you sure?" she asked. "It's late and dark."

"I'll be fine." I began walking and waved back at her. I was so upset that I didn't care that I was wearing a sheet and tennis shoes. My vision was blurred by the tears I was holding back and by a drizzling fog that covered the hillside.

The streets were unfamiliar, but I walked in the direction of Birch Grove, too miserable to care that I might be taking the wrong roads. I was caught up in my anguish when I noticed the hum of an engine on the street behind me. I slunk away from the curb, waiting for the car to drive by.

But it didn't. I peered back over my shoulder and saw the black shape of a car idling in the street with its headlights off, and that was all I needed to see. *Get away as soon as possible!* I hiked up my sheet and tore off as fast as I could, and the car followed, keeping back the same distance.

My only escape was getting off the street. To my left, hedges surrounded a property. I shoved the branches apart only to find my way blocked by a tall metal fence. The car was closer now and I began running again with the sheet winding on my legs, slowing me down.

The driver taunted me by staying close. My foot caught on the sheet and I lurched forward, the cloth ripping, and I windmilled my arms to stay upright.

The dark hedge seemed to go on forever, and my lungs ached and I didn't have the breath to scream even if anyone could hear. I wondered if I should turn back and try to make it to Catalina's. Then I saw the silhouette of the pines in front of the Radcliffes' house. I felt a sharp stabbing pain in my side, and the muscles in my legs burned, but I forced myself forward until I reached the driveway. I flung myself at the front door and pounded against it, gasping, "Help! Help!"

When the door opened, I threw myself into Mr. Radcliffe's arms.

"Jane! What's happened?"

Now I stared up the drive. The street was empty, and I couldn't hear an engine over my own strangled breaths.

My knees buckled and Mr. Radcliffe helped me to the living room. I collapsed on the sofa and he called out, "Hyacinth! Come quick."

I was vaguely aware of them bringing me a glass of water. I was shaking and sweating. "Lock it! Lock the door!" I managed to say.

"What? Jane, you're fine here. You're safe." Mrs. Radcliffe wiped my face with a cool wet cloth. "What's happened?"

Her expression made me look down at myself. Leaves and twigs from the hedges were stuck on my clothes and in my hair. I'd stepped in a puddle somewhere, because my shoes and clothes were muddy. I was drenched in sweat and my sheet had fallen off one arm. I gulped down the whole glass of water before saying, "I was at Latin Skit Night at Catalina's house. When I was walking back, a car followed me. I ran, but it kept following me."

"Why were you walking? Did you see who was driving?"
I shook my head.

"Jane, could it have been someone from the party, perhaps making sure you got home safely?" Mrs. Radcliffe said.

"The driver didn't have the headlights on and that means . . . it means a drive-by, something bad's going down."

Mr. and Mrs. Radcliffe exchanged a look, and she said, "Maybe in Helmsdale, but not here, Jane. Here it means some kid didn't turn on the lights. Or an elderly driver forgot to turn her headlights on and was concerned about a girl by herself late at night."

"Do you think so?" It sounded plausible.

"Yes, I think so." Mrs. Radcliffe smoothed back my hair. "We have never had a shooting here, Jane, or an abduction. It doesn't happen in Greenwood."

Mr. Radcliffe frowned. "It was enough to scare Jane, and we should call the police."

His wife gave him a look. "For all we know, someone thought Jane was the suspicious one, walking around like a ghost in that sheet."

Mr. Radcliffe went to a liquor cabinet and poured a tumbler full of amber liquid. "Would you like a drink, Jane, to collect yourself?"

"No."

He swirled the liquid in the glass and then tossed it back.

Mrs. Radcliffe said, "Jane, you'll feel better in the morning. I'll set up a room for you."

I couldn't bear to stay here lying awake and listening for Lucky to get home. "No, I want to go to my place."

"Only if Mr. Radcliffe sees you safely home. I'm going to call the police station and tell them there's a driver without lights scaring our students."

While she made the call, Mr. Radcliffe went with me to the front door and then said, "It's cold out. Wait here." He returned wearing a jacket and carrying an old sweatshirt with the Dog Waffle logo. I pulled off the toga and slipped on the sweatshirt. I knew whose it was immediately by the faint, comforting scent of leaves and fields.

Mr. Radcliffe seemed uneasy as we went down the hill. I stumbled and he caught me by the elbow to steady me. "I should have brought a flashlight. I forgot that you don't have our night vision."

"It's okay," I answered, but I let him guide me through the grove.

We were quiet until we got close to the amphitheater. "We haven't talked much, Jane, but I hope we'll get to know each other well."

I nodded. "Me, too."

"Did you have fun at Skit Night?"

"It was a class assignment," I answered too sharply.

He sighed heavily. "I know Lucky went to Catalina's. I asked him not to because we knew you'd be there. We've instructed him to keep his distance from you in public places until things settle down within the Family. It's been a disruptive year."

I was pitifully grateful to hear this. "Thanks for explaining. I didn't mind, Mr. Radcliffe."

"Call me Toby, Jane."

I saw the shine of his smile in the gloom. "I didn't want to stay anyway. I'm not a partyer, Toby." It felt awkward to call him that.

"Lucky is. I hope you'll be a good example to him, Jane. You have such a strong work ethic and you seem emotionally grounded and steady, which are the most important qualities in a Companion. And freshness, of course. When Claire was young, her blood was dazzlingly pure, so vibrant with health."

I heard him inhale deeply and then let out the breath. Then he said, "I'm glad we have the chance to have this talk."

"Yes, sir."

"Toby."

"Yes, I mean, it's been nice, Toby."

My nerves were jangling as we walked to my porch. The porch light was on and I could see now that he was a little drunk. Then his glazed eyes fixated on my throat and he said, "Would you like me to come in and check out the place for you?" He leaned so close to me that I could smell the whiskey on his breath. "Jane, I could tell you about my relationship with Claire, how amazing it was, how she fed me. You must be curious."

I had been misinterpreting so many things and I didn't know if I was misinterpreting his intentions. "No, thank you, no." I moved to one side. "I know you and Mrs. Radcliffe were probably enjoying an evening alone."

"You seemed very upset." He came close again. "We should get to know each other better, Jane."

I put my key in the lock and turned it so I wasn't facing him anymore. "We can talk another time. I overreacted because where I come from, you have to always be wary."

"Hellsdale. We rescued Claire from that."

My hand was on the doorknob, and I looked back. "Thank you for seeing me home, Mr. Radcliffe."

"Toby." Then he stared into the trees as they whispered in the breeze. "Mrs. Radcliffe and I want you to come to the house Sunday afternoon. A Council Director, our representative on our governing organization, will be interviewing you."

"I thought everything was approved."

"It is, but Lucky's a special young man, so special circumstances apply. Eventually my son will take over my seat on the Council's education committee, as well as the responsibility of Birch Grove Academy."

"But I thought the headmistress was in charge."

"Only of the school's administration. I'm president of the Board of Trustees. Officially, Birch Grove is a nonprofit corporation. In reality, I own it." Mr. Radcliffe's gaze lingered on my neck. "Sunday at three then."

"I'll be there. Good night."

To my relief, Mr. Radcliffe put his hands in his pockets and walked back toward his house.

When I got inside, I was so shaken up that I didn't notice for several minutes that the red light of my answering machine was blinking. I punched the button and could barely hear Lucky's voice because he was speaking quietly with lots of background noise. "Sorry I didn't say hi, but we gotta keep a low profile. Until it's official. Night."

The fact that he'd left a message was as soothing as the way he licked my wounds, and I played the message over and over again while I pressed the collar of the sweatshirt to my nose and breathed in the comforting green scent. Everything would be better when Lucky and I were official.

She spoke: a soft soothing voice, a voice that carried a spell with it, and affected us both strangely, particularly the rector. I wished to test as far as possible, without endangering our lives, the Vampire's power.

F. G. Loring, "The Tomb of Sarah" (1900)

Chapter 29 On Sunday, when I went to the Radcliffes', I saw a gleaming black Mercedes parked in the driveway.

My headmistress answered the door. "Come on in, Jane. The Director is talking to Lucian in Mr. Radcliffe's study. Let's wait in the family room."

As we passed the living room, I noticed vases of fresh flowers on the polished tables and a fire burning in the fireplace.

Mrs. Radcliffe said, "You look like a different girl than you did the other night, Jane. Quite the young lady."

"Hattie told me that I should wear LBDs to Family meetings. I'm sorry, but I left Jack's sweatshirt—Mr. Radcliffe loaned it to me—at the cottage. I can go back and get it."

"He's got a drawer full of them, and he won't miss it. Or maybe *I* won't miss it. Jacob's practicing with his band today." She nervously played with a long strand of pearls. "It will only be a little wait."

"Mrs. Radcliffe, what made you decide to teach Night Terrors?"

She looked pleased. "I started reading supernatural mythology when I was young. I was trying to find out why people hated and feared us so much. The more I read, the more I understood that literature reflects zeitgeist, which means the cultural climate of an age. I became fascinated with the progression of supernatural literature in conjunction with social and political movements, and that's how my course developed."

"What does current supernatural fiction tell you about our, uhm . . ."

"Zeitgeist." She spelled it out. "I'll tell you when I prepare my class for next year."

"In other words, you haven't figured it out yet."

Mrs. Radcliffe laughed, something she didn't do often. "You are an astute young woman, Jane. Is there anything else you'd like to ask me?"

"Have your kind always existed?"

"We've traced our people to villages on the Black Sea. When the traders on the Silk Road intermarried with the villagers, our genetic anomaly appeared in their children. Our kind migrated from those villages north and west. Our largest populations were in Eastern Europe." She paused. "Most of us were wiped out by genocidal campaigns instigated by those who wanted to take our lands and wealth, but you won't find that in the history books."

"That's what I told Hattie about history! It's inherently biased because it's always written by those who win the battles."

"That may be true, Jane, but we can still glean facts by analyzing a range of source material." Then we heard voices and movement at the front of the house, and Mrs. Radcliffe's hand went to her necklace again. "It's time. Be yourself, Jane, and you'll be fine."

She led me into the living room. I'd expected Lucky to be there, but there was only Mr. Radcliffe and another man, a man who made Tobias Radcliffe seem worn and shabby.

The visitor had deep brown curly hair, hooded brown eyes, strong features, and wore a flawless black suit and snowy-white shirt. Almost six feet and broad-chested, he emanated power even as he stood casually with a glass of red wine.

"This is Jane Williams," Mrs. Radcliffe said, but she didn't introduce him to me.

"Hello, Jane." The man's disarming smile made me feel that we had just shared a private joke. "Hyacinth and Tobias, I'd like to talk to Jane alone."

"Of course." Mrs. Radcliffe blushed prettily, and I wondered what she'd been like when she was my age.

When they left, the man waved to a tray of wine and soda on a side table. "Would you like something to drink, Jane?"

"No, thank you, sir. You know my name, but I don't know yours."

"I'm Ian Ducharme. I represent this region on the Council. Not that Hyacinth leaves much for us to do. She likes to control every detail of her school and the town operates quite smoothly." His voice was low and persuasive and, although his English was perfect, he seemed foreign. "Shall we sit?"

He waited until I sat on the sofa and then sat near me, making the hair on the back of my neck rise.

"Jane, you're too young to fully comprehend what a lifetime commitment is. No doubt, the Radcliffes have idealized the relationship in courting you, but Companions sometimes come to regret their decision. They rarely regret the generous compensation." He smiled cynically. "We buy loyalty, Jane. Most people are quite eager to sell it."

I studied him. "You remind me of Jack Radcliffe. He likes to say things to unnerve me. There's a physical resemblance, too."

"So I'm of a type?" he said wryly. "Now I must meet Jack to discover whether you've given me a compliment or not."

"It wasn't meant one way or the other."

"Why not? Don't you wish to cultivate my favor? I have influence in the world, you know, and I'm quite wealthy. Women find me extremely handsome."

His sexuality was as compelling as a riptide, and I wondered what it would be like to feel those white teeth biting into my throat. I glanced away. "For most people, being rich and powerful are synonymous with being handsome."

"That's been to my benefit, Jane. The very people who find me so attractive might decide they are quite mistaken should I ever lose my fortune."

I liked him because he treated me like an equal. "I think you'd get over it."

He had a rich, low laugh. "Now it's my turn to tell you what I think about you. I think Hyacinth may have miscalculated. The best Companions are those who are happiest when they're serving others. I think you do what is required to survive, but I doubt that subservience is your nature. Will you be loyal for a price?"

"Loyalty that can be bought isn't loyalty. I've already promised Lucky that I'll be his Companion. I keep my promises."

"Will you keep your promise for an eternity?"

"I won't live forever. I'll keep it for my lifetime."

"That will have to suffice," he said. "Hyacinth has reviewed your academic records, interviewed your teachers and social workers, and come to the conclusion that you are an ideal candidate for her son. However, when I look into your eyes, I see something other than the simple girl you appear to be."

"I thought Companions were selected because we've all survived unfortunate situations. I'm not special."

I didn't know why he seemed so amused, and he said, "It's a mystery to me why extraordinary young women insist that they're normal." He finished his wine and set down the glass. "I'm rarely contacted in these petty domestic affairs, but the Radcliffes have ambitions for their son and requested my approval."

"Mr. Radcliffe told me that Lucky will be on the Council's education committee and inherit Birch Grove."

"At the very least. The Radcliffes and their Greenwood branch have been petitioning for a new district to be formed and, with it, a new Council Director seat."

"So Lucky could replace you?"

"I'm irreplaceable, Jane, but he might be a colleague." Mr. Ducharme leaned toward me. "What would you like me to tell Hyacinth and Tobias?"

"What I want you to say doesn't matter, does it?"

"Not in the least, but I wondered if you would try to plead your case." He stood and so I stood, too. "Jane, a word of warning—this branch of the Family does not take betrayal lightly. *I* do not take betrayal lightly." He locked eyes with me and I felt the prickly rush of fear. "You may go now."

"Good-bye, Mr. Ducharme."

"Until we meet again, Jane Williams."

Mrs. Radcliffe asked me to wait in the family room. I nervously scraped off my nail polish and expected to be told to leave the school. When she returned, she was beaming. "Mr. Ducharme was absolutely satisfied that you'll be an excellent Companion, Jane! Isn't that wonderful?"

"Yes," I said, surprised, and I hadn't gotten over my surprise an hour later, when Hattie arrived.

"Jane, I heard you passed with flying colors. Congrats!" She gave me a hug. "We're going to run through your part of the ceremony. Only a week more! Can you believe it?"

"It's happening awfully fast. Is Lucky coming?"

Mrs. Radcliffe said, "He only has two lines and he already knows them. Jane, I have something for you." She handed me a small bag that had been on a side table. "A laptop is coming, but you should be able to log on to Birch Grove's computers with your name and student ID number."

I opened the bag to find a new phone and accessories. "Thank you!"

"It doesn't have all the new bells and whistles, but I

believe it's more than adequate for your needs. Your teachers and school numbers have already been entered. Nine-one-one gives you a hotline to *our* emergency services," Mrs. Radcliffe said. "Please respect our Birch Grove regulations about texting and phoning and, Jane, please don't contact your old friends."

She'd paid for the phone, so I nodded, because I could buy my own phone without restrictions later and wouldn't ever need to use the burner. Then Hattie and I walked down to the amphitheater.

"So what did you think of Ian Ducharme?"

"I liked him even though I get the feeling he's really dangerous. It's probably just my imagination."

"You should trust your instincts more. No one will talk about everything he actually does for the Council, but his nickname is the Dark Lord. The few times I've talked to him, I wanted to beg him to ravish me and he's not even my type!"

"Your type? But I thought he resembled Jack a bit."

"Oh, I *meant* that I like guys our age, not older guys."

The marble benches of the amphitheater almost glowed in the dusky light. Hattie pointed to one side. "The local Family members and friends will be standing here when you enter from over there. You walk around the outer circle and then to the center, where an officiate will be waiting. The Council will send someone who knows the ceremonies. You stand in front of him while he says the mumbo-jumbo, which translates into how much we cherish the Companions and the importance of family and duty."

"How do I know it really means that?"

"Because *all* of our ceremonies are about family and duty, but you can ask Mrs. Radcliffe to let you read the Family's ceremonies binder for the exact translation."

Hattie taught me the strange words I'd have to say and rehearsed them with me. I struggled through a sentence several times. "This language is all consonants and no vowels."

"Nobody can pronounce it except the officiates, and they're probably guessing," Hattie told me. "All you have to do is approximate the words, and the adults will be happy. Once you say your lines and Lucky says his lines, there's a tiny jab on your forefinger, enough to get a few drops of blood for symbolism. The officiate will give you a drink of this awful liquor made with herbs from one of the old recipes. You and Lucky each have to take a drink. Mrs. Radcliffe will make sure it's watered down and sweetened so you don't automatically spit it out."

"When I saw the harvest ceremony, everyone was wearing robes."

"You'll get one, and a pretty white dress to wear underneath for the party afterward." She smiled. "I picked it out myself when you were trying on clothes at the mall. The seamstress in town will hem them to the right length so you don't trip."

"That's good, because wearing a toga at Latin Skit Night was harder than I thought it would be. MV would say that it's my tragic fate to wear crazy robes and speak in dead languages."

Mary Violet might have been wrong about me having a good sense of humor, because Hattie barely smiled. "Anyway, the whole thing only takes fifteen minutes and then Lucky will be able to suck your blood happily ever after."

"Hattie, are you absolutely sure this is okay with you?"

She pressed her lips together before saying, "I think Lucky's not ready to have a Companion, but since he's decided to go through with this now, I'm glad it's with you because you'll keep him grounded."

"I'm going to try, but it's not going to be easy."

"Because he's such a prince, I know." She made a face and we laughed. "Jane, I've never told anyone else this, but . . ."

"Don't tell me anything you don't want to."

"I *want* to." Her face lit up. "My plan is to be the first female Council Director. Except for Ian Ducharme, they're ancient sexist geezers with outdated attitudes. They want us to stay hidden forever and stay the way we are. I have so many ideas on how to improve our lives, from political alliances to gene therapy for us and for Normals."

"That sounds amazing! But Mr. Ducharme said that the Radcliffes want Lucky to be a director of a new division."

"He told you that? It's true, but that may not be what Lucky wants. He's not interested in being a policy wonk, and I love all that stuff."

"I don't even know what a policy wonk is, but you can count on me to help any way I can."

"A policy wonk is someone who works out details and strategy to get things done. It will be great to have you on my side." She held her fist toward me. "Grrl power!"

"Grrl power!" I bumped fists with her and thought about the satisfied way Mr. Radcliffe had told me that *he* owned Birch Grove.

Chapter 30 The week before the Sunday ceremony was the longest in my life and I remember each day distinctly.

On Monday, I went to Mary Violet's and, since the sun was out, we studied on the lawn. My friend had raised her skirt and taken off her shoes and socks. "I need to get tan. These are the last rays of the year. I will never give in to the pasty aesthetic like Hattie, although she's the prettiest pasty girl I know. Pasty sounds ugly. She's the prettiest *pallid* girl I know."

"MV, do you ever go to Hattie's house?"

"I used to go sometimes, but I don't even want to anymore since Mrs. Tyler is a terrible horrible heinous snob and she said something mean about Mom's paintings." Mary Violet's blue eyes clouded in hurt. "No one's allowed to say how appalling they are, except us, and that's because we know they're actually marvelous. I think Hattie doesn't get along with her parents."

"Hattie's not snobby at all, though. She's so smart and thoughtful."

"She is, as Mrs. Radcliffe says, an exceptional girl." Mary Violet became more serious than I'd ever seen her. "You've been spending so much time with her. I think you like her better than you like me. Constance has all her other friends, and I thought you sort of *got* me, because I think I sort of *get* you. I know I'm too silly . . ." Her voice trailed off.

"MV, you're *fabulously* silly. I'm spending time with Hattie because Mrs. Radcliffe wants her to make sure I'm doing okay here." I wished I could have told MV more and then I decided to share something else. "I was lonely a lot in my life and I don't feel that way here. Please don't give up trying to funnify me. You're improving my vocabulary."

"I noticed!" Mary Violet leaned against me, her golden curls tickling my face. "You can share my family, but you have to agree to share the shame of the paintings."

"I love your mom's paintings."

"Pants on fire!" she said, and started tickling me.

"I love the *birch tree* paintings!" I said before laughter overtook me.

She jumped up. "Do you want to stay for dinner? I can see what we're having."

"Okay."

She went inside, swiping her skirt down and mooing, "Moooom!"

The Holidays chatted and bickered over dinner while I kept thinking that in a few days I would be initiated as Lucky's Companion. Mary Violet drove me back to campus and I asked her to leave me at the gate. I impulsively kissed her cheek before I got out of the car. "You smell good. What's that perfume?"

"Marc Jacobs Violet, because—"

"Because violet is your signature. Good night, MV!"

When I got close to my cottage, I saw Lucky standing on the porch. He was wearing a charcoal leather jacket over a black t-shirt and jeans. I admired his long athletic body even as I hurried my footsteps. He had his phone out and kept texting for a minute while I stood in front of him. He finally raised his head. "I was about to send you a message. Where were you?"

"At Mary Violet's. You could have told me earlier that you wanted to see me, and I would have been here."

He gave me an icy look. "I already have a mother."

"Then you *are* lucky, aren't you?" I snapped.

I could see his expression shift from irritated to regretful. "I'm sorry, Jane. I forgot what it must be like for you."

"You always do that, Lucky. You're rude and then apologetic. If you were more careful before speaking, you wouldn't have to apologize later."

"Correction noted," he said. "I have something for you."

"Come in." I unlocked the door and we went inside.

After I put down my book bag and turned to him, Lucky pulled a small red velvet box out of his pocket. "This is for you, Jane." I savored the surprise as I rubbed my fingers over the plush velvet box. Then I opened it and saw a gold ring with three small red stones, similar to the ring Ms. York had worn.

"It's a Companion ring from the Family. My mother said to tell you that the gold was mined from the Apuseni Mountains and the garnets come from the Banat Mountains in Romania."

I turned the lovely ring so that I could see the inscription inside. There was an *L* over a *J* in curlicue script. Lucian and Jane. Lucky took my hand and slipped the ring on my right ring finger. It fit perfectly. "Is this why Hattie made me try on rings?"

Lucky nodded. "You'll need to take it to the initiation and you can wear it after that. All the Companions have them."

I threw my arms around him. "Thank you, Lucky."

After a moment, he hugged me, too, and said in a husky voice, "Why don't you change into something that shows a little skin?"

I felt suddenly shy. "Okay."

He waited in the living room while I went to the bedroom. On my shopping trip with Hattie, I'd bought rose-pink silk boxers and a matching cami. I put them on and moved my hair forward to cover my scar. I rubbed lotion over my skin and put on lip gloss and mascara. My dresser mirror reflected the same plain Jane I'd always been.

I wanted to be sexy for Lucky, but I felt awkward and nervous. Maybe things would change when he kissed me. I opened the bedroom door and said, "Lucky," twisting the ring on my finger.

He came to the bedroom and his eyes skimmed over my body. "You look good, Jane. I like seeing your skin." He touched the lilac and yellow bruise on my inner arm. Then he kicked off his shoes and peeled off his jacket. His hair shone golden against the black t-shirt.

"You're right and I'm too rude. Maybe I should have paid more attention to Bebe and been nicer and she wouldn't have left." He sat on the bed and said softly, "I'm not going to make that mistake again, Jane. Come here."

I stood in front of him and he pulled me onto his lap. "I want you to enjoy this with me." He stroked my arms slowly and let his fingers linger on the blue veins at my wrists and elbows. Then he pushed me back down onto the bed and I shivered with nerves.

He took off his own shirt and revealed his sleek chest, toned abs, and flat stomach. He was so gorgeous, but I tensed as he lay beside me and ran his hand up my leg and up along my thigh.

"Lucky . . ."

"Ssh." He nuzzled and bit and sucked hard at my neck. One hand went under my cami and I gasped as he began caressing me. His hand edged under the waistband of my silk boxers.

I was turned on, but suddenly I knew I didn't want Lucky. I wasn't even sure I liked him. I gripped his wrist before his hand went any farther. "Stop it!"

Lucky drew back. "I thought you wanted that."

I sat up and scooted away from him, bewildered at my

own reaction. "I did, but it's all gotten too confusing and it's happened too fast. I know you don't . . ." It was all so impersonal and he'd never even kissed me. "We don't feel that way about each other, Lucky. Can't we just be friends for now?"

He let out a relieved breath. "Sure. Jane, I really like you, but . . . I like your *blood*. Anyway, there's someone else."

Catalina, of course. "It's okay. I don't want a . . . a pity coitus."

"Hey, guys think *any* coitus is good coitus, and if this was only a hookup, I'd go for it, sure." He laughed and the tension between us eased. "But we're going to be with each other a long time so why mess it up now?"

I'd turned down sex with Lucky Radcliffe and all I felt was a surprising sense of relief. "I totally agree."

"Great. Is it okay to draw a taste since I'm already here?"

"Sure."

He went to the bathroom and came back with the venipuncture tube. "Can I do it behind your knee? I want to tap that vein."

I rolled onto my stomach and remembered that I was doing this for a college education and a career, for a home, for security. There was the sharp jab of the needle and I heard Lucky's intake of breath. A few seconds later, I felt him slide the needle out. He said, "No sense wasting any," and bent to lick at the puncture mark before disinfecting and treating it.

"You've gotten good at it. That hardly hurt at all."

"Thanks. It's better this way anyway, isn't it? Less complications." He gazed yearningly at the tube of blood.

"Maybe we can set up a regular schedule, or I can withdraw the blood myself and you can pick it up, so it won't interfere with our classes and other things."

"Sure. We'll figure it out. Gotta go."

I watched Lucky putting his shirt on. I had craved him the way some girls crave a diamond ring, or an expensive car, or a closet full of designer clothes. I'd wanted to possess him as a spectacular and precious *thing*—a TSB, a Trendy Status Boyfriend, to impress others and boost my ego.

Lucky was not a possession. He was a person with his own issues . . . and that's what Jack had been trying to tell me when he'd driven me home from the county club. But I hadn't believed him. Now I wondered about all the other things Jack had said to me, and wondered what else was true.

He found himself more and more attached to the almost fairy form before him. He would tear himself at times from her . . . but he always found it impossible to fix his attention upon the ruins around him, whilst in his mind he retained an image that seemed alone the rightful possessor of his thoughts.

John William Polidori, "The Vampyre" (1819)

Chapter 31

On Tuesday, I had to stay late in the Flounder classroom to finish my story about the school's upgrade of water faucets for the *Birch Grove Weekly*. I filed a copy in the archives and then helped proofread the other articles. As I walked out of the empty building, I got the spider-crawling-on-my-spine feeling that someone was watching me.

I didn't see a soul as I went around the outside of the building to the drive. When I reached the grove I listened for sounds other than the trees. I thought I heard a footstep on gravel and then I heard that soft crunching sound again. I was close enough to make it to the cottage if I ran.

But I was sick of being chased, being harassed, being scared.

I whirled around just in time to see someone in a hooded sweatshirt step off the path into the bushes. I dropped my bag as I ran, and I hurled myself at the person. We both tumbled backward into the shrubs.

"Damn!" As he rolled over, I wiggled so that I stayed on top, but we were both trying to get our balance and I was saying, "What the hell!" as I recognized a too-familiar grin.

Jack Radcliffe said, "I'm a troll taken down by an elf in her magical forest."

I became excruciatingly aware that our bodies were intertwined. It was too dark to see the color of his eyes, but I saw the shine of them and the shadow of his black lashes. I felt the strength of his arms around me, and my hands were braced on his chest as it rose and fell. One side of his mouth lifted upward, showing the gleam of white teeth, and desire surged in me, more powerful than anything I'd ever felt for his brother. Because Jack always made me *feel*.

"I can't believe you're laughing about this!" I was angry and confused, pushing up from his body and standing.

"Come on, it *is* kind of funny." He stayed lying on the ground. "You're such a tiny thug, assaulting an innocent pedestrian."

"Since when have you been innocent, Jacob Radcliffe?"

"Well, when you put it that way . . ." He stood up and swatted at the dirt and leaves on his jeans. "See you around."

"No, you don't. You're coming with me." I grabbed a handful of his sweatshirt and yanked it as I walked back to my book bag.

"When did you get so bossy? I kind of like it. Beat me, whip me, make me write bad checks."

"I'd like to slap the sass right out of you." My heart was racing and I was glad it was too dark for him to see my face. I picked up my bag and put the strap over my shoulder. I let go of his sweatshirt. "Why, Jack? Why do you hate me?"

He stepped so close that I had to tilt my head back to look at his face. "I don't hate you, Jane. I'm trying to save you."

I was overwhelmed by the nearness of him, and I breathed in the chill night air, and resisted the crazy urge to press myself against Jack and feel the roughness of his beard on my face and taste his lips. "Lucky won't hurt me."

"Not intentionally. Let's get out of here. We need to talk."

I don't know why I went with him. As we walked toward the street, I saw the chem lab's lights on in the main building.

Jack pulled the strap of my book bag from me. "I'll

carry it." He hefted it onto his shoulder. "What the hell do you have in here?"

"Books."

"You could have said something funny, like 'the weight of the world.' "

"You're the king's fool, not me." I glanced at his profile. I wanted to touch his hair and his jawline. "Were you the one following me in the car the other day?"

"You know that I would have used my bike." His expression became serious. "My parents told me about it. It seemed strange."

"They think I'm paranoid because I freaked out about a car trailing me. Evidently the last crime in Greenwood was when Mrs. Holiday ran over a possum."

"Did MV recite her poem? It's genius. I think you're cranky, but not paranoid."

"Where are you taking me?"

"Okay, maybe you are paranoid. I'm not taking you anywhere. You're a consenting emancipated minor coming along with me for pizza."

"Why can't you say whatever you're going to say now?"

"I think better when I'm consuming melted cheese and tomatoey crust."

We walked silently for a block. Jack lifted his face toward the sky. "Beautiful night, isn't it?" The moon had risen and shone icily among gauzy clouds. Jack whistled and I recognized the tune as "My Titania." He said, "It was my childhood dream to take a midnight walk with a halfling."

"It's not midnight."

"It's midnight somewhere in the world. Maybe we'll meet your kin, pixies and elves, and you can sing one of your fairy songs to me. I don't have pretty ribbons to give you, but I can play music for you."

I turned my head so he wouldn't see my smile.

Once down the hill, Jack led me to a narrow lane off the

main street. A little restaurant was tucked between brick buildings. He opened the door for me and we went inside to a place with red-and-white-checked tablecloths and candles in wine bottles. Clusters of plastic grapes hung from a trellis on the ceiling, and the walls were painted with murals of gondolas on canals. The other customers were old.

A waiter came to us. "Hi, Jack. Here or to go?"

"We'll get a table, thanks."

"Wherever you want is fine."

Jack chose a cozy table in an empty corner and pulled my chair out for me. He sat across from me. The candle-light accentuated his cheekbones, his strong nose, his firm jaw, and his sensuous, expressive mouth. Lucky was a stunning boy, an overindulged, petulant boy, but Jack was a man already, with a man's confidence and ease.

I recalled the day we'd met and how his touch warmed me. When I'd walked up the hill, I'd seen Lucky and I'd associated him with my heightened perceptions. But it had been Jack's touch and voice and being that made colors brighter, sounds clearer, and sensations sharper. Now I knew why I had stopped Lucky the other night. Because I wanted someone else. Because I cared for someone else.

Jack said, "Only me and the old codgers come here. The food is good. What do you like on pizza?"

"Pepperoni and mushrooms."

He ordered and we were quiet while the waiter returned with a basket of breadsticks, a beer for Jack, and a soda for me. When the waiter had gone, Jack stared at me. "You've got some dirt here, Halfling." He reached toward my shoulder, but I jerked away, afraid of how I'd react to his touch.

He sat back and took a drink.

"Okay, Jack, why were you stalking me?"

"It's a little complicated. What have you heard about Bebe?"

"That she was another scholarship girl who lived in the groundskeeper's cottage. She was supposed to be your brother's Companion, but then she went to Europe with her uncle."

"Does that sound entirely credible to you?"

"Which part?"

"The part where she goes to live with her uncle."

I shrugged. "I've known foster kids whose relatives show up out of nowhere. On the other hand, it's more likely that she did a runner with a boyfriend."

"Why would she run when she thought that Lucky was her ticket to the good life?"

"Because running is what you know. When something gets uncomfortable or scary, you know you can take off. When someone whips you or . . ." I put my hands under the table and clenched them hard, trying not to remember some of the houses I'd lived in. "Most fosters run at least once or twice."

Jack's expressive brows went together. "Did you run?" His hand moved across the tabletop toward mine, but he stopped before touching me. "Did anyone ever hurt you, Halfling?"

I kept my face down, but my voice was thick when I said, "We're talking about why you were following me."

"Okay." Although no one was nearby, he leaned forward and dropped his voice so that I had to lean toward him, too. My knee touched his under the small table and I let it stay there for a moment as I thought about the muscles in his legs, and then I shifted my leg away. Jack's eyebrows briefly rose—he knew I was avoiding his touch.

"On the weekend Bebe left, the band had a gig in San Francisco, and Lucky went with us. When we got back, my parents were meeting with the Council's security adviser behind locked doors." Jack hesitated. "I've thought all the things you're thinking now—that Bebe couldn't take the life here, or she decided that a faster way to make money was to blackmail the Family and they decided she was a liability."

"What would they do to her?" I knew what happened to snitches and blackmailers in Helmsdale.

"You'd have to ask Ian Ducharme, and that might be the last thing you'd ever ask. Not that I've met him, but nobody risks making him angry," he said. "I don't think she tried to extort the Family, though, because I get this sense of uncertainty from my parents, like they don't know what happened, either. They're committed to the long-lost-uncle story, even though I've told them I don't believe it."

"Bebe probably took off, end of story. Your parents reacted for the same reason I did when that car followed me—when you've been a victim, you respond to everything as a threat. And you called me paranoid."

Jack tipped his head by way of agreeing. "There's a real history of violence against us. That's why they built the school with secret tunnels and hidden corridors to escape in an emergency."

"Seriously? That explains one thing. I saw a girl near my locker once and thought she was trying to break in. She got away somehow."

"Did you see who she was?"

"No, and she vanished down a dead-end hallway. Maybe your mother asked one of the other Family girls to snoop on me."

"I can ask her about it."

"Don't. The next time something like that happens, I'll deal with it myself. I thought I was going crazy—it never occurred to me that there was another way out of the school."

"Our house has false walls and tunnels, too. My parents made us practice escape drills."

We stopped talking when the waiter came with the pizza and served us slices. Then we went over everything we knew, but for every concern, there was a reasonable explanation. This wasn't the conversation I wanted to have with Jack, but I was grateful for the chance to watch his face in the candlelight.

After we'd finished eating and there were a few slices of pizza left on the tray, I said, "When I first moved here and you brought pizza, I was worried you'd take or toss the leftovers, but I was too timid to say anything."

"I know, Halfling, that's why I left them." Jack pushed his hair away from his face. "Especially after you'd been so welcoming and shared your morbid analysis of life and death with me."

"But it's *not* morbid! Math, chemistry, and physics are part of nature and our existence. You can use them to understand everyday miracles like the flight of birds, and more astonishing things, like the mechanics of the universe. You can even use them to understand music." I leaned forward and gripped his wrist because I wanted him to know how I felt. "It's all connected. The more you look, the more you see the complexity, but those truths also exist on their own and they're amazing and beautiful!"

I was staring into Jack's eyes and I felt the way I had after the party—as if the rest of the world were slipping away. Flustered, I sat back in my chair and put my hands in my lap. "Sorry, I didn't mean to bore you."

"You never bore me, Jane."

Now he sounded like the headmistress's son, saying the polite thing to the hopeless geek girl. "We were talking about Bebe. You think there's something suspect about her leaving, so you're stalking me."

"Stalking makes it sound like I'm completely obsessed with you."

His eyes met mine and I became so nervous that I babbled, "So now you're getting caught up on semantics. What does your girlfriend think?"

Jack swigged his beer. "Hattie never thought Bebe was right for Lucky. She thought Bebe was too dazzled by his looks."

"That's why Hattie dates you instead of him," I said without thinking.

"Yes, why else would any girl go out with me?"

I could have told him—because you're funny and caring, because you're strange and wonderful, because you make my every nerve tingle, because I love the touch of you, the smell of you, the low roughness of your voice, your eyes the color of leaves and streams, your language of music, and the way the muscles move in your body. Because you're brilliant and beautiful.

I tried to think of something to make up for my clumsiness. "Hattie must like you very much to date you. I heard that Tyler girls only get serious about Evergreen boys, and Radcliffe boys only get serious about Birch Grove girls."

He smiled and a wave of yearning went through me. "I know I'm crazy mad for a Birch Grove girl. She's the only one I want and I can't stand the thought of anyone else having her. I think about her constantly, I dream about her. I can't imagine living without her."

Lucky, lucky Hattie, I thought, and my heart ached because I wanted what she had—not her beauty and status—I wanted Jack Radcliffe.

He asked the waiter to call a cab. By the time he'd paid the bill and we walked out to the sidewalk, I was able to talk nonchalantly again. "Jack, I don't think you can be so sure that Bebe didn't leave voluntarily. Maybe the money wasn't enough of a reason for her to stay. Maybe she decided that she didn't want to spend the rest of her life with Lucky, being subservient to him."

The cab rolled up and Jack opened the back door for me. He spoke quietly so that only I could hear him. "No, Halfling, because Bebe had something in common with you. She was a lonely damaged girl madly in love with a rich pretty boy and she had the smart-girl delusion that she could *think* her way into making Lucky fall in love with her, too. She was so infatuated that she didn't see that she'd never have a chance with my brother."

All of my elaborate words failed me, because none could

describe the depth of humiliation I felt now, and all I wanted to do was scream and strike at Jack until he took back the horrible things he'd said.

He bent into the cab, handed the driver money, and told him, "She's going up to Birch Grove." I got in the cab and Jack closed the door. I stared straight ahead and willed myself not to cry.

When I got home, I got the composition book from its hiding place and scrawled angrily over all the references to Jack, so that his name was unreadable and the ballpoint tore through the pages.

Then I ripped out the pages and tried to stop thinking of how it felt to lie atop his body. I threw the shreds of paper in the fireplace, lit a match, and watched them catch fire, curl in the flames, and turn to ash.

My pulse was racing and my skin was clammy. I knew I had to control my feelings and my thoughts. I would organize them and reduce them to what they were, mere facts based on the five *w*'s: who, what, where, when, and why.

I drew a new chart with myself in the center of this one. In the outer circle, I wrote down all the people I'd met at Birch Grove, our interactions, and auxiliary incidents. When I was done, the lines connected and intersected around me, like strands of a web entrapping a moth.

The lines tangled around Bebe and around one other person, too: Claire Mason. Were the disappearances of the two orphans connected? I had a sense of who Bebe was from my friends, but all I knew about Claire Mason was that she was heartbroken and unbalanced.

I got the cheap prepaid phone that 2Slim's driver had given me. There was a number listed in the address book, but no name. I keyed it and the call went to voice mail. "Sir, it's Mousie Girl. I have a question."

A few hours later, I was in bed, trying to sleep, when the phone beeped. "Yes?" said 2Slim.

"I'm sorry to bother you, but I'm trying to figure something out. The other Hellsdale girl who came here was Claire, but what was her maiden name?"

"Hmm, her tag was Stubby, cause she was short when she was young, and it was something like that. Stubbing. No, Stebbing. Claire Stebbing."

"Do you know anything else about her? Please, sir."

He let out an exasperated sigh. "Nothing 'cept she was an orphan. Someone broke into her house, knifed her folks, and jacked their drugs and cash while she hid under a bed or in a closet. Her folks cooked meth and fought pits, so everyone had motive. It must have been an associate to get past the guns and dogs. News called it 'Stabbing the Stebbings,' or some such. Don't call me again unless it's important." The phone clicked off.

2Slim's information just raised more questions. How badly had Claire been scarred by her vicious parents and their murder? Could she have done something that caused Bebe to leave at the end of the term? Or had Bebe learned something about Claire's suicide that made her run from Birch Grove and the Family? Or could they have plotted to disappear as part of a bigger scheme?

Mina was looking tired and pale, but she made a gallant effort to be bright and cheerful. It wrung my heart to think that I had had to keep anything from her and so caused her inquietude. Thank God, this will be the last night of her looking on at our conferences, and feeling the sting of our not showing our confidence. It took all my courage to hold to the wise resolution of keeping her out of our grim task.

Bram Stoker, Dracula (1897)

Chapter 32 On Wednesday, I skipped my first class and went to Flounder. The Expository Writing classroom was empty. I logged on to the computer using my name and student ID number. I couldn't find anything about Claire Stebbing or Bebe. I searched through archives in the old file cabinets by cross-referencing subjects. Under "Financial Aid," I located an article marked "incomplete" from the year before and I skimmed it for Bebe's name.

The article didn't mention her. I kept glancing up at the door, hoping I wouldn't get caught. I tried again, moving my finger under the words to make sure I caught everything. "Bebe, Bebe," I was saying to myself. Then I saw the name Breneeta Justine Browning. BB, like MV.

Breneeta was quoted as saying, "My parents were only children, and when they died in a car accident, I went into the foster care system because all of my grandparents were dead, too."

There was no uncle.

❧ I couldn't deal with anyone, so at lunchtime, I went to sit on a tree-shaded stone bench across from the school's entrance. I saw Hattie walking along the drive and she spotted me and waved. As she came toward me, I admired once again her perfect body, beautiful face, and her shining hair. Of course Jack was in love with her, but I didn't want to think of them together. I didn't want to think of her mouth on him, drinking his blood. I didn't want to think of him kissing her, touching her . . .

It would have been easier if I hated Hattie. In the seconds before she reached me, I tried to tap into my anger and despise her for all she was, all she had. But all I could think of was that Hattie could never go in the sun without protection. She could never be honest with anyone about who she was and would have to hide her "strangeness" for the rest of her life. She could only have relationships with Family members. She might never have a child.

And I felt sorry for the beautiful, rich, sophisticated girl.

"Here you are!" She smiled and sat on the shadiest side of the bench.

I looked across the drive to the majestic stone angels guarding the school's entrance. I read aloud, *"Ut incepit fidelis sic permanent."*

" 'As loyal as she began, so she remains.' The perfect motto for a school established to educate Family girls and Companions. Jack told me he was horrible to you yesterday."

"I really don't care what Jacob Radcliffe says or does," I said with a calm expression that was like a mask suffocating me. "BB stood for Breneeta Browning, right? I dug up an interview she gave for the newspaper. Her parents were only children and she had no living relatives. Somehow I've become connected to her, even if it's only because other people associate me with her."

"Jane, BB might have decided to leave, and that's fine. But if she didn't leave willingly . . . we like you too much to want anything to happen to you. I know Jack likes you, Jane."

"He told me exactly what he thinks about me, Hattie. He believes that BB wouldn't voluntarily leave because she was stupidly in love with Lucky."

"That's because Jack thinks that *every* girl is stupidly in love with Lucky," Hattie said scornfully. "Actually, BB was obsessed with Lucky for a long time. Then something changed. She mentioned liking more mature men."

"Fosters are always trying to find Daddy. But what would happen to BB if she talked about the Family to a 'more mature' friend and the Family found out?"

Hattie understood my implication and spoke carefully. "I don't think the Council kills sources of healthy blood." She waited until I understood *her* implication. "I hope we're overreacting and BB ran away. But whatever happened, now that you're with the Family, you need to be careful. You watch my back and I'll watch yours." She looked both worried and hopeful as she held out her fist. "Grrl power?"

I bumped my fist against hers. "Grrl power."

❧ The day seemed like it would never end and I was out the classroom door before the final bell rang. I brought out my phone and texted Lucky. "Let's talk soon."

When I was at my locker, I got his message. "MayB 2mrw." Even with the initiation coming up, I wasn't worth his time.

"Jane!"

I turned to see Mary Violet coming toward me, holding out her hand.

"Let me see that message."

"It's just about my tutoring thing." I shoved my phone in my pocket.

She pouted. "When did you get a new phone and why didn't you instantly text me? Your tiny little fingers are perfect for texting."

"Mrs. Radcliffe gave it to me and I'm not supposed to 'abuse' my privileges."

"That doesn't mean you should ignore your besties!" she snipped. "What's going on with you, Jane? You're on another planet. Has something happened between you and my future husband? Does he want you to tutor him in the art of looove?"

"Is that how you see chemistry?"

"Of course. Passion is like dynamite—you need the right chemistry, then kaboom!"

I wanted so much to confide in her. "When I read Lucky's Chem syllabus, romance wasn't listed."

"Oh, please, JW, I have two devastatingly astute eyes in my fabulous head. I've seen girls fall for Lucian Radcliffe since he was eating Play-Doh in preschool, and I can diagnose the symptoms. The only reason *I'm* not madly in love with him is because he's too busy admiring himself in the mirror to worship me."

"I thought you were going to marry him."

"He's still one of my top candidates. I may hold out for a minor royal or potentate. Isn't that a good word? You'll be able to introduce me as Madame Potentate. Seriously, JW, is everything okay?"

"Seriously, MV, Lucky's gorgeous, but I'm more concerned about my grades right now."

"Yes, that's what BB used to say, too."

"I'm *not* BB! I never met her and I don't think I'm *anything* like her."

My friend blushed. "Sorry, Jane. I was comparing you two out of habit. It's like when people ask my mom why she keeps painting lady parts. She says, 'Old habits die hard.' But I'm going to kill this habit if I have to drown it in the toilet."

"It's okay, MV. I guess it's natural to compare foster girls on scholarship."

"You're not like her. She was more . . . opportunistic, I guess, and she liked to shock us." Mary Violet twirled a golden curl around her finger. "Jane, promise you won't ever leave that way, without saying good-bye?"

"I promise."

"Do you think I'm a frivolous rich brat?"

"No, I think you're a remarkable and fabulous poet and scholar."

"Just for that I'm going to make a promise, too. I promise to write a poem in honor of you."

"I'm scared, MV," I said as if I were joking, to cover the fact that I *was* scared—scared that I'd made an unfixable mistake by agreeing to be a Companion.

That evening, I kept staring at the same page of my chem book without seeing the words. All I could think of was what it would be like seeing Jack and Hattie together for the rest of my life. I tried to push all my emotions down far below the surface because old habits die hard.

Then it came to me: If old habits die hard, then BB *must* have had a stash. Hiding personal things is one of the first things a foster kid learns.

I began searching the cottage methodically. I started with the laundry room. I tapped on walls and floors, listening for any hollowness, and looked behind and under every item I could lift. I checked each floorboard and each outlet panel.

I went to the kitchen and pulled out the drawers to check above, beneath, and behind them. With great effort, I shoved the refrigerator away from the wall and felt the underside of the table. I got on the floor to see from that angle. In the living room, I tested each stone of the fireplace. I cleared all the books off the shelves and opened the big ones to look for any that might have been hollowed out.

I was so thorough that it took me two hours to get to the bathroom. I checked the predictable places, like the toilet tank. The tiles around the tub were secure, and there was nothing behind the medicine cabinet. I looked up to the ceiling.

The paint was scratched off on the screws that held a plaster wreath surrounding the light fixture. I got a screwdriver from the laundry room and carried a chair to the bathroom. The chair wasn't high enough to let me reach the ceiling, so I stacked books atop the seat.

The slick paper covers of the books slid under my feet as I clambered up.

I loosened the screws and removed the decoration, revealing an opening in the ceiling. I carefully got down off the chair while holding the plaster wreath, and I set it on the vanity.

Then I climbed back up. I reached through the gap in the ceiling. Nothing there. BB was probably taller, so I stretched as far as I could, too far, and the books slithered from beneath my feet. I crashed down and shrieked as my arm bashed against the tub and my left ankle twisted.

I rotated to my side, rubbing my elbow and blinking back tears. When I tried to stand, pain ratcheted from my ankle upward and I let out another cry. I got to my knees, grabbed the towel rack, and pulled myself up.

Someone pounded on the front door of the cottage. "Jane! Are you okay? Jane! It's Jack."

I hobbled around the fallen chair and slowly made my way to the front door as Jack kept pounding and shouting. "I know you're in there, Jane! Are you all right?"

I wiped away my tears and balanced on my right foot before I opened the door.

Jack had one hand on the door frame and the other raised to knock again.

"What was that crashing? I heard you scream." His eyes searched my face.

"Why are you here? Go away." My throat constricted. I hated him seeing me looking like a stupid mess.

"I'm not leaving until I know you're okay. What happened?"

"I fell." I leaned against the doorway. "Leave me alone."

Jack waited only a moment before he scooped me up in

his arms. "I've captured a wood sprite. Do I get to make a wish?"

"Dammit, Jack, put me down!" My skirt scrunched up around my thighs and I tried to push down the hem, which only brought me closer to his chest, and I felt the intoxicating heat and strength of his body.

"Do I get a pot of gold?" He set me sideways on the sofa with my feet up.

"I don't like you and I *never* want to see you ever again."

"You'll get over it. Now, I actually have some experience with busted ankles."

My ankle hurt so badly that I gave in. Or maybe I gave in because I wanted to be near him, even in this pitiful way. "Fine." I leaned back on my elbows and watched as he wiggled off my shoes and rolled off my socks. His calloused fingers gently explored my ankle, and I felt an agonizing amalgam of pleasure and fury. When he hit a tender spot, I flinched with a small sound.

His brows came together. "Sorry, Halfling, I didn't mean to hurt you." His fingers touched me more lightly. "It's swelling, but since you can put weight on it, I think it's probably okay. Let's ice you up." He went to the kitchen and I heard him banging the ice trays around on the counter. He came back with a plastic bag filled with cubes. "I always keep ice packs at home."

"And a first-aid kit."

"I'm the only one in the family who needs them." He placed a cushion under my foot to elevate it and arranged the ice bag so that it covered my ankle. "I'm here because I was thinking about apologizing to you. I shouldn't have said those things."

I looked away from him because I didn't want him to see my misery. "*Those things* like calling me damaged and delusional? I've been called worse all my life, and I don't give a damn what you think about me. I don't give a damn about you!" I struggled to keep my voice cold. "You were right about one thing. BB didn't have an uncle."

"Hattie told me."

"Do you tell each other everything?" I said, and my voice caught.

"Not everything." He grabbed another cushion and moved to put it under my head. As he was doing this, he touched my shoulder and the scar there throbbed warmly, as it had the day we'd met, when he'd braced himself against me to get on his bike.

Jack sat on the sofa close to my legs. The pressure of his body next to mine filled me with longing and regret and rage. I wanted him in a fierce way that I'd never wanted Lucky. My desire was primal yet couldn't be reduced to a calculation or described by pedantic words.

"Halfling, Lucky will never love you. You're not for him."

His words were a knife twisting in my ribs. "*That's* the apology?" My emotions crashed together so violently that I couldn't distinguish anger from pain from love . . . I wanted to say something that would hurt him as much as he'd hurt me—but I couldn't, because he didn't care for me. "Maybe you're right, Jack, and no one will ever love me, but that doesn't mean I don't *want* to be loved. It doesn't mean that my heart can't break, because it can, and it does."

"Oh, Halfling," he said softly. "Please don't let it break for Lucky. Don't be in love with *him*. Because, from the first time I saw you standing there in the grove, I haven't been able to get you out of my mind."

I just looked at him, unable to comprehend what he was saying.

Jack stared deep into my eyes. "Jane, are you in love with Lucky? Do you and he—because it makes me crazy to think of you and him together . . ."

My words came out as a whisper. "I don't love Lucky. I don't want him. Why are you saying these things?"

"Because they're true. Because whenever I'm away from you, I want to be with you. Because whenever I'm with you, all I want to do is kiss that smart, sexy mouth of yours."

Then Jack Radcliffe leaned over and kissed me. His lips were soft and warm and his kiss was firm and eager. His tongue slipped into my mouth and the taste of him was wonderful and sent waves of delight through me. When he took me in his arms, I felt a sense of *rightness*. I put my arms around him and kissed him, my whole body arching up to him.

He stroked back my hair and cupped my face in his hands and his lips were on my eyelids, my temples, my brow. Then he held my hands and kissed each fingertip, and even his smallest touch sent astonishing shivers through me.

I reached under his shirt to feel the smooth skin on his back. I nuzzled my face against his rough chin. His curls tumbled across his face when he bent to kiss me. I wove my fingers in his hair, pulling him tighter to me.

His teeth tugged at my lower lip in a way that made me groan with desire, and his hands moved over my body, and I could hardly stand the clothing between my flesh and his.

Suddenly, I was aware that I was kissing my friend's boyfriend. I shoved Jack away. "No! I'm not doing this to Hattie."

"Hattie and I are friends, no benefits." He reached for me again, but I held off his hands.

"Why should I believe you?"

"Don't. Ask her. She'll tell you."

His fingers laced with mine, and I would have done anything with him at that moment. I knew he wanted me, too, as he pressed against me, because he was looking directly at me as if . . . as if I were pretty.

Then Jack's expression became somber. "Halfling, I need you to leave Birch Grove as soon as you can. Run away—because I'd rather lose you than see you hurt. I'll give you money if you need it and a ride wherever you want to go. We can go tonight."

I felt like he'd lured me to the edge of a cliff and pushed me off. I was falling, falling, falling. I jerked away from Jack and a snarl came from my throat, a sound from the feral child still within me. With my good leg, I shoved at him, until he got off the sofa and away from me.

"I *hate* you and your spoiled rich-boy games of messing with me. I don't know if you do this because you're bored, or because you don't think I'm good enough to be Lucky's Companion. But you're a liar and you're cruel because you like to trick me, you like to *hurt* me. How does it feel? Does it make you feel special to humiliate me?"

"Jane, let me explain—" He tried to come close.

I grabbed the closest book on the coffee table and threw it at his head, but he caught it and set it down. "I don't want to hear another word from your lying mouth! Go now, or I'll tell everyone that you're sabotaging Lucky. I'll tell your parents and Hattie and Ian Ducharme. Get out!"

He took a step toward the door, then turned back to me. "This is for you, Jane." He pulled the chain out of his shirt and lifted it over his head.

The colors in the room dimmed. My voice went flat and my blood was ice. "I don't want anything from you."

He dropped it into my lap and I saw a silver leaf dangling from the chain. "I want you to have it anyway. I'll lock the door. Keep it locked."

When Jack Radcliffe walked out and closed the door, I cried. I cried so hard that something broke in me. I cried because I was missing *something,* but I didn't know what it was, and because I was so alone, but I was too afraid to let anyone near me.

I cried for Hosea, who died so unnecessarily. I cried for Wilde, selling her body to survive. I cried for my mother, whose existence was reduced to a single vague memory.

And I cried for myself, because losing the possibility of

love hurt more than living without love. I cried because my heart was broken. I cried because I was lonely and damaged, and I didn't think I could ever be fixed.

And I cried because the world was cruel and capricious, and I was small and poor and powerless and unloved.

There is no point, among the many incomprehensible anomalies of the science of mind, more thrillingly exciting than
the fact—never, I believe, noticed in the schools—that, in
our endeavors to recall to memory something long forgotten,
we often find ourselves upon the very verge of remembrance,
without being able, in the end, to remember . . .

Edgar Allan Poe, "Ligeia" (1838)

Chapter 33 My ankle was swollen and tender the next morning, Thursday, and my emotions were as deadened as they had been before I'd come to Birch Grove. Colors seemed to have faded overnight and noises were muffled. I hadn't slept much and my exhaustion helped me feign calmness.

I was about to leave my cottage when I saw the silver necklace on the sofa, where I'd left it.

The leaf hanging from it was as delicately detailed as the leaves on the birches. *JFR* was engraved on the stem. I wanted to remember my mistake so that I would not be stupid enough ever to leave myself vulnerable. I put the chain over my head and hid the medallion under my blouse. The metal heated my skin like Jack's touch always did, which was just as impossible as believing for those few delirious minutes that he'd cared for me.

I limped to the nurse's station before my first class.

She felt my ankle. "It's a sprain, but you should rest at home and keep it elevated as much as you can." As she bound my ankle and foot with a stretchy beige bandage, I noticed the certificates on the walls, which I hadn't seen since Mrs. Radcliffe gave me a tour.

"No, I need to go to class. Are all those certificates for Mrs. Mason?"

"Yes, she was wonderful. Any medical school would

have been glad to have her, but she came back to serve us at Birch Grove." The nurse handed me a packet of Advil. "Take this for the swelling. How did you hurt yourself?"

"I fell off a chair when I was changing a lightbulb."

"Use a ladder next time. Would you like crutches?"

"No thanks, ma'am. I can get around."

I had to hold on to the stairwell banister and hop on one foot to get to the third floor for Chem. Mr. Mason was at the front of the classroom. "Good morning, Jane. Is that a limp?"

"I sprained my ankle. I'll be fine in a few days." I moved my face into a smile. Then I hopped over to take my seat by Mary Violet. Her perfectly arched eyebrows knit in concern, and that made me feel a little better . . . that someone cared.

"Good heavens, JW! What happened?"

"I fell off a chair trying to change a lightbulb. It's only a sprain."

"That is a disappointingly dull accident. My mother is extremely concerned that you aren't eating proper home-cooked meals and she wants you to come over more. I told her that her gallery of giganto hoo-has upsets your sensitive digestive system and offends your delicate modesty."

"You didn't!"

"Yes, and I wrote the poem I promised. It's called 'Ode to an Innocent.' I'll recite it to you later. It's dreadfully poignant, but you inspire me."

I saw the affection on her face and wished I could tell her everything.

"Class, may we begin?" Mr. Mason directed the comment to Mary Violet and she took out her pen with violet ink.

❧ When I got a message during history that Mrs. Radcliffe wanted to see me, I thought Jack might have started some trouble.

I hobbled miserably to the administrative offices, and the school secretary told me to go right in.

Mrs. Radcliffe, sitting at her desk, placed a folder in a drawer. "Good morning, Jane. Please close the door behind you."

I lowered myself onto the chair opposite her desk. "Is anything wrong, ma'am?" I smiled. Adults liked it when you smiled.

She returned my smile with her own serene one. "Nurse said you'd sprained your ankle changing a lightbulb. I wanted to make sure you're feeling all right."

"The bulb didn't even need changing. I screwed it in tighter and it was fine. I'm fine."

"I'll have one of the staff take a stepladder to you and I'm sure you'll be more careful from now on. Lucian needs you to be careful."

"Yes, ma'am, I'll be more careful."

"Wonderful. Hattie says you've rehearsed your lines for the initiation."

"I have, but my pronunciation isn't very good."

"Your best effort will be good enough, Jane. How are things between you and Lucian?"

"Everything is going well. I think we'll be very good friends."

"He's said the same." Then her brow wrinkled. "Jacob has been so moody lately, and he's usually my sunny one. Maybe he feels left out, but he hasn't expressed any wish to participate in Lucky's Companion initiation." She tapped a silver pen against her desk. It was the first time I'd ever seen her fidget. "He seems to have a . . . an affinity with you. Has he said anything to you about . . . what could be bothering him?"

In chemistry, affinity was the force of attraction that could bind dissimilar substances. "No, there's no affinity— I'm just close by and he's bored." I willed myself to keep my expression even. When I looked at the headmistress, I wondered what she really knew about BB's disappearance. "Sorry."

She sighed. "Well, I'd like to take you to brunch on Saturday. We can go over everything that will happen at the initiation that night and have some one-on-one time."

"Yes, ma'am."

"Are you tired, Jane, or nervous? We can use the injury as an excuse to postpone your midterms so you can rest and relax."

"Thank you, but it's important to me to keep up with my classwork."

"That's the right attitude, Jane."

I could barely function through the day that didn't end until the *Birch Grove Weekly* was put to bed. I hobbled to my cottage and wished I could slow down everything— including the initiation that would connect me forever to Lucky . . . and to Jack.

A ladder was leaning against the railing by my front door, and a box wrapped in gold paper was on the chair on the porch. I picked up the box and went inside. A gift card was slipped under the red satin ribbon and it said, "Best wishes, the Radcliffe Family." When I opened the box, I found an embroidered white robe and a beautiful long ivory dress made of fine, gauzy material. It was the sort of dress a girl would wear to her first special event. I put the dress and the robe in my closet, not wanting to think of the initiation.

I had no appetite, so I did my homework until almost midnight. My Latin translations were accurate and my trig equations balanced perfectly: I could control this part of my life, and becoming a Companion would ensure my success. Time would heal my broken heart, just as it had healed the wound in my shoulder, leaving thick scar tissue in place of a child's delicate skin.

When I went to the bathroom, I saw the plaster wreath

sitting on the sink counter. I decided to put it back on the ceiling so no one would know what I'd been doing.

I lugged the ladder inside the cottage, banging the door and furniture as I maneuvered it to the bathroom. I placed the plaster piece, screws, and screwdriver on the ladder shelf. My ankle hurt as I climbed up. I was higher now than I had been on the chair. On impulse, I put my arm into the opening of the ceiling and felt around.

My hand hit something solid and rectangular. I dragged it to the opening. It was a jewelry box. I climbed down awkwardly and took the box to my desk to examine it.

Glued-on rhinestones formed the letters *BB*. I opened the lid and took out programs from student plays, birthday cards from Birch Grove girls, wristbands from parties, and a dried rose corsage. These were atop a framed family photo of the Radcliffe men. Lucky could have been a model, but my heart ached at the sight of Jack. Mr. Radcliffe was smiling and had his arms around his sons.

When I took out the photo, I saw a thick stack of cash, mostly twenties, but also tens and several fifties, bound by a rubber band. A lock of golden hair was tied with a red satin ribbon. At the bottom of the box was a passport. I opened it and saw a photo of a smiling girl. Breneeta Justine Browning was ordinary-looking, like me, the sort of sad, broken girl who had fantasies of love. The passport's pages didn't have any travel stamps.

None of the items mattered as much as the money. No one who'd grown up poor would ever leave so much cash behind. Which meant that something terrible had happened to BB.

I needed to do something, but what?

There was one person who knew about the Family and had always been understanding. I thought I could trust him to help me now. I got my new phone and scrolled to Albert Mason's phone number. I called him and when my call went to voice mail, I said, "Mr. Mason, this is Jane Williams. I really need to talk to you. I've learned something disturbing about . . . I really need to talk to you. It's about Breneeta Browning. Call ASAP."

When the phone rang a minute later, I answered it without looking at the incoming number. "Mr. Mason!"

"It's Jack."

I ended the call.

He called again, and then a third time. I answered his fourth call. "What?"

"Is Lucky there?"

"No."

"He's not answering his phone."

"Maybe he doesn't want to talk to you. I know I don't. Don't *ever* call me again." I hung up and then stared at the phone, even though Mr. Mason was probably asleep.

Ten minutes later, I got a text from my teacher. "I'm in the lab. Come see me now." He must have forgotten about my sprain. I texted him and called him, but he didn't answer, so I left my cottage with the jewelry box under my arm. The birches shifted and swayed in the wind. A sturdy branch was lying near the path, so I used it as a cane.

The main building was dark except for the lights on in the third-floor chem lab. I went around to the only unlocked entrance, a side door by a stairwell. I was tired and, as I climbed the stairs, I frequently leaned against the wall to rest.

The lab room door was ajar and I went in saying, "Mr. Mason?" The windows reflected the room and I saw someone moving behind me. I spun around as the door slammed shut and then there was a click.

The woman who stood there was about forty, wearing navy slacks, a blue sweater, and sleek mahogany pumps. Her hair was in a low ponytail and she wore gold and ruby teardrop earrings. She had style so it was easy not to notice that she was ordinary-looking under the discreet makeup. Her smile was friendly, but her expression made me uneasy.

"I'm meeting Mr. Mason here," I said.

"You must be Jane. Mr. Mason is indisposed right now."

I noticed a stack of papers and a phone on Mr. Mason's desk. His phone? "Does he know that I called? I can talk to him tomorrow." I edged toward the door.

She smoothed back her hair with a hand and I saw the gold and red stone ring on her right hand. A gold bracelet set with red stones glittered on her wrist. "Don't you want to know who I am, Jane?"

"You're Claire Mason."

"The Companions are always so bright! That's why they pick us, of course. What has your agile little mind figured out so far?"

Locate the danger. "Nothing," I said, trying to cover BB's box with my arm.

" 'Nothing' and that's why you came to see your chemistry instructor at midnight?" Her laugh had a manic edge. "By the way, the door is locked and I'm faster than you. You look uncomfortable. Take a seat."

I needed to rest my ankle so I dropped into a chair close to the door and kept the branch in my hand.

"What do you have there?" Claire pried away the box, took it to the desk, and dumped the contents out. "Nice find, Jane. I searched all over for BB's stash."

Don't panic. "It was in the bathroom ceiling. Where is she?"

Claire opened a drawer of the desk and brought out a hunting knife. "I'd like to know that, too. I left her body in the grove after I saw her with my man. Give me your phone."

I took it out of my pocket and she snatched it from me. "BB and Mr. Mason?"

"Oh, please. I could barely tolerate Albert! The Family chose him for me because he'd put up with any amount of abuse," Claire said. "BB decided that being Toby's

Companion was a better gig than dealing with his moody brat. Toby's rich and not too demanding. He'd have kept me, old as I am, but Hyacinth decided to replace me."

"But Companions are for life."

"*Our* lives, not theirs. They live longer and if they want to upgrade us, there's always another orphan girl." She ran her finger along the knife's blade. "Hyacinth was petrified that I might do the impossible and carry one of Toby's babies to full-term. Then he'd be mine forever."

Don't show fear. "I wasn't brought here to replace you, Claire."

"I saw the way Toby was looking at you the night he walked you home. He likes young blood, smooth new skin." She set the knife on the desk and lifted her sweater so I could see her torso. At first I thought she was wearing a sheer embroidered top. Then I realized that the pale raised lines were an intricate network of *scars.* She stroked her skin, letting her fingers run along the ridges. "I remember each one, each time, Jane."

Talk respectfully. "They're a map of your love for him, love that is like poison." Claire stared at me, and I saw the pain and surprise in her eyes. I needed her to like me. "I found your letter to Mr. Mason. Your words haunted me because . . . because we're alike. We know things. We've *lived* things, horrible things that no child should ever have to endure. They talk about 'deserving.' They say, 'You deserve to be here.' Does that mean we deserved our suffering, too?"

"They say, 'You're special, we'll take care of you,'" Claire sneered. "Where the hell were they when my parents locked me in a closet for days?"

"Where were they when my mother was being beaten by a vicious drunk? I couldn't do anything." Memories I had repressed for a decade came rushing at me. I remembered my stepfather's fists, his shouting, my mother's screams, and the way she drew him away to protect me from his blows.

I remembered packed bags by the front door. We were going to run away and she'd whispered, "Shush, shush, be quiet! It will be all right." But he'd caught us.

I said, "No one stopped him and I couldn't do anything. I was too small to stop him from beating her. I was too afraid of him, and no one would help us."

"He deserved to die, Jane. Even a child can kill a man. You go to the library and find a book about human anatomy. You wait until the bastards are passed out. The throat is good and under the ribs, too. The eye requires precision. You use the anger you have from the times they beat you and left you cold and hungry, and those times were better than when they traded you for meth or to pay for a lost bet."

"Oh, Claire."

"We do what we have to do to survive." She picked up the knife again.

"BB was only doing what was necessary, the same as us, Claire."

"She should have settled for Lucky. He was gone the weekend I came back. I watched BB in the grove with Toby. I watched him drinking from her and listened to her telling him she wanted to be his. Afterward, I tried to talk her into leaving. But she wouldn't and things got . . . out of hand."

"The Radcliffes don't know you're alive, do they? Then you're in the clear. You can leave and start over."

"That was my plan. I have one thing to do first: take from Hyacinth the thing she loves best, the thing I never had, Toby's child."

"Jack," I whispered, horrified.

"Jack? No, he's not even one of them. Who knows *what* he is." Claire stabbed the desk with the knife. "Lucky. He and Albert are knocked out and tied up in the auditorium.

I was going to set it up to look like Lucky killed Albert by draining him of blood, and then killed himself in self-loathing. It would *destroy* Hyacinth." Claire gloated. "But I didn't expect you to show up tonight."

"You don't want to kill me, Claire."

"Oh, yes, I do. I would have done it before, but Jack spent nights sleeping near your cottage. Toby must have sent him there to guard you."

In my terror, I felt a sense of elation—Jack had watched out for me! Colors and sounds became sharper and adrenaline shivered through me. My mind raced as I tried to figure out how to save Lucky and Mr. Mason—and get back to Jack. "I can be helpful to you, Claire—unless you've lived with the rich people so long you're used to throwing valuable things away, the way they do."

She tilted her head and deliberated for a few seconds. "If you can think of a way that we can both benefit from this situation, I'll consider letting you live. It will be a pop quiz and you must present an equation that solves for X, which is the sum of A, dead Albert, plus B, dead Lucky. Bonus points for constructing a scenario implicating Lucky in BB's murder. However, selling Lucky to the hunters is not an option. Death is better than that."

"Who are the hunters?"

"Different groups at different times, but there are always hunters."

"May I use a paper and pencil?"

"Be my guest." Claire waved the knife toward one of the lab tables, where there was a stack of papers and a box of pencils. "You have fifteen minutes starting *now*!"

I limped toward the table, leaning heavily on the branch. I remembered sitting here for the first time and Mary Violet's cheery lilting voice telling me, "Knowledge is power."

I faltered clumsily and clutched at the wooden stand with the old cloth periodic table, knocking it over so that it fell between me and Claire. "Sorry!"

"Tick tock, Jane, tick tock."

A beaker of water had been left on a table. I took a pencil and several sheets of paper and sat down. I feigned that I was figuring out an answer, scribbling on pages before crumpling them. I tossed the pages on the chart until there was a small pile.

"You've got five minutes left, Jane."

"Almost done. There are so many variables." I stood and pretended that I was going over my calculations.

Then, while Claire was examining BB's mementos, I lunged toward the shelf of chemicals. I grabbed the jar with mineral oil encasing a lump of potassium with its red oxidized edge. I hurled the jar at the fallen cloth chart and crumpled papers. As it shattered, I threw the beaker of water on it, praying that my aim would be good enough. The instant the water splashed away the oil, the reactive metal combusted in a dazzling burst of violet flames.

"Damn you!" Claire shouted, and came toward me with the knife. I pushed chairs down to block her and threw more bottles of chemicals toward the burning cloth.

By the time Claire got to me, the entire chart was aflame. I gripped my stick in both hands and struck her knees with all my strength. The blow made her scream in anger and lurch to the side, but she kept hold of the knife.

I smashed a bottle of alcohol at her feet. The alcohol splattered across her shoes and pants and spilled across the floor to the fire. In less than a second, the flames crawled back to Claire and swarmed up her legs. She shrieked and fell, trying to roll and suffocate the blaze.

I used the stick to knock over the bottles of acids, sulfates, alcohols, chlorides . . . For every action, there is an equal and opposite reaction, and everything that was flammable ignited, and everything that was combustible exploded.

Claire's screaming was an unholy sound. The sprinkler system went off and water fell, but not enough to douse the flames. The fire devoured the oxygen and light, and the noise was thunderous—crashing, creaking, rumbling. I scuttled toward the windows holding my breath against the scorching, poisonous air, dragging the branch with me.

I hauled myself up and opened a window. The air rushed in, feeding the voracious fire, and the flames blazed fiercer than before. I climbed onto the window ledge and surveyed the dark trees below me.

The sprinklers rained down, the screaming, the explosions, my terror, and the trees below . . . the incredible trees . . .

And I finally remembered *everything*.

Come away, O human child!
To the waters and the wild
With a faery, hand in hand,
For the world's more full of weeping than you can
    understand.

William Butler Yeats, "The Stolen Child" (1886)

Chapter 34

On the night that I die, the storm raging outside is not as fierce as my stepfather raging inside.

His hand is so sweaty that I am able to pull out of his grip. I run through the kitchen, past my mother's body. My foot slides in the pool of scarlet blood on the cracked yellow linoleum floor. I wrench open the back door and run outside.

The darkness is unfathomable and rain beats down and I am small and terrified.

"Come back here!" my stepfather bellows, and his heavy steps splash through the mud as he comes after me.

The neglected yard is fenced, and he is closer to the gate leading to the street than I am. I slosh toward my secret place among three enormous trees at the far end of the yard. It is too dark to see, yet I know when I have reached the largest, and I creep around it, hiding behind the wide trunk.

"Jane!"

Though I can't hear his movements, I know he's somewhere near. I peer around the tree trunk as lightning flashes, briefly illuminating the monster that he's become.

His face is contorted by madness, and his sweatshirt is soaked with my mother's blood and rain. The dull metal of a gun glints in his hand.

I shake uncontrollably with fear. I move behind another

tree and grip the rough bark, struggling to climb, but the smooth soles of my sneakers slide and even the lowest branches are beyond my grasp.

An earsplitting blast stuns me and throws me back against the third tree. I think it's lightning. A second later, pain radiates from below my shoulder to every part of my body. My knees buckle with the agony. I know that if I fall to the ground, I will die.

I twist my body toward the tree and blood seeps from my shoulder to the trunk, and the rain washes it down to the soil, the tree's roots. *Help me,* I think, *help me.*

As I begin to black out, I feel arms—no, *not arms.* I feel something take me and lift me high into the wet green branches.

Lightning explodes, deafening me and cleansing the air with pure ozone. In that burst of brilliant white light, I gaze far down to the yard and see my stepfather's body jerk violently as electricity rips through him.

Later, I hear the sirens approaching and then the voices amplified by bullhorns. The storm has passed and the rain falls through the branches in a soft drizzle. I want to sleep.

"The girl, the neighbors say there's a kid here," someone says.

They call my name and I hear them rushing through the house and into the yard. "Jane! Jane!"

I don't answer because I am safe.

"Here," a man says. "A shoe."

They are close now and they move below me. A woman says, "On the tree. Blood. Oh, God, a lot of blood."

"Where does it lead?"

"Up. Is there something up there? Turn the light this way."

"Where?"

"In the tree! Way up there."

I nestle closer to the trunk, so they won't find me. I feel as if I'm drifting somewhere.

Then the pain in my body vanishes. I can't hear the noise or the voices any longer.

I open my eyes and I'm in a glorious shady wood. I inhale air that smells of green things—pine, cedar, newly cut grass, sage and mint, the aromatic anise scent of wild fennel. I want to stay here forever.

I see someone coming toward me. I know she's a woman by her gentle movements, but she's not human. Her dress falls down to the brown earth and tendrils of the hem burrow into the soil. I can feel her kindness and she begins leading me out of the lush world.

"I don't want to leave," I tell her.

"You've found the way here. You can find the way back whenever you need us," she tells me in a language like wind. "Breathe, Jane."

I gasp and open my eyes. Pain suffuses my body. I'm lying on a hard surface and a cloth is covering me. Through it, I see flashing lights. I hear the crackle of voices on police radios, and someone is crying nearby.

I push the cloth away with my right arm and a man shouts, "She's alive! Oh, my God, she's alive!"

The sirens blare on the ride to the hospital, and I lose consciousness. When I wake next, I'm in a room, hooked up to IVs. Doctors talk nearby. One says, "Poor little thing. It would be best if she forgets what happened."

And so I had forgotten that night and everything before . . . until now.

Just as I'd heard the sirens then, I heard them in the distance now. But they wouldn't get to Birch Grove in time. Flames flicked out of the room to steal the air. I tried to breathe but my lungs hurt, my throat burned, the ledge was scorching. The thick dark branches of the trees seemed to be reaching up to me.

I wasn't afraid anymore because I believed the universe was beautiful and amazing.

So I leaped off the ledge.

There was a moment when I was suspended in air, like a feather on a breeze, and then I felt myself gently lowered and all around me I saw shades of green and brown. I was lying on the mossy bank of a shimmering stream. I inhaled deeply and the air had a delicious scent, verdant and earthy and sun-warmed like Jack, and I was in a lush forest. I stood and stretched, and then went to the stream, kneeling by it to drink the cold, pure water.

Something, *someone* moved toward me, and despite all the years that had passed, I recognized her immediately. I smiled at her and she smiled at me.

"You're the Lady of the Wood."

"That is one of my names, Daughter." Her voice was a silvery susurration.

"I forgot about you. I *thought* I forgot about you, but you were in the birch that night."

Her arms swung gracefully. "I've been here since you arrived, waiting for you to open your eyes."

I looked at her dancing arms, her leafy dress, and her fine, smooth skin, and I sighed with deep contentment. "Why me—that first time, why me?"

Her dress fluttered in a soft breeze. "You asked with a child's pure heart. You opened a door, Daughter."

Someone far off called out, "Jane! Jane!" The Lady of the Wood swayed toward his voice, as if asking me a question.

"Jack! I'm here, Jack!" I shouted, and then smiled at the Lady of the Wood. "I need to go back now. Will I ever see you again?"

"The doors are everywhere, Daughter. You only have to look and believe. Until next time."

❧ I was suddenly lying on the ground and Jack was lifting his mouth from mine. His hand was on my chest and when I placed mine over it, his face lit up. "Halfling!"

My throat felt like I'd swallowed burning coals as I

rasped, "Lucky and Mr. Mason, auditorium, save them!" and then I let myself sink into sweet darkness.

Sometime later I became aware of a wonderful coolness on my back. I was lying on the marble bench that faced the main building. Fire trucks and police cars crowded the drive and firefighters were being elevated on cranes toward the third floor.

Everything glowed orange, reflecting the flames coming from the third floor of the school. The stone angels on the façade seemed to be rising from the apocalypse.

Paramedics rushed toward me with medical equipment while they shouted instructions to each other. Jack was gripping my hand and watching them nervously.

"Lucky and Mr. Mason?" I began, and then coughed painfully.

"Jane!" Jack looked down at me with an amazed smile. "Lucky's still groggy, and Uncle Albert is being treated now." Then he shouted to the medical team, "She's conscious again!"

Paramedics hurried to give me oxygen, but I pushed them away. "No, I'm fine, I'm okay."

A crack, sharp as a gunshot, pierced the night as a hunk of burning wall tumbled from the building.

"You're lucky your boyfriend got you away from the building and knew CPR," a woman in a paramedic's uniform said.

"Not Lucky. Jack." I took Jack's hand. The paramedic wrapped a blanket around me as I began to shudder in my wet clothes.

A firefighter who had been hovering behind the medics came forward and asked, "Miss, was there anyone else inside?"

"Claire Mason was in the lab."

The firefighter shook his head and hurried back to talk to his crew.

"We're going to take you to the ER," the paramedic said.

"No." When I tried to sit up, Jack put his arm around my back and supported me. I leaned against him.

The paramedic told Jack, "We can treat her properly at the clinic and run diagnostics. Do you have her parents' number?"

"She's an emancipated minor. She makes her own decisions."

"I can get the authorization to force her to go to the clinic." The paramedic quickly checked my eyes, lungs, and pulse. Her experienced fingers discovered my telltale scabs. She turned to Jack. "Is she a *Companion* to the Radcliffe family?"

"She's our very special friend."

"That changes the situation." The paramedic came close to my face and spoke in a quiet but clear voice. "You suffered smoke inhalation, which could be serious because of the noxious fumes. You might have pulmonary irritation as well. We can take you to our private clinic."

"I've spent enough time in hospitals and I don't want to leave Jack."

"He can come with us. That fire ran hot and fast. It's a miracle you got out. How *did* you get out?"

"I jumped."

"You'd be dead if you jumped." She looked at Jack. "Her thinking is confused and she needs to be seen by a specialist."

"Jane's not confused. She's magic. She's a magical creature. If she doesn't want to go, I'll take care of her."

The woman frowned disapprovingly. "Whatever you say, Mr. Radcliffe." She packed her gear and went back to the ambulance, leaving us alone.

Jack kissed my brow. "I thought I lost you, Halfling. This is why I wanted you to leave—to keep you safe."

"I know." My voice was scratchy and it hurt to talk. "Claire killed BB. Lucky and Mr. Mason were next."

Jack was so stunned that it took him a long time to speak, and his voice came out rough and low. "Poor BB. My parents *couldn't* have known."

"They didn't know Claire was alive," I said, and each word was painful. "They *knew* someone killed BB."

Because I was so sensitive to some sounds that I could distinguish them through the chaos of a disaster, I heard someone weeping. I searched through the crowd and saw Mrs. Radcliffe. She stood gazing up at the building. Tobias Radcliffe was motionless beside her. Lucky was there, too, mesmerized by the fire. He was as striking as the stone angels in the eerie light, and I felt as much for him as I did for the angels.

The fire was horrible and magnificent, too, and I thought of the Family's blood ceremony to the harvest.

Jack said, "I need to talk to my parents and then I want to get you away from here. Will you be all right for a minute?"

I nodded and watched as he went to his family. While he spoke to them, Mr. Radcliffe put his arm around his wife's shoulders. Lucky covered his face with his hands, and Jack hugged him for a long time.

A police officer went to the Radcliffes and talked with them, and then Jack came back to me. "One of the officers is giving us a lift to the Holidays."

On the short ride, I saw all the neighbors standing outside of their homes, watching the fire at Birch Grove with the same fascination that neighbors in Hellsdale watched the aftermath of a shootout. Mary Violet and her family were waiting for us in their driveway.

"Jane!" MV cried out, and everyone talked in an excited jumble, asking if I was all right and wanting to know if I needed anything.

Mr. Holiday held his arms in a time-out signal. "All of you, quiet the heck down, and let Jane have some peace."

I didn't complain this time when Jack picked me up and carried me inside.

Mrs. Holiday led the way to a first-floor guest room and Jack set me on the bed and left to give us privacy. Mary

Violet helped her mother take off my shoes, my wet, charred clothes, and the dirty bandage on my ankle.

I sat on the edge of the bathtub as they ran cool water over my burns and wiped the soot and dirt off my hands and feet with a washcloth. Mrs. Holiday wrapped a clean stretch bandage over my ankle while Mary Violet lightly bandaged the burns and cuts. When Mary Violet brushed my hair back and braided it, she and her mother saw the scar that I always kept hidden. MV glanced at her mother, who shook her head.

As they lifted my arms to slip on a loose nightgown, I saw a pink, rose, and beige painting on the wall. I smiled, because now I understood that the painting celebrated life, and I was so happy that I was alive.

MV helped me into bed, and Mrs. Holiday held out two pills and a glass of water. "These will help the pain and help you sleep.'"

"Thanks, but no. I spent so long being afraid to feel. I want to *feel* things now."

Mary Violet placed a silver bell on the bedside. "Ring it and we'll come *tout de suite*, which is French for 'lickety-split.'"

When they moved aside, I saw Jack standing in the doorway in sweatpants and a clean t-shirt. "I'll stay with Jane tonight."

Mary Violet's rosy mouth opened in surprise.

"I want him here," I said.

Mrs. Holiday took Mary Violet by the hand, dragged her out of the room, and closed the door behind them.

Jack came to the bed and lay down beside me.

I asked, "How did you find me? Where was I?"

"I heard you calling me and followed your voice. You were under the trees below the chem lab. You weren't breathing, but you were smiling."

I curled toward him and gazed into his moss-and-sunlight eyes and I cupped his wonderful face in my hands and fell asleep.

Seven years ago we all went through the flames; and the happiness of some of us since then is, we think, well worth the pain we endured . . .

Bram Stoker, *Dracula* (1897)

Chapter 35

I heard a child say, "This room smells like a barbecue."

"You are an abominable pestilence upon this earth."

When I opened my eyes, it was late morning and Mary Violet and her brother were watching me.

"You're awake!" She came and sat on the bed, telling Bobby, "Tell Mom that Jane is awake."

He ran out of the room, shouting, "Moooom!"

"Where's Jack?" I asked MV in a hoarse voice.

"Your secret looover? He went to his house. He'll be back soon. I'm not supposed to bother you with questions even though I am consumed by curiosity." She blinked away tears. "You could have been killed, JW! What was Mrs. Mason doing here? I thought she was dead."

"I thought so, too."

"How did it start?"

It was such a simple question: how had it all started? Had it started with Birch Grove, or before that with Hosea's death, or on the night that I ran out into the storm?

Telling the truth wouldn't help BB and could hurt Mr. Mason, who had already suffered enough. "Mrs. Mason tried to run from the past, but couldn't live without Birch Grove. She wanted to surprise everyone by coming back.

We were helping Mr. Mason set up an experiment and that old table of elements chart caught on fire and started a chain reaction."

"We all guessed it was an accident. School is closed for a week and when we go back some of the classrooms will be moved to Flounder and the Gin."

I sniffed. "Your brother is right. I do smell like a barbecue. I must look awful."

MV picked up a book from atop a stack on the bedside table. "I brought these for you. They're my Beatrix Potter stories." She flipped it open to a bookmark. "See how pretty the mice are, like you."

I saw an illustration of a delicate brown mouse serving tea. "I still think you're crazy."

MV put her fists on her hips. "You little reverse-snob geek! Any dimwit can see how fabulous I am because I'm an *obvious* beauty. You're a *subtle* beauty. Most people will never notice you. But those of us who are perceptive think you're beautiful."

"Perceptive or deluded?"

She puffed out a breath. "Will you at least *consider* my theory?"

I thought about the way Jack looked at me. "Okay, I'll consider it."

"That's enough for me, Mousie. Interesting fact, Mousie sounds like *moi aussi,* which is French for 'me, too,' and that's a good nickname for you because you're one of us now. We'll help you remember things because we'll always be telling Jane stories now."

❧ The Holidays were careful with me, bringing chamomile tea with honey and letting me rest. Agnes peeked in holding a brand-new set of pink warm-ups with a matching pink sports bra, a new three-pack of panties, and lavender tennis shoes still in the box. "I think these will fit even though pink is for silly sissies and you're not a silly sissy."

"Thanks, Agnes." I couldn't resist saying, "Your sister is fanatical about pink."

Agnes laughed. "My sister is a secret genius. Don't tell anyone!"

"I promise!"

The warm-ups and shoes fit perfectly and the colors cheered me.

Jack rode his bike over at noon. I was resting on a lounge chair in the back garden, enjoying the mild gray day.

"Hey, Halfling." He sat down on the grass by my chair.

"Thanks for finding me last night. Were you already in the building?"

"No, I was lurking by your cottage because I thought Lucky might be there and then I'd have to beat him up. He's super strong, but I was planning to fight dirty."

"I *told* you he wasn't with me!"

"I was also thinking about apologizing again when I heard the fire alarm." He wove his strong, calloused fingers with mine. "I couldn't bear having my fairy creature hate me. She might cast a spell that changed me into a real jackass, instead of a guy who acts like a jackass. I had to awaken you with a kiss."

When I laughed, my lungs hurt. "Are you actually going to apologize or are you merely thinking about it?"

"I hereby issue an open-ended apology to Jane Williams for all my past, present, and future infractions and offenses."

"Apology accepted."

"Do you want to tell me what happened last night?"

"Yes." I told him about finding the jewelry box and getting the text from Mr. Mason. "Now I know why he didn't call me back. It was Claire texting."

"She logged on to an office computer using your ID and sent Lucky a message offering him a preceremony taste. When he went to the auditorium, there was a cup of drugged blood waiting. His craving overcame his common sense, as it usually does."

"Claire didn't want your mother to have a child when she couldn't . . ."

"It's okay. I knew about my father and Aunt Claire. We all knew, but we pretended that they were only friends."

"Was it awful for your mother?"

"It's hard to say. Most of her generation accepts it as normal for the Family men, and with Aunt Claire there, my mother didn't have to feel guilty about ignoring my dad." Jack ran his hand through his hair in the family gesture, and his fingers got caught in the curls. "My mother's real passion has always been for Birch Grove, her exceptional school for exceptional girls."

"Claire's passion was for your father. But she was damaged before. Her own parents did horrible things to her. No child deserved that agony."

"How did the fire start?"

"Knowledge is power. Even a small person can wreak havoc with the basics of chemistry." I thought about Claire as a girl, using her smarts to escape her parents. "I didn't expect it to catch so fast, but I wanted to set off the alarms and prevent Claire from hurting Lucky and Mr. Mason."

"Thank you for saving my brother. You protected him the way you promised, like a Companion." His thick brows lowered in resignation.

"You're welcome, but I'm *not* his Companion. I'll *never* be his or anyone's Companion."

Jack's smile was like sunshine. "Good. I didn't want that life for you and I don't want to share you."

"You were keeping guard outside my cottage."

"As much as I could, but it wasn't easy. Lucky and my parents were watching me. They figured out how I felt about you and thought I'd interfere with the initiation."

"They were right. We have an affinity." I ruffled his curls. "What now?"

"The Family's cleanup crew has already arrived and is doing damage control." He paused. "Jane, they didn't find

Aunt Claire's body in the classroom. Or *anywhere*. All the secret tunnels were searched. She'd been using them to hide and spy."

A breeze raised goose bumps on my skin. "So she's still out there."

Jack nodded. "But the official story is that she's dead. Otherwise . . . it gets complicated. My parents want you to come up to the house and talk to them. The Family will offer you something in exchange for your silence about the incident. Hattie will be here at three to take you to the meeting."

"Will you be there, too?"

"I wasn't invited, but if you want me there, I will be."

"I'd like that, but . . . Jack, are you *really* just friends with Hattie?"

"I'm *really* just friends with Hattie." When he stood up, strands of grass clung to his shorts. He kissed me softly. "I'll see you soon, Halfling."

After he left, Constance and Mary Violet joined me outside. They hauled lawn chairs beside mine.

"I absolutely can't stand it anymore," Mary Violet said. "You *have* to tell me what's happening, or I shall perish from insatiable nosiness."

"Mary Violet is going through gossip withdrawal." Constance kissed my cheek. "Everyone is asking her for details and she doesn't know any, except that Jack Radcliffe stayed with you last night, which she has told me repeatedly. Look in the dictionary under *mindless reiteration*, and you'll see her picture there."

"I'm stunned," Mary Violet said. "Except that Jack Radcliffe is a babe magnet. I thought you were lusting for Lucky. My photo is probably cross-indexed with *stunning* and *clueless*."

"Stunning*ly* clueless." Constance took off her glasses and polished them with the edge of her t-shirt. "The fire chief already made an announcement about the accident, and you don't have to tell us anything else. If you want to talk, though, we're here, Jane."

"You could have *died*, Jane." Mary Violet's eyes welled with tears. "Poor Mrs. Mason. The fire burned so hot there are no remains. I don't think she could stand living here, but this was the only home she knew, so she couldn't stay away. *Ut incepit fidelis sic permanet.*"

"It's only a dumb motto," Constance said. "You over-dramatize things."

"I think MV is right," I said. "When I first came here, I thought Mrs. Radcliffe was full of . . . was talking nonsense when she told me that Birch Grove relationships marked you for life. Now I know she was telling the truth."

"Speaking of relationships," Mary Violet began, and tilted her head, "JW, how *did* you steal Jack from Hattie?"

"He says they're only friends."

"I always thought so," Constance said.

"I thought it *first*," MV said, "so I win." She fluttered her hands frantically. "OMCG, Jane, *you're* Titania! Of course you are."

"I don't even know what that means, MV."

"Titania was the Queen of the Faeries in *A Midsummer Night's Dream*, and her jealous husband tells her, 'Ill met by moonlight, proud Titania,' but everything works out in the end and all the lovers are reunited," she said, the words rushing out of her mouth. "Oh, I can't wait until we do our Shakespeare scenes with Greenwood boys. You can be Titania and wear glittery wings."

"Jane, don't let MV force you to do anything you don't want to. She made me play Abraham Lincoln in seventh grade because she was dying to be crazy Mary Todd Lincoln."

"You were fabulous in a top hat and tails, like a Caribbean Marlene Dietrich," Mary Violet said. "Jane, my mother says I'm supposed to cheer you up, so I'll now recite the poem I wrote for you, 'Ode to an Innocent.'"

"Please don't! Save us!" Constance fell off her chair onto the grass as Mary Violet stood.

"She's going to throw her arms out now," I said. "I'm scared!"

"I am," MV said, and threw out her arms.

"Oh, sweet maiden Jane, so thoughtful and true,
Your heart was as pure as the morning dew
You sallied forth to an academic activity,
Only to find paintings of graphic proclivity.
Ladies' privates in size so crude and so vast
The vulgarity of which was unsurpassed,
The lesson you learned was not one expected,
No advance planning could keep you protected,
Because what's once seen cannot be unseen, alas,
Thus Birch Grove once more sullies a virtuous lass."

Laughing made me cough, and after Constance had patted me on the back and Mary Violet had held the garden hose for me to drink, I caught my breath. "I suppose I'm going to have to start writing poetry now just to defend myself. What rhymes with nitwit?"

"Illicit," Mary Violet said. "Permissive."

"Permissive does not rhyme with nitwit." Constance shook her head. "She's always forcing a rhyme."

"It's artistic license!"

I closed my eyes and, as I listened to their cheerful bickering, I felt an unfamiliar sense of relaxation and peace, something that had been missing in my life since Hosea had died. Because I *belonged*. I'd believed belonging meant being exactly like everyone around you, but I was wrong. Belonging was trusting others so much that I could finally be myself.

"I think you have had your share of the sunshine and the pleasures of the earth, and that you should spend your few remaining days in repenting your sins and trying to make atonement for the young lives that have been sacrificed to your love of life."

Mary Elizabeth Braddon, *Good Lady Ducayne* (1896)

Chapter 36 Hattie arrived at the Holidays' at a quarter to three. She hugged me for a long time before letting go. "I'm so glad that you're okay."

I leaned against her as we went to her car.

On the ride to the Radcliffes', Hattie was blasting some punk. "What is this?" I shouted.

"Bikini Kill, 'Don't Need You,'" she shouted back. "My mother hates my music." She pulled over to the curb, and we listened until the song ended. She lowered the volume and pulled back onto the street. "Jack told me what happened. I'm so sad for BB. I'd hoped that she'd run off with someone who loved her, because that's what she really wanted, love. If she'd stayed with Lucky and later married, her husband would always come second."

"Is that the way it always is with the Companions?"

"Not always. My father and his Companion have been long-distance friends for forever now. She's raising a family and doing real estate. But the Radcliffe men are egomaniacs—except for Jack."

I sighed. "Last night when I was watching the Radcliffes together, I thought, that's what family is, people who care for each other no matter what the circumstances, people who forgive each other."

"Jack says I'm supposed to tell you that we aren't really dating."

"Why did you pretend you were?"

"Because it made Lucky insane. Stupid, spoiled, selfish Lucky. He can go coitus himself, which he would if he could. Good luck to you with him."

"I'm not going through with the initiation, Hattie."

Her mouth dropped open. "Really? But why?"

"Because I don't want to put Lucky Radcliffe's needs ahead of my own."

"Well, it's about time!"

Hattie parked in the Radcliffes' drive behind a Crown Victoria with a police antenna and the black Mercedes. She helped me to the front door. "Time to face the firing squad." We bumped fists and said, "Grrl power," then she let out a breath and rang the doorbell.

Tobias Radcliffe, more worn out than ever, opened the door. "We're all here. Please join us. Hattie, you can wait in the family room."

"I'm coming to the meeting."

"It's not appropriate," he said listlessly.

"Mr. Radcliffe, you have some nerve trying to tell me what's appropriate." Then she tossed her head and marched into the living room.

Mrs. Radcliffe and her sons sat on one sofa. She was perfectly groomed and the only indication of a crisis was the tension in her jaw.

Jack smiled at us and I felt confident and hopeful. He was wearing a black t-shirt and clean jeans. He'd shaved so I could see all the wonderful lines of his face.

Lucky said "Hey" to me and gave a pleading look to Hattie, who remained near the doorway.

Ian Ducharme, the Council Director, wore an impeccable black suit and sat in a leather chair set back in the corner of the room. When he saw me watching him, he raised an eyebrow, once again giving me that in-on-a-joke-together feeling.

A man and a woman in business clothes stood by the fireplace. Mr. Radcliffe helped me to a chair and called the couple over. "Jane, this is Detective Fox and Officer Bateson, from the Evergreen Police Department. They're following up on the accident last night."

The woman, Detective Fox, said, "Miss Williams, we're grateful you weren't badly hurt. It's tragic that Mrs. Mason didn't make it out."

I waited for Mr. Radcliffe to say something, but he was preoccupied with staring at the carpet. "It's difficult for her friends to lose her twice."

Detective Fox nodded. "We have the fire chief's initial report, and we need your statement because there was a death. We know your memory may be hazy. People in crises have trouble recalling incidents."

I knew that she was providing me with cover. "Mrs. Mason desperately wanted to press the reset button and go on as if her recent loss and breakdown had never happened. That's why she was staying late in the lab to set up an experiment, because she used to help her husband all the time. The cloth chart caught fire and then the chemical supplies combusted. The rest happened so fast it's all a blur."

"Thank you. I have everything for my report. It's quite remarkable that you got out of the room and down the stairs." Detective Fox stepped toward Mrs. Radcliffe. "Headmistress, please give me a call if you need anything."

"I will, Katie."

The detective turned back to me. "Miss Williams, I know this has been traumatic, but I'm sure you're going to have a very successful life. I'm a Birch Grove alumna myself." When she shook my hand, I saw the gold and garnet ring shining on her finger.

After they had left, Mrs. Radcliffe said calmly, "What happened was a dreadful shock to all of us, Jane. We never expected that Claire Mason was alive and would try to hurt you."

"But you must have suspected that she killed her own parents." Her impassive face told me everything. "You *knew* someone had killed Breneeta Browning."

"We knew nothing of the sort. We assumed she left the school, which was her legal right as an emancipated minor."

"You helped us get out of the foster system to suit your own purposes." Although my throat was still sore, I didn't bother to hide my anger. "Without the protection of social workers, you could do whatever you liked without interference."

"That attitude is uncalled for, Jane!" she said, sitting up even straighter.

"*Your* attitude is uncalled for. You or Mr. Radcliffe found BB's body in the amphitheater. You fabricated a story to conceal her absence, and you've lied and told everyone that she's been in contact with you."

Ian Ducharme watched with interest as Mrs. Radcliffe's expression froze.

Mr. Radcliffe scowled at his wife. "I *told* you I didn't kill BB, but you wouldn't believe me."

The headmistress's face became paler than usual. "Accidents happen, Tobias. I only thought that you'd been overzealous because of her young blood. It would have been your right to take on another Companion . . ." Mrs. Radcliffe tugged so hard at her pearl necklace that it broke and pearls scattered all over the thick carpet and rolled across the hardwood floor.

Right then, Lucky understood what had happened. He glared at his father and shouted, "BB was *mine*! She was supposed to be mine!" Then he turned to his mother. "It's *your* fault. *You* wanted to get rid of Aunt Claire."

"Her behavior was increasingly erratic, Lucky, and she didn't want to retire," his mother said imploringly. "We tried to get her into treatment and relocated."

Lucky's face went red. "*This* was her home! She was our family! Family is supposed to be everything."

Jack put his arm around Lucky. Lucky leaned his golden head against his brother's dark head, and the room was so silent that I could hear the wind outside and the trees brushing against the windows.

Mr. Radcliffe ran both hands through his hair. "I can't deal with this anymore. Nothing's right since Claire . . . and I need a drink." He bolted from the room and we all waited for Mrs. Radcliffe to follow him.

But she had regained her composure. "Jane, this incident has nothing to do with the way we feel about you. We're postponing the initiation, and we're happy to do whatever we can to reassure you."

"I've decided that I don't want to be a Companion."

"Don't make a serious decision in your condition. You need to rest. You already have the week off, and you and Lucky can go somewhere, anywhere. We have a ski lodge, and autumn is beautiful in the mountains, or if you'd enjoy being by the ocean, we can arrange that. Why not see Paris, Jane?"

"A vacation won't change my mind and I've got to study for midterms."

"Lucky," Hattie began.

Mrs. Radcliffe turned her focus to Hattie, who stood in the doorway. "Harriet, you're not a part of this discussion."

"Yes, I am." Hattie moved to stand in front of Lucky. "Lucky, I'm giving you one last chance. Decide if you want to be a self-indulgent boy who spends his life partying and going through Companions or if you want to be a Family leader who is respected and trusted."

Lucky lowered his forehead and glowered. "I don't have to make this decision right now. I told you so in the grove the night you had that sleepover. There's no hurry and I'm entitled to my own Companion."

"Maybe someday, but not the way you want now—

taking her blood and treating her like a serf. I have plans and I'm not going to waste my life hoping that you might grow up." Hattie reached for his hands, clasping them. "You know that I have always loved you. There's so much good in you, Lucky . . . please don't let that slip away."

Lucky gawked at Hattie with all the adoration that I'd once hoped he'd have for me.

"Don't cheat yourself out of your birthright, Lucky," Mrs. Radcliffe said. "You can do better than Harriet Tyler."

Lucky snorted derisively. "You're crazy, Mom. There's *no one* better than Hattie. She's smarter than I am, she's nicer than I am, she's beautiful, and she's the most amazing girl I'll ever know. If she's willing to put up with me, then I'd be an idiot to let her go." He stood and put his arm around Hattie's waist. "Let's get out of here." Her face was radiant as they walked out of the room. We heard the front door slam a moment later.

Mrs. Radcliffe crossed her ankles gracefully, but her voice wavered when she spoke. "He'll change his mind, Jane. Lucian's always been impulsive, but he won't break an important custom."

I saw how she was trying to control her feelings, the same way I'd always tried to control mine. "Mrs. Radcliffe, I don't think you're monsters because you have a genetic anomaly, but I do think you've behaved monstrously. Your wealth does not give you the right to exploit the desperate. Hiding the bodies does not make you any nicer or cleaner than any common street thug."

Mrs. Radcliffe sat straight. "How very rude and ignorant—"

"Oh, give it up, darling," said Ian Ducharme in a low, languid voice.

"But—"

"Do you really want to argue with me, Hyacinth?" Even his smile seemed dangerous. "I'm suspending Birch Grove's Companion program indefinitely. Now, go give comfort to your husband so he doesn't have to seek it in a bottle. I'd like to talk to Jane."

Mr. Ducharme gave the headmistress a look, and she got up stiffly and left the room, crushing pearls in her steps.

Jack said, "I'm staying."

When the Council Director moved to the sofa with Jack, the resemblance I'd noticed before was more striking. They noticed it, too, studying each other for many seconds before Mr. Ducharme turned to me. "Well, Jane, you hardly gave me a chance to leave before you proved me right."

"Why did you tell them I'd be a satisfactory Companion?"

His eyes shone with amusement. "This branch needed a shakeup and I thought you might bring that."

"Where is Breneeta Browning's body?" I asked him.

"The dead are gone, their ashes scattered to the wind. However, we will try to locate Claire Mason and see that she does no more harm. We've increased security throughout this community. I suspect she won't appear here soon."

"Claire Mason is mentally ill. She needs care."

"We're cognizant of the circumstances surrounding her parents' death. The world is a better place without them. However, Claire Mason killed a Companion candidate and intended to murder a Family member, both extremely serious crimes. The Council will determine the appropriate action when she is apprehended."

He relaxed back against the sofa. "Let's move on to more pleasant matters. Since Lucky declines the privilege of a Companion, I don't think we have a problem. You'll be compensated for your trouble. What would you like?"

I knew immediately. "The chemistry lab at my old school is being reconstructed. I'd like you to upgrade it with state-of-the-art equipment in honor of a friend of mine, Hosea Sabatier. And I have a friend who needs treatment for drug addiction and counseling for abuse, and she might not want to go. She *does* want to go to beauty school, so I'd like that set up, too, and she'll need a safe house."

I had no idea how much these things would cost, but Mr. Ducharme didn't seem bothered. "Those are reasonable requests, although I'd asked what *you* wanted, Jane."

"I want to help others."

Jack looked from me to Mr. Ducharme. "Jane saved my brother's life and Albert Mason's life, and she could have died. She was promised a Birch Grove education, as well as funding through graduate school, including all living expenses, so she should get that in addition to the scholarship."

"You're her advocate?"

"The Halfling's usual legal counsel only comes out in moonlight."

"Ah, I thought I was the only one who noticed that in her, something not of this world," Mr. Ducharme said with a sly grin. "Yes, that would be fine. Jane, after you've completed your studies, we can revisit your relationship with the Family. We are not all as conformist as this particular branch, and we can always find a position for a trustworthy, intelligent ally, especially one with such composure in a crisis."

"Thank you, sir."

"I must be off. We'll work out the details through your advocate here." He gave Jack a long look. "I find it quite interesting that we haven't met prior to this, Jacob, but I'm sure there's a perfectly reasonable explanation."

Jack arched one eyebrow. "My mother says I don't take the ceremonies seriously."

"There you have it. Your good mother has provided a perfectly reasonable explanation. I shall be in contact soon," Mr. Ducharme said. "Jane, will you walk out with me?"

Mr. Ducharme offered his arm to me and we went outside. He paused in the shade of a pine. "I can trust in your silence?"

"There's no reason for me to expose the Family. I might even feel sorry for them if they showed any sympathy for others."

"That is very generous of you."

"You're making fun of me, Mr. Ducharme."

"I must, because you're such a solemn young woman. Don't stay so serious or you'll turn into someone like Hyacinth."

"I'll try to avoid that, sir. One of my friends here is on a mission to *funnify* me."

"That's excellent news!" He took my hand in his and despite his beautiful manners and elegance, I suspected he had done terrible things and I was glad that Claire had gotten away. I hoped she would never get caught.

"Jane, I hope that we will meet again under happier circumstances. I have a dear friend who would enjoy your company and I think you would enjoy her company, too. She's a rather remarkable creature, although, like you, she insists that she's an ordinary girl."

"Maybe she is, Mr. Ducharme. You know, I've always hated those stories about princes and princesses with some extraordinary ability, special because they're born special."

"Like me?" He smiled wickedly, making me laugh a little.

"I didn't see how those were happy stories, because life has given princes and princesses *enough* unearned advantages. I'd rather believe that anyone can accomplish remarkable things when she really tries. Maybe her accomplishments will never be recognized, but simply loving and caring for someone else, that's miraculous to me." And as I spoke, I remembered my mother taking my hand to help me cross the street.

"Let's continue this discussion next time, Jane. Perhaps then you'll tell me the secrets behind those brown eyes. I have something for you." He opened the trunk of his car and took out a sapling. "This survived the fire in the chemistry laboratory. I believe it's yours."

"Thank you." I took the branch and looked in wonder at the fragile new roots and leaves.

Then Ian Ducharme got in the Mercedes and drove away.

"You see me standing here beside you, and hear my voice; but I tell you that all these things—yes, from that star that has just shone out in the sky to the solid ground beneath our feet—I say that all these are but dreams and shadows; the shadows that hide the real world from our eyes. There is a real world, but it is beyond this glamour and this vision . . . beyond them all as beyond a veil . . ."

Arthur Machen, *The Great God Pan* (1890)

Chapter 37 Carrying the sapling carefully, I hobbled slowly around the house to the path through the grove. When I made it to the amphitheater, I sat on a marble bench to rest. I ran my finger along a gray vein in the pale stone.

What had Claire Mason and BB dreamed about when they came to Birch Grove and met the Family? What we all dream about: love and a haven from the cruel world.

I searched above me into the branches and saw a denser shadow there. It could have been the Lady of the Wood, or BB, or a trick of the light, but I wasn't frightened this time. The darkness expanded, growing more diffuse and fainter, and then it faded away.

Jack found me at the amphitheater. He sat beside me. "You left without telling me."

"I needed to spend some time here." We were only an inch apart, but I didn't touch him then because I needed to think over things.

Wind fluttered the autumn leaves, and a trio of deer came out of the trees toward us. They observed us for a few minutes before ambling off.

Jack said, "I'm glad you decided not to transform into a doe and leap away with your friends."

"I thought about it, but I'm fanatical about being with you."

"*Fanatical,* really?"

"A special word for a special person." I picked up the branch and stood with my weight on my right foot. "Can we go to the cottage?"

"Should you be walking? I can carry you."

"No, I want to do it on my own."

Jack was patient as I limped slowly down the hill. "Halfling, it would be easier for you to put the branch down or use it as a cane."

"It's already supported me. It helped save me last night and I want to plant it."

Once at the steps to the porch, I leaned against a column and set down the branch while Jack dashed ahead and opened the door. He raced back to swoop me up and carry me inside. When he set me on the sofa, I scanned the room. "Someone's been here. Things are moved."

"The Family's security team probably came through last night." He sat down, his strong thigh pressing against mine, sending blissful tingles throughout my body. "What now, Halfling?"

"I don't know. Even though I've still got the scholarship, I thought about transferring to another school, one without the Family, but there are things keeping me here."

"Such as?"

"Such as Mary Violet's poetry and lunch at the Free Pop and the *Birch Grove Weekly.*"

"Those are awesome reasons to stay. Anything else?"

"Yes, I love the grove and I have friends here and there's this guy . . . He's incredibly aggravating. He teases me and tells me to leave. But he brings me pizza and makes me laugh. He's amazingly sexy and talented. He's gorgeous and funny and thoughtful. He's really smart, too, but doesn't have an attitude about it."

"I'll never be able to compete with such a paragon. Is that one of your SAT words?"

"Actually, it *is* one of my SAT words, but you have a

chance because he's *not* a paragon. Sometimes he's a total jackass, in fact, and he's so inconsistent that I'm never sure if he really cares for me."

Jack put his arm lightly over my shoulders, and I nestled gingerly against him, conscious of my burns. "Maybe he's conflicted because he thought you loved someone else and he was trying to get you to safety, even though he really wanted you to stay. He wanted you for his own, not to share with anyone else."

"Does he want me to stay now?"

"Yes, because he's in love with you. He's never met a prettier, braver, smarter halfling, and all he wants, Jane, is to be with you."

I pulled Jack to me and kissed him.

When our lips parted, Jack's brows drew together. "You know this is going to be complicated."

"Compared to what I've been through, it will be a cake-walk."

"My beautiful elfkin is making jokes!"

"I have a fabulous sense of humor," I said, which sent him laughing.

Then he kissed me again and again, his mouth tasting like the stream from the Other World, his arms as strong as the branches that had raised me up on the night of the storm, and his eyes the color of spring and life.

I slid my hand under his shirt, feeling the heat of his smooth skin. I kissed his neck, then swept back his dark curls and kissed his temple.

He unzipped my pink warm-up jacket. I was wearing the borrowed sports bra, and Jack frowned with concern as he saw the scratches and bandages. His fingertips coursed around the small injuries, and I trembled with desire. His voice was husky: "Does your ankle hurt?"

"Some."

"I don't want to hurt you. Ever. So I'm going to have to wait, even though it's torturing me." He leaned to me and his lips brushed my ear, and he murmured, "But I *could* be very careful, Jane . . ." His mouth was hot on my neck, but he held his hands away as if afraid to be rough. When he pressed his cheek against mine, we were both breathing hard. "Tell me what you want."

I moved back so I could see his face. I ran my fingers across his marvelous lips, and he closed his eyes and groaned softly.

When he looked at me again, I said, "I want absolutely *everything*, Jack, but I need to explain something to you first." I waited until I saw that he was listening. "Before I came to Birch Grove, I was trying to grow up as fast as possible because that was the only way to protect myself. I was afraid *all* the time. Most of the people I knew didn't expect to live past eighteen, so they tried to experience everything while they could."

He began to open his mouth and I put my forefinger across his lips. He nipped it and I smiled. "But now I don't have to rush anymore. I can enjoy the things girls are supposed to enjoy. I can savor life. Besides, you only have your wisdom teeth taken out once."

His thick brows knit together. "Okay, I'm completely confused. What does that mean?"

I gazed into Jack's eyes. "It means that I want to go on a date with you, Jacob Radcliffe, our very first date, and I want to remember it forever. And then I want to go on *more* dates with you. I want to experience it all, and I don't want to skip ahead to the last page in the book. Is that okay?"

He nodded. "I can do that. I shouldn't have even asked now after what you've been through."

"That's okay. I like that you want me."

"So much that it drives me crazy. When you came into my bedroom that time, I thought, well, I thought you'd come to see me and tell me, I don't know, that you wanted me, too."

"I think I probably did want you, but you confused me

because you made my emotions go haywire. You still do. I better get back to the Holidays'."

He took a deep breath, letting it out slowly. "Do we have to go *right* away?"

"No, not *right* away."

Jack nuzzled, kissed, and stroked me as the early evening breeze brushed branches across the cottage, *shush, shush, shush*. Then Jack's rough fingers went to my scar, and it pulsed, responding to him as it had the first day we'd met. "What's this from?"

"My stepfather shot my mother and then shot me, and I climbed into a tree to escape," I said. "No, what really happened is that he shot me and the tree carried me up thirty feet into her branches and saved me. The paramedics had already declared me dead when I finally started breathing again. After surgery, they put me in an induced coma so I could recover. When I woke up three months later, I'd forgotten my whole life. I'd forgotten my mother."

"The scar is shaped exactly like a leaf."

"I think the Lady of the Wood gave it to me as a gift, a memento."

"So I was right, and you are magic."

"Not me. The Lady of the Wood." I listened to the branches sweeping against the cottage. "She watches over me. She watches over us all, but we forgot her. I stepped into that world when I died."

I thought about the gentle, maternal spirit. "I thought that my anger kept me alive, but it was love, I think, that sustained me. Even though I wasn't conscious of my mother's love, the memories were here." I placed my hand over my heart.

"You are like that, Halfling, a bit clueless about people who love you."

"I'm going to find the door to the Other World to visit." I ran my fingers over his eyebrows and down his nose, letting them rest on his lips.

He kissed my fingertips. "I think you already have. The day we met, I saw you magically appear on the path."

"I thought you were teasing."

"I thought I was *dreaming*." He held my hands. "The old stories say that magical creatures lived here hundreds of years ago. I think you're one, Halfling."

"I think what we call magic are really gateways to parallel universes with different laws of physics. Or maybe not parallel, but skewed universes that intersect."

"It really turns me on when you talk geek." His fingers traced my tattoo. "What does this *H* mean?"

I told him about Hosea. "He loved science and he loved God, and he was cross-referencing the Bible with his physics book. He wanted me to stop my incessant cussing, do my schoolwork, be nice, and *try*. He thought I should try to be a better person and I should try to figure out things."

"He sounds like he loved you."

I nodded. "I loved him, too."

"He also sounds like someone who wanted you to be happy. *H* is for happy and for hope, and . . ." Jack thought for a moment. "And for honey, which is both an endearment and nice with peanut butter in a sandwich."

"*H* is for hilarious, which you think you are."

"*H* is for Halfling, and I love Halfling," he said. "Jane, what happened to your stepfather?"

"He was hit by lightning in a storm."

"What are the chances of that?" Jack was silent for a long time. "We're dealing with a lot of improbabilities lately."

"You mean like how much you resemble Ian Ducharme?"

"That's one of them, but my mother says it's a coincidence and she may be telling the truth this time. Tobias Radcliffe is the only father I want and he needs me now. Besides, I don't heal up the way the Family does, and I do have kind of a common face."

"I don't think so."

"Well, you're a terrible judge of these things. Anytime I

tried to tell you how I felt, you thought I was talking about Hattie."

"It's because you were so elliptical."

"Okay, I'll be direct." Then he spoke slowly and carefully:

"sic erit; haeserunt tenues in corde sagittae,
et possessa ferus pectora versat Amor.
Cedimus, an subitum luctando accendimus ignem?
cedamus! leve fit, quod bene fertur, onus."

I translated the poem in my head as he spoke: "Thus it will be; slender arrows are lodged in my heart, and Love vexes the chest that it has seized. Shall I surrender or stir up the sudden flame by fighting it? I will surrender—a burden becomes light when it is carried willingly."

"Whew!" He wiped a hand across his forehead. "I mean, *vhev.* Hov vas my pronunciation?"

"You're supposed to pronounce the *v*'s like *w*'s, not *w*'s like *v*'s. Except for that, it was really the most genius Latin I've ever heard," I said, smiling. "*Te amo.* I love you, Jack."

❧ Jack helped me pack my sports bag with clothes and books. When he was in the bathroom, I snuck into the laundry room and pulled out the manila envelope holding my stash. All my money was still there.

"Jane, you ready?" Jack called.

"In a minute." I shoved the money in the envelope and hid it. Because old habits die hard.

I went out to the living room. "Ready."

Jack carried my sports bag and helped me hobble to the drive, where Mary Violet was waiting in her car.

❧ Mrs. Holiday was in the kitchen, arranging fruit in a basket, when MV and I came in. "Hi, girls! I'm so glad you're back, sweetie."

She had called me sweetie, the sort of ordinary nickname that mothers use, and I burst into tears. The tears became sobs, and the sobs racked my body. MV and her mother sat me in a chair.

"Jane, what is it? What is it?" MV asked, and handed me tissues.

Mrs. Holiday said, "She was in shock before. Everything's coming at her now."

I nodded and choked out, "It feels like she died yesterday."

"She *did* die yesterday," MV said.

"Not Claire, my mother. I remember . . ." The loss hurt so badly that I pulled up my knees and rocked.

The entirety of my memories came to me now.

But the memories came too fast, like the view from a roller coaster, and I could barely recognize one before I saw another, making me feel sick.

My mother's hand reaching out for mine at a street corner.

My stepfather's bloodshot eyes and ominous silence before he exploded.

Coming in from a cold day and smelling the rich aroma of chicken soup.

My mother's fingernail, painted deep rose, pointing out the words on a page of a picture book.

A striped cat that perched on the fence.

Playing by the trees at the back of the yard, where I couldn't hear the angry voices.

MV and her mother hugged me, murmuring, "Shush, shush, shush, shush," soothing me like the trees.

I stayed with the Holidays and grieved while my injuries healed and Jack dealt with his parents. I moved to a cot on the balcony, where I could look up at the night sky and think about everything that had happened.

MV and I studied and watched movies and talked constantly. I liked to visit Mrs. Holiday in her sunroom, letting the heat sink into my bones and watching her paint.

Mary Violet waited for me to tell her about my recovered memories. One night while she was sitting at the foot of my cot and we were both staring at the foggy night, I said, "You asked if I'd been camping. I hadn't, but I used to run away from foster homes. Sometimes I slept in homeless encampments in city parks. I liked being in places with trees."

"You can come camping with us this summer and help me meet boys who aren't from Greenwood."

"You're asking *me* to be your wingman?"

"Okay, maybe that idea needs some work." She grabbed my foot under the blanket. "Are you part Laplander?"

"No, but I know why my mother named me Jane." I remembered a daisy in a clear glass bottle on the windowsill. "She said Jane was simple and plain, and that all of her favorite things were simple."

"That's what I think, too! Like the best solution to a problem is an elegant solution—simple and true."

After five days, I felt well enough to return to my cottage.

Jack walked me from the Holidays'. I moved slowly because I felt tender all over, as if I'd been protected by a shell and it had cracked open, leaving me exposed. A large basket of orchids was set beside the door on the porch.

Jack picked up the basket and I plucked off the small white envelope attached to the cellophane. I took out the card and read aloud, "Get well soon, 2S."

Jack frowned. "Do you have another boyfriend?"

"He's more like a, well, a godfather."

"Sometimes I worry that I'm only an infatuation for you, like the way you felt about Lucky."

I opened the front door. "With all due respect, your brother's kind of a tool. I've seen pretty boys—we even have them in Hellsdale—and I thought Lucky was the one who made me feel alive again. But it was you, Jack, it was you."

❧ The next day, Mary Violet and Constance visited. "Where's your boyfriend?" Mary Violet sang as she waltzed in with a plate of cupcakes.

"He's at practice. We haven't even gone on a first date yet." I tried to sound blasé, even though I'd been wondering when Jack would ask me out.

Constance took a cupcake and nibbled at the purple frosting. "Do you know that you've become a Birch Grove legend? We'll need an iconic nickname for you. I thought of Firestarter, but MV thinks it's too Stephen King."

Mary Violet gave me an encouraging smile, so I let out a long sigh before saying, "Con, I actually have a nickname you can use. It's Mousie or Mousie Girl."

"That's cool," Constance said. "It fits because you're as neat and petite as a mouse."

"What's your iconic nickname, Constance?"

Mary Violet raised her hand and waved it. "I know! I know! Ooh, call on me, teacher!"

I nodded, and Mary Violet said, "Constant Comment, like the tea, because she's sweet and spicy."

"That is *not* my nickname! Constance is fine, thank you."

"Okay, not *so* sweet." Mary Violet sighed and sighed again. "Hattie's so busy with Lucky that we haven't seen her in years."

"She stopped by after you left yesterday." Constance winked an almond eye at me.

"Only for a nanosecond."

Constance mouthed "no" and said, "It was at least two hours."

MV held up a t-shirt that Jack had left on the floor and then she dropped it. "Everyone's doing the dance-with-no-pants except for me. Even Constance is seeing Joe, who's a junior at Evergreen. When we were in seventh grade, Joe laughed aloud when I got beaned in the head with a soccer ball at the Fourth of July picnic, which I thought was horrifically ungentlemanly. My self-esteem was in shambles."

"*We all* laughed when you got beaned, because you were wearing a ginormous pink hat with feathers."

"It was a captivating *chapeau*!"

Constance rolled her eyes. "*Chapeau* is French for ginormous pink hat with feathers. Three guys already asked MV to the Winter Ball."

"They don't count," MV said with a pout. "I've known them since we were all embryos and our mothers were in the same birthing classes. I think I'll dress my sister Agnes in a tux and take her as my date."

"You wouldn't!" Constance and I shouted.

"I *would*! Con, do you still have your Abe Lincoln costume?"

🪷 A few days later, the sun broke through the fog, and the sky cleared to a deep blue. Jack had gone off to do something, and I soaked languorously in the tub with lemon verbena bath salts. I suddenly remembered my mother rolling up her pants and sitting on the edge of the tub so she could soak her feet while I splashed in the water.

On impulse, I got out and tried on the pretty white dress that the Radcliffes had given me. The shoulder straps were so thin that my scar showed, but I didn't need to hide it anymore. The long skirt floated around my legs when I twirled. I heard Jack return and skipped out into the living room. Maybe this would remind him that I wanted to go on a date. "Hey, you!"

He grinned when he saw the dress and then he kissed me. "Come on. We're going for a walk."

"Let me change."

"No, you're dressed just right for a walk."

I tried not to be disappointed as I slipped on delicate silver sandals that I'd never worn before. "It's a beautiful day."

"A beautiful day with my beautiful pixie in her beautiful fairy dress."

We held hands, our fingers intertwined, as we walked up the path. Autumn had set in and leaves carpeted the ground. I kicked at them, watching them fly up. "Jack, you like me because I'm puny."

"I like you because you're fierce and brilliant. If I get a basket for my bike, you'd probably fit in it."

"That's hysterical."

"I *am* going to get you on a bike eventually." He veered off the path through the shrubs.

I slowed. "Lucky showed me this place."

"He probably took you to the boulder. He always liked to be up high, ruling the world. Come on." We veered around the boulder and deeper into the grove.

Rocks were set as stepping stones across the creek. Jack held on to my arm to steady me on the mossy surfaces. The air smelled incredibly fresh and the foliage was thick here with a mix of bushes and trees.

"Halfling?"

"Yes, Jack?"

"Do you remember saying you wanted to go on a date with me?"

"I recall that."

"Does the night at the pizza place count?"

"You mean the night you made me cry?" I snapped.

"Oh, you're a *cranky* pixie." He put his hand over my eyes and guided me forward. I felt branches and ferns brushing against me. "Where are you taking me?"

"You *axed* me that question when we went on our non-date. Are you absolutely *sure* that doesn't count?"

"I'm absolutely sure."

"What about this, then?"

When Jack removed his hand, I saw that we were standing in a tiny dell, only about eight feet wide, surrounded on all sides by greenery. A picnic lunch and pillows were set out on a blanket, and a green bottle and glasses chilled in a silver ice bucket. Small pink wild roses rambled up an old stump, their delicate blossoms honeying the air.

"It's a secret room!"

Jack plucked roses and fern fronds and laced the stems into my hair. "I've never brought anyone here before. The Family had their ceremonies in the amphitheater, and this was my private place. It always felt a little lonely before."

"It's so pretty!"

We sat on the blanket and he opened the bottle. "Sparkling cider, which I've heard is popular with pixies." He poured glasses of cider and lifted one to me and we clinked glasses and drank.

Then he put down his glass, bent his head toward me, and sniffed. "You smell better than lunch, and lunch can wait because I need to kiss you." Jack took my glass and set it aside. He pressed me back onto the blanket. I blinked at the sun that made an aura around his face. He kissed me, his mouth tasting of cider and autumn. He spread my hair out on the blanket. "Now you look like my fairy queen."

After lunch, Jack showed me a blackberry bramble and we plucked off the last sweet fruit of the season. The purple juices stained our fingers and we fed the berries to each other and then kissed and caressed and dozed in the sun.

A balmy breeze blew and leaves wafted down onto our bodies, as soft as sighs. I thought Jack looked like a wild creature, and perhaps I looked like one, too. I knew I would remember this afternoon forever.

❧ Diamonds form deep beneath the earth's surface and are carried up by rare and peculiar eruptions of molten lava. Jack's touch had brought forth all my suppressed emotions and feelings. I had seen the world through only one facet of a crystal and believed that I was seeing reality. Yet by turning the crystal, I had added a new dimension to my comprehension of my life and my experiences.

Every day brought more memories of my life *before:* my mother pushing me on swings at the park, making cookies together, blowing bubbles on a summer day, and going to the library for reading hour. She had loved me.

Now, too, I realized that some foster parents had attempted to draw me out and care for me, but I'd been too fearful and angry to accept their affection.

I'd fixated on Wilde's horrible misfortune instead of her indomitable cheer.

I had reduced Hosea's life to the injustice of his death, when I should have celebrated the wonder of his existence. I came to understand that I had never needed the tattoo to remind me of him, because he lived in my heart.

I saw the marvel of my new friends, too, and I no longer wondered why I liked Mary Violet so much: she had given me laughter, and I loved her for that.

I could say *love* now and I knew what it meant. I thought it was the most important and complicated word in the world. When Jack was with me, I felt such love for him. He might be rambling about his band, or filthy from a ride, or ranting about his family, or walking silently beside me on one of our night walks, and I felt such happiness.

And always in the back of my mind were 2Slim and Claire Mason, both damaged and deadly. Their childhood suffering in no way excused their murderous behavior, and I prayed that my own damaged soul was not incorrigible— that I would be healed.

All the parts of me were coming together, and I could even imagine the woman I would become: quiet, thorough Jane Williams, who loved solving problems in a laboratory and was happiest when she came home in the evening to her husband and their crazy-haired children.

On Saturday morning at breakfast, I said to Jack, "Classes

start on Monday, and I won't be able to study with you here all the time. People are gossiping that we're doing the dance-with-no-pants."

He laughed so hard that he choked on his coffee. "I wish! Who's saying that?"

"Never mind. Don't forget the regulation against moral turpitude. Mary Violet is already writing poems about my lost innocence."

"So you're her muse, too. I thought that if I stayed here, you would let me do the dance-with-no-pants with you."

Waiting to do more with Jack was exquisitely agonizing. "Don't go off topic. You need to go back to your house, and maybe you could start looking into colleges."

His smile vanished. "You're tired of me already?"

"Never! I want you to look for colleges with a good music program *and* a great chemistry department *and* terrific pizza. A college set in the woods. I want to live where there are trees. I want to be with you." I fiddled with the silver leaf necklace that Jack had given me. "JFR. What's your middle name?"

"Forrest," he said. "It's my birth name. Jacob Forrest Radcliffe."

In science and in math, one was always trying to find an elegant solution: an answer that is at once simple and true. Jack was that to me, my elegant solution.

But hark! here comes the sweeping sound over the wood-tops;—now it dies away;—how solemn the stillness that succeeds! Now the breeze swells again. It is like the voice of some supernatural being—the voice of the spirit of the woods, that watches over them by night.

Ann Radcliffe, *The Mysteries of Udolpho* (1794)

Epilogue   Possessing my memories again was both incredible and distressing.

I could be doing something as simple as changing my sheets and I'd remember folding laundry with my mother and how we'd toss sheets in the air and then fall on the bed. Other memories, like the sound of her voice and her scent, wouldn't come to me no matter how hard I tried to call them up.

Once, flipping through TV channels, a commercial played an old Stones song my stepfather had liked. I listened, frozen, and recalled a time when he'd been friendly and affectionate. I *didn't* want to think of my mother's murderer that way. I didn't want to think of him at all.

I wished I could have enjoyed the good memories and forgotten the bad ones, but each incident was inextricably intertwined with every other. Even when they had existed only in my subconscious, they were part of my life.

I came to accept my past; I didn't want to limit my experiences to the interior of a snow globe. I wouldn't forget where I came from, and I wouldn't stop exploring unknown territories because others feared there might be dragons.

Mrs. Holiday had said that the proper study of mankind is woman. I thought about my mother when I saw the loving way that Mrs. Radcliffe watched her sons, and how Mrs. Holiday cared for her family. Sometimes I talked to Teresa, the Holidays' housekeeper, about her children and I saw that look in her eyes, too, a mother's passion.

My teachers occasionally mentioned their families and friends, and I began to see them differently, as women with the complicated emotions and obligations and joys and loyalties that women have. Each one of them was a daughter.

Wilde was someone's daughter, too. I didn't know exactly how it happened, because she wouldn't take my phone calls, but she was forced into a treatment facility somewhere out in the desert. It's adjacent to a resort/spa, and, after six months clean and completion of a GED program, the salon there would give her a part-time job and sponsor her training at a school of cosmetology.

I had gotten over being mad at Jack, who had only wanted me to be safe, and I hoped that soon Wilde would get over being mad at me.

Hattie didn't say any more about her plans for the future, but I often saw her staring off into the distance, deep in thought. For most of my life, I'd accepted the old systems where the strongest and most ruthless men maintained power and used others for their purposes. I'd been complicit then, but now I questioned things.

I thought there was another way to live. Or a *million* other ways and a *million* other universes. And I had a feeling that I might find a door into the green world, and the Lady of the Wood could lead me toward some answers.

I was trying to be a better student and a better person, not because I wanted to escape my life, but because I believed that all the things that make up the world and the universe are beautiful and amazing.

I often dreamed about the nights that I died. Sometimes I had nightmares about the fire and Claire's screams. I saw her mutilated body consumed by violet flames, and I woke in a cold sweat, my heart pounding, and I would re-assure myself that she was alive, somewhere.

More often, though, I dreamed that I was in the grove.

The wind is blowing and the birches lift their roots from the soil and begin a lumbering yet graceful dance. They sing their whispery silver song in a language that predates time.

I am very young and playing Ring-Around-the-Rosy with other small girls. We're singing, "Ashes, ashes, all fall down."

Somehow I know that my playmates are Claire Mason and BB and Wilde. There are others girls here, too, and many wear Companion rings, the stones glinting like drop-lets of blood on our small hands. Our skin is yet unmarked by the scars and burns and wounds that will become our maps of pain.

We are the ghosts of childhoods lost and we will always haunt this place.

ACKNOWLEDGMENTS

My thanks to Paulette Jiles, who very kindly allowed me to use "Paper Matches." I first read this poem in the most unlikely of places—on bus signs as part of a public art project in San Francisco. The poem resonated with me, and I'm so happy to be able to include it in my book.

I'm deeply grateful to Susan Chang, my brilliant editor, who guided me through revisions, letting me find the heart and soul of my story and characters.

I wish I could name all the readers and bloggers who read the manuscript and gave me valuable feedback and support, but please know that I'm very grateful. A special thank-you to designer and reviewer Amanda Wright, who surprised me with wonderful cover art for my online manuscript.

Last, but not least, thanks to my beautiful son and the pack of wild and wonderful young men—Brian, Grayson, James, Roberto, Tyler, Shawn, Nick, Torren, et al—who invaded my house and constantly reminded me of what it is to be a teenager and why I value the company of girls.

TOR TEEN READER'S GUIDE

Dark Companion
by Marta Acosta

ABOUT THIS GUIDE

The information, activities, and discussion questions that follow are intended to enhance your reading of *Dark Companion*. Please feel free to adapt these materials to suit your needs and interests.

WRITING AND RESEARCH ACTIVITIES

I. Gothic Novels

A. The chapters of *Dark Companion* begin with quotations from gothic literature. Make a list of all of the novels, stories, and poems cited in the book. Beside each title, note the author, publication date, and a sentence describing the plot or theme relationship between the quote and the chapter it introduces.

B. Research the literary term "gothic novel" and then create an informational poster describing the main elements that make a novel gothic. Or, make a stack of at least six index cards, each featuring the name, biographical information, and notable works of a gothic author, such as Horace Walpole, Mary Shelley, Emily Brontë, or Bram Stoker.

C. Select one of the historical stories or novels from activity I.A above to read in its entirety. Write an essay comparing the main characters, supernatural elements, and/or settings of both stories. Conclude with your thoughts as to how the legacy of your chosen work can be seen in Marta Acosta's book.

II. *Names, Labels, and Families*

A. Names and nicknames play an important role in *Dark Companion*, both as clues to the mystery of Jane Williams's predecessor and as ways to clarify character traits and relationships. Write a short essay discussing the use of names and nicknames, citing at least four examples from the novel.

B. The main character of the novel has a very simple name: Jane Williams. This is also the name of a woman associated with the Romantic poet Percy Bysshe Shelley. Jane is also the protagonist of Charlotte Brontë's novel *Jane Eyre,* and Jane Austen created many young female characters who had limited options because of their economic status. Research these connections and more, if desired. Then, use your research along with observations from the novel to compose a short essay or poem entitled "The Legacy of *Jane.*"

C. Learn more about gothic novelist Ann Radcliffe. Then, create a short oral report noting at least three reasons Marta Acosta may have chosen to name the Radcliffe family in her novel for this author. Use PowerPoint or other visual aids to enliven your presentation.

D. BB, Claire, and Jane are all orphans. Write an interview with one of these characters in which you, as a reporter or guidance counselor, ask about the impact being parentless has had on her life.

E. In the course of the novel, Jane discovers her sense of "home." What is home to you? Create a song, poem, painting, or other creative work that represents your sense of home.

III. Vampires

A. The families of Birch Grove seem uncomfortable with the label of "vampire" and claim that the term, as a supernatural notion, is incorrect. Create a three-column chart comparing (column A) the vampirelike citizens of Birch Grove with (column B) the vampires from a contemporary paranormal novel of your choice, and (column C) a research-based description of the physical, psychological, and cultural characteristics of vampires from ancient folklore or Bram Stoker's character Dracula.

B. With friends or classmates, review the novel to find a list of the nonparanormal explanations the Radcliffe family gives for its vampirelike behaviors. Use this list to create a survey about whether being a vampire is a genetic defect or a supernatural phenomenon. Do people prefer a supernatural explanation or a scientific explanation, and why? Invite others from your school to take the survey, and create a chart summarizing your results.

C. Make a recommended viewing list of at least ten vampire movies, starting with a silent film and ending with a movie made in the last five years. At the top of your list, explain why you chose these movies and what you might learn by watching all of them.

D. Writing in the character of Lucky, create a defense of yourself and your kind entitled "Don't Call Me a Vampire."

E. Who is the "Dark Companion" of the novel's title? Draw, paint, sculpt, or craft your answer to this question.

IV. The Arts, Science, and Math

A. When Jane enters Birch Grove, she has no interest in the arts, yet she has several discussions about the value of literature, music, and painting. Cite these discussions and what they mean to Jane. Does her opinion change during the course of the novel?

B. Jane also discusses her love of science and math with several characters. What draws her to these fields? Write a poem or create a piece of art with a science or math theme.

DISCUSSION QUESTIONS

1. The novel's prologue is also a flashback. What questions do you take from the prologue into your reading of chapter one? Do you think it is important to be uncertain as to whether Jane is really alive or dead? Why or why not?

2. Describe the life that Jane lives in Helmsdale. What factors make her a very willing candidate for Birch Grove Academy?

3. Jane's limited early education leads her to constantly strive to increase her vocabulary. How does this effort give insight into her state of mind and emotions? What important new words does Jane discover in the course of the novel?

4. Describe the prep-school society into which Jane is inducted at Birch Grove. How is this similar to, or different from, Helmsdale? From your own school?

5. From "Mousie Girl" to "MV" to "Lucky," nicknames fill the novel. Do you have a nickname at home or at school? What roles do nicknames play in your social culture?

6. On page 55, Jack describes Jane as a "changeling." How does Jane react to this suggestion? What are her feelings toward Jack at this early point in the novel?

7. Describe how the author uses images of food, such as rare meat, to reflect key themes of the novel.

8. Jane seeks scientific knowledge as a way to understand life, and there are several references to perception, vision, and experience. What does Jane miss if she only relies upon what she sees?

9. Jane sees herself as a scientist and, as such, takes a binary

approach to ethics. For Jane, there is mostly a right or a wrong. Why is this perspective important to the story?

10. How does Jane weigh her options when she is offered the chance to be Lucky's Companion? Beyond his good looks, what does Lucky represent to her? Would you have made the choice she made? Why or why not?

11. Why do you think the author selected Paulette Jiles's "Paper Matches" to introduce her novel? How does the poem relate to Jane and other characters, including the men who appear in brief scenes?

12. Jane has a strong friendship with Wilde and she develops relationships with other female characters. Describe some of these relationships and what significance they might have to an orphan.

13. Compare the scenes in which Lucky uses bloodletting apparatus on Jane to the drug paraphernalia Jane sees when she flees to Wilde's place. She also sees a homeless person waiting to sell his blood at the plasma center. Is Jane's understanding of these various situations similar or different?

14. Who is Mr. Mason? Is it important that he is a science teacher? What is important about his grief over Claire? How does he help Jane realize some of the life complications that can evolve from one's Companion role?

15. As the novel draws to a close, the mystery of missing BB is clarified and Lucky confronts his father. Do you see Lucky as innocent or guilty? Redeemable or lost? Explain your answer.

16. What is the point Mrs. Radcliffe tries to make in the Night Terrors class? What might you and your classmates find useful or interesting about this class?

17. What finally makes Jane run away from Birch Grove? What draws her back?

18. Who is "The Lady of the Wood," and what is the role of nature in the story? What is Jane? Does MV's recital of Robert Frost's "Birches" poem (page 105) or

her reference to Shakespeare's *A Midsummer Night's Dream* (page 328) impact your answers? How do these literary allusions affect Jane?

19. The prologue of *Dark Companion* ends with the question, "who are we without our memories?" Later, in chapter eight, Hattie quotes Shakespeare to Jane, saying, "I love studying the past. . . . Whereof what's past is prologue." How can you understand *Dark Companion* in terms of these two notions?

20. At the end of the novel, Jane feels that Birch Grove is her home. Why does she feel this way? Do you think she is correct? How does this impact the choices she will make? What advice might you want to give Jane about her future?

ABOUT THE AUTHOR

Marta Acosta was born in the San Francisco Bay Area. As the only daughter in a family of boys, she sought sisterly companionship in books.

She is a graduate of Stanford University, where she studied creative writing and literature. Her feature articles and commentary have appeared frequently in the *San Francisco Chronicle* and the Contra Costa Newspapers. She is a Steinbeck Institute honoree, a University of California Latino Literary Contest winner, and her debut novel, *Happy Hour at Casa Dracula,* was named a Book Sense Pick by independent booksellers. *Dark Companion* is her sixth novel.

Marta lives in a fog belt near Berkeley with her family and rescued dogs, Bosco and Betty.

Visit her online at www.martaacosta.com.